Shakedown

By

Gregory Jonathan Scott

DEDICATION

This one is for Me & Scott

WARNING: This Book contains material that may be offensive to some, which includes graphic language and adult situations.

ACKNOWLEDGMENTS

Colton Haynes

Gregory Jonathan Scott

Prologue

It didn't happen every day, but there was a magnificent aroma in the air. I could sense it. Practically taste it. Springtime was always the best. New beginnings. New breezes. New everything. What was it about spring that made everybody so sexually active? For me, it was a hot as fuck black man taking his shirt off because the chilling weather of winter had gone away.

"Boner alert"

Gregory Jonathan Scott

Chapter 1

Monday had never been my favorite day of the week, and I could pretty much say it might have been the same for the entire population on the planet. My opinion.

A discouraging groan was all I could muster when I entered the office and sidestepped a busy body buzzing the hallway, fabricating nonsense and convincing listener's that what she had to say was the truth. In addition to her garb, I'd dealt with reprobates under house arrest who continually tried to convince me they hadn't done the crime. It was too late for that. The court sentences had been finalized.

That was a typical day for me as a parole officer—Mondays undoubtedly seemed to have been the downer. By the time the five o'clock bell had rung, I was in desperate need of liberation, such that of which would have been a shower experience to wash all the shit of the day away. The soap and rinse cycle concluded the highlight of my day-to-day ritual and seemed to have helped refresh my body as well as my worn out brain cells.

5

"Oh sweet surrender, I needed this," I released a low growl while leaning my head back into the hot shower stream. Everything that had happened at that moment felt perfectly amazing. The heat. The wetness. The incredible sensation of an increasing orgasm that had bombarded my entire body, from head to toe, and eventually spurted out the end of my dick.

I exhaled, and the sound of my deep voice, "so good, so fucking good," echoed off the tiles in the shower chamber, sounding musical, but with a low tortured rasp. I carried on, breathing heavily — my eyelids sealed tight, taking in every bit of the water as it assaulted my scalp and ran down my naked body. The hair that covered my chest and trailed my abs clung so tightly against my skin, the front of me appeared that of dark flesh when wet. I'd become turned on by my own wet body. The deep gutters over my sculpted torso caught most of the downpour, guiding it to my crotch like a flowing river.

I lifted both hands to the top of my head, massaging and smoothing back the soapy remains in my hair before gripping the back of my neck with locked fingers. I was in total paradise, moaning from the pleasure and heat that had taken me over.

"Oh gawd!" My low growling voice ricocheted off every wall. "Holy fuck!" rattled while propelling my hips back and forth, appreciating the way my nine inches of thick white meat looked and felt pile driving the rear end of my boyfriend's beautiful black butt.

Nykolson's chocolate-toned globes were solid muscle that hardly budged when my hips banged against them. His entire body was like that — built rock solid. Every inch of him had definition of being a healthy man. To sweeten the grasp he had on me, I smacked his hard ass with an open hand. He jerked. It was vice grip heaven on my cock.

Tensing up from the strike, Nykolson blurted, "Fuck! Yeah! Pound it out. Spank that black ass. Fuck it with that white meat. Hard like you mean it."

While he was bent over in front of me with both his hands fastened like suction cups against the tiled wall, I watched the raised ridges along his muscular back flex as I rammed my cock in and out of his ass. He was holding strong, supporting my thrusting weight like a champ. I banged, digging deep. The thick silver chain around his neck I'd given him a few months into our relationship swung back and forth in rhythm with my pelvic thrusting, the dangling strand thumping against his stocky chest. I hadn't lied when I growled from the depths of my throat, "Fuckin' damn, that ass is hot," at the same time he thrust his hard butt cheeks backward into my pelvis. His actions starving for all the dick I was able to put in him. I pounded my man like I was hammering at concrete.

The hold his asshole had on my cock pushed me closer and closer to bursting at the seams. I could feel myself getting ready to flood his guts with what he'd really been begging for — my boiling cum. As he stroked my dick with his fired up chute, my level of anxiety had gone so high, I couldn't help blurting out how much I loved seeing my cock sink in and then get pushed back out by his grunting forces. His continuous response when I fucked him was how addicted he was to my cock and couldn't survive without a daily dose of my sperm. Ever since the first time I'd entered his body without a condom, he'd made that perfectly clear. He'd never once objected to spreading those legs at a moment's notice like a good bottom would, nor had I ever opposed to a position switch whenever I felt the urge to have him ejaculate into me. We shared everything. Heart body and semen.

Since being with Nykolson, I'd become a versatile man, enjoying how great his black dick felt piercing me too, but as preferred, he was the power bottom in our relationship, and I was definitely his master top who he liked him that way. I couldn't get enough of his slick black hole. My personal cum dumpster. My breeding hole. It was skilled at sucking dick.

Pre-cum oozed from my slit whenever I so much as thought about sticking my hard-on into his butthole. On many occasions, his perfectly built body had me so wound up, I'd ejaculated the moment I slipped in, hardly getting my bulbous head past the sphincter ring. I blamed that body and that ass for lessening my ability to fuck him like the stud I thought I was.

I hollered out on the verge of crying, "Da'amn that cock sucking ass." The echo of my voice bounced around the shower walls, the acoustic tone sounding musical. His chocolate ass swallowed my white meat whole, pulling me in and spitting me out, over and over and over again—his body in rhythm with mine, moving back and forth—his back arched and flexed while his butthole had taken hold of my cock and sucked on it. His overactive body language had me believing he was enjoying my dick beating his prostate, inspiring satisfaction back on me by what his asshole had done to my pole. Every time he bowed his spine up or down, his rectum squeezed the fuck out of my cock, perfectly stroking my entire length like a genuine vacuum system. The friction was incredible.

Nykolson erratically hollered my name and squealed, "Fu-huck me-heee. Prod my black hole. Make me muthuh fuckin' cum." The thug-like order seemed to have spewed out of him uncontrollably and I always loved hearing his filthy mouth bossing me around when it pertained to jamming my cock into his ass. There was something about his brashness I liked and it made me want him even more. Perhaps it was because I'd always been a good white boy and his spontaneous recklessness was refreshing.

By then, my hands moved to his narrow hips where I gripped him tightly, my thumb pads pressing into the inward curve of his lower back and my forefingers running the ditches of the pelvic arrow leading to his dick. I held firm to aid my balance while I pummeled his sweet hole. My eagerness to drop my load inside my man's dark channel had begun to fire up. I could feel the surge coming to a head, sparking pleasured sensations from my nuts, up my spine to my brain, and charging back to my flexing prostate. I'd come moments from blasting his ass, plastering his rectum with my steaming semen.

Every time I shanked him, his bossy whimpers had proven how much he wanted my saucy cum flooding his hole. I couldn't deprive the desire from him—I wanted the same—wanted to keep my man marked with the best part of me—pass on my wolfen spore that would continue keeping the sniffing scoundrels off my property. He was my black bitch, no one else's, and I was damn well going to make that known. I continued fucking him so the both of us would, "*muthuh fucking cum*."

I reached a hand around to the front of Nykolson, giving his rock hard dick a few smooth strokes. His body aggressively thrashed, jacking my cock with his vibrating chute.

That fabulous squeezing sensation his slick hole had on me felt so damned good, and over the first couple of years we'd been fucking, I'd learned how to bring him to orgasm overload without a single hand even touching his dick. I knew how he liked getting fucked in the butt, I knew where my dick needed to nudge, how long to hold still inside him, when to probe, and how far I could push him until he was ready to get off. He liked having me plunge into him, pull out, tease with the head, and plunge back in again. The way he howled had told me everything I needed to know. He was always like a wolf in heat.

While intermittently jamming the crown of my dick into Nykolson's pulsing prostate, I heard his ranting cries, "Gah Dayum, right there. Fuck! Oy, yeah! Right there. Right there. Keep going. Keep going." He spread his legs wider that allowed me to dig in. Then he followed through like the bossy bottom I liked, ordering me to drive my dick deeper, still. Helping with penetration, he reared backward into my pelvis — the chestnut hair above my cock crushed by his hard black butt cheeks. Undoubtedly, he liked it when I shoved my cock in to the point of giving him my nuts too. He was a fuck machine, a pro at taking my thick white dick.

I could tell my cock was totally jacking up his prostate by the way he stirred and growled. I continued beefing him up the ass, driving intensity within his body higher. He curled his fingers into fists, planting his knuckles firmly against the tiled wall in front of us as though he was trying to push his way through it like Superman would have. His bunched triceps throbbed, getting thicker as the strain to stabilize himself increased, needing all the support he could get by the way I was pummeling his fuck hole from behind. I gripped his hips tighter and continued jamming my cock in and out of him.

"That's right, you better hold on," I growled at him as I skimmed my left hand upward along the cavernous crevice at the center of his spine, stopping when I reached his muscular shoulder where I clamped my fingers tightly over his thick trapezius. I leaned my wet hairy torso against his satin-smooth back and rested my chin on my fixed hand. I heavily breathed hot air into his ear. "Holy hot damn, I love the way your sweet ass sucks on my cock. So fucking good. You've trained it well." As though my man's ass had an automatic reaction to what I'd said, I felt him really bear down on my dick, almost locking me in place with an urge to get bred.

Slowing a bit but keeping my steady rhythm, I rolled my hips into him, anticipating my needed release, yet agonizingly held back for the thrill of it. As I slid in and out of his gripping channel, I moved my right hand to the side of his face and hooked two fingers in his mouth, feeling slippery teeth and tongue. His head rotated slightly, sucking them in. As a result of being skewered by my thick dick, the intense pleasure must have been what caused him to bite down. There was a sharp sting across my knuckles, but I liked it, and the pressure made my hips thrust harder into his butt cheeks, pushing my cock deeper, if that was possible. His moaning vibrated through my fingers and raced up my forearm where it fizzled at my elbow. Damn, he felt good. All over good. Inside and out. I needed him—desired him. I so badly wanted to ejaculate in him.

Nykolson's ass stroked up and down my dick, sucking and pulling as if trying to yank the sucker off, clearly hungry to feel my load blown up his butthole. What his ass was doing had fucked me up. I yelled, "Shit, Nyke. Gah, dayum, fucking, shit."

I slipped my hand from his mouth and reached for his gorgeous black cock. I squeezed his ten inch shaft, feeling the heated pulse in my grip. It was stone hard and burning hot. I matched hand strokes with my forward thrusts, sliding my fist into his wooly pelvis as I pushed my hips against his ass cheeks. "Hot. Fucking. Damn! Get that hole ready." I dug my cock into his hot asshole, making him answer breathlessly, "Yes. Give it up. Shoot me full. I muthuh fucking need your cum."

The way my thug of a husband begged just then had made me lose control. I was instantly ready to blow everything I had inside him, burn up his chute with my white-boy sperm. He squeezed my dick with his scorching channel and the incredible sensation made my entire body turn tense, every muscle ripped with definition as if every fat cell had instantly disappeared. I growled as though I suddenly had an angry streak. "Fuck, yeah. I'm dumping cum."

I viciously thumped my pelvis into my black man's rear end a few times before holding tightly against him as if trying to force my whole body into his rear end. Loud roars rushed from my throat as I pumped my usual thirteen spurts of semen into his cock wrecked channel, shooting every one of them so deeply that he'd have to spit from his mouth if he wanted to get rid of what I'd left him with.

I felt his ass channel flexing fitfully around my dick, validating he was ejaculating right along with me. I grittily rumbled against his ear, "That's my man. Cum for me."

Nykolson was a massive cum gusher, like that of a soda machine switched to full power. I was a fanatic for the immense amount of cum he ejected. Loved it from the first time he exploded all over my face and down my throat. It was as though I'd been hit with a high powered fire hose and I was the raging fire he was trying to put out. That was a memorable day since I'd never seen any dick squirt so much, except for my own. I was a close second, but Nykolson had definitely deserved the gold medal for most powerful shooter.

In time with each spurt Nykolson released, his thick cock expanded in my grasp. I couldn't see that gorgeous action from where I was hooked up behind him, but I'd known his glistening cream was flooding the floor at our feet and adding a pearled glaze to my knuckles.

"Fuck, that was intense." Breathing heavily, I collapsed across his back, still inside him. My nuts eventually dropped, sagging loosely between my wet thighs. I rocked gently, letting the water massage my backside as he jerked and roared under me.

Once I felt his prostate relax and his convulsions cease, he slowly stood, forcing me to stand with him, my chest slipping along his back. Regretfully, my semi hard dick snaked free from his ass as he spun to face me, our eyes meeting when he looked down at me and I glanced up at him.

Nykolson licked his semen from my fingers, sensually sucking each one with his soft brown lips. The visual was stunning. The contrast of his pearly sperm against his dark skin appeared as though it glowed. His Adam's apple bobbed each time he swallowed, and when he'd had enough, rotated my wet hand to my own mouth, sharing the pungent sweetness he'd ejected from his dick.

I'd taken his dark fingers between my lips and sucked, moaning with closed eyelids while the taste of him glazed my tongue. As I ingested his creamy goodness, he firmly hooked his fingers behind my lower teeth, holding me steady as he gently kissed my cum wet mouth.

Without pulling away, he whispered, "Dayum, we taste good."

I realized from the beginning we were cum sluts—I probably more than him at that moment—especially knowing the semen we were sharing had come from his beautiful black nuts.

Nykolson was a meaty man—muscular and strong, towered me by about six inches—the way I liked him, and because of how big and masculine he was, I found it amusing that he enjoyed being on the bottom more than doing time on top. His virile type, of which I shouldn't assume, was typically the dominant figure in a relationship—as in, the bigger guy manhandles and penetrates the smaller one. I recognized from the first time we made love that he desired having me inside him. He'd expressed to me a few times that the connection made him feel closer to me, like I was giving him a part of my soul to keep. I'd understood what he was saying, and I'd fallen in love with him at that moment, all six foot-three inches of his stunning black body. He was tough, masculine, on the edge of being gorgeously fearsome, but around me, that man was gentle and loving, totally devoted to ensuring my happiness.

As he faced me in the shower, which by then, the water had begun to cool, he pushed his beefy chest against mine, forcing me backward against the wall. I was pinned by the man I loved, couldn't breathe, but hadn't cared. Truthfully, without him, there was no reason for air.

I stood still behind the weight of his muscle-hard blackness, every part of our frames pressing against the other, apart from his hands, which were fastened to the wall above my head, and mine gripping hold of his waist.

In a matter of seconds, he covered my mouth with his, kissing me, transferring love and cum from his tongue to mine.

Backing off, probably to breathe, he blurted, "Gah, dayum, I love you... Gah, dayum!" His head snapping back and forth on every syllable—the chain I'd bought him banging against his massive chest.

"I know you do." I laughed, going in for more kissing to stop him from talking back the same way he'd done for the past two years since we'd met. I felt him grinning by what I said, so I whispered, "I do too."

"Do too, what?" he probed, jokingly?

"Love you," I confirmed, then cupped his deep dimpled pear shaped ass cheeks, kneading them with lustful admiration.

He then gripped the back of my neck with one hand and kissed me. The pressure intense. I'd felt his unreserved determination to have me, not letting me breathe until he was done using my mouth for what he needed it for.

Backing away slowly, he said, "Gah, dayum. I really do love you."

Chapter 2

That erotic moment in the shower had taken place soon after I'd met Nykolson two years earlier than the present day it was, and had happened frequently. Those had been some of my favorite times spent with him during our relationship, other than the days we simply held hands walking down the street or snuggling on the sofa watching a television movie while polishing off a bowl of popcorn.

Rewinding to the first day I'd met the man, I'd known then, there was no turning away once I'd gotten a glimpse of his piercing pale gray eyes. Those honeys had definitely been attention grabbers. For an African-American man, light colored irises were downright rare where I lived, but not uncommon, and I'd been one of the lucky few who'd snagged a man with such striking eyes typically only found on a snowy canine of the north.

Other than the hypnotizing glare from those gleaming eyes, his smile had a lock on me as well. That smoldering smirk and pearly grin lit him right up, practically turning the room into a flaming inferno. The man's smile was Cheshire wide, just right toothy, and in a crazy way, accentuated the sparkle in his eyes. All that whiteness had come at me like a shining beacon, pulling me in as if I was under some kind of spell and he'd been the one who'd zapped me.

I hadn't known what Nykolson Kannon had to smile about that Monday morning when he first walked into my office. He'd been put under house arrest by an ankle tether for a bum altercation he hadn't instigated, but had only gotten caught in the middle of because he was there.

That day had amounted to my typical Monday morning, one I dreaded as usual because it was the first day of work after a weekend of solitude. I imagined Mister Nykolson Kannon most likely was more perturbed about the day than I was. It'd been his scheduled day to meet with me, Michael Millhouse Jr., his parole officer, to review the ground rules and make sure he understood the upcoming community services he'd been sentenced with.

It hadn't hurt I found the man to be more than easy on my eyes, or for a better term, drop dead striking — in my opinion. He stood about a half head taller than me, and emitted a rugged air by the way he walked. His stride wasn't clunky by any means, but more that of a sturdy male fashion model on the runways of New York. Confidence and masculinity was written all over his tall light chocolate form. Just my bloody luck, and just my bloody type. How the shit would I have concentrated with him staring me down like he had, much less maintain my erection and keep the fucker free from spunking up my pressed trousers. That tall drink of creamed coffee was an ejaculation fest just waiting to happen.

"Sumbitch, I was so fucked." I put my best foot forward and hoped like hell I wouldn't trip all over the place like a newborn colt.

Well… *"Here goes nothing."*

I'd said, "Good Morning," to Mister Kannon a few moments after he'd stepped into my office, trying my damndest not to stare at him for an extended period of time, or run my gawping eyes up and down that perfectly built six-foot plus frame of his. He had a smile on his face as he entered, and yet again, I wasn't sure why that was. He should have been miserable and upset by the turn his life had taken. Perhaps his grin was due to meeting me since I might have been better than what he had expected.

Wishful thinking. A man can dream.

The expression on Nykolson's face had given me a good idea he liked what he had been looking at — an average, okay looking white guy with what I considered a decent body — one I'd worked hard at maintaining, but I knew for sure it wasn't as solid as his seemed to have been. *How dare he wear that form fitting shirt in front of me?*

I noticed he looked right into my eyes, held his gaze as if staring through them, like he was already in love.

Again, *Wishful thinking.*

I could have been mistaken, but his actions had that familiar gay male attraction thingy written all over it — the one where a man would hold his gaze for an extended period of time, exposing himself as being attracted to the same gender and allowing the other to reciprocate before looking away. That there was called collecting gay vibes and waiting for the gaydar pointer to land on, GAY AS FUCK.

I refrained from shaking Nykolson's hand for two good reasons. The first was to let him know I wasn't into sugary pleasantries with law breakers. The second and most concerning was, I hadn't wanted him to sense I'd found him amazingly attractive. I needed to keep that under wraps. For the time being, anyway. He was so damned good looking standing there with his mystic eyes gleaming. If his gaydar had been as in tune as mine had been, he'd have figured out the sexual desire I had for him if my hand at any moment had clasped with his. My grip would have unconsciously lingered with its release, and my sweating palm would have been another dead giveaway that I would have wanted more than just a handshake from that man.

It was important for Nykolson to know I was professional when it had come to my job, not notice I was some horn-dog of a man with a sudden schoolboy crush who wanted to fuck around with the hottest guy in gym class.

Oh, shit. Memory flashback. There he was. Hot and well developed, Thaddeus. Nude and dripping wet in the boys shower chamber. Waiting just for me.

Along with a swing of my arm as a directive instrument, I'd asked Nykolson to take a seat at the front side of my desk right before I confidently walked around to the back side to sit in my own chair. If I hadn't made my move on the fly, the guy would have given me a serious erection, *and* if I hadn't sat down when I thought I should, my manly tool would have invaded his personal space, or worse, had put his eye out. As much fun as that would have been to whip my dick out and give him all I had, he probably wasn't ready for my raging hard-on plunging into any of his manholes at the moment. *Or would he?*

As Nykolson sat, he greeted me with, "good morning, sir," as though he was addressing a high ranking Major, or he'd been hoping kindness would have gotten him off the hook with the law. With his sentence already set in stone, I had no power of any sort to dismiss the handsome gent. My role was to monitor and guide him through what had been outlined in his required program. Nykolson, however, could possibly persuade me to break a rule with that kick ass face and that come fuck me body. Shoot... All mister hot pants had to do was look me in the eyes and say, "Please, Sir," and I would have given him just about anything he'd asked for. My dick. My mouth. My whole body, that of which included my super tight hardly ever fucked asshole. Yes, that's right. I was basically unpenetrated at the rear, making me practically an unfucked virgin all over again. If my memory served me correctly, I might have been screwed twice during my gay as fuck life. But, I hadn't cared, though—decided to secure myself a long time ago after the last guy who tried to put his dick in me only wanted to use my butthole as a dumping ground, and then split to do it all over again with somebody else. I wanted more than that, not just give up my hole to any old whore.

Then Nykolson flashed them—those blessed eyes—struck me like a blinding solar eclipse and I couldn't seem to look away. I waited for him to say, "please", along with an order as to how he wanted me, but sadly, there was nothing.

"Sumbitch."

At that very moment, I was overly grateful to my colleague, Ashlund Butterfield, for passing such a hot number over to my office. I put it on my books to thank Ashlund personally, without giving away that I was already in love with the man—so to have spoken. I suppose I should also thank the office administrative assistant, Berdella, who had overbooked his schedule for the day, causing the need to transfer Nykolson over to me.

While I shuffled through the few papers on my desk, I hadn't any reason to have a look at Nykolson to know he was staring right at me. I felt his eyes digging right in, making my stomach release the sensation of those annoying butterflies. I'd even had to take a moment to clear my throat as if I'd just swallowed another man's spicy wad of cum.

Singsong thoughts had rolled around in my head the way they always had when I spotted a man I wanted to stick my dick into. Those musical words were, *"I'm in love. I'm in love. Holy fuck, I'm in love."* I hadn't really meant I was in love. The ditty was just my personal expression coming to life for wanting to bed a man I liked a whole lot. However, that man hit me a bit stronger than any of the others ever had. So, maybe I was in love, or at least adored.

I normally hadn't come across as being so obsessed when faced with a love struck state of mind, but, with that stunning creature on my doorstep, my entire body turned into a gah damned ball of nerves that outranked my ability to stay calm and collected. Shit... my cock had been leading that argument right toward his ass and I was sort of hoping there'd have been an open invitation.

As I flipped from one page to the next, I tried not to appear crazy, or desperate.

Breaking the monotony of my lunacy, I repetitively tapped the keyboard on my personal computer, trying to pull it out of sleep mode quicker than it wanted to. I told Nykolson my name, senselessly rapping the name plate on my desk as a visual aid to help him understand what I'd said. My name wasn't difficult to pronounce, I just had a strange urge to do that with my pencil, perhaps subconsciously wanting to make sure he wouldn't forget who I was.

I then briefed him on what my role was as his parole officer and the guidelines of the program—trying like mad to remain professional and not give out any signals I'd rather jump the desk and fuck his brains out right there on the floor at the foot of the sofa behind him. By the looks of him though, he might prefer being the fucker. If that had been the case. Game over. Maybe.

There was no need to go into detail with him regarding what he had done to land an ankle tether, he'd lived it and I had read it.

In case he wasn't aware, I explained how the strap around

his ankle worked, telling him it was the same as if being fully caged in a prison cell, only with more comforting amenities, and I'd be notified if he stepped more than a few yards outside his front door. His facial expression had given me the clue he'd already been briefed as to how that worked, so I ceased explanation with a drifting voice that faded off to silence and a clearing of my constricting throat. I wasn't placed as his P.O. to drudge up the past, only to help him move on, abide by the sentences placed on him, and guide him into a better future. Maybe along the way or sometime after his release, I could convince him I should be part of his yet to come.

I had a good idea the man was innocent regarding the dismissed account of assault and battery to another human being. To me, he hadn't shown evidence of a violent bone in his solid as fuck body. His pleasant smile the moment he stepped into my office and how he conducted himself while talking with me, justified my thoughts on his innocence, which aggressively fixed the not-guilty feeling I had about him in place.

At first I thought I'd misjudged Nykolson simply because my attraction toward him was messing with my ability to think clearly, but the more he'd spoken, I discovered the appearance of that man wasn't what swayed me. This guy wasn't guilty of anything other than giving me a raging hard-on. I, however, was super guilty for being thankful he was in the car when his brother's bitch of a girlfriend went crazy on their asses.

As we sat in my office, the sun coming in the window behind me lit his face right up, giving him a luster of holiness. At that moment, I knew there was a God and I decided to secretly give thanks for bringing that man to me. To keep myself sanctified for that moment anyway, it was my duty to do everything I could to hide my need to gawk at Nykolson's glory.

I noticed he was squinting one eye while we conversed, which had initiated my reason to adjust the way the sun shone in the window behind me. I needed to rectify the issue that was causing those beautiful pale gray eyes to close on me. Perhaps, that color was more sensitive to the golden rays than a darker pair like mine. I stood from where I had been seated and angled the blinds, moving the sunshine off his face with a quick twist of the dangling rod. I thought at first it would have been a real downer because he looked so good all bright and shiny, but, *"Oh... my... gawd,"* he changed from scowling to even more angelic when the fiery light left his charming face. *"So damned handsome. Bloody fucking Hell!"* How was that even possible? He was definitely blessed with the good genes, and to think there was another one roaming the streets who looked just like him had me thinking how unfairly my DNA cards had been dealt.

My brilliant brain had told me the man was totally my type, and moments after my mind had given into that fact, my effing cock had too. I immediately sat down before he noticed my dick was starting to stand stiff again. If I had spun to take my seat a few seconds later, my monster would have knocked lamps and shit off the desk for sure, proving to him I wanted to stick it where the sun wasn't able to shine.

I reasoned with myself, *"He's an offender, dumb ass. Put your dick back in your pants and move on with professionalism."*

I'd known I'd get screwed if I hadn't switched my thoughts in a more professional direction, taking them away from how great those beautiful lips would feel wrapped around my full blown dick, first nibbling on the bulbous knob and then swallowing my shaft whole. Man-oh-man, if he could fit all nine inches of me down his throat, I'd be in hog heaven. If gagging on me happened as it had with ninety percent of the guys who tried to blow me, there was always that high muscled butt of his I could go after instead, which from what I could tell through his navy dress slacks, was nice and tight the way I liked it. *"Oh, fuck. We're on again. Boner alert."*

I urgently corralled my thoughts from wandering any further, keeping it professional the way I was supposed to, and listened to Nykolson voluntarily tell me about how bad luck put him at the wrong place at the wrong time. For me on the other hand, his bad luck was my reward. That was selfish of me I knew, however, we'd get through the rough patch. Together. I smiled at that thought of togetherness. He looked at me with an appearance that indicated, *"What the hell is up with that smile? I'm in a crisis here."*

I knew everything he'd mentioned already, hadn't had any

reason to hear it again, but I wasn't going to stop him from opening up to me. I wanted to hear him, lose myself in the tone of his clear deep voice, get to know him, and make him feel at ease around me. As a result of telling me what was on his mind, enabled him to hang around for a while longer like I wanted him to.

As it turned out, his side of the story was lengthy and included an admission he wasn't a fan of his brother's bitch of a girlfriend. Even though he hadn't cared for her, he had no reason to push her out of a moving vehicle going ten miles an hour at a four way corner, nor had he had anything to do with planning such a thing. He was just as surprised by the event as the bitch who tried to pull off a fake accident and blame them for beating her ass had. I'd read in the documented folio given to me by the county that he was driving the girlfriends shitty Honda while his brother had taken the back seat. Nykolson was the only one in the car who wasn't hammered from drinking alcohol. He admitted he had a max of two beers, hardly finishing the second, and with that, he was the best of the three to take the wheel.

What originally hung the brothers to the wooden cross was that Nathaniel, Nykolson's identical twin, had been sitting in the back seat with strands of Dajana's fake hair clinging to his hands and a few loose weaves lying next to his feet on the floor. The evidence of that had made it appear he ripped them from her scalp while Nykolson pushed Dajana Washington out the front passenger door as she said he had. The domestic violence account hadn't been proven or what put Nykolson under arrest, but he'd been nailed for having a blood alcohol level of zero-point-zero-four. Due to his weight of one hundred seventy-five pounds, the intoxication measure fluctuated, tapping in at zero-point-zero-five, two out of the four times taken, putting him on the verge of being an impaired driver. Taking no chances by what the cop reported, the keys were confiscated and he was booked with a DUI. Since Nykolson couldn't talk his way out of having only two beers and getting behind the wheel of an automobile, the misdemeanor charge had gotten him one night in jail and an easy six months probationary house arrest, plus sponsored meetings with me, his good-looking probation officer. I'd been assigned to his case until the alarm strapped around his ankle was allowed to come off — a guaranteed six month love affair with a pretty ugly anklet.

"Strapped ankles. Strapped ankles." My thoughts had wandered again with delightful images of having my way with a bonded man, that time in which the fun included Nykolson Kannon. I was twenty-seven years old for the love of Pete, so why was I constantly thinking like a teenager — eager to stick my dick into every hot guy that walked by or rubbed up against me? Perhaps it was since I hadn't been laid in about a year. Well, that's exaggerating a little bit, but still, a guy gagging on my nine-incher doesn't exactly constitute as getting laid. I just hadn't connected with anybody that made me want to get into an hour's worth of meaningless ass banging. The job I held had put a halt on much of my social life, meaning, I'd been abridged to jerking off in front of gay porn actors on a television screen instead, dreaming I was part of the tag team. Okay, not as intimate, but it had done the trick and helped me move on.

"Strapped Ankles." Shit. The image had come to me again.

When the time comes to remove that tether from Nykolson's leg, I'd have no problem grabbing that foot in my fist, lifting it above my head and doing whatever it took to get it off, and at the same time, do whatever I needed to do to get him and me off. I started imagining how he'd look on his back with both my hands gripping his ankles, spreading those legs wide open into one magnificent wingspan that would allow me to successfully climb between them and do some masterful fucking. I'd make him beg to be fucked, never wanting me to pull out because reaming his ass felt too awesome to stop.

"Enough already. The handsome as fuck dude in front of me is not gay." I blinked away my fantasy, yet still observed the chocolate chunk of man with the beautiful white smile and strong square jawline, looking for any signals that might have given away his preference for the company of a man.

Up until that point, Nykolson had told me more of what I already knew about the case. His recollection reminded me it had been her who'd thrown a tantrum in the car, gripping the door handle and threatening to jump out if she hadn't gotten what she wanted from his brother, Nathaniel. Her idea that night was to get her so called big scary boyfriend tossed in the slammer for a domestic violence charge, one discovered to have never taken place, or probably ever would in lieu of how polite I understood Nykolson's twin brother to have been by the outline I'd read on him. I had a hard time believing a violent disposition was in either one of those two guys. Records indicated she'd had a few domestic reports filed on other boyfriends already, seemed as though she had issues with men all together and wanted revenge on them for many different reasons, and picked Nykolson's brother as her next victim.

That night, she was drunker than a stinking skunk in a trunk, apparently understanding booze would make her invincible, and the combination of a sick mind and alcohol had given her the courage to proceed with framing Nathaniel and Nykolson with a made up event. The passenger door on the car was never locked, and when she threateningly fooled with the handle, it unlatched, and she surprisingly rolled out the door as if snapped from a slingshot.

In my mind, the crazy bitch deserved it, and if it was me that had been driving, I'd have kept the car moving, leaving her ass to rot in the ditch.

Due to the bumps and scratches on her body from tumbling across the ground, and the way she wouldn't speak when the police showed up, appeared as though the two men beat the shit out of her, and the incident was documented as a life fearing situation for a fragile young lady, one who was afraid of being beaten at a later date by two vibrant thugs if she accused them of anything.

The cops practically pulled the cuffs that night, arresting Nykolson for the DUI and the alleged bodily harm to a female, taking his brother in as well by association and because he had those hairy hands as evidence.

Nykolson looked at me and proceeded telling me, "She wouldn't talk because she didn't want the police to know how drunk she was." His voice lowered, almost quivering after he told me about how his brother grabbed her shoulder to keep her from falling out of the car. During the bustle, a handful of weaves had come lose, the grip was lost altogether and out she'd gone.

Nathaniel was only trying to save the girl, but his heroic actions resulted in jail time.

I could tell Nykolson was traumatized by the ordeal. It was supposed to be a night of entertainment, but the booze had gotten the best of Dajana and it all turned uglier than any of them expected. It was a good thing the car was cornering at less than ten miles an hour, or her stupid stunt could have been much worse. For her. She limped away with scabby knees and elbows while Nykolson and his twin brother were thrown in the slammer for half the night.

I wanted to reach out and comfort him with a soothing embrace, maybe lock lips while I was at it, but I reminded myself I was a professional, in a professional setting, doing a professional job, on county time, so screwing around with someone who was detained wouldn't have been a good idea at all.

Nykolson hadn't seemed gay to me anyway, or my freaking gaydar was totally out of whack. That tender loving stunt of wanting to hug and kiss him, which might have been splendid for me, would have been another documented violent altercation added to his record when he knuckle busted me in the chops instead of kissing it. But... Jeez... those fucking eyes, and those beautiful brown lips were begging me to dive in and have at them. If only and as if. I lustfully licked my own lips and sat back in my chair before I'd gotten myself into trouble with him and the law.

I looked at the clock displayed on my computer screen and noticed we'd been holding down our conversation for close to an hour. Wow! Had that surprised me? No. But I couldn't believe time had flown by that quickly. It had, and it was time for him and me to get moving. I had other clients that day besides mister good-looking. But, I wasn't up to him leaving the office in a miserable state, or thinking his life as he knew it was crumbling, so I tried easing his mind by telling him it could only get better, and that I was around to help him get his life back on track, the way it was before *"that little bitch"* put him into the situation he hadn't deserved to have been in.

I'd scheduled his upcoming appointments that required physical appearances for the next several Monday mornings until the tether was allowed to come off, and told him I'd be available any other day of the week if he needed anything or somebody to talk to. Of course I wanted more than just a county reported visit from that black man, but when telling him he could call me anytime, I was honestly speaking as his parole officer.

His eyes had nearly glazed over when he looked at me. "Thank you, Mister Millhouse, Sir," — he glanced at my nameplate — "I'll take advantage of your offer for sure."

I felt the urge to hug that man, but instead, told him to call me Michael and dismiss addressing me as mister or sir. That made me feel dinosaur old, and for the record, I was actually two years younger than he was, so it hadn't felt right at all. I'd taken his hand in mine and had shaken it with compassion, unlike my colder character I'd shown him when he first arrived at my office. I'd done everything I could at that moment not to hold my gaze on those damned gray eyes, and if my gaydar served me correctly, he'd caught hold of the glint I had in my eyes for him.

On his way out, I wanted him to know I had a softer side to me as well — one that was keen on getting him through his dilemma while keeping true to my obligations as a parole officer.

His turn had come to show me his internal emotions. Nykolson held onto my hand and kept eye contact with me longer than a man who wasn't gay would have. In fact, he encased mine in both of his as though he never wanted to let it go until I vowed, "I do," and added his last name to mine.

Elaborated wishful thinking.

As I lingered woozily into his gray eyed gaze without blinking, my gaydar had instantly come back to life, making my brain do mad circus tricks. I silently argued with sexual urges racing through me at the same time I fought against releasing his strong hand. Admittedly, I wanted to hold on longer than a handshake was supposed to last, but regrettably, our manly bond had to come to an end. I hadn't wanted that, and I was hoping like hell he hadn't either.

"*Fuck my life.*" Another boner alert had come into play and I couldn't put the damn thing to use, like sticking it into the guy. I smoothly turned away for a moment, acting as if I purposely spun to view the sky outside the window, but had really done it to hide my growing erection trying to get at Nykolson's asshole. I wondered if he had noticed, and fuck me for missing the opportunity to see if he had one too. That there would have been my clue the man was gay and found my touch and beauty alluring enough to give him an erection.

As soon as my cock settled to the point I was comfortable enough with turning back around, I returned to his side and walked him out. I watched him go, his black ass calling for me as each cheek shifted with every step, making me wonder the entire time how tight he'd feel wrapped around my full blown stiffy.

While he strolled across the parking lot, he glanced over his shoulder with a smile directed right at me, and as long as my eyesight wasn't playing tricks on my homoerotic fucked up brain, I was sure he added a wink that I understood as, *"I'm so totally interested in you, good looking, and yes, you can put that white boy dick up my ass."*

"Maybe that tall, dark, masculine stud is gay." I thought at that splendid moment, opportunity might have just knocked on Michael Millhouse's front door.

Chapter 3

I'd gone back to my office to deliberate over what had just taken place, processing the bits of information Nykolson had passed on during our meeting, ignoring most of what he'd told me about the incident, except for the part where he mentioned he despised Nathaniel's girlfriend, Dajana Washington. I probably would have absorbed more if I wasn't thinking about fucking the guy. I couldn't get him, his face, or that penetrable ass of his out of my head. Until I'd done something about my sexual frustration, the rest of my day might have been shot to hell and I wouldn't have been able to concentrate on anything else.

"Jeez, that hard black ass of his." I hadn't touched it, but I could tell it was firm just by looking at the fucking thing.

After breathing the same air that Nykolson had and coming inches from locking lips with the man, I'd casually gone to the restroom down the hall to choke the chicken—privately eject the seeds from my loins while thinking about sticking my dick into any or all of Nykolson's hot inviting holes. I stiffened when I thought his butt might have been deprived of a man's cock slipping into it, and I'd gotten harder at the idea of my white dick sliding in, pulling out, and going back in again, breaking in that black hole with newfound force. I was more than ready to have been the one to bust that virgin manhole.

All those butt fucking thoughts about a virgin ass had caused me to leak pre-cum, and my only fix would have been to beat the meat... like straightaway.

The way Nykolson looked—which stereotyping by appearance alone was bad on my part—the man probably wasn't the type to spread his legs for another guy, but would have been the one who'd do all the banging. Either way, I bet myself he was one hell of a fucker and a lover.

If Nykolson was gay, as I'd hoped, he seemed more like the pitcher in a relationship than the catcher. A bit of a downer for me, but… either way, I so badly wanted to find out. I had no qualms about bottoming for that man if that's the way he played. I could learn to take a dick all over again. I assumed it was like riding a bicycle. Once mastered, it wasn't forgotten. I could just pick up right where I'd left off. In time, if he trusted me to be the man he'd like to hug and kiss, I'd help him discover the meaning of versatility, teach him to take mine for a joy ride as well, if in fact he'd never sat down on a dick before. He might find a liking for it and I could work on getting him to switch positions—bottom for me so hard, he'd never want to top again. Jolly ho for me.

When I reached the restroom down the hall from my office, I pushed the door open at a slower pace than I normally would have, backing into the abode while looking outward to make sure I wasn't being followed, hopeful I'd been left alone for the time I needed to relieve myself from the stone hard misery I'd been left with. The institutional style toilet room echoed when the door slammed shut and a haunting click of my heels across the tile floor rebounded off every wall as I walked. I hadn't heard anything other than my own noises, or noticed any of the four shitter doors had been closed and latched. All of them slightly left open. I was happy to see the three urinals were cold and free of pissers, too. The hollowness had proven I was the sole person hanging out in the crapper.

Even with my nerves pricking every part of my body for being daring enough to jerk off in a public place, my hard-on had still grown substantially in size by the time I reached one of the uninviting stalls where the chilly stool would feel like an ice block when first planting my bare ass down on the horseshoe shaped seat. Other than meeting up with a frightening vagina, a cold toilet seat was a close second for killing a gay man's erection… for me anyway. Men, who weren't gay, might think differently about coming in contact with the lady bits. Nothing wrong with that, though. Love is love. Godspeed.

As I spun to punch the lock into place, my projecting dick was nearly knocked off when the metal door swung into it. The electrifying jolt I had gotten from being smacked in the pecker actually felt pretty charming. In fact, I'd done it a couple more times for the fun of it before locking up and shucking it off as freaky foreplay. *"Jeez. Fucking a door? What is wrong with me? Am I that hard up for a piece of ass? Sit your hairy butt down and get to it already."*

Bopping my bologna in the restroom that time wasn't a first for me. Nope. I'd done it a few times before when I was in an aroused pinch, but never had I been as eager as I was that day after Nykolson left my office. He'd done something to me — turned my horny into super horny, gotten a rise out of me without even laying a hand on my body. With beauty like his burning up my brain, I couldn't help but playfully tell myself I was in love with all of that. Yep, that man was perfect, and I was sexually in love. Hornier than a toad. Ready to burst if I hadn't blown my load within the next few minutes.

While sitting in the crisp white chamber right handedly fisting my red hot erection, I weirdly whispered to myself, "that's it, Nykolson. Ride that dick." I closed my eyes and imagined my hand was Nykolson Kannon sitting center in my lap, his tight black ass gripping me, sliding up and down my dick, working that cum out of me.

When I'd reached that moment where I was totally into my jerkoff session, about to lose my nut, I had the shit scared out of me when an intrusive bang echoed on the outside of my stall.

"Fuck, me," I squeaked, hopefully had gone unheard by the idiot who crashed through the entry door so abruptly with intentions of adopting the bathroom for what it was meant to have been used for. By how violently he busted in, I supposed the guy had to pee like a pent up racehorse.

I'd almost taken another ghostly shit when the guy's cell phone skated across the floor and stopped a few inches from my shoe. I heard an, "Oh fuck," as a hand reached down and picked it up only moments before I was about to kick it back into the main chamber of the restroom.

Then I heard, "Whew. Oh yeah. That's good," while a powerful urine stream was playing music on the porcelain unit outside my stall. It was, Rusty Poindexter, the red headed intern who recently joined the office, hopeful to someday manage the place. A goal of his, I couldn't see ever happening for him. I could tell it was Rusty by his voice and the clumsy actions he'd been known for. The kid had always cracked me up. He was like a busy worker bee that hardly accomplished anything because he made such a mess of everything he touched. It was as if his nerves were always on fire.

I patiently waited for the intruder to empty what seemed to have been an oversized bladder and find his way back out of the bathroom so I could finish what I'd started. I really needed to shoot my load, thanks to Nykolson Kannon and those smoldering gray eyes with the come get me shimmer.

"For the love of Pete, Rusty. Come on already." I was wound up beyond raging at that point and it seemed as though Rusty's pee break was going to take an hour to complete.

Finally. Privacy crept back.

I was still bone hard, but waited a minute before going at it again. Then, more muted whispering had come out of my mouth, "Yeah. That's it, Nykolson. Ride that cock. Suck the cum out of me with that tight black ass." The sound of his name and the image of him taking my dick for a rodeo ride had made me lose my rocks in less than a minute. I was too far gone to count the spurts, but I knew it had to have been somewhere between ten to fifteen jets — the usual.

I tried like hell to prevent semen from getting on my clothes, but being lost in the mind blowing moment, my jiz flew all over the place. I'd even held a cupped hand out to catch most of it, but unfortunately, I wasn't successful during my spasmodic jerking. The amount I released flowed through my fingers and over the sides of my hand. Aside from the puddle in my palm, I saw pearly gobs had spotted my silk tie and was quickly soaking in.

"Fuck an A." The A was for asshole. There hadn't been much I could have done at that point other than remove the evidence of what I'd done. That was one of the times the heavy producer I was had been problematic.

Before leaving my semi-private masturbation chamber, I snaked the necktie from the confines of my collar and stuffed it into the inside pocket of my charcoal sport coat. When I made it safely to the sink to wash the thrill of the orgasm off my hands, I noticed a few small spots of cum had made it to my crisp white shirt. I vigorously brushed at the stains with paper towel, hopeful to influence a faster drying cycle, but miserably, that hadn't dried it one hundred percent. To help conceal the mess I'd made, I buttoned my jacket and proudly walked out of the restroom as if I'd done nothing out of the ordinary. *"Nykolson Kannon. I blame you and that rockin' hot body."*

Every few steps, I'd been able to smell the pungent scent of semen wafting into my septum. Call me a cum slut, but semen really smelled pleasant to me. I found it to mimic a fine cologne, an arousal inducer, and if I could have gotten away with it, I'd wear it as my signature fragrance.

On the way back to my private office, it had come as no surprise that Berdella Hutcherson, the office gossip queen had met up with me in the hallway, acting as though her thundering ass was just passing by. She stopped in front of me, pressed a pink pointy fingernail into my chest, jabbing a couple times before pulling it away, and at no skepticism to me, asked, "Didn't you have a pretty pink tie on when you went in there, Michael Millhouse?" She shifted from side to side in a way that prevented me from moving forward until I answered her.

That nosey wench must have watched me the moment I had come in the front door that morning, probably had her binoculars on Nykolson the entire time he was with me, and timed me while I jerked off in the bathroom, just waiting for me to come out. I knew what she was up to, so I lied and told her water had splashed from the faucet when I was washing my hands, giving me no other choice but to take it off. Her auburn-dyed hair swished in sticky hair-sprayed chunks as her head pivoted on top of her neck. As usual, she was being nosey, and I knew she had been trying to figure out where I'd stashed the tie and why. I refused to give her the satisfaction of seeing it, so instead, I'd given her something else to visualize.

She snarled after I mentioned I shouldn't have eaten spicy chicken wings the night before, which was what had given me the Hershey-squirts to shoot from my asshole in the restroom, practically flushing the toilet on splashdown. Another crock of shit—I was on a roll. But her reaction to what I'd said was funny as fuck.

I smirked when she gasped and brought her hand to her skinny neck to clutch pearls that weren't even there. She huffed and stormed off, probably bothered that I hadn't given her a story she was expecting to hear. That'll teach the queen of gossip, hopefully stop her from prying into my business. Who the fuck invited her to my sperm shooting party anyway? It sure as hell wasn't me.

Damn, I disliked that noise maker in a major way. I was only a jackass to her. For those who had opposite intentions than Berdella, I'd gone out of my way to be cordial, treated them with respect and communicated the truth. I was helpful beyond the norm of an average person, and naturally refrained from offending people. But that busybody bitch was always getting on my last nerve, poking her "bigass" nose into everybody's affairs, fabricating the story and blabbing about it to somebody else. She should have taken up a career as a rag columnist instead of a documents entry person at the CPPO, Cumberland Probation & Parole offices. I'm certain she would have been good at that rag job, and could embellish the stories the way she wanted, and put them into print for everyone to read. I guess her reason for holding the chair at CPPO was to get into the private files of people she didn't know, just to tell _both_ her friends about it so they could have helped her spread the news. I'd always sensed there had been more to that miserable piece of shit than what she had let us see. People like her always had a skeleton or two hidden in the closet. They'd spoken ill of others to divert attention off themselves.

Once I returned to my desk, shirt stained, smelling like cum, relieved and a little bit more comfortable, I'd been able to focus on what I was supposed to, like other offender's assigned to me. For the most part I'd been able to do that, but with Nykolson's folder wide open on my PCs second screen, which had allowed me to have looked at his mugshot all day long, had taken me away from being one hundred percent on top of what I should have been doing. It would have been better if he was scheduled closer to the end of the day, or best at five in the evening on Friday. That way, I could have been more focused on my work and gone straight home to privacy while imagining all the naked positions I'd put him in. That mugshot photo of him was pretty damned hot, even with a file arrest number under his chin. Maybe that'd been what had done it for me — a bad boy with a prison seal. With his face as my make-shift screen saver, that had set me into motion for breaking the CPPO's policies pertaining to fraternizing with detainee's and internal office personnel. But, I couldn't help like what I liked.

"Fuck, I was fucked."

Chapter 4

A few days had gone by since I'd first met Nykolson, and I was crazily fixated with seeing him again. I had no right to be obsessive over the guy, but he hadn't amounted to the type of person I could simply dismiss from my thoughts. He was too damned handsome. In fact, he hadn't left my mind since he winked at me in the parking lot on his way out that Monday morning. I was certain it was a wink, not caused by the blinding sunshine poking at his eye. I couldn't wait to see him again, to endorse my hopeful thoughts about him being just like me — a gay as fuck man with an interest for interracial love.

Before my introduction to Nykolson, Monday's had never been a favorite day of mine, but after meeting that man, I had good reason for wanting that blasted day to show its ugliness sooner than later. Nykolson certainly changed my mindset regarding the Monday blues and I wished for that day to arrive already. I had to tell myself that good things come to those who wait, and to help me make it through the week, I'd jerked myself off every chance I had to mind recollecting images of his perfect form and face. I could have phoned him before his appointment date, made something up as if it pertained to parole business, but figured my eager approach would have surely indicated my impatience for getting at what he had stuffed in the front of his pants.

I wondered what he'd been up to since the day he walked away from me, hoping he'd been jerking off to thoughts of me as

SHAKEDOWN

I'd been doing with him. Without any known facts, he must have been spending the days at home minding his Ps and Qs like the good man I seemed to have thought he was.

I had Nykolson's cell number, even his email address, but I had to kick myself in the big hairy nut sac to stay alert so I wouldn't mistakenly press send while I entered his number into my phone. I *had* to leave the guy alone, let him be the one to screw up—if he would. It shouldn't have been me, the professional, instigating the breakdown in protocol. Savagely, I continued with entering his house address into my phone in case a drive-by was necessary. No rules broken there, that was part of the deal for being connected to him as his P.O.

"Oh, Lawd. Connected to him." That for a fact I wanted to have been. Was it possible I could have been so horny that a simple word such as connected had given me a hard-on?

I released a shameful sigh, but had been startled out of it when my phone lit up with Nykolson's mug shot I'd downloaded to my contact list. On the second ring, I grinned. Hadn't meant to, but I had. My heart sped up, wondering what he was calling me about. I was praying it wasn't anything major—like he murdered the bitch who accused him of beating her up.

Ring number three was when I picked up the call, trying not to appear overly excited. Keeping the call professional, I answered, "Good afternoon, this is Michael Millhouse." I pinched my eyes shut, provoking contortion from forehead to chin and thought how corny I must have sounded with my firm tone.

"Hello, Michael, I mean, Mister Millhouse," Nykolson rattled. I heard a small amount of stress behind his voice, but had chosen not to elaborate on his character. I humbly let him tell me what the reason was for the call after I asked how he was doing.

The sound of his voice had gotten quieter as if somebody he hadn't wanted to hear had been standing over his shoulder listening to the conversation. For the first time since I'd met him, I hadn't thought about bending him over the printer and fucking him, but instead had become concerned.

After a few moments of silence, Nykolson told me his brother had come up against some trouble with that piece of shit girlfriend of his again, or ex-girlfriend if the brother was as smart

35

as I'd understood him to have been. After the ordeal she'd put them both through, I couldn't imagine Nathaniel hadn't already dumped the bitch back into the garbage bin she'd chosen to live in.

As though he'd been concerned, Nykolson asked where I was. I answered, "at the office," and told him he and Nathaniel were welcome to stop by anytime, or I could meet them at his home or someplace nearby. I was up in the air with the idea of getting involved with Nathaniel and his problems, but my instincts as a P.O. kicked in and I felt it was my job to help out even though I had no ties to any existing files on him.

Nykolson huffed in the phone before advising what I was already aware of, "I think it'll be a bit tough for me to leave the house with this tether on my ankle, Mikey. It might be a better idea if you come to us."

He had a point, but as is P.O., I could bend rules if I felt it was with due cause. *To say I was stunned just then was an understatement. Where had the nickname come from and what instigated Nykolson to call me that?* It was cute, and I liked it. A lot.

I felt a smidgen of warmth roll through me when I heard him call me Mikey as if we were good friends, or better yet, I was his boyfriend. *"Oh, Gawd, imagine that?"* With a smile tucked away behind my voice, I let him know if we decided to meet somewhere off his property, I had the authority to approve his prison break by putting it on record that *"the arrested"* was with me for observation purposes. My criminal label sounded "verge inappropriate", but it was what it was and made him laugh as soon as he commented on me calling him, "The Arrested." Since he found my verbiage comical, had only supplemented my inclinations about his innocence pertaining to the charges Miz Dajana Washington raised against him. Nykolson's laughter was sexier than shit and had given my entire body those soul caressing chills—from head to toe, with a few extra sparks igniting my crotch. I'd felt myself stiffen a little bit, and what I wanted at that moment was to hear his laughter and see his body in person. I recklessly mumbled, "Boner alert," and had just about gone into cardiac arrest when I heard Nykolson ask me what had just come out of my mouth.

"Aw, Fuck! He's onto me." Wasn't that what I wanted?

Steering the conversation away from my boner, I quickly asked if Starbucks or Panera Bread was a good place to meet with me. I liked both establishments and there were plenty of quiet areas inside either location where we could have a semi-private conversation and I could gawk at the man without too many people seeing me slobbering over him. Plus, a public place would prevent a full out attack on the man—help keeping my ass tamed.

Nykolson answered that either place would be okay. "How about you stop over here, pick us up, and the three of us can go together to whichever place you decide?"

"What? Three? Oh, the brother. Right. Okay. I can do three."

Nykolson's voice was so sexy over the phone I could hardly contain my interest, and I liked the way he'd given me the direct order. I was impressed, and that assured me he wouldn't hold back when telling me what he wanted if we had ever become a couple.

"Aw shit, he's a Dom. A top. Or, hopefully, maybe he's a bossy bottom." I could work with that.

After I'd heard Nykolson's identical voice in the background mentioning he preferred coffee over bread, I immediately said, "Starbucks it is."

I told them to stay put, and I'd be by to pick them up in about thirty to forty minutes. The timing couldn't have been better—Lunch breaks were finishing up, which would provide a less packed coffee house at two-thirty in the afternoon.

After Nykolson agreed with Starbucks and before ending the call, I'd told him it was okay to come as they were, no judgement would have been placed for the way he and his twin would have been dressed. It was a casual meeting, plus more about Nathaniel than Nykolson.

My heart rate increased a little bit because I was about to meet the identical brother. The miracle of twins had always fascinated me, and getting to view those two side by side made me wonder how close he and his brother really resembled one another. I'd seen a few pictures of Nathaniel in the file, but since I wasn't involved with him, I hadn't paid much attention to the grainy photos I'd been given. Oh, the joys of twins and how my imagination had run wild about the two of them in the same room... with me. There wasn't a negative thought as for how great the experience would have been being pinned between a pair of sexy male twins. Starbucks was in for a treat that afternoon and I was part of the trio.

As soon as I ended the call, I shut my office down and had taken off to the parking lot as though I'd had a tiger on my tail, and the sumbitch was freaking hungry. I punched Nykolson's home address into my navigation system, permanently storing it as a favorite stop, and then put the pedal to the metal. My tires laid rubber and the truck squealed away.

When I pulled up to Nykolson's modular home set on its own cement foundation, I was thoroughly impressed with how nice it seemed. I'd never imagined it would look the way it had. Anybody viewing it from the street would never guess it hadn't been built from the ground up under the elements of outdoors. I'd recently heard good things about those homes, but convincing myself a manufactured home was worthy of laying out the dollar had me second guessing ever investing in one. So it'd gone without further mention, I was rather impressed with Nykolson's stunning home. Either the guy was likely gay, had a secret passion for design with an artistic eye for curb appeal, or those homes had come a long way from the trailer on wheels I'd understood them to have been. I put a stop to those thoughts of it being either or, and concluded my hopes it was both.

Sitting in the drive with my currently leased pickup truck idling, I waited with the mindset of letting the two come out of the house when they were good and ready. I found myself having a difficult time waiting patiently since I was more than excited to see Nykolson again, meet his twin brother and start comparing the two of them side by side. As far as twins go, I could pretty much define they had the same eyes, the same smile, same bodies, and oh Gawd, the same dick. I was game for checking these guys out full Monty and claim proof to my thoughts on their similarities.

Yes, my mind had gone there. Whose wouldn't?

While I waited for Nathaniel and Nykolson to appear, I felt as though I'd set myself up on a sting operation, expecting a true crime lord to sight himself on the front doorstep of his hideout with surrendering arms held high above his head.

Then the moment I was waiting for had arrived.

"Oh sweet Mary mother of the baby Jesus, would you take a look at that." I nearly lost my mind when the two of them stepped through the front doorway wearing the same clothing. I wondered if that was socially planned or because their minds rode the same wave even when they were apart.

"Holy crap, I'm screwed," I said quietly as though preventing them from hearing me at thirty feet away.

I wasn't sure who had come out first, but I believed it was Nykolson leading the way. Since I'd lost my mind when they exited the house, fucking up my ability to pay attention or even think clearly, I hadn't given thought to check for the tether, which had been attached to the front brother's right ankle. I would have figured that out sooner if I hadn't been so busy checking out their muscular arms that were exposed because the navy Tee shirt with yellow Abercrombie & Fitch lettering across their chests had no sleeves. They might as well have walked off the pages of an A & F catalog with their tan cargo shorts and bill backward baseball caps on. I could have seriously screwed Nykolson right then, across the hood of my truck in broad daylight, maybe his brother, too, if he'd let me. But, which one would bend over for me first? Perhaps we could form a trio train and share the experience together. Since I hadn't been stuck in the ass for a very, very long time, and would run into a super tight butthole situation if holding a position as the middle car, I'd consider myself happiest hooking up at the rear.

The closer they had gotten, I was surprisingly able to snap out of my fantasy where I was trapped on a train ride with a pair of twins. As glorious as that would have been, I needed to turn those thoughts over to business as usual. I'd been called to their place for help or advice, not to be the meat in an identical twin sandwich. *"Oh gawd, that would be superb."*

To pull off politeness, I stepped out of the truck to greet them.

I looked like the father figure in my pressed shirt and purple tie and felt a tad bit out of place standing next to them in their casual Tee shirts and ball caps. I'd told Nykolson earlier by phone there'd be no judgement based on dress wear, which meant I had no choice other than to follow my own advice. Had I don't that? Hell no. I needed to relax or deal with my neck sweating consequences. So instead, I tugged at the tie's guppy nut, loosening it from around my neck to take my dressy appearance down a few notches.

"I wanted to blend."

Being cordial, I headed to the other side of the vehicle and introduced myself to Nykolson's brother, who amazingly looked exactly like him.

I noticed Nykolson watching every step I'd taken and I'd totally lost my nerves. What the fuck! I was usually confident when meeting new people, but having a crush on my offender made me blunder like a schoolboy who couldn't control his erections.

As expected, the introduction had gone quickly, and soon after, the three of us climbed into the truck and headed over to Starbucks for a coffee break and a chat. My secret desire had come true when Nykolson had taken the middle spot next to me. Our legs pressed up against each other's—his touch had given me anxiety—I silently cursed the long pants I was wearing, wishing I was in a pair of shorts so I'd be able to feel his brown flesh rubbing up against mine.

I glanced down at the defined muscles in Nykolson's legs, following his inner thigh as far as I could before the hem of his cargo shorts put a stop to my traveling gaze. Nykolson could have pulled away, but he hadn't. My thoughts had run wild. Was Nykolson's position and touch a subtle signal that let me know he was stricken with desire to be more than just my assignment? Or was I reading too much into the way his leg was touching mine? There wasn't much room in the cab, so I was likely imagining more than what was there.

I graciously moved my gaze back on the road where it belonged, leaving my leg where it was, tightly pressed against his.

I hadn't said much along the way and neither had the twins. I figured Nathaniel was shy at the moment, and as for Nykolson, I thought he might have remained reserved so I wouldn't figure out he had a crush on me.

One conversation we'd had, Nykolson expressed he liked my truck, and in the same sentence, confessed he was expecting a county official cruiser where he'd have been handcuffed to the back seat behind a caged wall for security purposes. After telling him P.O., hadn't stood for Police Officer, he chuckled and mentioned the cozy cab suited him just fine and he was happy with his position in the front instead of in the back.

Was that another subtle gaydar signal for me to have caught onto? I'd taken it as though it was, picturing him on all fours in front, with me hooking up in the back. Where was the lubricant when I needed a shit load? Not at the ready, that's for sure.

I'd gotten a kick out of Nykolson's reaction when I told him we'd either driven side by side in the truck or climbed aboard my motorcycle and the three of us could have traveled tandem. His excitement about the two-wheeled crotch rocket with a fast engine was instantaneous, and if I hadn't been wrong, he'd spurted in his shorts the moment I mentioned it.

I perked up when he showed so much interest in taking it for a spin with me. I was certainly up for that and was ready to get him on it. I pictured the two of us riding, fitting snugly in the seat, his chest pressed against my back, arms tightly wrapped around my waist with his chin resting on my shoulder from behind. Perhaps I had purchased that bike for a good reason, not just for my own pleasure—but to take my boyfriend for a rebel riding race. Maybe end up alone at a lakeside picnic where we could explore each other privately in the bush.

He bumped his shoulder up against mine and said, "Name the date and I'll hop right on."

"*Oh gawd.*" Gaydar overload. Hop on what? My mind had gone someplace else.

If he was working at trying to figure out if I was gay, he was certainly making all the right moves and asking all the right questions, some of course subliminally, others not so much.

I kept thinking, "*was he or wasn't he?*" That was the ultimate question.

I could stop pussyfooting around and just ask the man, "*Hey-hey. Are you a gay?*" That ridiculous cheer would have come out corny, yet would have gotten my question answered quicker than trying to put puzzle pieces together until I'd seen the full picture.

Statistically, there was an excellent chance that one of the identical born twins was attracted to the same gender. It happens quite often. Considering the process of elimination based on recent events—Nathaniel, who seemed to have taken interest in boobs and vaginas over a beautiful throbbing cock, a muscled chest, and excessive body hair, meant there was a very high gamble Nykolson was the twin who preferred a man to have and to hold.

Hot damn! I was totally high on luck and I hadn't any need to trip on over to Vegas.

Chapter 5

"I enjoy this place. The smell of ground coffee is like a warm hug," Nathaniel had finally spoken while breathing the aroma inside the Starbucks establishment.

I sat opposite the brothers in a corner booth secluded in the back. It was the perfect spot, allowing me to look at all the duplicate glory on the other side of the table. The two were sitting so tightly against each other they appeared to be one person with two heads—Nykolson practically in Nathaniel's lap.

It was charming how close the two of them were and I adored the way Nathaniel was single handedly massaging the back of Nykolson's neck, probably not even realizing he'd been doing it. I understood and presumed those types of actions had come naturally for twins, also heard stories about their incontestable connections—how they felt each other's mood swings, sensed the other's feelings, and thought on the same wavelength even when apart from one another. I could tell by observing their actions, there was some truth to those mysterious statistics.

With both of them appearing a little bit tense, I decided to initiate the conversation, starting out with how much I thought they resembled one another. After I'd mentioned that, I wished I could have taken it back, but it was already out and too late for a do over. Neither one of them replied, only smiled at each other before turning their gaze back at me, probably finding the statement somewhat annoying, and likely getting tired of hearing it on a daily basis from everyone else.

To mask that comment and hoping the next one wasn't as monotonous, I threw out, "Have you guys ever thought about a career as cover models? Like with Abercrombie or Aéropostale? I see you're already wearing the clothing and there's a cool resemblance to Colton Haynes. You have the same facial features — a strong jawline, come kiss me under the moonlight lips, sharp nose and a set of eyes that would reel in anybody's attention. You'd compliment those catalogs nicely."

I seemed to have gotten overly confident at getting them on the pages of a highly circulated catalog, and finally cooled down when Nykolson answered, "We would need an agent for that, and I don't think we're black enough for the messages those companies like to portray. We'd get lost on those pages, and it doesn't help I'm an awkward poser. Plus, Colton? Now *that* dude is far better looking than the two of us put together. With a face and kissable lips like that guy has, you have to agree he's more marketable than we'd ever be. Actually, you might have beaten us on those Colton Haynes moonlight kissable lips. Those babies of yours don't look half bad and look more like his than ours do." I caught Nykolson staring at mine before he smirked.

"Wait a minute." Had I heard Nykolson say Colton's lips were kissable and in a roundabout way, mine were too? I was sure I had, and believed I'd been given another gay AF signal that Nykolson was in tune with kissing men and knowing which types of lips he liked? I was sure I'd caught him running a tongue over his own lips after looking at mine.

I tried not to get any more excited than I already was about everything happening on the other side of that table. I cleared my constricted throat and said, "I'd say you two are just as marketable if not more, and in my opinion, as equally good looking as Mister Hayne's," — I put another bug in Nykolson's ear that would tell him I knew a handsome man when I saw one — "and the advantage you'd have would be double the pleasure... for everybody's eyes... men and women... and the clothing industry would benefit on those perks for sure. Don't get me started on being black enough either. From what I see, the two of you are every bit black enough. Sure you're skin tone is a little bit lighter, but still black. If you know it or not, you two are fresh and just what a catalog like A&F would be interested in. Trust me. The two of you are very editorial. We'll talk about that later."

Who had I thought I was? I'd spoken like an agent... their gay agent. I should have kept my mouth shut, but it seemed to have wanted to spit out what my head had been thinking. My verbal filter had worn thin, letting just about everything through. I rattle when I'm nervous. I only hoped Nykolson picked up on the hints I'd been handing him regarding me and my attraction toward men. They had been subtle, but I'd put them out there. Aside from my efforts on that, at least I'd gotten a smile out of the two of them—Nykolson's a smidgen bigger than Nathaniel's. Shit, those teeth. So bright and reflective. I knew just the trick to help keep them polished.

After taking a sip of my boiling hot coffee, nearly burning my lips and tongue in the process, I changed the subject and asked what their reason was for organizing our meet and greet, and I wondered what had made them think I'd be able to help them out.

Nykolson had spoken first, telling me I was the only person he'd thought of who had insight on a few laws and what could have been done to keep Dajana away from his brother. I'd already known the bitch was crazy and by the sounds of things, they'd known it too—first hand, actually.

My advice to Nathaniel had been to file a restraining order against the woman. That was, however, if he had proof one would have been necessary. If she'd gone against the courts orders after that, she'd have been the one put in jail instead of him. I'd gone on and asked Nathaniel what she'd done to him lately that had triggered such concern.

As I waited for an answer from Nathaniel, I noticed Nykolson looking directly at me, almost staring right through the back of my skull. His head slightly tilted as though stuck in a fantasy.

"*Sumbitch.*" Was he trying to figure me out, or had I captivated him so much, he'd instantly admitted to himself he liked what he'd seen? Praise Jesus in the glorious manger, I certainly hoped so.

As if the guy was a little bit nervous, I felt his knee bouncing up and down against mine, and the rhythm seemed to have been going a hundred miles an hour. I was certain he felt me under the table by the way I purposely shifted a few times to see if he'd jerk away.

Pulling his knee from mine, he hadn't, nor had he seemed interested in doing so. He seemed to be enjoying our itty bitty knee rubbing connection, and far be it from me to move my leg aside if touching me was what he wanted. I turned my head away from Nykolson at the very moment Nathaniel captured my attention with news if he hadn't paid the rent on Dajana's apartment, she'd beat herself up with a bag of oranges after self-fisting her twat.

I privately thought, *"What the fuck? Who does shit like that?"* Crazy people, that's who, and she was clearly a top notch lunatic as far as I was concerned. Anybody who would self-inflict injury and blame it on somebody else had something missing upstairs. I thought again, *"Who does shit like that?"*

I was pretty sure the expression on my face had told the two of them I was shocked by what I'd heard. Truth be told, I was grossed out about the fist to the twat, but overall stunned that somebody would actually pull something like that off to get what they wanted from another individual.

When Nathaniel told me he flat out refused her pathetic demand, which I'm glad to have heard that, she said he was only forcing her to go to the cops with a violence case against him again, bruises and all—the ones she'd done to herself with a dry fist and a bag of fruit.

After listening to that crazy story and remembering all the mismatched evidence against Nathaniel already in the file, I realized Dajana Washington was the typical freeloader, and if she hadn't gotten her way, would make trouble until she'd gotten it. I was surprised she hadn't already popped out six kids with six different fathers, just so she'd have been able to collect government dollars on each one of them. I'd seen similar cases, where the girl said no when she really meant yes, only to cry nonconsensual sex occurred when it really hadn't been that at all. Those are serious allegations and the court doesn't take those fake cries of sexual assault lightly anymore.

Anyway, I tried to convince Nathaniel that Dajana wouldn't stand a chance if there wasn't any true evidence that he'd done anything, such as possible knuckle imprints and bodily scratches on him from the attempt she would have made at fighting back. DNA extraction would have proven a lot, like maybe his flesh found under her fingernails or pre-ejaculate near her tampon packed vagina. That would have been the first thing looked at and a dead giveaway the innocent guy had never gone near her vicious tooth lined pussy. So far, I'd found Dajana to be a crack pot, probably a master at what she does, which meant she might have a plan with evidence already in place. I'd kept that bit from the twins, so not to cause panic.

"You have a point," Nathaniel said, but I could tell by the way he glanced at Nykolson, there was doubt with what I'd told him. He put his arm around Nykolson's shoulders and said, "If it wasn't for my bruh here giving me a realization whack to the head, that filthy *cunt*"—he whispered the word—"would have screwed up my life more than she already has. I guess I was too pussy-whipped to see that for myself." He used the word cunt very loosely, which to me was the ultimate term of disgust for a female, and in Dajana's case, well deserved. If he'd gone as far as to say that horrible word, I was pretty certain he'd reached his limit after the last stunt she pulled. Apart from that, I liked how the twins seemed to have each other's backs during a crisis. Nobody was going to fuck with either of them without the other. My question was—why on earth had it taken him so long to move away from the hussy if he knew she was bad news? Can lady bits fuck up a man's head that easily, clamp down so hard on his pecker that he couldn't seem to pull away? Could a,—pardon my use of the word—"cunt", be that desirable? Oy! That was something I'd never be acquainted with or ever wanted to find out. I'm totally hooked on big dicks and tight man-asses.

Nathaniel gripped Nykolson's chin and shook his jaw before giving him a few slaps on the cheek. "I'm right about you, eh, bruh?"

Nykolson smiled, his expression presenting knowledge that what his brother had said was true. They fist bumped and then wiggled their fingers as their hands pulled apart. Damn, they were effing cute. I wanted to chow down on them both and then fuck the hell out of Nykolson while his brother watched. Jeez, that guy was putting shit in my head I hadn't even known was in me.

Before I finished my coffee, I assured them I'd do whatever I could to help get Dajana off Nathaniel's back. She was a class A trouble maker of the worst kind, and I'd already disliked her without even meeting her—or meeting *"IT"*—face to face in order to form my own opinion of IT—I mean her. No way in tarnation would that filthy wench mess with who could very well be my future boyfriend. There were easy fixes to the brother's problems, which I hadn't divulged, but would fill them in on legal processes soon enough, if any would have been necessary.

"Is that all you wanted to tell me?" I asked and waited for an answer with one curious eyebrow lifted. They both blinked at the same time, in harmony, flashing me those beautiful grays. They really are in sync. Freaking amazing. It was super cool to have witnessed the twin connection first hand.

"Um... Almost. One more thing." Nykolson surprised me when he shyly asked for a picture of me, mentioning he needed it for the contact tile he had of me on his phone. I smirked when Nathaniel nudged Nykolson's shoulder, sneaking in a smug grin and a half assed wink. What had just happened then looked like an uncontrollable response out of Nathaniel when he realized his brother was making his moves on another guy. If my intuition had been on the mark, I'd have said Nykolson was getting the mating ritual going with me, and his identical brother was pushing him closer to the starting line.

I said, "Of course. How do you want me?" *On my knees, perhaps? Over top of you, perhaps?*

Nykolson's reaction to my question returned a certain appearance of greed, like he wanted more than a pose out of me, or I looked like a perfectly braised lamb chop he needed to take a bite out of. I was certainly game if he was, whether his intentions were to fuck me or to eat me. Shoot, if I had my way, I'd have bent Nykolson over that table we were sitting at, swabbed his hole with butter, and skewered him like he was the meat on my shish kabob grilling stick. Then I was hit with an intrusive reality alert when he told me to act natural and say cheese. That wasn't exactly what I wanted to hear, but I'd done as he asked, smiling at him as he lifted his phone into position and snapped my picture.

He showed it to Nathaniel who smiled and said, "Not bad. You photograph pretty well."

I smirked because I knew damned well I always looked much better in person than I ever had in a two dimensional photo. I only hoped that picture wouldn't dismantle Nykolson's opinion of me once he was away from the real McCoy. I hadn't asked to have a look at it because I really disliked seeing my face in photos, and if I'd seen it, would most likely insist it be deleted. My smile always appeared forced, as though I was trying to take a constipated shit at the moment the flash had finally gone off. I'd rather imagine that picture was a good one and leave it at that.

As Nykolson thumbed the faceplate on his phone, most likely putting my face where he wanted it to be, he said he'd text a shot of himself to me so I could link it to his name on my phone, or do whatever with it I wanted once received. He glanced up at me with what looked to be a smug smile, just like his brother had done a few minutes before that, and I spotted Nathaniel nudging him with his shoulder again. I nodded calmly, trying not to seem overly eager about getting a hot photo of my future boyfriend. The picture I already had was a good one, but I wasn't up to refusing another. I silently pleaded, *"Shirtless please. I only accept shirtless chest shots."*

Chapter 6

The return ride to Nykolson and Nathaniel's home was better than the trip going to Starbucks. We had become more relaxed, and I was sure Nykolson had sat himself even closer to me than on the way there. I'd felt the pressure from shoulder to knee. Any snugger, he'd have been in my lap or at least draped over one knee. My guess, that was where he was headed, and I totally wouldn't have objected. If he'd have wanted a seat dead center, I'd have been fine with that too. He'd only needed to prepare himself for a butt load of semen.

Another surprise once we arrived at the house was when Nathaniel asked if I'd like to come inside, see what Nykolson had done to the place with his creative eye for design. He told me if I was mesmerized by what I'd seen on the outside, I'd really be impressed by what I'd find once I walked through the door.

Admittedly, I was eager to spend more time with Nykolson, as well as Nathaniel, so of course I graciously accepted the invitation. My mind wandered, wondering if these two cats were up to something, like into a three way. I'd never been involved with a triad before, but what the heck, I could seriously get it on with those two striking creatures. Stick me in the middle and call us an Oreo cookie sandwich. There was something about Nykolson, as well as his brother that put the idea I might be game for giving up my once fucked asshole to either of them. That of course, if they were into sharing the toys they played with.

Shit, there it was again. Boner alert. However, that time my asshole was twitching, too. Never had that happen before, and it kind of caught me off guard. What the heck was going on with my sphincter? At that moment I figured I was bottoming out—like really getting into the idea of being this tough guy's bitch. Was my body preparing to carry out whatever it needed to have done to take on that stunning black man? I figured as much, since my asshole had actively gone into high gear twitching mode again. I'd become damned with happiness that I'd discovered my asshole was able to do that all on its own. It felt like my asshole had the mouth of a fish going crazy for oxygen.

Thank God Nathaniel interrupted my fantasy with a question of drink selections. I'd taken a look at my watch and discovered it was only four in the afternoon, thinking it was too early for a stiff one, but right then, I seemed to have needed it, hopeful it'd douse the fire in my pants—front and back.

"Yeah, sure. Why not," I answered. "I might as well get my weekend started early."

Nykolson chuckled and said, "Great. What would you like?" I wanted to reply, *"You. That ass, and maybe your brother's, too,"* but instead just said, "Do you have whisky?"

Was I shocked when Nykolson said that was the favored drink of his brother, which was different from his, a man who downs the classic martini? Yes I was, because I thought they'd done everything alike. I guess booze and sexual partners were their only differences. I hoped. That's when I'd gone back to thinking, *"What the heck was I doing inside their house and what was the real plan these two had in store for me?"* I hoped they had plenty of lube and condoms stashed in the bedside drawer, because the way I imagined it, the rendezvous was going to be an all-nighter.

Interrupting my gang bang fantasy, I heard Nathaniel telling Nykolson to show me around the house while he mixed the thirst-quenchers. I was happy to hear we were moving along since the front entry was feeling a bit congested, and I wanted to peek around during the tour to see if there was any evidence of Nykolson being gay, like a picture or reference to rainbows or ruby slippers.

After Nathaniel squeezed around us and headed to wherever they kept the alcohol, Nykolson said, "Follow me,

Mikey."

Damn, I liked hearing him call me by that nickname the way he had, and hoped he remembered to holler it during friendlier moments. I'd usually gotten no more than a, "YEAH! Fuck me!" shouted from the men I'd buried my dick into. Maybe Nykolson would have been different and added my name to the profane words of order when I'd given him all I had, pounding roughly to see what would have come out of his mouth—perhaps cause him to lose his mind so I'd undoubtedly gotten that screaming name I wanted to hear.

The first thing I blurted out as we walked the hall was, "Holy crap, this place is nice." I enjoyed all the soothing gray tones and bits of complimenting shades strategically placed. I was mesmerized, to say it bluntly. Nathaniel had been spot on as to how I'd react to Nykolson's brilliance. It was like a work of art that shouldn't have been touched or messed up. Another thought was, where would I have sat once I'd been asked?

"Do you both own it?" I wasn't being nosey, just looking for something to say.

"Yep. That half is his and this half is mine." Nykolson turned away as I said, "Nice."

As Nykolson walked ahead of me, I looked at this and that, and many times, caught myself checking out his cute as fuck ass as he sauntered in front of me. It looked so inviting from my angle, and I kept picturing how appealing it'd look with those blasted shorts out of the way.

Pulling my eyes away from his sweet butt and back to the surrounding decor, there was no evidence of rainbow paraphernalia or paintings of half-naked men on any of the walls. Even though there had been none of that, I sensed that somebody with a designer's point of view had loaned a hand in decorating the home in such a fabulous manner. I could have been wrong, but knowing Nykolson decorated the place, had me tipping my gaydar pointer closer to the side that indicated he could have been gay.

I'd despised the idea that I had been thinking on a stereotypical level, but I couldn't help it. Maybe that was because I was hoping so hard the man was gay, bringing about all the unconfirmed characteristics that influenced me into believing he wasn't gay.

The hottie I had been following around was certainly masculine, somewhat disengaging my gaydar, for which by that meant simply looking at him hadn't convinced me he'd have been one who would have hopped on my big white dick and taken it for a rump ranging joy ride the way I wanted him to. If he was gay, my intrusive doubts had gotten the better of me and he seemed more like the one who'd have been doing all the banging. I was usually better at the intro ritual than how I'd been managing it. What was wrong with me? I wanted him to be my gay bottom so badly, the idea of him not being gay was throwing me all off balance, that's what.

If I wasn't such a chicken shit, I'd have come out and asked him if he was gay or not, or I'd have snuck in a few hints during conversation about myself that would have gotten him to take the bait and come clean with his own confession. But instead, I'd chosen to remain a timid investigator who was having a go at solving a secret mystery.

Along the home tour, I commented on how meticulous the place was and that he'd done an outstanding job filling the place with his and his brother's personal interests. I'd been able to identify in his bashful-like actions that he'd blushed a couple of times, even though his smooth dark skin prevented me from seeing any tones of red.

The last room he showed me was his shadow-gray bedroom at the end of the house where we lingered the longest. I could have stayed there the rest of the evening, throughout the night *and* into the bright blue morning, while showing him how great of a fucker I was. I breathed deeply several times, taking in his personal scent clearly evident everywhere. As I glanced around the room, I noticed he had a king sized bed and wondered why a single man needed one that large. Perhaps he sprawled out or he enjoyed a lot of sleep overs where that much mattress space was needed. With that image in my head, I immediately fought with depression, thinking he was already in a relationship and the big bed was meant for more than just him. He was quite handsome, making it difficult for me to believe he was a single man. Could have been true. Maybe there was something wrong with him that kept him single. That could have been true, too. I had no problem clearing that up straightaway when I jokingly asked him how many people slept in that great big bed of his.

He smirked and said it was for him only, but many nights he shared it with Nathaniel. Was he having me on?

"Oh?" My eyes nearly popped from their sockets when he mentioned that so calmly. I started visualizing a pleasing fantasy involving twins.

"Oh, gawd. No, not that." He partially spit on me when he laughed, then proceeded filling me in how Nathaniel would fall asleep until morning while they watched television in his room. The double bed he had before the bigger one was beginning to get too cramped for two big guys like them. One of my eyebrows lifted as I nodded.

I'd wanted to stay, tackle Nykolson onto that massive bed and tear into him with every part of my body, but figured we shouldn't have kept Nathaniel waiting in the kitchen watching the ice cubes dilute the beverages he'd made. Yeah... that was the reason.

We'd both had gone for the door at the same time, bumping into one another, and when we turned to politely allow the other to head out first, I inadvertently grabbed his waist to prevent either of us from stumbling. My nose graced his lower lip and skimmed his jaw. His five o'clock shadow was abrasive, but I'd dismissed the biting scratch since he smelled so damned good. If I'd only been a few inches taller, our lips would have perfectly aligned, leaving me to follow through with only one thing—a kiss, or at least I'd take his winter-fresh breath home with me.

He stayed in place and eloquently said with a smile, "After you, Michael. Sir." His warm tone traveled across my ear.

I exhaled slowly. *"Fuck me. I'm in love. I'm in love. I'm fucking in love."*

                  CB BO

"Didn't I tell you my brother was a fantastic designer?"

Nathaniel repeated as I found myself back at the kitchen island with Nykolson. I was so enthralled by Nykolson's gentle voice in my ear back at the doorway, the walk back to the kitchen was a hazy blur.

Nathaniel added, "I'd always told him he should have pursued that skill instead of what he's doing. He's too talented for that word game crap." I loved how honest Nathaniel was with his opinions, and I completely agreed with him. Nykolson knew how to style a home and with the right connections, could have probably made serious money at it.

Taking the spotlight off himself, Nykolson suggested we take the party out to the back patio and cool down, take a load off and forget about all they'd been dealing with.

As soon as we sat in the chairs skirting a large round table, there was continuous banging on the front door along with the entry chime repeatedly echoing all the way through the house to where we'd been sitting. Mixed in with all that noise was one of the most annoying voices I'd ever heard in my life.

"What the hell was nagging?" No, really. Not who, but what?

I had a good idea who it was, but sat tight and squeezed hold of my glass, almost cracking it in my grasp if that high octave squealing at the door hadn't taken care of that first. I was damned sure I'd rather have been hearing that fist banging on the door than that uneducated squawking coming out of the mouth behind it.

The yelling had immediately gotten louder as soon as the door was flung open. Dajana screeched, "Get out here you miserable piece of shit and pay me my money. I know you and your gay-ass brother gots it, cuz you can't have a house like dis widout a few extra pieces of coin in yer pockets. Now get me some money or I swear you will go to jail."

I'd sworn I heard gum chewing after she spewed all that noise, and I was surprised she hadn't invited herself all the way to the back patio where we were seated.

There went my suspicions about Nykolson being gay or not. The voice of a crude individual just announced he was, and coming from a person like her, I was pretty sure it had come out because mean bitches like her couldn't keep something like that bottled up if they themselves thought it'd boost their own confidence and popularity. Nykolson looked at me and the expression on his face indicated—now you know, but not how I wanted you to find out.

Nathaniel and Nykolson had both gotten up at the same time and had taken off like major league athletes for the front door. I'd overheard them telling her to get off the property before they called the cops, and her reply was if they proceeded with that, she'd follow through on her threat with the oranges, making it all the more believable since they had already shown anger about her visit. I'd even overheard she'd start the shit right on the front doorstep and would finish before the police had a chance to arrive. She was definitely a piece of work, and I was the silent witness behind her plan. I honestly couldn't believe what I'd heard. Who would have done something like that unless they were so disjointed with themselves they needed to destroy somebody else's life along with their own? I wondered what had happened to her that made her the way she turned out. All I knew for sure was that girl needed to have been put in her place and exposed for the vindictive person she was.

"Put your phone away you bigass homo-gay. I'm leaving this dump," she hatefully blasted in her uneducated voice.

I figured she was talking to Nykolson, which had broken my heart because verbal bashing was just as bad as being struck with a fist. I felt the stab in my own gut as if she had said it to me. Coming from a person with such low class, I was hopeful he wouldn't have taken the vulgarity of her statement too seriously. I was totally put off by her and couldn't figure out how an intelligent man like Nathaniel had gotten mixed up with such trash.

I had a difficult time keeping my opinion to myself. "You guys weren't kidding when you mentioned she was off her rocker," I said as they returned and sat back down at the table. Nykolson reached for his martini and instead of sipping like he should have, he'd taken a good sized gulp, gnashing his teeth as he swallowed. My guess was, that first swig of gin had gone down his throat as harshly as if he'd ingested the pine cone it smelled like.

"I'm toast," Nathaniel said.

I replied, "No you're not."

"How can you be so sure?"

I held up my phone and wiggled it. "Evidence of her plan has been recorded. That bitch is going down if she attempts her self-inflicted stunt and tries blaming it on anyone at this table."

Those beautiful smiles and gleaming gray eyes were back, and I was damned well going to make sure they stayed bright and cheery no matter what I had to do. I was well connected within the system to keep those two out of any more trouble with that girl, as well as have the restraining order put in effect on her if she followed through with beating herself up with the bag of oranges. We had to let her follow through to prove she was cracked in the head. That girl was only hours away from starting her own jail sentence by falsifying a crime that wouldn't have been committed by either Nathaniel or Nykolson. We already had our dated evidence of the event about to occur. We only needed to wait for her to squeeze her own trigger.

Nathaniel pointed at me and said, "I could kiss you right now for what you just did." Then he moved his finger toward Nykolson. "But I'll leave that up to him. How about I hug you instead?"

"I have a better idea. How about that Oreo sandwich instead?" I reached for my whisky on ice as though I was uncomfortable with the whole situation. Not a chance. I grinned and was definitely all for whatever either of them had in mind. I'd spoken truthfully to Nathaniel, "I'll take that hug"—I then turned to Nykolson—"and that kiss."

Nathaniel blurted out, "Well isn't this special. At least something good had come out of all this B.S., and it's about freaking time. I was becoming exhausted waiting on which one of you was going to make the first damned move." Nathaniel seemed as excited about the mating ritual crossing the startup line as I had.

What had happened wasn't the best way to break the ice, but I was glad it finally had come out into the open. My thoughts had been Nykolson wouldn't have gone for a guy like me. I was simple, okay good looking, far from being drop dead gorgeous like he was. How could I even measure up to somebody like Nykolson? He was A&F model material and I was just an average gymster who seemed to have to work three times harder than everybody else had just to gain a pound of muscle. I never dated guys like Nykolson, much less had become their boyfriend. I only fantasized about them. Could Nykolson and I really happen?

My heart nearly stopped when Nykolson said, "I don't think it's a good idea that I kiss you until we'd gone on a first date. But since I'm out in the open, if you hadn't figured it out by now, how about we get together sometime and see where it goes." He wiggled his ankle out front of me. "I can't go far, so perhaps we could meet here for a drink and dinner. Nathaniel can cook."

"Who the, what the?" Nathaniel had come close to choking on his tongue. "Hope you like eggs and toast with your wine."

I tried my hardest to contain my excitement and the gleam in my eyes, then softly said, "I'd like that. Just say when."

As shocking as thunder on a sunny day, Nathaniel exhaled hot air like a hissing cat at the same moment his arms had gone up in the air like football goal posts. "Yessss. Score. Finally, my brother." Nathaniel was older than I me, but somehow acted younger as though he was still in college and was hanging out with his heterosexual buddies that understood his gesture of defeat. I hadn't minded. I found it refreshing, and those muscular arms weren't bad to look at either. I had to force myself to look away because it was Nykolson I'd found interest in. But since Nathaniel was as hot as his identical twin, he could easily come in as a close second on my list of fuckables.

"It's a date." I smiled. Oh no. Wait. Protocol. Shit.

Chapter 7

The lonely ride back to my own home was agonizing for one good reason—I couldn't get Nykolson out of my head and all the things I wanted to do to his naked body. He was an offender I had been assigned to, and I'd have been totally going against the rules of fraternizing, but shit, I had a dick that wanted that man's lips and asshole. How the hell was I supposed to deny what my body and mind wanted? I was a man's man. A rump rider. A cock sucker. My plan was to proceed with our sweet little date, in which I'd make it well known to keep our fling on the down-low until his probation period ended. It was proper protocol and would have been one ball busting task to have kept my dick out of his ass if I'd gone anywhere near it.

I looked at my crotch that was trying like mad to pitch a tent beneath my constricting slacks, and noticed a wet spot where the knob of my boner was pushing upward along my inner thigh. Just the thought of Nykolson had caused pre-cum to seep through the heavy fabric of my pants. Thankfully, I was on my way home where I would finish off what Nykolson unknowingly started with his good looks, body and charm.

I never cared for the phrase, "pinch me," but I had stupidly thought it to make sure I wasn't dreaming. Nykolson was very handsome, so beyond the type of man I would normally hook up with, and I couldn't believe he was interested in someone as average as me. My dick twitched just thinking about seeing the rest of him, like his chest, his abs and everything he had going on

59

below that trim waistline. I wondered if he met the legends of most black men, where his cock was of substantial size and he fucked like a beast on steroids. I couldn't wait to find out for myself, and if everything had gone the way I wanted, it would have happened soon. At that thoughtful moment, my phone lit up with a text message from Nykolson.

"Oh shit."

I waited until I pulled into my drive before viewing the incoming message. I wanted good news, but feared he might have changed his mind about dating his parole officer.

I had taken a deep soothing breath before I'd punched the message open. "Oh my shit," I said again. How could I have forgotten about the photo he said he'd send me? The minute I saw the colored picture, my boner had a zoinks moment, gone even harder than it had and feeling like it squeezed out another sluggish wad of pre-cum. I knew his brother put him up to that photo shot — there was no doubt about it. I could see it was taken sometime after I'd left those two alone in their back yard. I recognized everything, right down to my empty glass on the table in front of Nykolson's beautiful shirtless chest. He had risen from the seat, leaning at an angle against the backrest. I could see the best of him, from the waist band of his low riding cargo shorts to that beautiful baseball capped head of his. "Oh... my... gawd." He hadn't taken his shirt off completely, just lifted and looped the bottom hem over and behind his head to expose his hard as fuck chest and six pack. The man looked as though he'd just returned from an all-day workout at the fucking gym.

"Damn that hottie."

All I could think about was rubbing my dick back and forth between the deep crease of his puffed up pectorals, using his chest to jack myself off until I ejaculated all over his beautiful face. I looked down at my thigh and saw the wet spot of semen getting larger. "Damn him and his brother. They are masters at turning me on."

I'd stuffed the phone in my front shirt pocket and quickly ran into the house like I was hiding a sick secret from the neighbors. I was desperate to have a better look at Nykolson's body in private and jerk off to his photo before my balls blew up in the front seat of my truck.

I slammed and locked the front door, turning my back on it as though I had just run away from the cops.

There he was. My soon to be boyfriend—I hoped. His chest and abdomen were chiseled exactly as I had imagined. Chocked with muscle. Hard as fuck. No fat that I could even identify.

He was smoother than I was, except for a line of black hair traveling from his navel into his shorts. He was grinning with his pink tongue extended, still had his hat on backwards, adding to that boyish charm, disguising that he was definitely all man. His arms were bent with balled fists on either side of his head that had given me an erotic glimpse of his swollen guns—the damn things actually had mountain peaks. I had to check for snowcaps on those crests. I knew they were impressive from what I'd already seen, but the way he was propped at an angle had really put them on display. He was built to perfection, just the way I liked, and hot damn, his sensual underarms were identical to what I'd already seen on his brother. I wanted to bury my face in them before moving on to licking the mounds of his biceps, trailing my tongue across his chest and over every other part of his stunning A & F body.

What those brothers had done to me with that photo wasn't fair. No gay man in his right mind would have been able to resist that bit of art. I had an erection so stiff, if I hadn't let it loose immediately, the fucker would have surely torn the shit out of my slacks the same way The Hulk would have made an appearance during an angered state. It wouldn't have surprised me one bit if my cock had turned big and green.

I couldn't wait another minute. I needed release before I exploded.

Off went my belt, down went the zipper, and my big Johnson popped free like it was gasping for air. That was it. I'd reached my sweltering moment. I needed to finish what the twins had started.

As I gazed at Nykolson's square stocky chest, not feeling one bit guilty about what I was about to do, I grabbed my nine-incher, fell back on my sofa and started stroking enthusiastically from tip to base, growling the entire time, working that cum from within me. I imagined being inside Nykolson, fucking him like a raging gorilla. My craziness had gotten the best of me and as if he was actually on me, I blurted out, "Yeah, ride that cock. Let me cream that ass." I was full of it.

In a matter of minutes I'd lost the grip on the phone, dropping it to the cushion next to me while shooting cum toward my face and chin, leaving pearly streaks across my shirted chest. My entire body convulsed, every muscle bunched and bulged. I roared between gnashed teeth until every spurt had been ejected. I was dripping wet with semen. Face, chest and abs. I'd even had it clinging to my hair. I breathed heavily as I'd begun to slow my strokes, luring the last spurts of semen from my pulsating cock. My throat felt raw from every, "huh, huh, huh," that had come with each jet of semen pumped from my erection. Soon after the last spurt lazily oozed over my knuckles, slugged down my cock and burrowed into the pelvic hair at the base of my cock, I laid there a few minutes longer, waiting for my quaking body to settle and my heart rate to reset to normal. I licked my lips, tasting cum that had hit the roof of my mouth. I swallowed all of it, lapping at what had thickly gummed up my knuckles.

I reached over my wet chest with my dry left hand and picked up the phone at my right, looked at Nykolson's photo again and warned, "Mister Kannon," I huffed, "I hope you can handle nine thick inches of dick crammed in that black butt of yours. If not, I'm ready to train you."

Chapter 8

The next day, I'd gotten that call from Nykolson I was somewhat expecting. He told me she'd done it—the crazy bitch beat the crap out of herself with a bag of oranges, or fruit, or potatoes, or whatever. It hadn't mattered what she used, at least the job was done. Part of me was in disbelief she followed through on what she said, and the other part of me was glad she had. That put Nathaniel in an excellent position, and was what we needed her to do to get him off the hook with an easy restraining order placed against her irrational twat. Dajana Washington was in for one rude awakening, an unexpected twist to her mad plot at taking another man's money she hadn't deserved or had any right to.

"I'll be right there, Nykolson." I couldn't wait to see him again, but wished it was under different circumstances.

I'd driven to Nykolson's home where it appeared he and Nathaniel were being questioned by the police. I knew I'd been spotted when Nykolson waved. The half-smile on his face had gotten to me, tugged like mad at my heart and I couldn't look away for the life of me.

After parking my truck in a vacant spot across the street, an officer blocked me from getting to Nykolson, sternly blurting out, "No visitors beyond this point."

I'd told the man I wasn't a spectator, that I was Nykolson's parole officer. When I flashed him the truthful proof he need to see, giving him a moment to digest what I'd said, scrutinizing and registering my identity, he eventually let me pass.

"I'm glad to see you, Michael," Nykolson said, his arms were crossed against his chest, but I knew it was more of a protective gesture instead of feeling cold or not wanting to wrap them around me.

I turned and found Nathaniel in the back seat of a cruiser as though he'd already been convicted of the crime I knew he hadn't committed. His face lit up when the moment he looked at me. I figured that grin was because he knew I had the evidence to clear all the crap up and send the crazy bitch to the sewer where she was trying to put him and the future love of my life. No way will that hussy mess with my men without an all-out fist fight. My dukes had already gone up.

I placed my hand on Nykolson's shoulder, squeezed in a bit of comfort, and said, "It's gonna be okay. We've got this." He angled his gaze down at me with thankful eyes, giving me a look as though he was in love with me, his expression seemed to have reached my soul right then. My weakness for him had grown a little bit more at that moment, and before I'd done anything stupid, like kiss him smack dab on the lips, I removed my hand from his shoulder like a responsible man. I so badly wanted to hug him, and for the love of Pete, I wanted to kiss him even more. I moved my hands to my hips, positioning them like I was a crime fighting tough guy, at the same time clearing my throat as if that would have helped get the idea of locking lips with Nykolson off my mind.

As if Nykolson wanted me to proceed with comforting him, he inched closer to my side and whispered, "I know you do."

"Hu — what?" He caught me off guard because I thought he had actually read my mind.

"You got this," he defined, repeating what I had said earlier.

"Oh. Yeah. Right. I thought…"

"Thought what?"

"Nothing. My mind was wandering."

I held back mentioning to anybody I had a recording of the planned event that caused the police to come to somebody's rescue, even knowing it would have probably gotten Nathaniel out of that cruiser and back in his own house sooner than later. To make sure the recording would have been officially documented, I needed to wait until we were taken downtown to the police station to release the evidence. It was too risky to give it up in the driveway of the twins' home. Doing it properly would ensure everybody remained honest and committed to putting Dajana where she belonged. Who knew if Dajana had any of those cops under her pussy clenching spell? For all I'd known, any one of them could have been in on the bitch's scam.

On the way downtown, I cradled my phone securely inside my chest pocket to make sure that thing stayed safe. I wouldn't even answer it when a call had come in, fearing my nervous hands would punch the wrong button and I'd erroneously delete the recording. Or I'd drop and break the phone, spoiling everything. I really needed to learn how to store my shit in that rain cloud thingy in the sky so if anything happened along the way, I could retrieve it from up above. But that safeguard for some reason seemed inconvenient as shit.

oX €O

By the time we arrived at the police station late that afternoon, Nathaniel was in the process of getting booked for the incident Dajana reported he'd committed. It chilled my bones to see him sitting in the criminals chair like that, the image as though I was looking at Nykolson. It was remarkable how closely they resembled each other. In general, twins simply astonished me.

We hadn't been allowed to get near Nathaniel, but, being under the same roof with him was all that mattered. At least we were together and able to get glimpses of him while he remained detained. We had to wait it out, remain on standby until called out with our side of the story that would hopefully prove his alibi. We'd known the truth and were aware of the evidence that would verify whatever Dajana said was inconclusive. The solid proof that would shut her shit down was hidden in my pocket. I could hardly wait to give up what we had on her and put this crap-shoot mess to rest. For good. That girl needed to be stopped.

An hour or so after we arrived, I was thrilled to hear an officer calling my name. His voice was big, bursting through the cold room like he'd been holding a megaphone to his mouth. I practically skipped with joy to the place I'd be questioned. On my way, I turned back and winked at Nykolson, hopeful he'd taken it as a distance kiss as well as an, "I got this," gesture.

I wasn't at all unfamiliar with the grimy interrogation room with the bright overhead light and mirrored wall, so taking my seat in the small institutional green four cornered cube wasn't as intimidating to me as it might have been for somebody put there for the first time. I was glad to have been where I was, especially knowing I held the incriminating evidence that would get Nathaniel off the hook and all the fabricated charges tossed in the trash. I wasn't certain they knew what I had yet, but figured Nathaniel might have given them some kind of tipoff or the request for my assistance wouldn't have been so speedy. I was eager to have the question asked about the recording, and hopeful I wouldn't have to sit through a bunch of crap-shoot questions before they brought it up. If they hadn't, I was ready to slip them the phone to move the interrogation process into high gear.

Within the first two minutes, the eye smoldering detective looked down on me and said, "I know you're familiar with how this goes Millhouse, so I'll spare you the dramatics and get to the point about the recording your boyfriend's brother mentioned." Before anything he said had sunk in, all I heard was your boyfriend. *"My boyfriend?"* Where'd he come up with that? Was it obvious I had the hots for Nykolson? Was it my actions toward him that had given me away? It probably was, and I guessed it hadn't mattered — I liked hearing it.

Fidgeting as if impatient, the detective asked again, "Millhouse? What do you know about a recording?" By his enthusiasm with skipping the initial formalities and hop to the main reason we were both put in that room, I'd gotten the feeling he wanted to get the hell out of there as badly as I wanted to help unlock those shackles from Nathaniel's ankles. Before pulling my phone out and pressing play, I'd first told detective, Wannabe Hard-ass, about that night, with hopes my story would have collaborated with Nathaniel's. I'd almost burst out laughing when I looked at the disgusted and impatient look on the detectives face while I'd given him the long version of the truth.

He interrupted me by boldly pressing, "We know all that, Millhouse. Just give up the recording." I'd done as he asked and finally let him have it. It'd taken me a minute to get it going, but when I had, the distant confession from Dajana about her plan to set Nathaniel up on another domestic dispute played clearly, declaring she would rough herself up if he hadn't paid her stinking rent.

Before the detective confiscated my phone as evidence, he politely asked, "May I?" while holding a finger on it so I couldn't refuse and drag it back toward myself across the tabletop. I pushed it closer to him and watched the light on the faceplate slowly fade to black, as if it had died from separation anxiety. I figured I'd get it back eventually, but I was more than happy to give it up for the justice it would serve. I'd also been glad to have been done with the interrogation, and just as happy to have gotten back to Nykolson.

It hadn't taken much longer after I returned to the waiting area to find Nathaniel being released. He was all smiles, and seeing him like that put a grin on my face that mimicked the Grinch's at that pivotal moment when he discovered he actually had a heart.

While the three of us reunited in the front part of the precinct, waiting for Nathaniel's confiscated personal belongings to be returned to him, we heard screaming that topped all the other noise in the entire place. It was a sad screech combined with wicked anger, and it had come from the furthest end of the corridor, one of which was brought on by the individual it had come out of. We recognized the voice and knew why it had wailed at that time. It was Dajana—who deserved being dragged away by those weaves for what she tried to get away with.

 C3   ᏠꙨ

On our way across the parking lot to my three person

pickup truck, Nathaniel walked between me and Nykolson. Perhaps it was an instinctive move at his doing, taking the middle spot where he felt the need for somebody else's protection.

There was a position swap once we reached the truck. Nykolson hopped in the seat and sat next to me again, so close at my side, I felt every bit of him from shoulder to knee. I'd hoped he occupied that middle spot to crowd a bit of my personal space because he really wanted to be next to me, not because the interior of my truck was so small and it was the only place for him to have sat. I was polling for his need at being crammed against my side, but the other thought still crossed my mind. Having his body so tightly pressed to mine was heartwarming—made me feel as though we were already a cuter than shit couple, and his actions proved he couldn't have gotten enough of my body heat.

After Nykolson checked with his brother, making sure he was doing okay, he expressed how thankful he was for what I'd done. Then..., "Oh my gawd," his hand reached for mine and held it. "Holy fuck!" Was it happening? Really happening? That stupid phrase about pinching me assaulted my mind again, but before it stuck there with annoyance, I erased it straightaway with an entwined five fingered grip to his hand. No stupid pinch was needed to make what was happening feel real.

I fought with my oncoming anxieties and perpetual erection that popped up every time I thought about or had been around Nykolson, but I was certain he'd already noticed the beast in my pants snaking down my inner thigh like a python. He had to have seen it, even his brother must have noticed. I hadn't the dick that could easily be hidden when the fucker hardened, nor was I the type of guy other men made fun of in the locker room. I silently begged for it to go away, but Nykolson's touch wouldn't let that happen. "Sumbitch!" The last thing I wanted was for Nykolson to think my main interest had been to stuff the expanding part of my body inside his. That wasn't it. Well, from the very start it was... but... not at that moment. He was so genuine, and kind, and stunning, and handsome... and he had those inviting eyes that drew me in. I couldn't help how my body reacted to any of his features and how his touch made me feel. I was a man for fuck sake—a horny man who thought about fucking nearly twenty-four-seven. My sex drive heightened beyond my comprehension when I was around Nykolson. The electrical forces that generated between us were over and above what I'd ever felt before, pretty much confirming I was meant to be with that man, leaving me to believe I'd be shocked if he hadn't felt the same way.

"Home. Yes. Here we are." I heard Nathaniel gloriously comment, and it was a good thing he had, since my head was on automatic pilot — in a trance, and I would have missed the drive if he hadn't spoken up.

I replied, "That was fast." *Too fast.* Then I felt wounded when Nykolson's hand separated from mine. The warmth of it missed desperately. *"Yep, too fast."*

First it was my erection I'd fought with, and then the undesirable release of his hand. I wondered if Nykolson would have objected if I'd leaned in for a kiss. I wanted to so badly, but figured it might have been way too soon and I should just let him go. My confusion burst into flames and I started to lose my fucking mind. He. Was. Fucking. Me. Up… Seriously. I needed to pull back on the reigns a little bit, or they just might have strangled him.

The twins had gotten out of the truck first and I'd followed suit, but I, not having a clue what to do next, stood in the open driver's side doorway feeling a bit awkward. *"Do I stay or do I go?"* That wasn't meant to be a sing-song phrase.

After Nykolson closed the passenger door, he asked if I was planning on standing and looking handsome under the streetlight or had I planned on joining them inside. That was the prompt I needed to hear. My anxiety spiked… in a good way.

Containing a jackrabbit approach, I closed the door with ease and casually walked beside Nykolson into the house. Being respectful of the guys tidy home, I removed my shoes at the door before going further. Even though Nykolson said there was no need to have done that, I felt obligated as a guest to keep the place free of my personal dirt.

I remember thinking that night was going to be a good one. I'd felt it in my bones, not just my pecker. I hadn't any idea what the plan was, but, as long as I was with Nykolson, it hadn't mattered. I wanted to get to know him, find out his interests, and see what made him tick. After I used the restroom down the hall, I returned to the kitchen and found the two of them side by side making a martini and two whisky-waters on ice. I hadn't asked for one, but that day was one of those times I honestly needed a stiff drink. I'd begun to think their spare time was all about drinking adult beverages. To me, having alcohol two nights in a row was an insurgent's way of life, and I was becoming a guzzling rebel in that tribe. *"What... the freaking hell! I wasn't like this."*

Nykolson handed me one of the glasses of whisky and told me to enjoy. The sting of the first swig added fire to my throat, but when I exhaled with an, "Aaaaaah," the burn that had gone down was magically soothing on the way out. Nykolson had done the same—a swig and what sounded like that fiery blow. His waft of alcohol swirled into my face, and I could almost taste what he was drinking.

Nathaniel set his glass down on the granite with a clatter and blurted words that seemed to have come out of nowhere, "What was I thinking when I decided to bang that bitch? I should have known to back off by the way she clamped those claws around my throat the first time I screwed her." He'd seemed to have realized what he'd done at that very moment, like something in that drink tapped on his noggin. Had he been blinded all that time by a pussy that had an open invitation? I hadn't mentioned anything, but Nykolson on the other hand told him her stretched out twat with an echoing effect should have been his clue to stay clear of it. Just because a trinket looked like gold, hadn't meant it was real gold. Unfortunately, Nathaniel found that out later than sooner.

"Okay, guys," Nathaniel breathed. "Let's go outdoors and enjoy what's left of the evening, forget about the shitty day we just had and let that wicked wench of the west get what's owed her."

His idea sounded great to me, so I kicked back, "I'm in."

Within a snap, I was caught off guard when Nykolson grabbed my hand and whirled me toward the back door, whisky sloshing in my glass as I spun, some spilling to my hand. Before reaching the spot Nykolson wanted me, I collided with his chest where we stood face to face. I felt his breath, absorbed his heartbeat beneath his shirt. Our lips only millimeters apart.

"Damn!" So close.

I stared into his eyes, finding him gazing back at me. He hadn't moved. I hadn't moved. I couldn't breathe for several seconds, and I hadn't believed he'd taken in air either.

Should I kiss him? Yes? No? Maybe? Will he let me? I stammered for something to say, but couldn't find the right words. Then, I shyly dropped my gaze, my head moving in the direction my eyes had traveled, and my forehead bumped the bridge of his nose, forcing him to back away. "Oh. I'm sorry, Nykolson. I... Fudge! Are you okay?" I glanced at his face, catching the sight of his hand reaching where my big head landed.

Nykolson rubbed the bridge of his nose and started chuckling, his eyes a bit misty. "Fudge? Where'd that come from? Are you not allowed to speak bad words?"

"Oh, gawd. I'm such a klutz. You caught me off guard with... Sorry about... that."

"No big deal. I'll survive. Next time I'll be sure to warn you before I make a move like that."

Wait. Warn me about what? Was he talking about whisking me away in a surprising twirl, or trying to find a way to get a kiss out of me? Was that moment a tricky plan of his? Gah! Of course I fucked up his perfect opportunity at nabbing a kiss.

There was a moment of silence before he stepped aside, opening a pathway to the back door. "After you," he said. His head tilted in the direction I was supposed to follow.

The outside air felt good, the cool breeze showing up at the perfect time, almost as if it had come to knock back the steam that had billowed throughout the day and between me and Nykolson inside the house.

He led me to the patio furniture and we sat in the settee opposite Nathaniel. I couldn't have been more pleased by Nathaniel's natural reaction at seeing his brother's interest toward me. I'd noticed he actually seemed thrilled when we held hands on the ride over, and when we sat like companions on the two-seater across from him. It had me wondering what he'd do once we finally followed through with a kiss.

While I sat with Nykolson, I attempted one of those cheesy first date-night maneuvers where I lifted my arm as if I was stretching and sneakily brought it down behind Nykolson, hoping he'd take the bait and lean into my chest where it was warm and cozy. Then I thought, *"Warm and cozy? Hope he likes a man with a hairy chest."* Why had I kept thinking things that would send him walking? Fear of not being as perfect as he was, that's why.

As luck had bestowed itself down on me, he fell for my smooth move without a single moment of reluctance. I felt the weight of his body settling in against mine.

When he shifted, I'd brought the palm of my hand against his chest, feeling him breathing and the rapid thump of his heartbeat. He seemed as comfortable as a cat on a downed packed pillow. I couldn't have been more surprised that I hadn't exhibited another erection. Perhaps I was more nervous than I thought. As with all our previous engagements, my big boner that always had a mind of its own was the first thing that had come to life. I felt content at that moment, even with his brother overseeing what was happening between us.

While sitting comfortably looking at stars, one thing I'd mentioned was how talented I found Nykolson as an interior decorator and asked why he hadn't followed a career as a designer. His answer was logical. He enjoyed it so much that if he'd done it day after day, the demand would have put a damper on doing it for fun. I understood that since clay sculpting was my hobby, and I couldn't see myself obstructing the enjoyment by turning it into a demanding occupation either. After I'd mentioned his wises decision with keeping his interest solely to himself, he filled me in on his professional editing career at a fashion magazine based out of New York, and that had given him the opportunity to work remotely at home. In my opinion, that was a dream job, and had allowed him the freedom to craft a schedule that suited him.

After that little bit of chitchat, Nykolson sat up, looked me in the eyes and asked when I was going to make a move and kiss him. He said he'd been waiting all day and if another minute had gone by without one, he'd burst into flames. Of course I wanted his lips touching mine from the moment I first laid eyes on him at my office, so with his mouth only inches in front of me, I wasn't wasting another second at giving him what he'd been waiting for.

We had an onlooker, but I hadn't given a shit, since Nykolson hadn't seemed to either.

I shifted to level my gaze with his, finding his gray irises glowing from the moons light above and his centers staring right back at me. I nervously swallowed, and as soon as our lips met, Nykolson was on top of me like a woolen blanket, the weight of his body heavy as it pressed down on mine. He felt good covering me. I kissed with an appetite, keeping my connection tight while his head aggressively rotated opposite mine, his tongue forcefully prying my lips apart to get inside. In a lustful rage, I pushed into his advances, giving him my tongue in exchange for his. It was exactly the way I thought it'd be. Masculine and reckless. Forceful and aggressive. Yet gentle in a way. His touch had once again caused my dick to harden.

Then, my eyes sprung wide open when Nykolson quickly pulled away and shrieked, "What the shit, bitch?" He gripped the front of my shirt as he lifted himself up, causing me to scowl when his twisting fist tugged at the hair on my chest.

I followed his shrieking by yelling, "Aw, shit. Gah, that smarts." To sooth the itching pain, I massaged my chest where I probably lost a handful of hair.

Like a scary monster, Nathaniel was standing over us with an empty glass that a moment earlier held the whisky he'd tossed across Nykolson's back. "Don't forget I'm still here, you whores." Nathaniel's so called brilliant idea had broken us apart the same way a water hose would have separated two mating dogs. If he hadn't, the heavy kissing might have turned into nudity and deep dick penetration. I chuckled at what had taken place, which I shouldn't have, but I was relieved it wasn't me who made Nykolson so urgently withdraw from one of the best kisses I'd ever had.

Nykolson yelled, "You mangy scoundrel. Couldn't you tell I was getting the kiss I'd been waiting for all my life? Go get yourself a refill so I can finish what I started."

I wondered if Nykolson had any idea how he just made me feel after his illuminating comment. If I could, I'd have kissed him until the crack of dawn.

While Nathaniel was away on a refill run, Nykolson leaned into me, scraping his scruffy jaw against mine until his mouth met my ear. He whispered in that deep voice I'd already grown to love, "You... kissed exactly the way I thought you would."

Should I have been worried? "Hope you mean it was as good for you as it was for me?"

"Oh, Yeah." Then Nykolson slowly backed away, telling me to ignore his brother's comment about the two of us acting like whores.

I really hadn't cared because when with Nykolson, that label his brother had given us, or me, was the truth. I'd concluded already that I was a, Gah damned slut, when it would involve a man like Nykolson—ready to get naked with the guy, feel his smooth black skin against mine.

Even though I wanted to rip Nykolson's clothes off and tear into his body at that moment, I sat up and behaved myself, giving the respect to his brother I thought the guy deserved. I'd been still unconsciously rubbing my chest, drawing Nykolson's gaze to where my hand was at. He commented, "Sorry about that. Please tell me I hadn't done any damage."

"Nah. Ya hadn't," I answered, glancing down beneath my lifted shirt collar. "Now I know what waxing feels like."

"Oh, shit. Then I did inflict havoc to one of my favorite parts of your hot body?"

"I wouldn't exactly call my body hot, but be assured, the hair removed from my chest will grow back in no time."

"Thank God, because I like a handsome man with a hairy chest. And don't correct me cuz I'm not wrong about you being totally hot. I knew that the first time I met you in your office."

"Totally?"

"M-hmm." Nykolson smiled.

Damn, that toothy sheen. Angelic and blinding.

Before Nathaniel returned with his refill, Nykolson asked me if I'd consider spending the night. His argument was that I had plenty to drink and it wasn't a good idea to sit myself behind the wheel of a moving vehicle and drive into the dark scary night.

He had a point, and I sarcastically thought, *"Yeah... that single drink had certainly gotten me hammered."*

Nykolson mentioned it would be a casual overnighter, no hanky-panky, and if I preferred, I could take the sofa in his bedroom or the one in the living room.

At first, I him-hawed with my answer, making believe I should have gotten out of there so not to become an imposition to him and Nathaniel. I knew they both needed some down time after the events of the day, let their over worked brains get some much needed rest.

I was really thinking, *"How the Sam-hell was I going to sleep in the same room with such a stunning man without trying to slip my dick into his asshole?"* I'd bed that stud in a split second if he so much as winked at me, or better yet, spread those beautiful legs of his and showed me that point of entry. I imagined how warm and snug it would have been. If I stayed, I anticipated being up all night fighting down a raging hard-on.

I'd eventually given in and answered, "Don't be silly, Nykolson. We can share that great big bed of yours. Like brothers. I'll stay on my side if you promise to keep to yours." I rolled into the seat where I was before he lunged at me. He followed and quickly kissed me one more time before his brother had gotten back.

I concluded, "Great. That's settled. For the rest of the night and into morning, there will be no more incidences like we just had. Deal?"

"Deal."

Chapter 9

"Oh boy." I inhaled as I stepped into Nykolson's bedroom, picking up his scent everywhere I turned. The masculine traces of his body found its way to my brain, and because of that, would have made my earlier pact about sleeping on my side of the bed even harder to uphold. It was like walking into the men's locker room and not putting my mouth on a single one of the guys. Could I have done a sleep over with an attractive man without sticking my cock into him? I was surely going to give it a go. There was nothing I wanted more at that point than to spend time with Nykolson, either wide awake in dreamland or with my eyelids clamped shut in total despair.

I'd taken another inconspicuous whiff of the place with my forward steps. *"Yep. I'm in love, I'm in love, I'm fucking in love."* That ditty had gotten more and more real every time I met up with Nykolson. Everything about him I'd come across was pulling me closer.

"Are you a righty or a lefty?" Nykolson asked.

"Um... I'm sorry, what?" Was it the dangle of my dick he was asking about or the hand I used to write letters and jerk off with. I was momentarily confused by the question.

He looked at me funny and pointed to the bed. "Which side do you prefer? Right or left?"

"Oh that. Yes... Um..." I'd noticed Nykolson was frequently at Nathaniel's left, giving me notion that was where he felt most natural all his life, so I quickly answered, "I'm a righty." Was that the correct answer? Shit if I knew. I hadn't been in a relationship long enough to find that out or had anybody concerned enough to ask. I really just slept in the middle where I belonged. *That's what loners do, right?*

"Great. Me, lefty." A tribal accent had come out of Nykolson and I suddenly pictured Tarzan banging a fist against his thick chest. That private image made me smirk as I nervously repeated what he said. "Great."

After my obviously senseless reply, he asked if I fell asleep to the television or if I preferred total darkness.

Like many guys I'd known, I found it more relaxing to doze off with the flickering light and noise of a boring movie playing. I kept a couple of other reasons to myself for wanting the television running—where the distraction would curb my filthy thoughts of what I wanted to do to his black body as well as prevent me from finding a comfortable place on top of him.

"OMG. Not the shirt. FUCK ME!" Then he started.

I watched him cross drop his arms to grip the hem of his shirt and slowly pull it up over his head in a fluid motion. He kept eye contact with me, watching my reaction the entire time until he disconnected behind the rising fabric. His tight muscled torso swayed from side to side as if performing a stripper's dance. The glow of the lamp lights reflecting against his chocolate skin was hotter than hot, giving me clear glimpses of every ripple from waist to chest. Had he just worked out or what? Had I missed a push up or two before he started undressing? That body certainly looked as though he had. Every damned muscle was swollen.

If that wasn't the best boner alert I'd ever witnessed, I hadn't known what was. It was like watching a real live porn flick right there in front of me and the good stuff was about to get started.

"Holy shit! If he keeps going, I'm totally dead."

He tossed his shirt into the chair next to him, tilted his head to the side while smiling at me. Every freaking muscle on his body flexed as he breathed, catching glints of light, as well as my full attention. I couldn't look away, nor could I have spoken if there had been any reason to.

As if he was a trained stripper, he single handedly snapped open the top button on his jeans and slowly dragged the zipper down as far is it would go. His pure white Calvin's sweetly exposed and looking splendid against his dark skin.

"You beautiful bastard, how could you?" I was convinced he was purposely putting on a show, wanting me to cum where I stood. His malevolent smile convinced me as well.

To make my situation worse, he confessed he usually slept in the nude, but to maintain his scruples, told me the briefs would have to stay on throughout the night, but I was welcomed to get as comfortable however I wanted.

He dropped his pants and threw back his side of the covers.

"Oh, Gawd." Before he had a chance to jump into hiding, my eyes focused straight on the outline of his dick where I'd found it nicely thick and of substantial length, just the way I fucking liked it. Where the head crowned, it looked like a gah damned fist crammed in those briefs. From what I'd seen in relaxed form helped me understand that fucker was going to grow to an enormous size when rock hard. There'd have been a hurried need for some serious training on my part if he'd planned on stuffing that beast of a thing up my ass. Until the rear ended challenge presented itself, I would have been glad, however, starting with a mouthful. I was ready to have a go at that big black cock on way or another. Like straightaway ready. I wanted to feel the weight of it lying over my tongue and slipping down my throat to test my gag reflex. But, a promise was a promise. No touching during the night. *"Damnit! Why had I agreed to that stupid rule?"*

His confidence astounded me, which I guessed had come from being so fucking gorgeous. Something I hadn't possessed, but wished I had.

After he crawled beneath the covers, resting on the pillow with one arm tucked behind his head, he asked, "Are you going to sleep fully clothed or did you need a little help getting comfortable?" There was that confidence of his, elevated to the next level with a verbal command.

Like an eye popping schoolboy about to get laid for the first time, I stared at his curled arm with the bulging bicep, and fantasized about burying my face in that deep delectable pit before taking it upon myself to blow a load of cum into the well. *"I am so screwed. Like literally screwed."*

As he smiled up at me, I murmured, "No, no. I got this." *Had I really?*

Unlike his money making strip tease, I unbuttoned the top of my shirt with clumsy fingers, and without finishing, pulled it straight up over my head and tossed it onto the sofa behind me. I stood there in front of him and watched the way he mechanically ran his tongue over his lips. That reaction had given me a bit of my own confidence to drop my pants. My stage performance hadn't been as grand as his, but the good thing by what I'd seen from his reaction, he enjoyed what I had offered.

Nykolson observed every step I'd made right up until I laid down beside him and pulled the blanket to my waist, covering up my boxer concealed dick before it had any chance to grow any bigger than it already had. I'd always felt like a freak because of my size, which I shouldn't, because I'd known myself I had a prize packed behind my zippers.

Nykolson rolled onto his side and faced me, propping himself on his elbow and said, "You have the most attractive body I'd ever seen." Then he embarrassed me when he mentioned everything he was looking at was perfect, expressing how much he liked the bulk of my hairy chest, and really liked the feathered trail running down the center of my abdomen.

I blushed, clearly turning beet red from head to toe. I could feel the burn across my flesh as if my nerve endings had caught fire.

I thought, *"If you think that's impressive, wait til you get a gander at my dick when it's stiff?"* I wasn't bragging by any means, just thinking the obvious.

Many of the men I'd been with—*uh, replay*—the "couple" of guys I'd been with thought they could handle the oversized fucker between my legs, but when I attempted to ease it into the port of entry, they discovered taking my entire cock wasn't the easy task they'd thought it would have been. I'd barely gotten the crown passed those greased up sphincters and it always pissed me off how much resistance I'd felt after they said they could have taken it all the way in. A lot of guys desired a big dick, wanted a big dick, and acted as though they could take a big dick, but when the time had come to open up for my thick nine inches, they nearly passed out from the agony of the grand intrusion. With those guys who weren't as stretchable at the rear as they claimed, I'd been left jerking off beside them while they fingered their wannabe fist banged buttholes. The only satisfaction I'd ever gotten out of those size queens was seeing their greedy faces light up when they first laid eyes on my erection. Too bad it all turned into tooth-contorting mugs when I tried to push my donkey sized dick into their buttholes.

After reminiscing about my previous failed butt fucking encounters, it dawned on me that my monster cock could scare Nykolson as well if taking a big dick up the ass was one of his hang-ups. I surely liked the guy, so perhaps I could work at pulling a switch-a-roo. I hadn't bottomed much, only because I really had to like him and needed to completely trust him to open myself up like that. The very few times I'd let a guy climb on top of me with a decent sized dick, I'd been able to handle it with minimal scrap. But, could I take Nykolson's? His cock from what I could see through his briefs was fucking huge. A better thought I had since I am mostly a top. Could Nykolson be as accommodating and take mine inside him? Gawd, I hoped so. If not, that just might be the deal breaker in our potential relationship. Jerking off together just won't cut it for me. I needed total connection with the man I'd be spending my life with. There was a powerful sensation that had come when one man's cock was buried inside the other. One that of a spiritual connection. A complete feeling of closeness, like joining two souls.

For some reason, something told me Nykolson would give all he had to make what we were about to start, work. He seemed to like me, and I couldn't have seen either one of us turning back, even with the obstacle of two monster cocks erected between us.

I decided to push that horrifying scenario out of my head and simply enjoy the no sex evening with Nykolson and worry about giving him the gigantic Johnson later.

Sleeping in the same bed beside a handsome man without dipping my dick into his goods would definitely challenge me for the first time. But... I was determined to pull it off, wake up fresh in the morning, and remain happy with the decision of not making our first sleepover a wham-bam-thankyou-man kind of night. That was something to have been proud of in those days.

Nykolson asked if he could kiss me one more time before laying back and drifting off into dreamland. There was certainly no reluctance with my, "go for it," answer, so he leaned in with a palm to my chest and planted one of the most intimate kisses to my lips I'd ever been given. It softly lingered. There was no tongue, no slaver, just a dry wholesome farm boy kiss with meaning so deep I thought I'd seen sugar plum fairies dancing overhead.

He backed away slowly and smiled, leaving his hand where it was, leisurely moving it side to side, his fanned fingers petting the feathery hair beneath them. The sensation was pleasing. His dick twitched against my thigh, proving he liked being in bed with me.

Then he told me, "Gawd, I love your chest." He dragged his fingers down the trail at the center of my guttered abdomen. "This too. Sooo, sexy." The last part had come out as a whisper.

I don't think I'd ever had another man touch me like that. Keeping it gentle. With desire. The sensation sent the most pleasurable sparks through my entire body. I wanted to shout how good his touch felt. But instead, I just laid still and let him enjoy my chest and abs while my rising erection consumed my body and my mind.

After exhaling with a whistled, "Phweoooow", Nykolson had fallen back into the pillow and turned his focus to the film, Tarzan, playing on the big screen. I outright knew that probably wasn't the best selection to be watching since Tarzan was shirtless during more than half the film and we were lying next to one another nearly naked. With erections. That shit was a sexcapade waiting to happen.

I was burning up inside, like a frustrated sexually deprived hot mess. I sat up and said, "If our no touch sleeping arrangement is going to work, I need to do this." I immediately karate chopped an indentation down the center of the bed that represented a division line between the two of us. "This line right here?" — I pointed from top to bottom — "Don't cross it" — then my finger moved from him to me — "Your side. My side. Capiche?"

I dropped back against the pillow, landing hard, gluing both my arms to each side of me. Right after I sort of settled down to hopefully get a decent nights rest, I heard a couple of sharp claps come from Nykolson's side of the bed, and just like that, the lights had gone out. I cracked up and thundered, "What the fuck?" because I hadn't realized those things actually existed.

Nykolson chucked, "What? It's funny, and works great from anywhere in the room. Now lay still, keep quiet and watch Tarzan swing from vine to vine in his tiny underpants."

To be funny, I musically recited, "The Clapper," in a singsong voice that matched the silly commercials, and I laughed again. "You do realize there are voice activated devices on the market these days, don't you? Those things can be programmed to turn just about anything on and off. As a matter of fact, you can get them through Amazon. Her name is Alexa and she likes to be told what to do without an argument."

Nykolson smirked, rolled his head to look at me. His gaze traveled up and down my entire body. I'd seen lust as he'd spoken, "Well then. I will invest in one of those in the morning and connect you to it."

Chapter 10

I'd woken up alone in bed that Sunday morning with a hard-on so massive it could have drilled a hole through steel if I'd humped it. I was proud of myself in regards to holding on to my scruples and not trying to fuck Nykolson while he was sleeping. That there sounded insanely creepy but, it had crossed my mind several times throughout the night. I would have wakened him of course, since I'm not one who'd fuck the dead.

At one point during our sleep, I'd woken to find myself spooning Nykolson — my chest pressed to his back, my stone hard cock cradled between his butt cheeks and climbing his spine. My arm had been holding him so tightly he couldn't have gotten away if he tried. I'd felt his grip on my wrist against the well of his chest and a single leg tangled around mine as though he was locking me in place. I wondered if he backed into my body like that, or had I pulled him against me. All I knew was, having him in my arms like that felt as natural as breathing air. After I'd realized I was latched onto him and breathing in his sporty scent, I unhooked myself and rolled over so I wouldn't mistakenly penetrate the man of my dreams. No yet, anyway. If I hadn't had boxer briefs on to absorb all the pre-cum that leaked from my prick during the night, the man I was clinging to would have been fertilized with at least nine children by morning.

"Sumbitch! Why in the world had we settled on that crazy idea of a sexless sleepover?" My battling thoughts had gone there again.

That morning, the sun coming through the glass patio doors

seemed brighter than bright as the piercing light tried to bore a hole straight to my brain by way of my eyes.

I stretched with a low grumble, making limitless efforts to rise and shine without first expelling the usual wads of semen from my erection. I was a morning shooter, enjoyed my regular jerk off sessions, sometimes ejaculating twice before the crack of dawn. That waking moment behind Nykolson, I was so fucking horny that I'd have surely burst if I'd so much as thought about giving my stiffy some sort of relief. Since I was harder than a damned steel pipe, I had to do something about it—perhaps a gentle rub with the thumb pad a few times to appease my mind into believing I was going to go all the way with a flooding load across my chest and abs. However, being a guest in someone else's home, and in a bed other than my own, I wasn't comfortable with jerking myself to that explosive finish like I really wanted to. The furthest I'd gone that morning was extricating pre-ejaculate, and to trick my brain into partial satisfaction, I'd taken pleasure in transferring the glistening spunk to my tongue and swallowing every bit of it. It worked like a charm. No visible mess to the sheets and I was fulfilled with the musky offering that had gone down my throat. A better alternative to jerking off by myself would have been to shoot the full load up inside Nykolson's rear end. I decided to save my spunk for him, if and whenever that would happen.

Figuring Nykolson might have been in the kitchen or at the outdoor patio, I put on my jeans and headed there. I announced, "Good morning, Guys," as I stretched again, blocking the sun from my eyes with one raised arm.

Nathaniel barely looked up when he mumbled his lame ass reply, "G.M.," but Nykolson on the other hand grinned and couldn't seem to take his eyes off of me. His gaze traveled downward, hung out at my dick for a few lick lipping moments, then back to my chest. He was hooked. I could tell.

Feeling out of place when I noticed they were both wearing those blue A&F Tee's, I excused myself and mentioned I'd be right back after I put on a shirt. Nathaniel had given me the thumbs up signal at the same moment Nykolson sprung from the chair and blurted, "NO!" followed by immediately lowering his tone,

"Um… You're fine the way you are."

Nathaniel glanced over the top of his coffee mug as he sipped. He grumbled, "You look like a hairball a cat spit up." I laughed, because it was probably true.

By Nykolson's reaction, I'd known full well he wanted me to remain the way I arrived — shirtless for his own enjoyment. I had to laugh when Nathaniel told me to go trim that shit, and Nykolson hollered, "Shut the hell up, bruh. He's perfect the way he is. Plus, he's mine, not yours."

"*Mine?*" Okay, I liked the sound of that. Nykolson can own me, and likewise.

Nykolson's opinion was the only one that mattered to me, even though I knew Nathaniel was just having fun by telling me to groom my hair covered muscles. What care of Nathaniel's was it anyway? His brother was the one I wanted to please. My bare chest was only the preview to a much bigger and hairier package Nykolson would have the pleasure of tackling later.

I heard the clink of a coffee mug on the stone table top after I'd turned away to get my dirty shirt from yesterday, not happy about putting that thing back on, but it was all I'd come with. Seconds after that clink, I heard the sound of a chair scooting across the concrete floor, followed by Nykolson's voice saying, "Wait up, hot stuff. I'll get you a clean shirt. You can wear one of mine."

"Hot stuff? Wha-aat?" Nathaniel's unfiltered mouth blurted out, "Did you two go to town and back, last night? Not that I need to know, but all this crap happening right now is making me believe you two had banged."

"No bruh. We were respectable gentlemen. The entire night."

Nathaniel nodded a few times. "M-hmmm."

Nykolson answered back with a fuck-you finger. He probably deserved that.

"As expected," Nathaniel returned the same lifted finger.

03 80

"I'm not thrilled at the thought of covering up all this exquisiteness, but here you go, put this on." Nykolson tossed me a deep V-neck tee he'd pulled from his chest of drawers. I caught it in flight before it had a chance to pass over my shoulder, snapped it open and approved it as wearable material. While I started putting it on, I was surprised to see Nykolson standing in front of me once the fabric dropped below my eyes. "Whoa! Did you fly across the room or what?"

He laughed and had taken hold of the shirts bottom hem, helping me inch it down my body as if I was a child getting dressed on the first day of school and I had been doing it all wrong. I trembled a little bit when the backs of his knuckles gently traced my chest and skated across my nipples. *Oh shit. That felt good.* Had he done that on purpose? I thought he had, but might have been for his enjoyment as well as mine.

He tugged the tee into place at my waist, telling me, "You're good to go, and this bit of chest right here is for me to enjoy." Nykolson gently ran his fingertips along the shirt's deep V neck, pointing out what he was referring to—my hairy chest. I let him have his moment, refraining from depriving the part of me he liked so richly.

"So you chose this one purposely, did you?" I squeezed into it, puffing up my chest.

Nykolson grinned, then begun to back away.

"Wait!" I firmly seized him by the shoulders before he had a chance to escape. I spun the bill of his baseball cap to the nape of his neck the way I liked it and kissed him, holding my lips to his for several moments while inhaling the scent of him through my nose. His impressive erection had come to life in an instant, pushing into what I had growing between my own legs as if trying to pick a fight. I wanted to clutch hold of that fucker and play with it, but kept my shit under control for a better time. I had those fucking scruples to deal with first.

He sweetly moaned into my mouth, "Gah, dayum! You're killing me, Michael. Simply killing me, you know that?" The tone of his confession had just about put me six feet under.

He looked down at my hard-on invading his space and said, "I was going to say something about that thing last night, but I didn't want to make you feel uncomfortable, but holy fuck, I want to manhandle that beast in the baddest way."

Those were the words I'd been waiting to hear, making me feel like I'd just won the lottery. I knew then he was anticipating the challenge I'd someday put him up against, or better yet, put up inside him. I was beginning to believe we were a match made out of heaven. Had to have been.

I silently begged, *"Please, please, please, be a bottom."*

ᘒ ᘔ

Before heading for the patio to enjoy the morning sunrise with Nathaniel, Nykolson and I stopped in the kitchen to get ourselves fresh cups of Java-Joe's. I snatched the coffee kettle in case Nathaniel was in need of a warmup, too.

Smartly, Nathaniel said, "It took you long enough to put a shirt on. But I get it. You two are just getting started. The lust overpowers the brain in the first trimester."

"Are you nuts?" Nykolson wailed. "Trimester is a division defining the duration of pregnancy. Nobody here is pregnant."

Nathaniel leaned back in his chair, locking his fingers across the front of his zippered fly and said, "Not yet anyway." He glanced at Nykolson with a pirates glare.

I almost huffed at what Nathaniel said and added, "But the term can be associated with each of the three terms in an academic year, so technically the term he used is valid."

One night over and we were having our first debate. The way Nykolson looked at me after I said that was as if he had planned to tape my lips shut. Glaring at me, he said, "As an F.Y.I., my love. You never take his side, NEV-VER. Even if he's right. After three months pass, you'll know exactly what I'm talking about and will wholly agree with me."

All I heard was "my love" and "three months", nothing else,

which meant, Nykolson had a future in store for the two of us.

Looking a little bit cross, Nykolson asked me, "What *ARE* you grinning at?"

Like a well-polished couple who'd been together for years, I told Nykolson to sit down, drink his coffee and to enjoy the sunrise before he missed out on it. When he'd done as told and surrendered a half smile up one side of his face, I'd understood he liked me bossing him around. *Jeez. He was cute as fuck smiling like that.* Maybe I should spank his bare bottom. See what comes of it.

Silence lingered at the table, but hadn't lasted long. Nathaniel had disrupted that when he asked about how to process the restraining order against his ex-girlfriend, Dajana. That name could really put a damper on all things going well, like it was a pile of shit on a pastry cart. I'd taken a deep breath and cringed before speaking. "First thing Monday morning, I'll present it to the court."

Nykolson interrupted, "Shouldn't a lawyer do that?"

I followed through with assurance, "I can technically be legal representation in a small case like this, as counsel, not a lawyer. We already have the solid evidence we need against her, and it's documented, so it should be quick without the expense of hiring a lawyer to do the same thing I could do for free."

Nykolson leaned into the conversation. "I'll be happy to take the burden of payment for the help you're giving my brother. Call it a freebee if you'd like, but please know, I insist on giving you what you deserve in return for your good deed done. I have no objections whatsoever with paying you any way you'd like." He lifted a brow and accentuated, "_Anything_ you'd like."

"*Aw, shit!*" I grinned and tried to hold down my erection at the same time Nathaniel chimed in with, "I'm sure you will, Bruh, and I sincerely thank you for your marvelous contribution with giving up that powerful cock sucking ass to counsel."

So much for my erection taking a break—Nathaniel's term of endearment about Nykolson's ass sucking a cock put the wood back into my stick in a hurry. Had that been the evidence I was after that meant he was a bottom? I believed it was, or at least his black hole was familiar with riding a dick—hopefully a big one.

"Would you shut the fuck up, Bruh. Drink your coffee and

leave it to the adults to handle your dilemma? We got 'dis. And, thanks by the way for letting the cat out of the bag about me being a power bottom. I wanted to surprise him with that little secret myself." As though a flip had been switched, Nykolson turned to me and calmly said, "You were saying?"

All that came out of me was, "Uh… that's all." I couldn't think past Nykolson blurting out he liked getting fucked in the ass, referring to himself as a power bottom. Those fantastic words had indicated to me he could handle my full nine inches without a doubt. I was too far gone at that mention, and since he roundabout confessed he'd have no issues with the size of my dick, I knew right then we were going to be a seamless match.

Nathaniel smirked in my direction, giving me the idea he knew what had entered my mind regarding his brother's accommodating asshole.

Damn, he had me pegged, and damn I was thrilled about fucking his brother.

Chapter 11

"I need to make a trip home to clean up. I'm starting to smell like a pig farmer who lives in a chicken coop full of bird droppings," I'd exaggerated. Other than the fresh shirt I had on, what I said was the truth. There were no fragrance resembling daisies and pine cones coming off my body.

"Okay, that's nasty and untrue," Nykolson said. "You can clean up here, and I have other clothes you can wear. More so, I like seeing you running around in my gear—makes me feel like you're already mine."

Whoa! Another surprising strike to the noggin. Nykolson expressed a hint he was infatuated with me. I could tell. Absorbing his mention that he owned me, which I adored hearing, I commented, "But, you're a few inches taller than me so I might have issues with fit." I wasn't making excuses, because God knew I wanted to wear Nykolson's clothing. I only needed to argue the case to show I wasn't around to take advantage of either of their generosity, or overstay my welcome.

"Come on, now. Stick around. We're pretty close in size— same shoulder widths, chests and asses, so everything else will be manageable. We can always roll up the pant cuffs if we need to, or you can wear a pair of my shorts. What'll it be? Stay?"

Nykolson was so damned cute when he begged, and with that, I couldn't wait to get him down on all fours and hear him beg then. "All right. Enough pleading. I'll wear whatever you have available."

Nykolson led me to his en-suite off the master bedroom, pointing out where everything was that he thought I'd need. Then he handed me a towel and a fresh soap bar, mentioning if I dropped it, all I needed to do was holler and he'd be in straightaway to pick it up for me. *Jeez, he and his sexual innuendoes wouldn't stop. But, I adored every one of them and they kept me alert.*

I'd been left alone in the bathroom to do my business, and when I'd finished, found Nykolson sitting on the bedroom sofa next to a pile of clothing he'd laid out. He looked up from his second cup of coffee and said, "I knew you'd look awesome wrapped in a towel. Gah, dayum!" I'd left all the goods exposed from the waist up, with the white towel cinched low on my hips and swishing just below my knees like a pencil skirt. Admittedly, I felt sexy like Nykolson seemed to have thought.

"You held back those clothes purposely, didn't you? You don't fool me one itty bit. I know your game plan, wise guy." I figured Nykolson would have been waiting for me when I finished my shower, so I made it a point to give him a better look at what he'd have on top of him someday soon. Since I recently discovered he liked his men hairy, I made sure the towel rode low on my hips to give him as much of my furry manhood as possible without giving too much away, letting him in on the part of a man's body that drove most of us bloody crazy. It was all about that deep V pointing to our dicks, like it was put on us as an invitation arrow to the greatest find on the planet. I worked hard at keeping mine defined, and I was finally happy I had the chance to share it with someone who cared and would enjoy my labors. I saw him staring at my hair covered V, and by the lust on his face, I knew my hard work had paid off effectively. As long as *he* liked what he saw, I could care less if anyone else had.

I sauntered toward Nykolson, trying my best to look sexy as hell with my wet chest and damp pelvic hair sprouting above the low cinched towel. On my approach, Nykolson stood and said, "Well… it's my turn. I'll leave you to dressing while I have a go at the rinse and repeat."

I reached for his arm and ordered, "Stick around and show me what you picked out, and for the love of Pete, don't run away when the party's gittin' good. You're going to see all this soon anyway, so why not get a preview to save you from a shit load of shock when that big moment between us arrives."

As if Nykolson was afraid, he whispered, "oh my gawd", so quietly I could hardly make out what he said. His tension must have been rising, noticed by his hands landing on his thighs where he rubbed them up and down as though drying sweat drenched palms.

I hadn't been sure what I was about pull would help Nykolson relax, but I proceeded to step closer to him, putting my damp chest to his, tilting my head up toward his lips to kiss him. His hands transferred from his thighs to the bare flesh above my hips, and the delightful moaning coming from him assured me everything would turn out fine. With our lips lightly touching, I asked, "Okay, pass me those panties." I was glad to hear him laugh, even though I was sure he'd hand me briefs.

I casually removed the towel, dropping it at my feet and stood on it. Nykolson turned with the briefs in his hand, not once expressing the shock I thought I'd have gotten from him. There was a smile though, one that confirmed he was no longer afraid. I stepped one foot at a time into the leg holes, and before lifting my pole into place, Nykolson asked, "Do you need a hand with that fucking thing?"

"I knew you wouldn't be able to hold your comments back for too long, and I'm glad you've recognized your biggest challenge in this relationship."

Nykolson replied in a favorable way, "Challenge my ass, or *up* my ass. I'm definitely a fan of that fucker and trust me, I can handle it." He pointed at my dick and then proceeded to head to the bathroom to take over where I'd left off. As he walked away, I saw his reflection in the bathroom mirror coming back at me. He was mouthing, "oh, my, gawd", behind one of the biggest grins I'd ever seen. His irises rolled under his upper lids as he sharply inhaled, and I understood by that, he was overly excited about his upcoming encounter and he'd have to spread those legs pretty wide to let me in.

A short time passed by the time Nykolson had come out of the bathroom completely nude, not trying to hide any part of his body from me. I was happier than all get out with the decision he'd made and all I wanted to do right then was have at that chocolate man from head to toe, paying close attention to his midsection. My gaze had gone straight to his black sagging nuts that resembled two avocados, and his large dick dangling like the trunk of an elephant. I wailed, "Holy fuck!" I'd gotten right up and charged him, walking him backward into the wall. I gripped his dick because I needed to, had to feel that black beauty in my hand. It was warm and heavy, perfectly thick, a complete pleasure to hold, pretty much like my own. I was addicted straightaway. I wanted it in my mouth—to feel it snaking down my throat. Ejaculating. Maybe someday taking it up my ass.

I grasped the nape of his neck, turning his ear toward my lips. I quietly breathed into it, "That challenge you mentioned earlier? I'm ready to lay out the offer, right up that sweet ass of yours." I wasn't holding back what I wanted. Not anymore. Fuck my scruples.

I smoothly moved my hand back and forth over his thick as fuck shaft, keeping him hard as stone while luring glistening dribble from the slit of his velvety crown. I wanted to finish him off, watch him cum, but preferred our first time to have been more meaningful. I wanted to make love to him, face to face with elegant kisses, see his expression when I slipped inside him. I hadn't wanted to just fuck him from behind, or jerk him off and be done.

As he stood with his back against the wall, breathing in air like he'd been deprived of it for weeks, I back stepped the entire way to the sofa. I sat observing every part of that tall chocolate stud with the shoulders of a weightlifter, fantasizing about plugging his hole so perfectly I'd make him cum by butt fucking him alone.

"You, mother fucker," I heard him groan as he stared me down. His breathing still labored as his dick slowly started drooping toward the floor as it deflated.

Putting all my fantasies aside about getting my dick inside him, I mentioned it would have been a good idea if he'd gotten his sweet black ass dressed. As long as that ass remained exposed, it was easier for my cock to find a way in.

Was I nuts? Yes. For sure. But it hadn't always been about lust with me as it seemed. I wanted more. Especially from him. I wanted his love.

"You know you're incredibly sexy, right?" I made sure he heard me the first time, but I said it again with a slight whisper. "You're so fucking sexy that it makes me crazy. I want you right now, Nykolson. I want to put myself inside you. So badly."

"So badly, huh?" Nykolson hadn't seemed very eager to get dressed, but I needed him to. If he hadn't, I might have destroyed my streak of maintaining my stupid scruples. He'd become hard again, and I had, too.

"Yes. If you let me. But, I don't want to just shove my dick in and pound your ass, however, when that time comes, you'll feel like you'd gotten one hell of an ass kicking. I'd rather give you passion and smooth sweet love. It's important that I make you feel good. You'd already begun to mean that much to me, Nykolson, and I want your first time with me to be our memorable best."

Nykolson wandered over to me, stood for a few seconds before straddling my lap with an arm locked around the back of my neck. Looking down on me with his hard cock digging into my abdomen, he reached for and lifted my chin. "I will let you, and it will be our best, and will be amazingly memorable." He planted a kiss to my lips so sensual that I was having one hell of time letting him go.

Chapter 12

That day had flown by like it was carried away by a windstorm. I felt as though I had just gotten my ass out of bed an hour ago, when in all actuality, the three of us had already taken in a brunch kind of breakfast and a late afternoon lunch, or super early dinner while doing a bit of shopping together in the design district where I'd only driven through once or twice.

I was aware that allowing a detained outlaw to stray outside the fence line was cutting into the rule books, but since I had clout, and as long as I documented the release as a controlled visit, his outdoor excursion would meet approval.

While roaming in and out of the high-end shops along the avenue where nobody dropped less than a thousand dollars at each visit, Nykolson looked at everything as if he were planning to attend fifty dinner parties over the next three days and he had to find that perfect outfit where he'd stand out in the crowd. He appeared extremely focused on what he'd been doing, Nathaniel and I hadn't seemed as though we existed. If I wanted his attention during his shopping spree, I'd have to pull my dick out and start jacking it in his face. That was just an idea and one that made a whole lot of sense when it'd come to working at getting a gay man's gaze to shift. I'd known most of the tricks.

"Oh, fuck." The mere thought of actually doing that in a public place had given me a stiffy. Plus, knowing in the end, I'd have been dousing his mouth with a load of cum made pre-ejaculate ooze a little bit. I felt the cooling drizzle on my inner

thigh. The solution for that was to find a way to conceal my rising erection from Nathaniel and anybody who might have been looking at my jam packed crotch. It amazed me how easily I was aroused by Nykolson. He was able to bring out the best in me.

Shopping seemed to have agreed with Nykolson, something I supposed I'd have to get used to if I planned on sticking around. A minor setback if it was really considered one at all.

Nathaniel and I were about as thrilled to have been shopping as much as Humpty Dumpty was about that wall he'd sat on. The two of us hung out together in the lounges of those fancy-schmancy shops Nykolson dragged us into. To pass the time, we'd drunk mimosas and whatever other kind of beverages that had been served. I felt like the husband who'd given his studly mate the credit card and then sat back waiting for it all to be over.

I'd never been interested in shopping. Never had been. Even though the stereotypical label of a homosexual specified I should have been. I was the type who wanted to get in, get the shit I'd gone in for, and get the hell out—finish the entire experience in less time than it would have taken me to pee.

Every boutique we visited had lounges situated inside the dressing rooms, which I hadn't minded. Not only had I been given the chance to watch Nykolson undress and redress, providing me with an eye popping show, I had the pleasure of sneaking glances at countless men making their own wardrobe changes as well. I was mind boggled by how many men in that room were New York catwalk material. How was that possible and I wondered if any of them knew how stunning they really were?

For minutes on end I thought the changing room was where all the golden genes had been dealt out, and my A&F boys had dibs on a few of them, and they'd frequented the place for a gene rejuvenation regimen that would keep them young and gorgeous. The twins had fit right in without a doubt. I was fascinated by the experience of the places we'd visited and how it appeared not to have been gender specific. I figured that out when there were men *and* women in the dressing rooms together, and the best part was, nobody seemed to bat an eye in the same way somebody would if we'd gone to the neighborhood mall.

I'd caught on quickly as to how it worked for the rich and famous. The whole process made me feel as though I was backstage at a fashion show, even the runway music that had been piped in from above helped enhance the glamorous vibe, a drum beat matching every footfall. It was as if the clothing changes had been choreographed.

Everything Nykolson tried on made him look fantastic. He was one of the lucky ones who could wear anything as though it was made just for him. He could put on a freaking trash bag and make it look like a million bucks. I on the other hand would simply look like trash in a bag.

I'd never been into fashion, even though the gay man's sacred scriptures mentioned I should have been. I preferred a well-worn pair of jeans, a decent fitting Tee shirt, and a favorite set of sneakers. Now that was comfort and suited me just fine.

The entire day, Nathaniel and I repeated, "Yes dear. You look great in that, dear." Toward the end of the show, we started saying it without looking up at what he had on. I was shocked the guy hadn't pooped himself out. It was similar to a challenging triathlon from what I could tell. Sweat, and all. No wonder Nykolson was so fit. Keeping up appearances was a major workout.

Even though we'd only been shopping for less than an hour, it felt like four.

"How much longer will this go on?" I whined under my breath, but must have been loud enough for Nathaniel to hear because he leaned into my ear and said, "If you're going to be my brother's boyfriend, your ass better get used to this shit."

I sarcastically replied, "So you're telling me this will go on forever?" My head fell back against the wall behind me. The thump shocked me a little bit, but I still stared into the light above me as if I was waiting for Scotty to beam me up.

Relaxing deeper into the sofa as though planning to hang out there all day, Nathaniel leaned back with both hands locked together at the nape of his neck, and his feet stretched out as far as they could go on the floor in front of him. "I foresee that handsome as hell brother of mine — who coincidentally looks just like me—will be doing this until our hair turns gray. Mark my words, white boy. Then, these fashion shows will go all orthopedic on our asses. I hope when the time comes, those shoes and shit will have bling. Cuz dis dude ain't ready to be wearin' no flesh toned footwearz."

On occasion when Nathaniel had spoken, the thug-like jargon had come out of him almost naturally. I wasn't quite sure if he realized that, but the short time I'd known him, that gangster edge popped right into a conversation nearly every time. I'd heard him and Nykolson speaking very intelligently several times, which led me to the realization that the "gangsta shit" was part of his "home boy" wannabe act.

"You seem comfortable." I glanced over at Nathaniel who was still laid back on the sofa with his feet extended so far out in front of him on the floor he looked like a skateboard speedway ramp. I shouldn't have looked, but I had. That fucking crotch of his was so jam packed and bulging with deliciousness, I knew everything under that denim was identical to his brothers.

As though he had caught me looking, he sprung from his stretched out position and grumbled, "That's it. I've had enough of this parade. Go get your man. His black ass needs to speed 'dis bow-shit up. I need new gym shoes, and this place doesn't have anything I want, and if it did, there's no way in hell I'm paying two thousand dollars for the left one and another three for the right. That amount of money for a pair of soles is sum-pin seer-ee-us."

There it was. More Gansta.

Over the past couple of days, I'd come to enjoy the way Nathaniel spoke. During our shopping excursion, I certainly had gotten a full dose of it. He was a funny guy if he'd been aware of it or not. The way he talked to Nykolson was just as comical, always point blank with all kinds of sarcastic love attached to everything he said. I'd heard a bit of it out of Nykolson as well, but he seemed more reserved at times. If he was "the Gansta" wannabe type like his brother, he hadn't let it all hang out in front of me yet. Come to think of it, I'd only heard them talk to each other like that, so I'm guessing it might have just been a brother to brother thing as it was with that hand bumping maneuver I'd seen them pull off a while back.

Nykolson had come out of the frosted glass dressing compartment wearing what I hoped to have been the last costume he'd planned on showing us. Holy crap he looked hot as fuck in refined leather. Then I saw the beautiful package between his legs. The light reflecting off his fly had nicely shaped his oversized bulge, pushing his meat to one side of the zipper and taking over part of his thigh.

"Fucking, damn." I was getting wet all over—pretty sure my asshole was self lubing, too.

Snapping me out of my fantasy, Nathaniel had given a backhanded smack to my upper thigh and harped, "If you don't say it, I will."

"Whaaa...?" I had totally gone blank, probably mumbling words out of order.

I hadn't given Nathaniel an answer, but my thoughts asked, *"Say what? That I want to feel what it's like to have your brother's leather bound cock fucking me in the ass?"* That just might happen if he continues doing what he's doing.

The way Nykolson had smiled at me, I must have mumbled something, like telling him to purchase what he had on because he looked so damned hot in it. I forced a dry swallow in order to have forced my gaping mouth to close, and soon after, had eventually come back to life when Nykolson finally decided to swagger back to his changing room. That's when I'd gotten a good look at his leather packed ass. Damn, I wanted to fuck it. Like real bad.

"Hey, Chump...? Brozo who wants my brudder," Nathaniel boasted, fist popping me again, aiming for the bicep, but striking my elbow instead because I moved. "Get your white butt off that chair and tell him we're done. Drag his sorry black ass to the street."

I was still stunned by how good Nykolson looked in those black leather pants and form fitting dress vest. His good looks had me stumbling to find the right words, "Yeah. Yep. Sure. I will."

Nathaniel grabbed my arm as if he was holding me steady. "You okay there, big guy?"

"Of course. Yeah. I got 'dis." I banged a two fingered piece sign against my chest. Okay, maybe not the coolest gangsta move ever, but I was trying. Right then I felt shadowed by Nathaniel's ability to be cooler than me. He was the real phony gansta. I was the first to admit, I wasn't as funny as if Nathaniel had said and done it, so I winced and told him to ignore what I'd just tried to pull off as a cool move.

Nathaniel laughed at me, which was well deserved. "You blow true, white boy. Now, go get him. But remember. If this shit between you two works out as I think it will, you get me, too." He forked his two fingers and double pumped them against his chest. "Check dis. That's how it's done." He slowly nodded at me with pursed lips, like a stoned headed dude who had just partied on the Jamaican island.

I nodded back, accepting that I'd be getting two for the price of one, and answered, "I can live with that."

Before I stood to go get Nykolson out of the leather and into his street clothes, Nathaniel remarked, "I know it's only been a few days, but on a serious note, it's nice to see that huge smile on Nykolson's face. He's always had it, but it's much bigger now. Fact be known, it has a lot to do with you being around. Don't stop doing what you're doing, okay? Keep that crap up. He likes it. I can tell he's hooked."

I was moved by Nathaniel's genuine lyrics. Someone other than me felt the love in the air.

It had taken bit of enticing and sexual promises to finally get Nykolson outdoors and onto the streets of San Francisco where we could get the fresh air we'd been deprived of for the past hour... or so. Being situated in a big city flooded with diverse culture had given us the freedom to hold hands while walking the avenue. Nobody we were aware of seemed to have thought two men holding hands was anywhere close to being out of place, and I respected the feeling that support had given me. I'd never done it before, nor had I met anybody I cared to do it with, but with Nykolson's hand in mine, that all changed, and not once had I sensed a need to pull away. I squeezed his hand, locking his long fingers between mine, believing wholeheartedly that the embrace would embed the memory of my first time holding hands in public into my head forever.

While walking, partially caught up in my own little world, I had suddenly been jerked into a spin to find myself facing a miniature window display in the front of Cartier's diamonds are forever jewelry shop. As soon as I had a chance to focus, Nykolson said, "I've been eyeing those commitment bracelets for quite some time, and I just might finally get the chance to wear one of them." He kissed me on the cheek before turning back to the window where our reflections bounced back at us. It just so happened, the way the bracelets had been displayed in the window formed halos above both our heads. *"Holy crap! Was that a sign? Had I finally found my angel?"* I was certain I had, and he was standing next to me holding my hand.

Nathaniel groaned, almost spoiling the moment, but I chuckled at his slang, "Oh. My. Gawd! I think I'm gonna upchuck my samitch."

Nykolson reacted by barking, "You don't be meanin' dat, dawg!" His head sharply snapped forward and back a few times, the shopping bags in his hand and the ones in mine swished back and forth along with the motion of his jerking head.

I laughed at the gesticulated dramatics that had come out of Nykolson—all of it appearing as though he was forcing his point of view with a full bodied exclamation mark.

Returning to our reflections, the mirrored image so clear, it seemed as though I was looking at the real thing, no glass to haze the brilliance. I'd gotten lost in Nykolson's eyes looking back at me. I was captivated all over again by the cool crisp color of them as I believed I always would be, and I'd probably see them that way until the day I died. They were just one of the many things I loved about him, my attraction fixed from the moment I first saw those sparkling grays. Like... I loved them a lot. They were shiny and stood out so brightly against his dark skin, and the outline of his long black lashes made them practically look silver. Mine on the other hand were an unusual shade of brown, not auburn, not chocolate, but somewhere in between, almost matching the chestnut color of my hair.

As we walked, I enjoyed the way people looked at us, most zooming straight in on Nykolson's unusual eyes first, then over at mine. The couple of times somebody felt comfortable enough to comment on the color, I told them it was because our souls had recently traded places—I'd gotten his and he'd gotten mine. I think Nykolson enjoyed hearing that because each time I said it, he grinned so wide I thought the corners of his mouth would reach his ears.

During our jaunt, I'd noticed the twins attracted a lot of attention, even when standing still, which made me realize it'd become an all-out mission once I'd bound myself exclusively with Nykolson. It was a boyfriend challenge I was willing to put myself through since I liked him that much, and my attraction toward him had gone beyond how I'd seen him leaning against the bedroom wall earlier that day. I was persuaded into liking him well before I'd gotten a peek at his stunning body, all naked and brown. I figured I'd better start preparing myself for a few fist fights, as well as start collecting those much needed fighting sticks to take out all the men *and women* who'd come sniffing around my property. Because of the way he looked, there'd be a lot of people who'd find it difficult to look away. That hypnotizing gaze of his had taken me right into his center and would definitely do the same to somebody else once they'd gotten a glimpse of those baby grays. Thank my lucky stars, however, I was the one who kept him looking back.

When both Nykolson and Nathaniel were together, wearing identical threads, doing the twin thing—holy crap, it was like fighting off killer birds in a Hitchcock film. People swarmed in circles just to have a gander at the stunning duo.

I kissed Nykolson, planting a soft one on his cheek, followed by my skating lips across his jaw until I reached his ear to whisper, "One of those bracelets would look magnificent on your wrist." Shoot, if only I could afford it. Maybe not at that moment, but I was sure as shit going to try.

Chapter 13

"Summm-bitch! My feet are on fire. So much for these two hunert and fitty dolluh athletic sport-playa's B-court shoes." Nathaniel cracked me up when he blurted out how the shopping spree the three of us had gone on seemed to have roughed up his feet, even though he and I were the ones who'd sat most of the time tossing back beverages and taking pee breaks while Nykolson carried out eighty percent of the foot work. In my eyes, those fitty-center's needed to be on Nykolson's feet, not his brother Nathaniel's.

Our trio was still quite new, which meant, I hadn't reached the point where I felt comfortable teasing Nathaniel about the bad day he seemed to have thought he had. Even with the comforting feeling that I'd known those two most of my life, and any noise I'd made about him most likely would have been invited, I still held my tongue and refrained from blasting out my opinion of whose day of the three was roughest.

The little bit I'd known about the twins, I hadn't noticed either of them having the typical amplified ego that one would find in good looking men like them. It wasn't difficult for me to be myself around Nykolson and Nathaniel, and undoubtedly, I was grateful. I could talk to them as easily as if we'd been long time friends. People like those two weren't easy to find.

Putting a finish to the day, Nathaniel and Nykolson dropped backward like cement blocks onto the sofa in the living room. I headed to the bathroom down the hall for another much needed pee break.

"Are you spending the night or what?" With my back to the twins, I wasn't quite certain which one of them had asked that question. I'd hoped it was Nykolson, but the emphasized question mark made me think it was Nathaniel. I'd figured out while being around them all day that if I wasn't looking directly at them, it was a tossup as to who had been the speaker. The tones of their voices were so identical — same highs, same lows. That would be a task I was going to have to work on, observing their quirks to figure out how to tell them apart. Until then, I answered them both, "That depends on which one of you is asking." Excited either way, I kept walking. My full bloated bladder wasn't getting any less painful and really needed to be emptied. If I said yes to staying the night as I had wanted, it was a sure bet I was getting laid.

"Oh my gawd, I have GOT to pee."

Finally, I'd come closer to whipping out the pecker to hose down the porcelain, practically limping through the entranceway of the bathroom because I had to pee so bad. I flipped the light on and shut the door. Once I'd found my place behind closed doors, and just for fun, I clapped my hands, only to discover the lights stayed on — Thank God. I laughed under my breath, thinking I was silly for exploring the Clapper test in the bathroom. If the lights flashed, I was definitely investing in a smart home system for my man — that boy needed to step into the space age.

Standing in front of the porcelain throne before letting the flood gates break free, I decided I needed a few private moments alone. It wasn't to jerk off, but to conduct a little office business I would have preferred to have done on company time. But at times, the nature of my job called for working overtime off site. I'm not one who squatted to pee since my freakish endowment between my legs had always made it near impossible to keep my peckers crown from taking a dip in toilet-water. A seated position was workable if I shifted my ass further back toward the water tank and elevated one thigh several inches off the seat, giving me those few extra inches I needed for my dick to dangle. While I awkwardly sat off to one side, holding the front half of my prick in one hand, giving a go at a seated wiz, I single handedly sent a brief text message to Ashlund, telling him I needed to urgently meet first thing in the morning at the office. I sat there waiting for his response and in less than thirty seconds, he replied, "Okay. Seven thirty sharp."

☙ ❧

Since I was able to identify traces of outdoor noxious ozone clinging to my person, I was sure Nykolson would have been able, too. I'd always found that odor to be offensive, so I asked if it was all right to use his shower. It wasn't meant to be a question, but more of an advisory I was heading in there to take one.

As soon as Nykolson entered the shower chamber and turned on the water, I understood that was him giving me the okay. A more confirmed approval as though he had a plan to jump in there with me was when his shirt had come off, exposing that beautiful brown chest.

Wow!

I was close to being star struck and wanted to dive right in and rub my hands over every part of that chocolate chest, followed by gliding my wet mouth from nipple to nipple, sucking and nipping. I knew what that felt like and hoped he liked it, too.

He pulled two towels from the closet, giving me the idea it was truly going to be a joint showering event, and that great big tiled chamber was meant for the two of us.

I acted stupid and questioned, "Two towels? Are you calling me huge?"

After glancing at my crotch and smiling, Nykolson hung the towels on the side-by-side robe hooks near the entry and quirkily advised, "No, no. One's for me."

I inhaled deeper than I normally would have and looked into the heat lamp above us as means of melting away the image in my head of what I really wanted to happen—a gorgeous naked black man in my shower, soaped up, spread eagle, bent over, showing tight ass, downright ready for me to fuck the shit out of him.

Putting a stop to my rump-riding fantasy, I said, "Soooo,

would you like to go first?"

Nykolson sleekly stepped toward me like a dangerous panther—a beautiful black one—put a hand under my shirt and caressed my chest. His eyelids smoothly lowered halfway, giving me a seductive glare. He'd spoken with soothing conviction, assuring me there was room in the shower chamber for two, and bathing together would conserve precious water.

I felt his hand slide a few inches to the left, rubbing a gentle thumb over top of my tit. I gasped sharply, followed by a drawn out release. His voice lowered as he proceeded to say, "It'll be no different than an athletic locker room, like the one in school, where we openly showered with other boys, painstakingly keeping to ourselves, while secretly aching to fuck or be fucked by a soaped up buddy showering next to us. You must know what I mean?"

I could feel my temperature swiftly rising as his voice against my ear changed to a raspy whisper, "It'll be just like that, Michael. In... and out. That's all."

The heat of his breath left my ear, and at that moment my dick was about to burst through the fabric of my jeans, and if it had, steel zipper fragments resembling shrapnel would have blown clear across the bathroom, cracking mirrors and wall tiles. I shimmied around Nykolson, trying to keep my raging erection inside my pants until the right time had presented itself to let it loose. Showering together might not have been a good idea if either of us were planning on maintaining our stupid scruples. My body wanted to fuck the man, but my effing mind kept interrupting my efforts with a big fat, NO!

Within a flash, I transported back to my senior year in high school, thanks to Nykolson for bringing up those days and the lust I had for all the hot guys who showered with me after gym class. I suddenly sensed those familiar echoes a locker room had. It was as if I was there all over again. I had distinguished the rising humidity of a community shower chamber, heard the continual downpours pinging against the tiled flooring, and I even smelled the dirty jockstraps wafting into my septum. All of those attractive pleasures had come to me at once. The images so clear, and included the high school quarterback, Thaddeus

Oxemberg, who had once given himself a soapy rubdown and a one handed wash job up and down his dick as I stood watching across the way. To this day, I was pretty damn certain he knew exactly what he was doing, and was probably pissed that I hadn't acted on his attempt at turning me on, like dropping to my knees and taking him down my throat, or bending over to let him fill my ass with his beefed up schlong.

Those lustful secrets had been locked away for a long time, but miraculously had come to life all over again as though it was the day they had taken place. My cock instantly turned harder, feeling like solid steel, as in, needing to seek out a hot tight manhole to pummel until I'd shot off a few good rounds. My dick pushed, pushed, and kept pushing, determined to break free from the zippered restraint. If I hadn't let it loose, that shrapnel would have been flying.

My head rung, *"You're gonna cum any second, Michael Allen Millhouse."* I would have if I hadn't immediately severed the sexual tension building between Nykolson and me. That was a no brainer and had to be done pronto. I turned away, but, even doing that, I still was so ready to bend Nykolson's sweet black ass over the countertop and shove my fuck pole so far up inside him that he'd feel me in his throat. He would have gotten one hell of a jolt when my semen flooded his mouth at my entered position from his behind. I wanted to cum, but I needed to wait. A much needed shock to my system had come when my head echoed *"Stop"*, and it continued resonating over and over again.

I knew a fast reckless fuck wasn't how I wanted to start my affair with Nykolson. I had better things in store for him. Such that as, wanting to enter him slow and sensual. To move inside him so he knew I was there. To give him a moment filled with passion so great that he'd never have been able to forget what I'd done to him. That's what I wanted for the man I adored. A good, slow, passionate screw.

When I turned back around to face Nykolson, he was fully nude with a cock of steel pointed right at me, one that was surely ready to be used and abused. I found his behavior to have been demanding, which I liked. There'd have been no guessing what and how the fuck he wanted me. With a stern domineering voice, he ordered me to get my clothes off right before he said, "Tonight this black body is yours to do with whatever you please."

Was I really ready to hear Nykolson tell me that? Fuck yeah, I was ready. So ready to put... All. Hands. And mouth. On. Dick. There was no possible way I'd have been able to wait another day, or much longer than that. The more I looked at him, the harder it was to keep my dick from leading my brain.

"Be a good chap and control that cock."

I'd done well containing my urge to go down on his big beautiful prick by changing my manner of thinking. Following a much-needed, head-clearing deep breath, I held strong and told him, "Let's make this soapy adventure about foreplay, could we? A little soap here. A little soap there. That's it. I have better plans waiting for you in that king sized bed."

I smiled and added, "How limber are you?"

That phrase had gotten his attention like a firecracker had gone off at his feet. I noticed that when his dick jumped and bobbed as if it was an antsy thoroughbred at the gates of the Kentucky derby. That fucker was eager to come and get me, or the idea of having me prod his prostate made that black fucker twitch.

I could tell by Nykolson's actions he was gluttonous for my erection and wanted me to take him into the shower and blow his mind with a furious fuck. I'd known from what he mentioned earlier, he preferred the idea of me making love to him instead of a ride on my cock to simply get his rocks off. From what I'd detected so far, Nykolson was a passionate man—a lover of meaningful things—a precious gem that needed to be delicately handled and treated with care. I was the man who could and would have given him all of that.

As we showered together under the near scalding downpour, I held him with tenderness, kissed him with passion, and let him allow what was taking place to only go as far as he wanted it to go. I started out by spooning him from behind, then turned and held him face to face, kissing and caressing nearly every part of him from the neck up. The pressure of his strong body against mine was more than I could handle. I wanted to connect with him in a bad way, slide inside his body to let him know I wanted to be with him.

Albeit, as my dick held on to its stone-like quality and ached to feel him on it, I still seized my desires, and only fantasized about what was yet to come and how intense the moment was going to be when I finally put myself inside Nykolson where I knew I belonged.

Outside the chamber, wet sparkling rivulets trickled down both our bodies. I wrapped a single towel around the two of us, concentrating on Nykolson's eyes looking down at mine. I ran my knuckles over his dark bare chest before moving both hands around his back where I locked my fingers to hold him close. I kissed him softly, sharing the gentleness before moving on and giving him the moment in his life that would seal our deal and confirm we were an everlasting couple.

ᘓ ᘔ

With my body letting off a soapy scent that was fresher than before we bathed, I hopped into bed next to Nykolson's naked body after I had set the alarm on my cell phone to go off at the crack of dawn.

The room was prepared for a night of romance by Nykolson, who'd flipped off every light in the room except for the lamps on each side of the bed. The fixtures let off a soft white glow that fused with the silver shimmer seeping through the window from the moon outside. The way Nykolson stared at me as I lay nude in bed above the covers was clear he liked the way I looked, and he commented how nicely the light reflected across my skin. The side of my body closest to the window excelled a silver tone from the moons glow and my other side closest to the lamp shone a few shades whiter.

"Could you be any more stunning, Mikey?" Nykolson said as his hand reached forward and dragged a slender finger along the center of my chest, following the trail of hair down my abdomen that was dividing the two radiant hues of light over my body.

Nykolson's light chocolate skin looked dark blue under the mixture of the two light sources, and up against mine, there was the contrast between us that I found erotic beyond the extreme. Where my attraction for a handsome black man had come from, I'll never know, but I couldn't have been happier with the way I was. That's how I am, and I can't make it, nor would I want it to, go away.

Because of the way Nykolson touched me, my erection had grown in thickness and in length, climbing heavily up the center of my abdomen past my navel. Pre-cum oozed from my slit, fusing with the hairy trail a few inches below my sternum.

Nykolson had gotten to his hands and knees, his own erect dick projected forward, heavily arcing downward beneath him. He shifted, slowly lowering himself, sliding his chest against mine and situating a bent leg over my hip. He gently slipped his tongue into my mouth instead of viciously jamming it in. The slickness set my mouth on fire, and I fought like a dog not to charge in and bite.

Without taking his mouth off mine, Nykolson repositioned his body over me. I huffed when he lay prone on top, pressing down, holding me hostage. We continued kissing with unrestrained passion, containing as much of the imprisoned lust that would kill us if we let it run free all at once.

He made me feel wanted, as though I was only his. His soft lips caressed my soul, and the flavor of him cut straight to the bone. My heart beat faster and faster, wrapping me with the sensation of breaking in two. The amount of desire I had for Nykolson was almost too much, pushing my need to connect with him to a height I hadn't expected. My sexual desires perked up, had come out of nowhere, speeding through me like a supercharged train. I battled the urges, cursed them, put them into hiding until the time was right to set them free.

The continuous touch of Nykolson's mouth over mine had punched me with exuberant cravings, over and above anything I'd ever felt before. By his exploit, my masculine veneer had been peeled away. I cupped his jaw with one hand and confessed, "If another second had gone by without feeling you against me, I'd have surely gone insane." I dived back into his mouth, keeping it passionate—the heat of his breath flowed into my lungs as if helping me breathe.

The way Nykolson felt to me, I could have kissed him for hours, but it seemed he had a different plan when he pressed his open palms against my chest and sat up, saddle-striding my hips the way a cowboy would ride a horse. I'd taken pleasure in the way his body weight bared down on me, pinning my stone hard erection to my abdomen, forcing it deeper into the gutter. I reached forward and gripped his cock, pushing his darkened meat into the centered indentation of his six-pack abs, feeling the delight of his thick erection in my hand and how nicely it had come to life by my touch.

I moved slowly under him, rotating my hips to keep him hard, sliding my erection back and forth between his nuts that loosely dangled at either side of my swollen cock. My own balls sagging between my thighs.

I looked up at Nykolson, observing every bit of his defined body, tracing the outlines of every muscle, seeing him once again as a stunning man—so brutally masculine, powerfully built, and appearing statuesque. Visually inspired, his splendor and fluid movements were more than I could take and there was no stopping any of the reactions he'd lured out of me.

I lay back while wrapping my mind around Nykolson's magnificence, finding he'd focused his gaze on my chest, giving me the idea he was fascinated all over again by its strength and the soft chestnut hair that spread across it like fine feathers. His hands felt good as he combed them over it. I'd caught a gleam in his eyes when he slid them further along, stopping a few inches below my sternum next to where the bulbous crown of my dick had found it's resting place—pre-ejaculate leaking from the slit. He swirled his thumb pad through my slick discharge before transferring my flavor to his tongue.

Holding back no longer, I reached for Nykolson's broad shoulders and drew him down to me. He felt strong in my grasp, his muscles bunched under my grip. I quietly embraced him in the dim light, loving and kissing him, keeping our connection filled with passion. A deep timbered moan rattled from my throat as his smooth body and erection glided back and forth over my torso.

He shifted, panting into the pocket of my neck as his body grew tense from what I recognized as his mounting orgasm. I indulged him with what he was begging for—my chest hair scrubbing his smooth flesh, bringing his level of exhilaration higher. I paid attention, keeping my rhythm even, pushing sparks of pleasure through every part of his perked up core. I felt him tremble as if he was about to cum. Then I heard a muffled moan. A gratified groan. Then a whispered, "Ohmigawd."

Had my outer body felt that good to Nykolson that he'd be able to cum without me penetrating him? The thought of that struck me in a barren way and I wanted to prove I could go at him like a wild gorilla. I had enough of the sweet tender foreplay. I was a cock-hard horny man and I needed to really fuck the guy sitting on me. By the way my flesh burned and I started sweating, the levels of my testosterone must have shot off the charts. The urge to mate with him intensified, and all I could think about was power driving all nine inches of my stone hard meat into the man who wanted it.

Nykolson covered my mouth with his again, probing for my tongue. His moaning and rock hard cock confirmed his satisfaction for how I'd made him feel. He pushed up, sitting on me. "Fuck me, Michael. I've got to know how good you're going to feel inside me."

That, I could guarantee I'd do.

I observed Nykolson's body as he sat on top of me, running my hands along the deep crease below his muscled pectorals, keeping my touch moving gently from left to right. "You're fucking stunning, Nykolson." I expressed the facts that I was sure of and it seemed to cause his dick to pulse and grow stiffer, still.

I pinched and twisted each of Nykolson's brown nubs, first the left, then the right, making him whimper as though they were linked to his prostate. By the way he pushed his chest into my hands, I recognized he wanted more. I'd given him more, pinching harder, twisting, and he cried, "Yeah," at the same time his body quaked and his dick popped upward and back down again, banging against his rolling abs and then thumping against my cock that lay prone against my own hard six-pack. I twisted his nipple again, and his cock shot upward, pre-ejaculate oozing.

With gracious subtlety, I moved a hand further along, palm stroking the deep impression of his sternum. Moving downward a few inches more, I was forced to stop when I reached the crown of his tall standing dick. The pre-cum leaking from the slit glazed my palm and I brought it to my tongue and licked it clean. I moaned from his musky flavor, then I rattled erratically, "Fuck... You're so damned hot, Nykolson. I've got to get inside you... Right now! I can't wait another second. Are you ready for my thick cock to be shoved up that black ass? I need it. So fucking bad. I want to make you cum." I carried on, couldn't believe what he'd done to me — couldn't believe what was coming out of my mouth. I was so wound up, wanted to talk dirty, to make us both insanely impatient to have at each other.

Appearing as eager as I was, Nykolson swiftly reached above my head and seized a magnum prophylactic and the tube of super lube he'd already put out on the nightstand next to his side of the bed. While climbing, his big black dick poked me in the chin before snaking up side my ear. His heavy black nuts dangled alongside my cheek. The muskiness of his manhood blew my brain cells to bits and the scent made me want to fuck him even more.

On his way back, the reverse had taken place, but after his retreating cock slid down my face, he skimmed his lips across my ear and whispered in a raspy tone, "I'm more than ready, you sexy fuck. I want that cock shoved inside me. Right now."

I grabbed Nykolson by the chin, pulling him into a kiss I just had to have. His mouth felt so good against mine, and he tasted like the greatest chocolate chunk on the planet. I had given that kiss to him hard and hungrily, locking him in with my rotating jaw and chewing mouth, gripping the nape of his neck to keep him where I needed him.

My breathing had gone sharp and I listened to the voice in my head that kept prodding me to fuck my man, fuck my man, fuck my man hard, pierce him with my thick white cock and make him cum.

I lay under Nykolson, chest to chest, my arm angled behind his neck in a ruling headlock. Without any interruption of our tongue locked kiss, I rolled Nykolson onto his back. The quick shift forcing me down on him, and I dropped between his legs as if I weighed three hundred pounds.

Releasing the kiss, I pushed myself to my knees, towering above the man I was about to fuck.

Beautifully spread out under me, Nykolson laid waiting. His voice quivered when he said, "If you don't slide that dick inside me soon, I'm going to burst. Please... screw my brains out. Hurry."

His orders made me crazy for him. I needed to feel the burning sensation of his channel hugging me. My dick flopped next to his, hitting him in the stomach with a smack. I moved my dick so it touched his, rubbing it alongside his hard-edged shaft. The contrast between my thick white prick with prominent veins and upward curve, and his extensive caramel sausage with the wrist thick width and the fist-like head, had gotten me wet and dripping pre-cum. When seeing our two cocks side by side, it was clear he was the bigger man. Knowing for sure I was nine, he was at least ten inches, maybe eleven. I growled, "Fuck an A! Your cock. So huge."

My hand gripped both of our dicks, struggling to meet finger to thumb, squeezing and stroking as best I could.

Aiding my strokes, I rocked back and forth, sliding my stiff cock over top of his. I looked down on Nykolson, watching his expression change between blowing air through an Oh shaped mouth to growling behind gritted teeth that resembled an angry grin. It was me who made that happen. I picked up the pace, gliding my dick back and forth, instigating another groan out of Nykolson that sounded like a cry for help.

He followed with, "Please fuck me, Mikey... I need you to fuck me. Don't keep me waiting."

At that moment, I knew I had him, and when I sensed his meaty dick pulsating against mine, actively trying to spit the load he had, I eased back, slowing my strokes before he ejaculated too soon. I wasn't ready. I wanted what we were doing to last.

To bring Nykolson's body to the verge of release, I concentrated on every spot I touched, paying attention to each kiss I'd pressed to his chest, upward along his neck, under his ear. More pleasured whimpers had broken free as I lured the sensation of a climax from deep inside his body with each lap of my tongue to his sensitive nipples. The intensity inside him had surely grown, identified in the way he moved. I craved him badly, wanted and desired him, needed to make that connection with him, to slide my cock into his lonesome hole.

Anxiety spread through me, and the desire to fuck Nykolson overpowered my ability to hold back any longer.

He moaned and thrust uncontrollably — breaking the full fisted grip I had on both of us. He'd gone wild, yelling to be fucked in the butt.

Nykolson's hard-on throbbed up and down against his abs as he watched me position myself between his open legs. "You want this cock, don't you?" There was no need to ask, but I'd done it anyway. His actions and his blaring vocals had told me that much. He nodded as his hand reached up and stroked my chest. His rough touch and vigorous petting made me tremble. When he pulled my chest hair, the pain felt more like pleasure.

I hurriedly stretched the magnum down my dick and added several coats of lubricant with my excited hand, stroking it, keeping it stiff while aiming it at Nykolson's black inviting star. The fucking knot was winking, or begging, clearly needing dick.

When my oily hand brushed across his anxious hole, getting it ready for penetration, his vocals let out an, "Oo-oh. Yee-aaah. Gawd, I nee-eed you." His low drawn growl motivated me, pushing my enthusiasm to fuck his butt even further. I'd gone on with probing him, circling, rubbing, and sticking his manly bullet hole with a single finger. The sensation felt magnificent. It was soft, like a warm glazed doughnut. I felt his pulse from inside and an incredible suction around my finger.

I made sure Nykolson was good and ready before I shocked his system with my oversized dick. He said he could take it, but my past experiences still forced me to prep my victim first, and then slide my thick dick in slow and gentle.

Adding to my single digit, I punched another one into him, making it a pair, sliding and twisting inward, pulling them out and pushing them in all over again. I felt his backdoor gripping my fingers, pulling them in and spitting them out as though his ass was a sucking machine. I fucking lost it when I saw the desperate look on his face, that of which had made me want to plug him with my donkey dick.

By the way his tight hole gripped my two fingers, I knew then he was almost ready. "Jeez, Nykolson. You're fucking hot in there. Fire pit hot."

While I stroked myself with one hand, my other continued reaming with twisting movements in the depths of Nykolson's chute.

He squirmed, acting as though he needed more. I'd given it to him, adding a third.

I rotated my hand, turning the three fingers stuffed inside him, hooking them into his prostate. I pressed the pads of my fingers upward with massaging strokes, making his body quake with need, causing him to curse and holler, "Gah, Dayum. FUCK! Michael. FUCK!"

His back arched, forcing his butthole downward onto my hand.

By his reaction while I warmed him up, I sensed he wanted to be stuck for good, not with my few curved fingers, but with the enlarged tool between my legs—my rod shoved deep until he felt the course hair above my cock scrubbing his taint.

Nykolson's impatient actions were clear, and from that, I no longer held back. I gripped my cock and aimed the glistening fuck-post at his brown flexing knot. It was more gorgeous than I thought it'd have been, nicely slick, appearing greedy, and completely inviting.

Pulling his knees to his chest, Nykolson exposed his twinkling star to me even more. It was most enticing, flexing as if aching to be pummeled, seemed as though it needed me. His whimpered cries spurred me on. I'd taken the lead and teased him, tapping my glossy hood against his dark manhole, punching softly, just enough to breach the seal with the tip of my head.

Then I'd given him more, pressing harder at the same time Nykolson pushed into me. His vocal moaning had gotten louder when my bulbous cap opened him up and sunk beyond his spasmodic ring. His legs opened wider and I could feel the suction of his black hole pulling me in. As great as his asshole felt squeezing my dick, I still only wanted to give it to him slowly, make sure he felt me digging in. His sphincter snapped tightly around my crown, strangling the head. The rest of my shaft remained outside his body, appearing as though there was over a foot yet to slip inside him. Was I really that big? It sure looked like I was.

I blurted, "Whoa, Hun. I'll get in there soon enough." I leaned down and kissed him, and when I managed the short jabs that inched me in with little effort, he looked me in the eyes with tremendous desire.

He bawled, "I can't take it, Michael. You did this to me. You made me like this," — he gasped — "I need you to jam it in. Fuck me up. Cock plow my hole. Do my ass some long awaited good. It's been too long." He sounded crazy.

As much as I wanted to shove right in and pound his black ass like he'd been begging for, my intuition had told me he might regret it once I had. To hold him steady, I pulled my cock all the way out, gripped his ankles and produced the wingspan I knew a man like him was capable of, he was wide open like a wishbone and my wish had come true.

His large black balls sagged long and heavy, blocking his sweet slippery hole I wanted to get back inside of so badly. Moving that nut sack aside, I slipped back in, slowly giving my dick to him, gliding in and out with care, slipping a little bit deeper each time I pushed forward. Within a moment of effortless guidance, I was all the way in. Even though I had loosened him up with slow perpetual motions, he still felt tighter than a clamp on my dick, that ass so tight, his farts needed a password to get out. He'd given good ass for sure, making my dick feel right at home, allowing my thick prick to pry him open like I was breaking the lock on a steel vault door. Spread eagle, trembling, and begging, indicated he wanted my cock real bad.

That's when I really let him have it, jacking his rear like I was drilling for oil, pulling out and shoving back in, hammering hard like the master fucker he'd wanted. Between ball busting thrusts, I grittily asked, "How's that butthole doing? You like how my fucking feels? You gonna cum soon?" I wasn't sure he heard a word I'd said, and since I'd gotten no answers, I figured he hadn't, or he was so deep in fuck-lust to realize anything was going on around him.

In what seemed to have been brain altering ecstasy,

Nykolson fist gripped the pillows above his head, whimpering and whining, spreading his legs wider than what they had been. Those extreme actions had shown he would have said yes to everything I'd asked if he'd been of sound mind and able. He seemed too far gone at that moment to breathe evenly, spearheading toward an outstanding orgasm that I had been working out of him with my plunging up-curved cock. He acted like his asshole was real hungry, going plum wild as I tormented his prostate with the head of my dick. His butthole sucked the fuck out of my reaming rod as if determined to swallow me whole. I was factually in love with his cock starved chute.

Nykolson's body rhythmically shimmied under me, his head bumping against the headboard every time I banged my pelvis into his rump.

I blurted out, "Jeez, you're cock sucking asshole feel gorgeous. I'm about to dump my spunk up that butt."

He appeared on the verge of crying, and from that facial expression, I knew he was battling an orgasm by what I had done to him. His head hinged back, chin pointing toward the ceiling.

I had come so close to releasing my load, and I sensed he had too. To prolong ejaculation, I pulled all the way out for a few seconds then plunged back in again. That intense maneuver caused him to holler, "Gah, FUCK! FUCK!" That outburst immediately changed to more whining. The roller-coaster torture must have been too great.

I wanted to keep it up, please him until he reached that volatile finale. I snaked my cock back a few inches and followed through with jamming my hips into him, banging my hips against the back of his thighs, enabling my nine inches to reach for his heart. He felt so good, I was certain I'd remain stiff even after I ejaculated.

Keeping him stimulated and under my control, I remained submerged, my thumping rhythm on fire, like a stud that couldn't give up. I rocked and rolled against him. Grinding, gyrating, and shifting my hips to change the angle. I pulled out and dug back in, ensuring he would feel satisfied with being well-bred.

Illuminating my desire to get closer to him, I nuzzled Nykolson's neck, sucking and kissing while I rutted my hard cock with slow loving strokes in and out of his contracting chute. I couldn't get over hearing Nykolson's enraptured whimpers that had turned louder as I bore down on him, penetrating him with both cock and tongue. His legs locked tightly around my hips, holding me secure, lodging me permanently inside of him.

Our pace had changed to slow penetrating love for nearly an hour, and amazingly, Nykolson had been able to hold me inside him pretty much the entire time without flinching. I'd become certain he was the best bottom I'd ever put my cock into. I pulled out briefly so he could revisit the pleasures of the initial penetration all over again, and I wanted to make sure he felt what I'd done to him well into the next day, hopeful he'd come back for more. From his reactions and vocals cries, everything I had done seemed to have worked.

After giving my gentle dick to Nykolson for as long as I had, it was time to cross the finish line and flood the man I adored with my white man genes. Without warning, I pulled my tongue from Nykolson's mouth, rose to my knees, grabbed each ankle to spread his legs and increased my hip action—pounding him, matching a drumbeat, banging, pumping, thrusting and thumping. Like that of an auto piston, my cock tunneled in and out of Nykolson's sucking channel. I heard butt-fucking slurping and thigh against thigh spanking. It felt like hot pleasure to me— super hot cock-sucking pleasure. Rough and dirty, on the verge of a violent ass attack. I was fucking him so hard that as soon as I finished him off, his body impression would forever be embedded into the mattress under him.

Suddenly and unexpectedly, the lights on either side of the bed begun to flash as if ghosts were in the room or there was a short in the wiring. On. Off. On. Off. On. Off.

Losing a little bit of my rhythm, I griped, "What the fuck?" without letting whatever was happening stop me from pile driving my dick in and out of Nykolson.

On again. Off again. On. Off. On… off. It was like a lightning show and I was the pounding thunder.

Ghost or no ghost, I couldn't break my rhythm. I was too invested in getting Nykolson to cum. I wanted to get that sauce out of him so badly, see what he had and how much he'd let loose. I groaned when it dawned on me what had caused the flashing lights. It was about my thighs slapping repeatedly against the back of Nykolson's ass, sounding as if I was clapping my hands. My mood was nearly yanked clean out of the zone when I started to chuckle. "That fucking —" I hadn't finished saying what I knew it was. But instead, I kept my dick inside Nykolson and made sure I fucked the shit out of him the way he wanted me to.

"Fuck those lights and fuck me harder!" Nykolson turned bossy. "Pound that ass!" His legs opened wider, helping me stay inside.

I reciprocated without protest, banging Nykolson with all I had, shoving my dick as deep as I could, drilling him like I was an oil rig that knew I'd get a money making eruption at any moment. I wanted that. Badly. My power-driving dick was busting up his hole, mimicking the steel shaft that pounded deep into the ground. I wouldn't give up. The headboard above Nykolson wobbled, boogying in time with our rocking bodies, keeping perfect rhythm with my wild thrusting. I hollered out another truth, "Holy shit, your ass is sweet. Fucking slick."

I grabbed his ankle tether like it was a handle meant to aid our fucking, holding his leg up and out, making room for my body to move the way I needed it to. I drilled him. Slap. Slap. Slap. Slap. Slap. In rhythm with our meeting flesh, the lights had turned, On. Off. On. Off. On. Off. On...

Between the flares of light that had changed my perspective on just about everything, mimicking a disco tech, I caught glimpses of how wide open Nykolson's mouth had sprung during his bouts of orgasmic frenzy.

He lay moaning and whimpering. No words. Practically crying.

It must have been my amazing ball busting ream job that had taken away his ability to speak. I stared down at him, watching his reaction as my thick white cock bored into him, igniting that sweet spot inside his slippery channel.

I knew I'd never get tired of sticking my white dick into a black man's ass — more than ever, since I'd found Nykolson and the way it made him feel when I'd done it. I planned on sticking him from that day forward — getting off on the contrast between our flesh tones. My white cock sinking inside his black hole would always be as erotic to me as the sexual act itself.

The experience would have been a whole lot better if the fucking lights would have stopped blinking. That's when a grand solution had come to me. I spanked my thighs against Nykolson's ass one more time to get the lights to turn on. Then without hitting him up with a flesh connecting bang a second time, I shifted my position to soften the blows that would keep the lights from flashing off.

Genius.

It worked.

I was home free and back on track, banging my hot man's ass like a champ without the distraction of a dance-disco strobe light.

Nykolson grabbed hold of his own cock with a gripping fist that looked to be tighter than a steel vice. Then he'd begun jerking himself, jacking so fast his hand was a blur. He hollered with a raspy voice, "Yeah. Keep that dick in me. Right there. Keep going." There was no need for him to give such an order, I wasn't pulling out of him until we were both shooting semen and totally satisfied.

I turned my attention to his prostate, stimulating the gland with the head of my prodding cock. As soon as I'd given him the first punch, he started quaking, his legs opened wider, and it appeared as though he was being netted by the mind wrangling orgasm that started in the groin and raced to the brain and back to his knotting nuts. He convulsed, his abdomen crunched and his upper body jerked upward off the mattress. When he growled, "Gah, Dayum, fucking, FUCK, that's good," I knew he was that much closer to reaching that sperm shooting event I wanted to see blast from his big black dick.

I pushed my cock as deep as I could, giving him every large inch of me. I groaned with gusto each time I felt Nykolson's asshole sucking my dick in a starving manner.

I begged for the lights to stay on and then pleaded, "Come on, Nykolson. Let me have it. Let me have that load. Paint that beautiful chest."

Luring what was still inside him, I thrust my hips like a

madman, banging into his ass with the speed of a fuel powered ramrod, my dick getting sucked and stroked beyond the point of any possible return. I repeatedly jammed my hips into him, wildly using his hole to get myself off, working at bringing my massive explosion to the brink of a major release, as well as his. I was growling. I was reaming. I wanted to cum.

Possessing Nykolson, intensely kissing him with rising desire, I hummed broken words into his ear as I started to tremble on top of him. "Are you ready?" — I groaned, — "oh gawd," — I grunted, — "for my load?" I could feel my face had changed to a contorted knot that matched my extreme pleasure. I was on the verge of my typical release, and Nykolson's ass was exactly what I needed to get me there.

Nykolson's orgasmic pleasures echoed mine, almost drowning me out. I heard him struggle for an answer. "Huh. Huh. Fu..," — he whined, — "shoot me... in the ass." The friction I felt from being inside him made me lose any control I had left. I kept after that sweet spot inside him, bumping into it again and again, prodding to keep his body trembling under me. Then it surfaced all at once. The mind blowing moment I'd been waiting for.

As I watched his hand-cranked orgasm bubble up and shoot from his dick, spraying streams of hot semen across his chest that soaked his smooth chocolate skin with ribbons of his frothy white cream, I continued fucking his ass as I ranted, "Damn. Fucking, BEAUTIFUL... Gah. Damn. FUCKIN'. BEAUTIFUL!!!" I couldn't add enough exclamation points, or fucks and damns to what I'd seen. *"I'm in love, I'm in love, I'm Gah damn fucking in love."* There was so much cum.

Like a strike to the head, I was then hit with them mind busting sensation.

"Shit!"

The scent of Nykolson's ejaculate was spunkily pungent and charged at me like a favored dessert, fucking me up, and because of that, the extraordinary orgasmic buzz that was already in me boiled from my hairy pelvis. It had taken me to a place so fast I hadn't had time to think about its arrival. I burst, blowing sizzling semen into the magnum up inside Nykolson's sucking channel, spurting over and over and over again, loading up that rubber, filling the fleshy condom to the point of bursting, stretching it to the magnanimous max. My breathing was quick, matching irregular roars in time with each forceful spurt. I fist gripped the hem of the condom near the base of my cock, but my semen still squirted out and oozed down the crack of Nycholson's ass.

As I continued spurting, Nykolson begged me not to pull out.

My jerking body bucked and had gone warm as soon as I felt my surging cock spew the final surge. I was a mess. Worn out beyond comprehension. Huffing like I'd ran a marathon. Surrendering to my orgasm, I lay down on top of Nykolson, tightly against him, sensitive and trembling. I ground my teeth together as I let go of my final growl. My back arched, forcing my pelvis hard against Nykolson, pushing my cock to the farthest depths of his rectal chute.

I needed to kiss Nykolson while I was still emptying myself into him. My mouth met his and I inhaled his breath as he breathed out. I kissed him. Passionately. Deeply.

I lifted myself up, looked at the man I helped cum and saw more pearly white glory across his chest and abs than what I'd ever seen on another man before. "Wow, Nykolson. I thought I was a gusher, but this? All this cum? Holy!" — I fucking loved it — "When was the last time you ejaculated?" I was shocked by how much semen had come out of him, and when he told me he jerked off that same morning because he couldn't get me out of his mind, I was convinced by the mess he'd made, the man was fertile. There was so much cum. Like a lot, as if he'd been hit with a gallon of milk to the face and chest.

Nykolson exhaled deeply, as if he'd been holding his breath for a while, and then he laughed. His laughter had taken me by surprise and I hoped it wasn't how he had really felt about the way I screwed him in the butt. I hadn't thought it was that, but since it was our first time fucking, that very well could have been his reaction to an explosive orgasm. He seemed to have enjoyed the position I'd put him in — on his back, legs wide open, with me, the handsome hairy stud on top and inside of him.

Once he brought up, "those damn lights," I knew why he had laughed. The disco show and the time it had started was something he and I could have done without. It was comedy in the making, however, wasn't the way I had imagined my first time with him being. Thinking back on the flashing light show, I mentioned it made for a funny highlight of such a serious fuck job. If I hadn't been so into fucking Nykolson, I probably would have laughed about it at the time it was happening.

I decided not to pull out of Nykolson's body even while we chuckled, and before that reluctant time had come, I gently moved my hips in small circles as I casually carried on a conversation with him. He gasped a little bit, probably from the relentless pleasure I was able to give him and his exquisitely accepting sphincter. I liked making him feel that good, so I continued rolling my hips, keeping it gentle, smoothly sliding in and out of my new man, who I was totally planning on keeping if he knew it or not.

Nykolson laid his palms against my chest and said, "I can't believe that light show happened while you—the guy I couldn't wait to impress with my fantastic bottoming skills—were cock-ramming my ass. Apart from that crazy disco incident, I loved every second of what you did to me. You were such a stud and so fucking good at it." Nykolson opened up and laid his legs flatter against the mattress, putting a tighter squeeze on my cock that was still inside him. I heard the juicy sputtering of my semen spitting from the condom around my dick.

"I suppose the light show could count as fans clapping based on how fantastic we performed." I'd gone back down on Nykolson, locking lips with his, and it wasn't long after I had given him my tongue that he'd taken hold of mine and sucked on it. His eagerness to fulfill my fantasies had made me want to go a second round with him, but after the drilling I had just put him through, I wasn't too positive he could handle another hour of my nine-incher boning his ass.

Still hard, I pushed my hips into Nykolson again, going as deep as I had gone earlier, which once again, had made his eyelids flutter and his head fall back. He'd shown the same gratifying signs as before when my talented erection hit that magic spot inside him. He gasped and howled, "Gah, Dayum, that's excellent." He exhaled with rasp.

"Hey... Stud... How do you feel about being on top?" My

voice was deep and sexy, the way Nykolson seemed to like it. He hadn't answered me right away because I had immediately grabbed him by the shoulders and rolled him over. His eye's instantly connected with mine, looking down at me with only a smile, and I figured his answer about giving it a try would have come in time. What man doesn't like sticking his dick into a tight warm hole?

To ease the pressure of giving me an answer, I crunched my abs, rising to meet his lips with a kiss.

Fucking for over an hour was physically arduous and I hadn't noticed the strain it put on my body until it was over. It had been a while since I'd gone at it with another man in my bed, but shoot, I couldn't believe how my entire body had felt like rubber once we called it quits. "Holy shit, I'm wrecked." I released the kiss and fell back against the mattress, my arm flinging above my head against the pillow.

"I can certainly understand how you'd feel that way. I just laid there with my legs in the air while you did most of the work, including fist gripping my ankles that helped me hold them open." Nykolson rolled off of me and collapsed face up. "I suppose it wouldn't kill me if we traded places someday, but not forever, because I'm the fucking bottom in this relationship. You got that, stud?"

That was the subtle answer I was looking for, and was thrilled when he mentioned, relationship. To me, that meant we were going places... together. *"Jeez, I was loving this guy, more and more."* Then I started wondering if I'd be able to take his size cock up my back door. I was game for just about anything with him and was definitely willing to give that thick fucker a try. The way I noticed how good my cock made Nykolson feel, I might feel the same and not want to get off his once I'd hopped on. If I found riding the donkey dick wouldn't work out, there'd have been nothing lost and Nykolson could regain one hundred percent of his title as the bottom in our, "relationship".

Clearing my mind of the top going bottom scenario, I lay waiting for my erection to relax, even though I preferred it was still tucked up inside Nykolson's sweet, tight, black, hole. It really had felt so much better there.

As soon as I settled down from my orgasmic tremors, Nykolson propped himself onto his elbow and looked at me. He tugged my chin in his hand so I was facing him directly and confessed, "That was the best finish to a terrific day. An amazing fuck by one hot guy."

Right after he said that, I followed him by saying, "That's good to hear. I was worried when the time had come to stick my dick into you, my size would be a bust and I'd never get in."

Nykolson exhaled while glancing down at my dick. "Listen, I'm a talented bottom—can take a good sized cock without flinching. Yours felt fantastic and I could have gone longer. I'd spread my legs wide open for you anytime, probably anyplace. Just say the word and my hole is there for you to use."

I noticed he sighed, but was pretty sure it was due to disappointment that my white beast was no longer sliding in and out of his stunning black ass. My beast of a dick lay stiffly up the center of my six-pack, cradled comfortably in my cum-gutter, but in time, would work its way back to a more reasonable size once I was able to get Nykolson's naked body out of my thoughts. By the way Nykolson gazed at what I believed was his favorite play toy, made me think he was impressed with the fucking thing. His dick was a few inches bigger by length and width, so I hadn't quite understood his envy with mine. Maybe my whiteness was what fascinated him like his blackness was to me? Instead of guessing, I asked him what he liked about it. I rolled to my side, and my dick went with me, flopping off my abs and slumping over my hip bone with the rubber covered head mashing into the mattress.

"You have to ask?" He nearly squealed.

"Meh. Just curious."

"If you must know. Firstly, I love its perfect size. Hot damn I do. Length and thickness. Secondly, I'm thrilled with how it makes me feel when I'm connected to it. Thirdly, that it's attached to a perfect man like you."

I smirked at all his good answers, then questioned, "I made third, huh?"

Nykolson chucked breathily. "Not a bad ranking, but you'll have many chances to bump yourself up on that scale."

"You liked taking me up your ass didn't you?" I asked him.

"Um. Fuck yeah," he answered greedily. "That fat fucker is going back in there soon, too."

"Happy to hear that because I definitely want to put it back in there again, and again... and again. No flashing lights though. Promise?" I pointed at him and he replied, "Note to self: ditch, The Clapper."

I rolled my head toward Nykolson, and caught his sparkling eyes looking at my dick as if he wanted to hop back on it. "What are you looking at?" I waited a few seconds until he answered, "Is there a reason you are keeping that thing on?"

I looked down at my big boner still wrapped in rubber and sniggered, "Oh shit, that's right. Go ahead, do the honors."

Chapter 14

"You two did it last night, didn't you?" Nathaniel uttered.

Any clue that his brother and I had gotten sexually active must have been by the way we were standing wrapped around each other at the kitchen counter, or because we had smiles on our faces that made us look guilty as shit. Another tipoff might have been Nykolson's horse riders bowed legs since I'd been between them with my jackhammering cock for over an hour. Anybody would have come out of that ass ramming with a whole different stance.

Nathaniel's doubting face was scrunched when he said, "But I'm confused, right now. Why are you behind Michael? Shouldn't it be the other way around? I mean… isn't that how it works for you, Nyckol?" He wiggled a finger at us and before he continued with anymore crazy questions as to who should be hunched behind whom, I answered, "Things aren't always what they seem, Masseur Nathaniel."

Sure, our night in the sack felt natural, with me on top of him, but at that moment I found it comforting having his body curled over mine while we stood. It felt good having his long arms along my sides with his hands flatly planted on the granite, pinning me in place as though he was dominating the situation. I felt safe the way his open shirt dangled at my sides, covering me as if I was wrapped in his blanket. At the moment it made perfect sense, the same way it had in bed where it all played out quite the opposite.

Because Nathaniel knew his brother was a bottom—and from what I found out the night before, an active and talented one—hadn't meant I should be dragging him around by a collar because I'm the one who stuck him with the big white woody while he was spread eagle on his back under me. It was clearly visible I was a few inches shorter than Nykolson, him being more muscular, and the order of our bedroom activity would seem to physically work better with him on top of me, but the bigger guy just so happened to be the eager bottom in our promising relationship, and I was happier than shit to be the one on top.

Nykolson looked like the big strong black man, chocked full of muscles and shit, and I appeared to be the short submissive white boy, but that doesn't automatically make him the one who would fuck me in the ass on a sweet September morn, or whenever. Things in life aren't always what they seem, which had brought up the question I'd asked, "How does the way two people stand together indicate the prone positions they put themselves into while intimately connecting their bodies, or in our case, a beastly light show butt fuck?" I laughed at butt fuck, wondering if it might shock Nathaniel when he heard me blurt that out.

"It doesn't, but... the dominant person in a relationship usually stands over the subservient one, no matter what either of their sizes are. Of course when I saw you tucked under my brother like that, my initial thought was, oh shit, two bottoms, how's that going to work? I was concerned more than anything when I saw you guys like that, because... I want this to work out with the two of you, dammit."

"Don't worry, bruh, it's working out the way it should. I'm still the enthusiastic bottom I told you I was, and, omigawd, that definitely won't change with this one," Gleaming, Nykolson said, remaining hunched against my backside—protecting what I wanted him to own—and tilted his head down around my neck and kissed that sensitive spot below my ear. His rough facial stubble tickled, causing me to go fucking nuts by his touch. It was a good thing I was behind the counter then or Nathaniel would have seen how big I really was and why his brother had such a crush on me. Plus, it was probably a good idea Nykolson wasn't in front of me, or things would have been a whole lot different, like my stiff rod stuffed deep inside him instead of just cradled in the crack of his ass.

"That's what I needed to hear." Nathaniel pointed at me and said, "Little white top" — then moved his finger toward Nykolson — "does big black bottom."

"Now you've got it," I replied. I could feel Nykolson smile against my cheek. I grinned back when he shifted his sweat-pant covered hips that pressed his long dangling dick and heavy avocado nuts into the crack of my ass.

Nathaniel had given two agreeing thumbs up and had then gone on telling us why his metrosexual brain thought the way it had. "With guys and girls, there's a pretty good chance of figuring out who and what fits where, but with two guys, it's a freaking guessing game." Nathaniel had a good point with a solid base, but then came the tricky part when he filled us in on one of his experiences. He started off chuckling when he told us, "What broke down a bit of the boy-girl theory was, I'd been with some pretty kinky females, and as I'd told my brother before, one of the bitches I was with had come at me with a strap on dildo. At that time I thought, meh, no big deal. If my brother can do it, then so could I. We were identical twins after all, and everything about us was pretty much the same. Whatever he could do, I could do better. So I'd thought. Well… That fucker only made it so far into what you guys call the pleasure emporium. As soon as that girl popped what I think was only the dildos head into my asshole, I nearly shot across the bed on all fours and then flew out the fucking window without a set of wings. I couldn't even call that ass invasion my début. How the fuck do you guys do it? Shit, that was a shock to my system I hadn't expected." His head was tilted, eyes squinting at the ceiling as if trying to picture that magnificent moment all over again. "Maybe I'll give it another try someday, but the bitch better use a lot more lube."

"Oh my gawd!" I laughed louder than I usually would have because that was one hysterical story I was going to keep with me forever. I pictured him on all fours waiting for that dildo to make contact. There was probably a nervous smile on his face in the beginning that turned into horror when the rubber schlong tried entering him from behind. I would have paid to see his facial expression more than watching the dildo going in. First timers are usually a bit stunned when a dick is aiming to get into their tight sphincter with force.

I was glad to find Nathaniel hadn't had any hangups when it had come to me and Nykolson having sex. It was refreshing to know that about him and I liked him even more because of that. I could tell, however, that his knowledge about two men humping each other was limited when he commented, "Don't you guys refer to it like playing baseball and other sports? Like… I know for sure my brother is a catcher, but I'm not certain where your place is on the playing field."

Were Nathaniel and I involved in some sort of a debate? "Does it matter who's behind home plate and who's on the pitching mound?" And why was Nykolson's brother so interested?

"No, but I get a kick out of trying to figure that shit out. Not that I really give a crap, but it gives me a project when I have spare time, and I want to make sure my brother is taken care of with a man who'll be his perfect match."

Nykolson intervened, "Trust me, brother. After last night's undoubtedly amazing connection, I'm pretty sure we are the perfect match. If it was up to me, I'd still have my legs over this man's shoulders, letting him take full advantage of my hole. That's what it's there for, now — his personal use."

Stunned by the conversation the twins were having, I lowered my head to avoid awkward feelings. I'd never come across anybody, including brothers, who shared such information with one another, and I was in the middle at that moment beating down an erection because it was actually turning me on.

"That's my bruthuh." Nathaniel suddenly perked up and said, "Oh, hey… Speaking of pitchers and catchers, unrelated to the two of you, the three of us should go to a ball game."

Then I perked up, rubbing my chest as if dusting it off. "Absolutely. I'm down with watching men chase each other on a ball field in tight pants and jam packed jock straps."

Nykolson bumped me in the bum with his hips. "None of that anymore. You've got what you need right here."

I liked hearing Nykolson take claim to me, and since it seemed I was no longer single, I needed to be cognizant about sneaking peeks at other men from that day forward.

Nathaniel shifted his mood suddenly with a curled lip, going from excited about baseball to disturbed about something else.

"What the heck just happened?"

He cleared up that sudden mood swing when he insisted I go put on a shirt to keep my white boy hair off his food counter. Okay, I get it. Nathaniel preferred a set of milk jugs over what testosterone had done to my chest. I shifted while grumbling about putting a shirt on. I had actually stamped a foot, madly crossed my arms and tisked a little bit. I was more put off because I wouldn't have been able to feel Nykolson's bare chest against me.

"Oh, no you don't." Nykolson grabbed me around the waist, pulling me back into him, my back slamming against his hardened torso and brick-like chest. "You aren't going anywhere." He rubbed a hand over my abs, finishing by tucking the tips of his fingers down the front of my lounge pants and kissing the twisty network of my ear.

Nykolson wouldn't have needed to lasso me in place the way he had since I would have come back to him without force. I stood at the island wrapped in his one armed grip and had taken a few sips of my piping hot morning brew, savoring its blackness the same way I had done when I slept with my new beau the night before. His touch was a pleasure and I could have hung out in the warm pocket of his body all day long, but that idea was quickly interrupted when I glanced at the time on the microwave and had seen it was closing in on ten past six in the morning.

It had been our third consecutive day together on that Monday Morning — the most dreaded day of the week. As agreed with most of the human race, the clock needed to stop ticking and return back to five o'clock on Friday evening. I despised the first day of the work week and I argued my obligation to earn what was needed to survive — that which being, spending five or more days per week behind a desk at an understaffed office. Nykolson, who was one of the lucky few, had the pleasure of working remotely from home, permitting him to skip pretty much all of the office politics.

I spun in Nykolson's arms—getting caught up in the tails of his dangling shirt much like I had when I looked into those eyes of his—and had given him the signal it was time for me to get moving.

Jeez, I adored his touch.

My body temperature had risen when he encased his hands over top of mine at the rim of my coffee mug. Between all the warmth stemming from our centers, the combined heat vied through my arms and lassoed my fast beating heart.

Nykolson looked down at me, intensely gazing into my eyes and whispered, "I wish you could stay." He was already close, but he moved in tighter, lightly touched his lips to mine, and slowly, very slowly pulled away. My breathy words, "gawd you taste good," left with the kiss he'd taken from me. His handsome face softened when I glanced up at him, giving me every reason to accept his wish and stay.

He cradled the back of my head in his hand, bringing me in for another kiss, one so passionate that it seemed doused with sheer pureness. He smoothly rotated his head to the left and then back to the right, breathing deeply with flaring nostrils. I reciprocated, giving in to his supreme desire.

When we finally disconnected, I'd been left with a strong feeling I was given a piece of his soul. Breathless I was by the engagement we'd shared and the realization I would have become devoted to just him.

"sumbitch, I wanted to stay."

Chapter 15

I walked the hallway toward my wide-angled-view-of-the-city office, feeling Berdella burning a hole in my back with her green-faced wicked glare. As I continued putting distance between the two of us with every step I'd taken, I hadn't needed to see her face to know she was watching every move I made, and jamming daggers into my back. It was much too often that I'd catch her laser eyes pinned on somebody else as they walked by her for me not to know she was judging me, too.

I'd been cordial to her when there was call for it, however, most of the time only wishing her a good morning, good day, or good evening. That was all she'd gotten out of me—nothing more unless she struck up a conversation first, but even then, I'd kept my replies limited. Every so often I'd throw in a, "God bless you," just to see if she'd go up in flames one of those times. It hadn't happened yet, but I was determined to keep trying until it had. Even though I understood she was a frequent church squatter, when I mentioned a blessing from the glorious man above, her sneer back at me was a look I read as, "How dare you exalt me with your God!" She had come off as the devil's spawn to me after all.

Before I had a chance to reach my office door, Berdella hollered from thirty or so feet behind me, "I haven't seen you in those clothes in the past. Did you go shopping over the weekend?" Her noisy tone dug right into my eardrums like a dull shank blade hacking its way through sheet metal. The sound of her voice probably wouldn't have been that bad to people who hadn't known her, but to me, it was fucking annoying and I'd much rather had listened to the sound of a chainsaw blaring next to my skull.

I arc rolled my eyeballs from one corner to the other before I turned around to answer her with, "these old rags?" followed by a silent, *"fuck you bitch,"* under my Nykolson flavored breath.

I'd always been on to her, knowing she wasn't interested in what I was wearing, but simply trying to find out how I'd spent my weekend. There was no chance in tarnation I was telling her the clothes I had on belonged to the guy who rode my dick for an hour and a half. It had, however, surprised me how she missed Nykolson's cologne I'd splashed on. Much of everything must have been visual for her, I supposed.

Over the few years that I'd known Berdella, I'd said and thought many times how much I detested that lady and her busybody behaviors, and because of that, I could never in a million years get close to her. She wasn't anyone I could trust. In fact, many times I'd thought she was planted in the office for other reasons. She'd never really been good at her job, only hung onto it because of who she was connected to. If she wasn't a distant cousin of the civil suit judge on the fourth floor, I was pretty positive she'd have been working someplace else, such a place of which she'd be managing incoming waste at the local landfill, probably joyfully sitting at the top of the largest dung heap with the rest of the nasty flies.

It was a good thing I handled my own scheduling and only needed her when the new arrivals had been placed. Undoubtedly, my confrontations with Berdella hadn't always been the worst. She and I had a few okay days, not many, but they had existed. Many of them were downright bad, and that was due to her ruthless ways. She emitted such bad energy most of the time and I just couldn't get used to her bullshit and how she purposely tried to add misery to almost everybody she met. I never understood that. Was she that miserable with herself that dawging people was her main goal in life? It had certainly appeared so. Since she seemed to have been swimming in the dirty part of the pond along with the most offensive detainees who walked through the front door, I supposed the place at Cumberland Probation & Parole offices suited her. It had given her time to mingle with those whom were truly her own kind. Anyplace else, she wouldn't have lasted a day and a half. Yep, her malicious soul was that repulsive.

As soon as I arrived at the office and before I'd started anything, I recapped my recently discussed client swap with Ashlund, passing over all my hand written notes as well as emailing the electronic file I had on Nykolson.

That morning I'd met with a couple of my regulars—two offenders to be exact—one who I'd come to adore because he obeyed the guidelines precisely, and in my opinion, which shouldn't have mattered, he hadn't seemed to have deserved that tether around his ankle. I never had found him to display any characteristics of a beer-drinking tank-top-wearing spouse-beater, but the records of the court had proven the guy whaled on his live-in boyfriend like a banana deprived ape, not only once, but more than a half dozen times. Could have been more, but none of those had been proven. He was a cute young guy, tow-head blond with pretty blue eyes, who hadn't displayed any kind of angry streak in front of me. I'd always been a good judge of character and I learned then that judging a book by its cover was not what I should have been doing. If I had, that kid in my eyes would have been an angel and set free long ago.

Something about that breakdown in the kids past had pushed him to his limit and he'd gone all ape-shit on his boyfriend with violent fists and a broken broomstick. When the police arrived at his apartment that night, there was food all over the kitchen walls and floor, sporadic peas and carrots around the living room, and a single dinner roll lying in the hallway. I'd seen the photos, and it was unprofessional of me to have laughed, but the lonely buttered roll had tickled my funny bone lying there all alone.

It had been documented the two guys had started the argument that led to a food fight. The kid was covered in mashed potatoes and gravy, along with a few kernels of corn wedged in his golden locks. Once again I laughed at the pictures I'd seen, but shouldn't have. They'd also found he locked his food covered boyfriend in the bathroom, telling them he'd done that to keep himself off the evening news for being a gay basher or worse, a killer. He'd known he snapped, coming that close to putting his mate out of his misery for throwing a turkey leg at his head. I'd understood that nights brawl between the two had started because the kid farted in the kitchen during dinner, something his boyfriend found offensive and worthy of an argument that led to a fist fight. There had to have been more to their relationship than either of them had mentioned. It seemed to me, a fart and an airborne turkey leg wouldn't have justified one wanting to kill the other. The whole scenario was comical, and if on film would have been the highlight of the movie.

Killer was the operative word in the situation, as in attempted murder, and because the boyfriend accused the kid of trying to execute him by shoving a broomstick up his ass, off to jail he'd been dragged.

To me, the kid deserved a little credit for calling the cops on himself, which was why the sentence hadn't gone where it could have. He'd been given a second chance at street life, which was how I had gotten hold of his case. The poor thing was a wreck when he first arrived at my office, not knowing which way was up or down, and seemed to have wanted help getting the bit of anger he had for his boyfriend out of his system and under control. I truly believed there was more to the boyfriend that set this kid off, and might have been festering for quite some time.

He hadn't said much to me about his past, as though he was protecting the guy for some reason, but my feelings about the whole thing told me the other one was more trouble than the kid I was paroling. When I recognized that, I'd become instrumental in setting him down a better path, aligning him with a therapist who could help him understand there was more than one person who would love and care for him, proving to him there was no reason to stay in an abusive relationship if he hadn't had to. Some people felt trapped and needed a nudge to understand their hands and feet weren't tied down. Sometimes it would take just one person to help them realize that, and once they'd come across them, they would wonder why they stuck around all that time in the first place.

Dealing with troubled individuals had been the way I'd spent numerous days of my life, a few within the office and many from the streets. Even though several people abused the system or tried to challenge it, producing a bad outcome, I still found it gratifying when a single positive achievement manifested by what I'd done. There'd been a few, and with that, I couldn't imagine doing anything different as my occupation. I remained persistence with helping every case that had come through my door, and if I hadn't, I might not have met one offender in particular, who coincidentally turned into the man I'm falling for faster than a landslide raging toward the base of a mountain.

I smiled when I saw a text on my phone from Nykolson, letting me know he was on time for his scheduled Monday morning appointment. I had recently left him, but I was aching to see him again.

When I walked the blue eyed tow-headed kid to the door, I greeted and collected Nykolson on the way back, trying my best to remain professional the way I was supposed to, and not reach out to hold his hand like I really wanted to, or kiss those gah dayum beautiful lips. Any indication whatsoever I'd slept with Nykolson, "you know who" with the flapping lips would have blabbed it all over the complex before I was able to finish our meeting and get him out of the building.

As we walked, I quietly mentioned, "No... TOO young... and... just you," after Nykolson whispered that the kid I just escorted to the door was cute. As soon as he seemed quickly appeased, I mentioned, "You're early."

I smirked when Nykolson smartly answered, "yeah, so???" followed by a wink that only I thought I could have seen.

Keeping our meeting on track and official, I asked, Mister Kannon, to have a seat in one of the two chairs positioned at the front side of my desk. When I said his name so formally, he'd given me a look as if I sprayed him in the face with a garden hose, then he mouthed *"What the fuck?"* at me while lowering that sweet ass of his into the chair.

Then I'd given him the sprayed by a hose look when he stopped halfway into his seated position, stood back up and asked, "Do you mind if I take the sofa instead?"

I told him it would be no problem if that made him feel more at ease.

He let out a cola guzzling, "Aaaah," as he sat, then said, "This is better."

I watched the entire process unfold while he adjusted himself into the seat. He brought one leg over the other, resting the tethered ankle against the top of his knee. It had slipped my mind that somebody might have been watching from the outside looking in, and my gaze had still mindlessly gone straight to his lumpy crotch when his legs splayed apart. My thoughts roamed, *"Oh yeah. That's it. Let me see that monster cock."* There hadn't really been any need to say what was on my mind since I knew exactly what was between those thighs already. I released a disappointing sigh since the time and place wasn't good for diving into all that gorgeousness face first. Every wall around us was set in glass, giving anybody on the outside easy viewing and snapshot photo opportunities that would gain a million hits if posted.

I gulped because I really needed to clear my throat. I'd seen Nykolson's full unclothed body earlier and noticed then he was definitely a black man to be reckoned with. All the characteristics were visibly clear, especially his ten-plus inches of rock hard cock I'd already had the pleasure of putting my hands on. I prized that part of him, yes I did, and seeing how nicely it was packed in those jeans made me fantasize about having at it all over again. I wanted that fucker badly, like... on the double. In my hand. Down my throat. And treasuring the challenge I'd have once I'd taken the entire meaty schlong up my ass. I gasped and admitted to myself I'd have a go at all of the above, anytime, anywhere.

At that very moment, and certain I wasn't imagining it, I'd felt my asshole twitching. The guy had been able to give me erotic thoughts of being his bottom man, and I'd gone into wondering if he'd go for letting me put my ass out there for him or would he maintain his greediness at keeping his seemed favored position underneath me—legs over my shoulders, taking my dick.

Nykolson let out a low rumbling chuckle when the evidence of me looking at the lump in his pants was clear. He couldn't have been that stupid how much I wanted that big dick, and could probably tell by the way I circled my tongue over my lips. Before I looked away, he pointed at his bulge and then at me, moving his mouth silently that I could tell said, "All yours. But Later."

Jeez, why had he selected to torture me like that, knowing I'd have been stuck at the office all damned day, blanketed by frustration because I was in one place and his tight ass was in another?

Clearing my head, I disclosed to Nykolson, "Down to business, Mister Kannon." There was that hose in the face appearance again he'd shown me earlier, but that second time the look crossed his mug had made me laugh.

I hadn't found anything odd with Nykolson saluting back at me. The meeting *was* formal after all.

Conducting the official record-keeping meeting, I asked him the standard questions—those where I'd see body language that would help me identify if the perpetrator was lying to me or not. The first question I asked was for him to elaborate on what had entertained him over the weekend, as if I hadn't known, followed by more inquiries that seemed monotonously unnecessary.

Everything I'd asked was mandatory and essential for court reporting. Since I'd been with him the entire time, I could have easily conducted the meeting without him, but that wouldn't have been nearly as enjoyable as having him present—sitting in front of me. Looking at me. Legs open. Appearing so damned enticing. I was required to make sure protocol had been followed with proven documentation.

I'd gone over several matters of interest with Mister Kannon that morning, finishing the meeting with his obligatory community service duties, which had been scheduled for Tuesday of that week.

That's when Nykolson's jaw literally dropped into his chest followed by an aggravated blurt, "Shit, that's tomorrow. Damnit! Can you get me out of it? What could I do that would set me free?" He'd snuck in a glinting wink and lowered his foot to the floor that had given me full wide open access to his jam packed crotch.

Damn him. He knew exactly how to use his body to persuade me into giving him anything he wanted. My voice cracked, almost coming out as a squeal when I contested, "No I can't get you out of it!" After realizing I'd raised my voice, I lowered it to a whisper and repeated what I'd said.

He couldn't have been serious when he said, "then you're no use to me."

"Yeah right, I'm no use to you? That was an understatement if I'd ever heard one." I immediately reminded him how I made the flashing lamps go crazy the night before. I proceeded to "professionally" outline the next day's community service requirements—confirming work time would be four hours on Tuesday, starting at eight in the morning, and the final four hours on Thursday at the same times.

He threw his head back into the pillowed sofa and started whining, "Gah. Nooooo. I doen' wanna go." He tossed his head forward in a snap. "Let me guess, I'll be picking up trash and shit."

I stopped his blubbering and said, "Yep. Nailed it." I walked around to the front of my desk and propped my butt on the edge, crossed my legs at my ankles, in which pushed my wadded up dick and ball sack up and forward, nearly busting my zipper open and giving Nykolson a delightful eye level crotch shot, similar to the one he'd given me earlier, only closer. I saw him looking, that of which I hadn't minded him doing, and knew he would. His eyelids retracted way back, forcing his eyeballs to project forward from the sockets, coming at me so fast they appeared to have instantly inflated with air. At the same time, his greedy pink tongue made a far-reaching appearance and that slippery sucker curved downward and touched his chin.

"Jeez." That delightful trick stopped my breathing. I was astonished more than I had expected, hadn't realized he had such a talent of extending his tongue so far. I was seriously impressed... and hot... and pleasingly bothered. Shoot... I'd heard what men could do with a tongue like that. With all honesty, I was willing to find out. A surprise to me was when my mind so quickly imagined myself stripped naked, lying on my back across my desk with my legs in the air, ready for Nykolson to go to town on my sphincter, demonstrating his tunneling abilities with that fucking tongue. Fo-sheezie. Was I bottoming out again? Jeez, the shit that man was able to get me thinking about

was so far out of my typical comfort zone. That right there had told me he was the man for me. I *would have,* done anything for him.

Before he put me in a compromising position where I'd gone into full erection mode and forced to deal with a discouraged boner in my wide open office, I told him to put his tongue away, but convinced him to crack that whip later in the day. I couldn't continue feeling exasperated about my dick having no place to go. It was like a traffic jam in my pants that had me downright frustrated. Having somebody like Berdella catch him waving that fabulous tongue around might not have been a good idea.

Damnit. Too late.

Sure enough, the worst person on the planet walked by my windowed office before Nykolson had a chance to retract his wet pink appendage.

That freaking Berdella slinked passed, dropping a glare as if she was looking over the rim of invisible spectacles balancing on the end of her pointy nose. I was certain she spotted Nykolson flicking his tongue at me… er… lapping toward my jam packed crotch. I was sure as shit she had me and him marked for lude behavior. I could have gotten fired for that. Really. Instantly canned. I could tell that bitch was plotting something by the way she lifted that single eyebrow of hers, prepping a list of questions about Nykolson and why he'd done what he had. If she confronted me, I was ready to make something up. I would. I had time to think. In her slow nosey walk back to her desk, she looked through the glass walls surrounding my office again, but I'd already found my place at my seat behind the desk and told Nykolson to cool it with the cock rising gestures—there was a better place and time for that.

Berdella sat at her chair for about thirty seconds before she'd taken off around her desk like her ass had been set on fire. My imagination spotted a charged flame shooting straight out of her butthole, propelling her forward. There she'd gone, the totally invasive Berdella, bitch on an imaginary broomstick, off to nab the first person she saw with a plan to embellish smack about the recent office incident between Nykolson and me. She most likely would have burst into flames if she hadn't been able to tell somebody what she'd seen. Her victim was Sandrine, nicknamed Sandra Dee due to her innocent and virgin-like qualities. The lady seemed so pure, and hadn't seemed bothered by the moniker or the significance of the iconic person, completely uncomplaining, which I found odd she'd been so accepting with being made fun of. Her real name was Sandrine Concepcion Courtney Dexter, so the short version wasn't too far off from her originally born-given name, not to mention, easier to remember and say. Come to think of it, maybe she was clueless and simply understood it as cutting her first and last name short.

I'd probably come off as being challenged when I passed on a combination salute that turned into a messy wave at the two women chatting, but I wanted them to know I noticed what they were doing. For all they knew, I was reading their painted lips.

Whatever the gossip queen was feeding Sandra Dee, and I was sure it wasn't about the past Sunday's sermon at the church I knew they both attended together, Berdella had probably put two and two together about her recent theory on Nykolson and me, and was filling Sandra in on my personal sex life with the guy she assumed I was sticking my dick into.

To me, Sandrine appeared to have been a listener more than a talker, absorbing and keeping what she heard to herself. I could almost see her brain churning as if she was some sort of recording device. Sandrine most likely understood the lip flapper in front of her stirred up trouble like nobody's business, and she probably found it was in her best interest to stand and listen only, keep herself at arm's length so she wasn't one who ended up as part of what the wench spewed.

If I had a penny for every time she hurt somebody with the shit she pulled, I'd seriously would have been a billionaire by now, which amounted to a lot of gossip considering I had only asked for one measly cent per news flash from that woman's blow hole.

While keeping my eyes angled on the two ladies, I mumbled to Nykolson from the side of my mouth, "Don't look now, but the gossip queen of this office is on the loose. She saw your tongue hanging out a moment ago, looking like it was after my dick, and

I'm almost certain she's heading off to exalt the scenario into more than what it actually was."

"But... it was exactly that, I do want your dick. Front and back. I'm certain of that. So she wouldn't exactly be fabricating a story." Nykolson backed away from my finger pointed at his face, meant to stop him from saying or doing anything more.

My blood started to boil—like hot-hot—turning my ears beet red and probably my sunken cheeks as well when I pursed my lips in disgust. I hadn't heated up because of Nykolson's cute sexual innuendos in my office space, but because of the damage Berdella could have one to me for fraternizing with a tethered offender.

I told Nykolson straight up, "No more messing around." Right then I saw Nykolson's face turn somber, he stiffened like a board, swiftly nodded, and let me finish. "I have a few more things to finalize straightaway before I let you go, and hopefully, she'll be out of our way while I'm walking you to the door."

Nykolson made me laugh when he said, "Why don't you toss a dead rat in front of her. That should redirect that vulture's attention and get her out of the way for a few minutes."

Could I have turned him against Berdella that quickly? Or was he as good at judging character as I was? I bet on his judgement being spot on track that swiftly.

"Brilliant plan," I replied, tapping my temple as if I really would have tried something like that with her. I snapped out of my daydream put there by Nykolson and said, "Down to business."

I gathered Nykolson's community service packet, highlighted the address where he needed to go, stuffed it into an envelope and handed it to him. As he reached for it, he stood, and without him asking, I told him what it was and mentioned he could review it at home. If he had questions about any of it, I'd be around later to answer them. I needed to get him out the door to prevent Berdella from scrutinizing the two of us any further.

I'd gotten out of my chair and stood in the doorway, holding up a finger for Nykolson to stay put. I scanned the hallway in both directions, thrilled that I wasn't able to see Berdella anywhere, or smell the rankness of her cheap perfume that always burned holes in my septum.

I looked Nykolson square in the eyes, then cocked my head with a quick jerk to the left, enticing him to start moving.

"This is so fucking stupid. Seriously!" I felt as though I'd been locked up behind bars, and was pulling off my own office prison break. All of my ridiculous actions were instigated by the cruel intentions of a single person's twisted mind, Berdella *Deville*, sister wannabe of Cruella the eminent. Even though Berdella was foul in her own means, there was no way she could ever live up to Cruella's malevolent manic methods. Now, that queen was a bitch.

Stopping at the doorway leading to the outdoors, I couldn't pull my eyes away from Nykolson's lips. They were beyond luscious as he slowly ran his wet tongue over the bottom and then the top. Was he doing that intentionally? I believed it was done subconsciously because the guy seemed to want me so desperately, and a kiss right then would have been just the sendoff he needed, as well as I.

My eyes darted panic-like from side to side, checking every corner of our surroundings. I whispered so low it resembled breathing, "Gah Damn, Nykolson, I want to kiss you so badly right now." The super fucking cute smile I'd gotten back from him was partial, only half of his mouth curled upward. *Sumbitch.* My imagination had taken off in a wild as shit direction.

As hushed as I'd spoken a moment earlier, he said, "I'll save this mouth for when you get home, hot stuff."

"Fuck. Fuck... Fuck, fuck, fuck. He's got me totally under his control." I wondered if he realized what he'd done to me.

ఆ ఎ

After I watched Nykolson walk away, I'd met the office witch face to face in the entryway on the half spin. I was sure Berdella heard me groan when I realized she was there, and when she sarcastically sung, "Miss him already, do you?"

I wanted to sucker punch her in the face with an upper cut to the chin, followed by a major choke hold around her skinny neck before I dropped her ass to the ground and toe kicked her in the ribs. If I'd followed through with what I really wanted to have done to her, my cute as fuck ass would certainly become an overflowing cumdumpster while doing time in a prison cell.

Everybody had limits to what they could withstand, and my escalating rage for Berdella was quickly rising. If she continued with her crude shenanigans, I'd have been wearing a tether right next to the guy I had banged. One positive thought about that, Nykolson and I would have the matching bracelets he'd always wanted.

Berdella backed out of my way and slithered like a serpent behind her workstation where she belonged. I angrily followed her, standing at the counter and stared her down. She had her perky face aimed at her computer screen, but her eyes rolled upward and stared me down. Her voice wasn't always all bad, in fact, sounded pleasantly churchy at times, but I recognized that funk ugly tone when she asked in a snarky manner, "Can I help you?"

My eyelids dropped, hooding my irises with half slits as my head lowered to look down on "*Her, Bitchness.*" I waited a few seconds before giving her a long overdue piece of my mind.

I wasn't the type who caused trouble in the office, or for that matter, anywhere else, but I finally reached my limit with that woman, and if I was tossed to the street because I spoke my mind, I could have cared less that day. I was about to do what so many people had probably wanted to do for a very long time, but might have been too reserved to follow through because of the people she had ties with. At that point, I hadn't much given a rat's ass. She needed to be stopped or at least told people knew the sneaky shit she'd been pulling.

I drew in a lung full of air before I blasted her with the long overdue verbal abuse she well deserved.

"You couldn't be helpful if you tried, you miserable woman. You make me sick with your unfavorable behavior and trouble making sessions of gossip that most people don't even care to hear." My voice had come out on the verge of demonic, spewing with rage toward that nasty woman. "Why are you always in everybody's business, flitting around like a little bug, hopping from one pile of crap to the next, dropping dung on everyone you trap into listening, and infecting them with the twisted diseases you've collected from the shit mounds you'd visited?" That wasn't a question.

Her mouth gaped open in the shape of an oblong circle as if someone just shoved her own broomstick up her ass and it was about to make an appearance out of her rancid blow hole.

I leaned in closer to keep her mouth from ejecting whatever her mind was thinking. I continued by telling her, "What I do outside these walls is my business, not yours or your gossip absorbing hags."

She stood erect, the chair almost tipping over behind her. "How dare you speak to me like that, you fucking honkey faggot. Who do you think you are?" Her words dug into my soul as if she had just tried to carve out my heart with a rubber spoon. That word was one of the ugliest on the planet next to her well-deserved label at being a cunt. My level of class was low at that point, but if it had been right down there with hers, I would have screamed "you cunt" right to her face. I hadn't even backed away from her wretched words, not giving her any satisfaction that she affected me. Actually, it made me lean into her even more. That's when I noticed her breath was as bad as her attitude.

She really needed help, so I'd given her advice. "When was the last time you had a man near your ass? That might just be the ticket you need to get you out of that pond of misery you're floundering in."

She reached for her bird-like neck and gasped. "You gays disgust me, every single one of you. Including that felon who just walked out of here." — she tisked angrily — "A dick" — she lowered her tone to a whisper — "has never gone near my ass. Blasphemy."

I wondered if she realized how sad that sounded, but I wasn't surprised to hear that her so called sacred ass had gone untouched by a cock her entire life. I was pretty damned certain one hadn't come close to her stankin' vagina either.

At that moment, sudden realization hit me.

"Oh my gawd."

I might have figured out what her hang ups were. She was a forty-one year old virgin who stood doomed to wear that chastity belt for the rest of her life.

She raved as if she knew everything about me, telling me I was a gay whore and probably had every sexually transmitted disease ever named, and that I deserved every one of them. Her ugly tone even spouted that she knew I'd already screwed around with Nykolson and I'd be paying for that by the end of the day. Her noise continued by saying she had many other secrets about me, claiming everybody knew of them, thanks to her.

Okay… There's the proof I'd already known.

She was honest to goodness proud of spreading rumors as if it was a talent.

Disgusting.

She practically had a two second orgasm after telling me all she thought she knew as being the truth. Some she mentioned were true, but not all of it. But still, peoples' business wasn't for her to blab.

Again, *"disgusting."*

Having at her had definitely started my boxing career. I wanted to punch her in the throat when she said she'd get me fired for dating a fugitive, reminding me of what I already knew — that it goes against the guidelines of getting involved with the detained. But, damned her thundering butt crack, why does she have to be so vindictive all the time with minor shit that doesn't affect her life?

I told her, "You have no proof of anything." But she answered by saying she had, which I knew was bullshit and she was guessing by what she had seen a few moments earlier when I walked Nykolson to the door.

I hated the thought of lying, it wasn't my practice and never gets me anywhere when all is said and done, but her word against mine would never stand without solid evidence. If she hadn't any pictures showing Nykolson's legs over my shoulders, then she's got nothing on us.

Note to self: Close the drapes next time I slide my dick in and out of Nykolson's asshole.

Berdella was merely trying to scare me into cowering, or apologizing, taking back what I'd said, or whatever. But I, being a master of holding onto a secret or two, especially learning how to keep many of them to myself due to growing up gay, I was several steps ahead of that wench at covering my tracks and keeping my relationship with Nykolson under wraps.

She picked up the phone and said, "It'll only take me a minute to call the man upstairs and fill him in on that filthy, Nykolson Kannon, character you'd been screwing around with. I could ruin both your lives with a press of a button."

And the purpose of that would benefit her how? My guess, she was just a bitch and wanted to prove she was more of a cunt that I'd thought.

Whatever she meant by that hadn't frightened me one bit. What could a button on a phone do to destroy two guys fucking each other? To me, it was just another one of Berdella's scare tactics, trying to make me believe she was put on the planet to clean up what she understood to have been trash and sinners. Was she really stupid enough to have made that call right there in front of me? I had half a mind to reach out and chop off her hand before it punched a single number. Instead of acting like a guerrilla leader, I leaned in, propped both sweaty palms on the granite in a pose much like her preacher father does at his pulpit, cocked my head to one side as if I was her evil twin and had given her a piece of my mind.

"You listen to me, bitch. You may have secrets on me and everybody else inside and outside this office, and for some fucked up reason, it makes your lonely vagina spit piss when you go out flapping those ass-fat filled lips of yours. But starting today, you'll agonize more over wondering what fucked up secrets I have on you and am keeping to myself until a rainy day, which I suspect will be soon by the rolling thunder I hear creeping in above that big head of hair of yours. Oh Yeah"—I manically perked up—"I've got shit on you. Quite a bit. So… If you push that button and send whatever garbage you think you have on me to *the man upstairs*", that'll be the last time you ever raise a weapon to me and walk the streets of San Francisco to talk about it. Capiche, you honkey bitch?"

Berdella set the phone in its cradle and back stepped away from me, appearing frightened as if she was looking at her leader, the devil. The expression on her face displayed terror I'd never seen before. I was pleased with myself for making her feel that way and it made me realize right then, she really was hiding something major. I just hadn't known what, but for the love of Pete, she thought I had. It was about time somebody put that horrid wench in her place. I grinned when she sat in her chair like a frightened feline cornered by wolves and said, "Are you threatening me?"

"Oh... That wasn't a threat, Miss Thang." I'd most likely never follow through with any of what I said, but she wouldn't ever know that. I spun around, leaving her to figure out how to shut that gaping food trap of hers.

I merrily walked to my sunlight filled office, feeling good about myself while thinking the entire time how the hell I let her get to me like that. The smile on my face had given me the relief I needed, which helped put the bottled up stress of many other things to rest as well. I'm far from being a hurtful person, but she touched a nerve that must have been waiting to blow up for a very long time. I shamefully regretted much of what I'd said to her, but for criminy sakes out loud, she deserved it and hopefully would put a stop to what she'd been doing to so many people behind their backs—or at least put the shit on hold for a little while.

Had I made a mistake by screeching at her? I wondered if she would press that button to send the bat signal to HR. I'm sure I'd find out soon enough, once the swat team barged in my office to carry me away.

Chapter 16

"That was one fucked up day," I announced the moment I stepped through the front door of Nykolson's home and walked right into that handsome man's greeting arms. The low voice in my ear rumbled, "Well, hello to you, too." He'd given me a tight squeeze that felt spectacularly good. Damn those strong arms. I hadn't cared he smelled differently than I was used to. A new soap all over his fabulous body had been used, perhaps?

I looked up, prepping for the kiss I really needed and saw a jokers grin staring down at me. "Oh shit, sorry Nathaniel. I thought you were Nykolson." I pulled away once Nathaniel had finished topping my chestnut head with one hand and smacking me on the ass with the other. I'd taken it. Nothing wrong with a little brotherly love.

"Not a big deal, bruh. We get mixed up all the time. By the looks of things, you really needed that hug from me, anyway. Well overdue." He called me bruh? Did I hear him right? Was I part of their secret triad brotherhood? I knew I'd get the two of them mixed up someday and I'd accidentally give the wrong guy a kiss or a hug, but hadn't expected it to happen so soon. I should have known it wasn't Nykolson since I hadn't felt his usual erection when I pressed my body against him, and the fact he smelled like a basic soap instead of lavender or a woodland spiced blend. I should have known instantly just by that.

It was mind boggling how the two were so identical. Were they scientifically cloned in a lab or what?

I spotted Nykolson in the near distance laughing at what had happened, jovially poking fun at my expense. I was glad he found it funny, and that he hadn't displayed any signs of being jealous by me manhandling and trying to lock lips with his brother. I was a tad embarrassed by the erection Nathaniel had lured from my crotch when I held my body against his. My dire hope was that he hadn't felt my snake trying to invade his private space or get all up inside his ass if I'd snuck up and hugged him from behind. In all fairness, however, and I'm sure he understood, I honestly thought he was Nykolson.

"Jeez, I need a bottle to the head," I blurted out.

Immediately after I said that, I heard Nykolson chuckle and question, "What the hell does that mean? Am I supposed to hit you with one?"

I'd imagine if anybody heard that phrase for the first time wouldn't have realized what it meant. I laughed because getting beaned in the noggin with a bottle was exactly what it sounded like. I cleared that up, explaining it meant to throw my head back and chug the booze right from the bottle—I hadn't the time to wait for a glass. That's when it struck me I'd become an alcoholic over the past few days. For some reason, I'd been tipping the bottle back a few too many times lately. Actually, it wasn't for some reason, I knew why. I was finally having a little fun with guys I enjoyed being around, and adding a bit of booze in moderation wouldn't hurt as long as my shit hadn't gotten out of control. Once I'd gotten over the stress of my work related fraternizing, the habit of throwing my head back for that drink would subside, I hoped. Until then, I ordered a whisky on ice as if I was yelling my order to a bartender at a restaurant bar & grill.

"Coming right up," Nathaniel publicized as if he was at a ball stadium. By his overly excited actions to get the mixing started, he must have been waiting all day for one of us to ask. While he mixed and poured our favored cocktails, Nykolson came to me with seizing arms and planted the kiss on my lips I'd been expecting from the moment I stepped into the house. I desperately needed it—and was thankful it had come from him.

Without removing my mouth from his, I teased, "Almost as good as your brother."

152

He'd given me a spanking to the butt cheek, adding a loving full fingered squeeze as if trying to sooth the inflicted pain he'd stricken me with.

"Now that's the smack to the ass I'd been wanting," I honestly clowned. Sure Nathaniel had the talent and was my first, but Nykolson had the touch I'd been interested in. That's my man, *and* there's my boner. Damn him. That hadn't taken long. All that man had to do was look in my direction to get an erection out of me. Laying a hand on me—forget it—my dick sprung to life within seconds and could find his asshole without me directing it to the glorious playground. I had no control of my cock or my thoughts whenever he was around. My body reacted as it wished and I followed.

Once I had my first sip of fire and released that legendary "Aaaaah" that sounded like it started as deep as my asshole, I asked Nykolson if he'd had a chance to review the community service papers I'd sent him home with. Noticing the envelope lying on the countertop had an untouched appearance, and him telling me he'd been editing four articles for the magazine all afternoon, finishing that about five minutes before I walked in the door, indicated he hadn't looked at the papers yet.

I reached for and opened the packet. "It'll only take a few minutes. Take a seat while you slurp and I explain." I opened my laptop to google maps, but once I found the website listed on the form, everything he needed to know was laid out there.

He groaned a little when he found out he had to drive several miles north to a place called Bodega Bay, but then settled down after realizing it was the best situation overall. "I guess it'll be fine. Nobody knows me up there, which leaves me some privacy while picking at everybody else's trash."

"I take it you'd never been there?" I understood his answer to have been, "no," when he'd shaken his head from side to side.

He leaned into his martini glass and lapped at the liquid inside with his tongue. He looked ridiculous and adorable all at the same time, and what he was doing made me laugh. I looked at the top of his head and wondered what possessed him to lick at it instead of drinking it like a normal person would. Instead of asking the question and waiting for a smart-ass answer, I revealed that the village on the bay was stunning and I thought he'd like it there.

"So you've been there?" he asked while biting a small chunk from the green olive he fished from the bottom of the glass.

I answered, "A couple of times," and left it at that. It was pointless to go into detail about my previous rendezvous that involved my dick plowing a huge black man's ass on the rocky coast during a summer hiking trip I'd taken with a few friends. I was much younger then, which I considered those to have been my guy fucking training days, and at that moment in time when my cock was inside that chocolate skinned beast of a man, I knew I'd forever go black and never turn back. He was so much bigger and muscular than I was and seemed it would have been him fucking the shit out of me with his horse sized cock. I vaguely remembered that day, but the one thing that had stood out vividly was how much that great big guy loved getting reamed up the ass by my white dick. I could tell by the way I made him holler and cry out for it. All of the ruckus he was making while I fucked him certainly made me feel like one hell of a stud with a talented cock. I never knew I had it in me, but was thrilled I could make another man scream for more like that. The incredible sensation of having that man's ass sucking cum from my dick had made me want to have at every black man's ass I'd come across.

I'm not sure if it's just the guys I'd been with, but the black dude's sure go plum wild when they have a cock fucking the shit out of their assholes. It was as though they couldn't get enough dick once it was plunged inside them, going crazy and shit— hollering, out of control, begging and growling, whining a little, and cumming like they hadn't shot a load in over a month. Everything about it was a turn on for me. White pearly cum on the chest of a black man? So fucking hot. And when sperm glazed their tight black holes, even hotter.

I handed Nykolson the pages and told him not to worry about upcoming changes with his case.

"Changes? What changes?" His voice definitely sounded on the verge of being alarmed.

I'd never been good at passing on unwelcoming news, so that was my cowardly way of preparing him for what was about to be revealed, even though it might appear to have been the worst.

While he flipped through pages of paper, I'd added a few more splashes of whisky to the cubes in my glass. I knew I was going to need that extra bite to dull my nerves for what was yet to come. As I spun the cap on the bottle back into place with a single finger, Nykolson asked, "Who's Ashlund and why isn't your name on these papers?"

There it was. I knew he'd ask that once he'd come across Ashlund's stamp and signature at the bottom instead of mine, so I'd given him the honest answer, "An executive decision." I then told him, "I want this relationship of ours to move forward sooner than later. After spending time with you over the weekend, I asked Ashlund to take your case through the end of its term. I decided that was the best thing to do, otherwise if I hadn't, I wouldn't be able to see you outside the office any longer. It's the fraternizing decree to prevent corruption within the system. If I hadn't given you back to Ashlund, I'd have to wait six months to be with you again."

Then Nykolson asked me what I meant by giving him back to Ashlund.

"Wait a second, what did I miss?" I hadn't realized I said anything about Ashlund having him before I had gotten his file. How'd this get so complicated? My words were coming out of my mouth before I thought about saying them. That's why I never let alcohol get into my system too often. It fucks shit up and what's said and heard contradicted what I really meant and should have mentioned. The perspective of everything gets blurred, unlike when sober.

"Why hadn't you told me before I found out from seeing his name on these papers?" Nykolson's face had told me he was taken back, but before he lost total trust in me, I immediately cleared it up with my personal version, comparing myself to the cowardly lion from The Wizard of Oz—I hadn't the courage. I couldn't quite figure a way to break it to him verbally, fearing he might not agree with what I knew to have been the right decision. It shouldn't have been that difficult since the outcome could have been worse for us in so many ways if I hadn't made the change. It was either see him formally once a week for the next six months or be with him every chance I had on a daily basis. With those differences brought up, the whole tiff between us had come to an end rather quickly, and Nykolson seemed to understand the reasons why.

I had to admit, I was worried by his reaction at first, but when he came around with his wet tongue polishing my lips before taking a plunge to the inside of my mouth, I accepted that as his way of forgiveness. With that disagreement out of the way, I vowed I'd find better ways of breaking what I thought would have been upsetting news to Nykolson and never let what occurred happen again. I couldn't risk breaking any trust between us. Nykolson had become too important to me in the few days I'd known him and I wanted it to blossom into more and hopefully continue well into the future.

It was good that Nathaniel interrupted us by speaking a few words in the background. If he hadn't, he would have remained forgotten. I'd become so captivated with Nykolson whenever I was near him that I started missing out on much of what was going on around me. It was incredible how he was able to do that to me. I was pretty sure it had a lot to do with me not wanting to miss out on any of his life anymore. I needed to know everything about him and what he was up to next. Not as a stalker, but as a boyfriend who was closing in on loving him.

"Oh, shit. Hey, brother. Where for art thou been?" Nykolson's staggered expression led me to believe he'd overlooked Nathaniel's presence as well. My guess was, his absent mindedness was probably like mine, staying focused on me so he wouldn't miss out on any of my life either.

Nathaniel answered, "Yeah, brozo, Thou-ist hath-ist been-ist here-ist." I'd found the guff between those two invigorating. I knew it sounded like street slang, almost difficult for me to understand, but the humor they delivered when hashing it out had me laughing at their idiotic slander most of the time.

After discovering Nathaniel had never left the room, Nykolson spun around, sat on the stool at the island and pulled me backward between his thick thighs. It felt so good having him holding me like that, with his strong arms wrapped around my waist as though keeping me captive. The warmth of his body seeped straight into mine. I almost ruined the intimate moment when he surprised me with delicate butterfly kisses down the side of my neck.

Was I that into the guy that he made me giggly weak? *I'm a man. I don't giggle. What the fuck?* I was definitely planning to clean up that silly feature straightaway. I'd proceed to demonstrate the stronger side of me in bed later on, the one where I'd be one hundred percent stud with a dick that wouldn't quit, jamming my cock in and out of him until his brains were blown clear to the stars. Until that time had come, I'd gone all macho on his ass by slugging back my whisky on ice before lunging for his mouth and grinding viperously over top of his.

To keep him where I wanted him, I fist gripped his pants at the front waistband as I powerfully cupped my other hand at the back of his neck. I felt reckless and pretty damn proud of myself for coming off in such a strong manner. By his reaction, he seemed to really like the way I manhandled him. That had gotten me thinking about introducing him to a few bits of leather. Why not? Could be fun. Shoot, he sure reacted positively when I smacked is ass during sex the other night. Perhaps I'd introduce a horse crop to get things moving along.

My dynamic drive into my man was abruptly broken when Nathaniel decided it was his moment to speak again. I was so involved with Nykolson, I hadn't heard him ask if I'd made time during the day to work up whatever was required to put the restraints on his ex-wench, Dajana. I thought he actually repeated himself more than once. Not sure though. I was too enthralled with hustling his brother.

Still holding Nykolson in my forceful grasp, I leaned back a few inches and tilted my head at Nathaniel, wiped my wet mouth with the back of my wrist and growled like an irritated tiger. Supposing I should, but not wanting to, I let Nykolson loose and told him, "We'll continue this later, my stud." Jeez, my dick hurt.

I'd promised Nathaniel I'd help him out, and so I would do just that. I stayed between Nykolson's legs where I was most comfortable, however, spun toward Nathaniel to guide him with processing the restraining order. I'd first told him he might not need it, since Dajana the bitch was still under scrutinized watch for what she'd recently done to him. If the order was needed, and as I'd told him before, the law offers protection for victims caught up with acts of domestic violence. Even though he was originally thought to have been the felonious one in the case and ended up being the victim, he still had the right to petition an injunction against her for inflicting the violence. The look Nathaniel had given me was weedy, but he appeared to have understood most of what I had told him. It really wasn't that difficult, only time consuming if any of his ducks weren't properly lined up when filing that specific ban against her.

Nykolson seemed to have understood the process a little more than Nathaniel had. I noticed that when he chimed in saying, "That's great news. Now he can finally get rid of, Her Royal Cuntness, for good, with your help, right?"

Of course but, "I can't actually do it for him, but by law, I can provide clerical assistance for preparing and filing a petition for the injunction. Once you have the paperwork completed and presented, the court will determine if you are in danger of being victimized, and if so, a temporary sanction would be prepared." The way Nykolson and Nathaniel were looking at me, I'd sworn they thought I was a master at putting people away, or they had no idea what I just told them. Either way, I had no problem helping Nathaniel get the proceedings started, and if he needed me to go with him to submit the order, I'd do that too. What I'd come across and witnessed so far, I was all for putting a person like Dajana away. She was deceitfully crafty and shouldn't have been allowed near anybody with a dollar in their pocket. "You can save time by going on line and printing the Domestic Violence Questionnaire forms before visiting the Clerk's office. Bring the completed documents to the intake location to obtain the order against her. It's that easy. The tough part would be convincing the court of the case's validity, which, with everything already filed on her, it should be a no brainer that she needs to be kept more than one hundred miles away from you or anybody with a penny in their purse."

I figured Nathaniel understood when he said, "Sounds simple enough, but can you keep your tongue out of my brother long enough to help me get it started?"

I had to laugh at that, because it was the bloody truth—my tongue and dick were constantly trying to get inside my man. "Now you're asking a bit much, don't you think?" I replied, and no, that wasn't a joke.

"Too much would be if I had asked you to keep your dick out of his ass. I only asked for your tongue."

Nykolson laughed.

I was shocked. That's when I knew I really needed to get used to how open those two were with each other. Everything was shared so freely, like an open book. So, if I fucked Nykolson, his brother would know about it as if he'd been there filming it.

For only knowing the Kannon twins for three days, I'd come to enjoy being around them, admittedly so, one more than the other, but that goes without saying. Other than the two of them being extremely handsome, in my opinion, they were genuinely kind individuals, and finding they were appreciative of the smallest things, only confirmed who they really were.

Nykolson had even gone as far as asking me where I'd been all his life and what had taken me so long to find my way to his doorstep.

Did I cry when he said that? Just about and I would have if I wasn't such a manly man... in my opinion—whatever. I explained my viewpoint on that, telling him love can't be rushed, that fate had a way of pushing people together at the right time and in ways not understood. Such like with our case of meeting unexpectedly and under circumstances out of the ordinary. Who would have thought that a vicious person would have been the sole factor with connecting two people that were destined to be together? I supposed the world needed the good and the bad to make it move forward.

I was a good person, almost always, but never considered myself tied to any religion, nor had I wanted to have been. Mainly because I despised how each eroding organization continued to pit themselves against each other and drag many good hearted people with them. They seemed to understand that judging and hating those who weren't like themselves guaranteed their ticket into heaven. No... I'm pretty certain that wasn't the way it worked. Undiluted hatred wasn't going to get anybody passed Saint Peter and through the pearly gates—true and honest love would.

I may only visit a church once or twice a year, which I don't deem going at all was necessary in order to be a believer of the almighty, however, I still lived the Christian life as best I knew how—giving, accepting, loving, believing, and cherishing everything I'd been given. One thing I'd always remembered, spoken many times by my mother was that, God works in mysterious ways. That applies to just about everything and I wholeheartedly believe that statement. So I continue believing a shit storm might not just be a shit storm, but an eye opening experience to lead us where we're supposed to end up—and it can't always be candied flowers and pretty butterflies. Nykolson and I are proof of that example and I had sensed Nathaniel's good day was coming soon, too. What he'd been dealing with might have been a lesson being taught that can't be explained today, but might be understood tomorrow.

After we'd gotten Dajana worked out of our systems, the DV forms printed and ready to go, the question of the evening had come up and I was pleased it was Nykolson who asked, "Are you spending the night?"

I excitedly answered, "Yes," almost yelling it out. "Of course. Why wouldn't I?"

The tone in his voice to me was more of a demand than a question, so next time I hoped to hear, "You're spending the night, so don't think about heading for the door," and if he wanted to add a smack to my ass, that would be welcomed, too.

Smiling on the inside, I thought back on how easy it was for him to bark out orders, especially in bed when I fucked him, wondering if he'd continue being that bossy bottom all over again once I'd gotten those legs in the air and his ankles propped over my shoulders. I'd loved his ass, worshiped his ass, and the sweet thing felt so incredible when I fucked it.

Nathaniel raised his arm as if he was a student in a classroom full of noisy kids, and if he hadn't waved a hand, nobody would have known he was there. The added jumping fit and, "Oo-oo-oo," helped with getting him noticed a little better. I supposed he had good reason for doing that, since we'd forgotten he'd been hanging in the kitchen earlier, and seemed whenever he'd spoken, we were too busy groping each other to hear any of what he'd said. A preannouncement or gesture in advance always worked well in a haggard situation, by which with all his hoopla he'd released, had figured that out on his own.

Once we acknowledged Nathaniel's existence, which at that time wasn't hard to do, he put in a request that we might not follow. "This is probably a senseless question, but are you two doing it again tonight?"

I agreed — stupid question. *"Um, yeah, and none of his business."*

Nathaniel had a grin on his face when he said, "If you are, could you do me a huge ass favor and unplug that strobe light this time? I don't know what that did for the two of you, but that beacon signal coming through my window was more annoying than hearing my brother beg for your throbbing manhood."

I glanced at Nathaniel with stink eyes and groused, "Oh my gawd, you heard him?" If I wasn't such a fuck machine, none of what was being discussed would have been an issue. That's the price I had to pay for being a gah damned stud, I guess.

Stud? My fantasy and I'm sticking with it.

"Yes, I heard you. Even with my head buried in the pillow," Nathaniel was a jokester and I knew he had a point. From what I recalled, Nykolson had a set of pipes on him that reached a register off the charts when my dick hit that prostate of his. He'd come off to me as being one of those guys who lost his mind when he had cock in the ass — all buttons go, no matter which one I punched. That there was confirmation of another black man who loved getting my white dick up his keester.

I was first to have been made aware Nykolson needed to get to bed early, sympathetic with how he had to be in Bodega Bay by seven in the morning, which meant he should probably be up and at it no later than five. I was definitely planning on a repeat performance of the other night, however, without the blinking effects of those blasted table lamps, which reminded me at that moment to whisper in Nykolson's ear, "Did you get rid of, The Clapper?"

He just about threw his head back with laughter, probably remembering how it turned his night of getting laid into anarchy, mayhem and downright mind blowing disorder. I on the other hand found the sudden shock of it all to have been exciting and hysterically erotic. It literally seemed like chaos and undoubtedly made our first fuck a memorable moment that neither one of us would ever forget.

As much as I would have liked to have taken things slowly on our second night together, making love to him so he felt every bit of me, I settled with the idea of giving him a quickie so he'd crash early enough to get a full nights rest before the barnyard cock doodle doo'ed.

Comically, Nathaniel had given me a tip that was more to his benefit than ours, telling me to stuff my jockstrap into Nykolson's mouth while I pounded his ass with the big one.

I was thrilled to discover how comfortable Nathaniel was about two men having sex, and that he wasn't fazed by how much his brother enjoyed taking another man's dick up his ass. In fact, he seemed to promote it, which made me believe Nathaniel was happy about it being me who was sticking it to his brother. It definitely made the two of us becoming a couple a whole lot easier, and the amount of sex we'd be having would burn up his brain if he wasn't cool with it.

Knowing Nathaniel hadn't had a problem with me burying my erection inside his brother's butt, I'd given my guarantee to Nykolson that I'd be doing it to him as often as I could, like fucking him at least once every night if not more.

Nykolson grinned, so I set my mind on giving him another ride of his life. Although, be it a quickie, would blow his mind just the same.

Chapter 17

"Did I really hear a rooster do the cock-a-doodle-doo?" If I hadn't and it was some form of wakeup alarm, I'd be tripping on down to the electronics store to pick up a new bedside clock for Nykolson, or better yet, one of those Amazon Echo devices that would tell his sweet ass to get out of bed at a specific time. The broken bell I might have heard more or less belonged in a chicken coop meant to fool the egg laying hens into thinking they were about to be embarked upon by a cock. *"Clappers, and now Cluckers? Where was I?"*

I heard Nykolson groan, "Crap. Five already?"

While I tried to fight with the idea that I was getting out of bed before the crack of dawn, thinking, *"Who does that?"*, I sat up rubbing my eyes as my mouth stretched to one of the biggest yawns of my life, soon to have become practical reality once I'd tried sucking Nykolson's huge cock. I'd woken with my dick was so hard and straight, it nearly punched a hole in my chest when my body bowed forward into a seated position. Another inch and a half, the head of my prick would have been in my mouth like it had been so many times before I'd met Nykolson. Yes, I've been sucking my own dick since I was about sixteen, and yes I'd been swallowing my own cum like it was meal snacks since then as well, all owed to my length and self-sucking abilities. A flexible gymnast with a big dick has its perks.

Even though I thoroughly enjoyed swallowing my own semen while blowing myself, I thankfully had Nykolson around to do that for me now and far into the future. Thank my lucky stars he lived up to being a fantastic cocksucker. He was so much better at giving me head than I was, plus he was able to take my entire dick, not just the first four stupid inches that I was only able to get into my mouth. Sure I was flexible, but not that bendy.

I'd given Nykolson a nudge to the shoulder, hearing him groan face down in the pillow when I thumped him. He wouldn't move, forcing the need to nudge him again, harder, and that time his body rolled away from me and rocked back to where he was before I'd pushed him. "Leave me-eee alo-oone," he whined, as if he really meant that, but I kept at him because I knew the importance of fulfilling his obligation of doing time at the roadside.

"Not happening, buster." I threw the covers off him, exposing every bit of his chocolate form, secretly wanting nothing more than to get a glimpse of that high and tight butt I'd had the exclusive pleasure of sticking my dick into.

Unfortunately for me, the room was still dark, leaving it up to my imagination to visualize what his ass cheeks looked like. His undefended ass was probably still slick with the previous evening's oil and in the perfect position to take my dick again that morning. I couldn't resist giving it a light smack, and once my hand landed, I battled with pulling it away. His firm brown pear shaped orb was so taut and deliciously alluring, my hand wouldn't have budged even if I was forced to. I felt him go tense, but relaxed when I said, "Get up before I fuck that thang." That might not have been the right thing to say, because knowing him, he'd sway for the butt fuck.

As I'd thought it, my hand had gone up with his rising ass, surely giving me a clear invitation to have at his hole. I'd gone for it.

"How dare you torture me like that?" I massaged his muscled butt cheek, gliding my hand downward between his slippery crack where I sunk my thumb into his hot hole, feeling the pulse of his heart as his ring gripped hold of me, his rectum flexed, manically sucking me in. His body twitched the second I pushed my thumb pad into his prostate and two of my fingers pressed downward along each side of his saggy black nut sack where I squeezed and kneaded his furry taint as if I was pulling taffy. That had done a number on him. He squealed out an, "Oh gawd, Yea-ess. Fuck!"

It was less than three minutes after my thumb had gone inside that I felt his body jerking and convulsing. So quickly, he growled, "Fuck. I'm cumming. Fuck. How'd you...?"

"...get you to cum so fast?" I finished his sentence, grinning because I knew the right spot to apply pressure and knew if he was anything like me, he was really fucking horny in the morning. Dropping a load had never taken more than a few strokes after a solid nights rest.

After he released the last few spurts of cum, catching some of it in his open palm pinned beneath him, he twitched, heaved, and hoarsely huffed, "Fuck. Fuck, Fuck. Holy Fuck. Gah, dayum, Michael."

I was satisfied as all get out when I was done with him, smacked his ass one more time and ordered, "Get up. Its bath time." He was instantly wide awake after getting off, the sheet beneath him soaked with his semen. He flipped over, gripped my dick with his cum damp hand and said, "Your turn. Spray my face, will Ya?"

"I'm good with what just happened," I fibbed, but still enjoyed making him cum with only my thumb up his ass.

He replied, "Are you sure?"

I was jealous when he licked his own cum off his hand.

"Of course. Now go. You can't be late."

He kissed me quickly and swiveled to a seated position on the edge of the bed. As he walked, I heard, "Fuck. What the...?" I laughed out loud as I watched him peel my cum filled magnum from the bottom of his foot. I honestly thought I had wrapped it in a towel after our previous evenings screw, but I guess I missed that part.

As Nykolson walked away, I was already stroking my worked up cock that was going to spurt cum if I'd touched it or not. As usual, I was horny as fuck in the morning and after what I'd done to Nykolson with my thumb, I'd gone rock hard and seeping pre-cum like it was a leaky faucet.

"Damn, he was so fucking hot."

I really would have rather climbed aboard and chipped that ass, but I had to let him go so he'd keep in check with his sentence and arrive to the site of punishment on time. Because of that, I'd been left alone with a stone hard cock. Nykolson had me so horny, I needed to do something about my predicament. A decision had been made without further argument. My dick would feel so much better once I stroked it, and since I was so worked up, it would take but a minute to ejaculate.

I rolled over and laid my face into where Nykolson's semen had soaked the sheets. The wet pungent scent destroyed me, instantly turning me into a jackoff maniac, and within less than a minute, I was growling, "Fuck. Fucking, FUCK!" I shot semen like the Buckingham fountain in Chicago had exploded, adding wads of cum next to and on top of Nykolson's, making the stain he had already left, a much larger one.

I huffed, breathing the tang of his spunk deep into my septum, keeping me damaged. "Fucking, fuck," was all I could mutter. "Fuck!"

Then I'd taken another breath that was more like a sigh. I rattled, "Holy Shhh-it! *I'm in love, I'm in... love... I'm fucking in love!*" I inhaled. I couldn't move. I hadn't wanted to.

Like an impaired lump, I left my face in the wet patch where my boyfriend sprayed his cum, inhaling his scent even deeper than before, loving how good that part of him smelled.

I rolled onto my back above the mussed sheets, spread eagle, legs and arms spanning toward the four corners of the bed. I huffed until my breathing returned to normal.

I popped my head up from the pillow and saw Nykolson standing at the foot of the bed looking down on my naked body. He announced, "Oh my gawd. You look amazing. What the shit did I miss? Is that cum on your chest?"

I chuckled at how good he thought I looked, laying in a pool of sperm with my hand giving my dick a few final strokes, advancing a hint that I had just jerked off in his bed.

Nykolson stepped into a pair of briefs while standing over me, and seemed to elevate his excitement when he saw the huge stain at the side of my ass. His voice was on the verge of laughing when he said, "Holy shit! Is that all me, or did you add to it while I was in the shower?"

I squeezed my eyes shut and started snickering.

Then he added, "You jerked off, didn't you?"

I aimed my wet dick at him, letting him see the drizzle of remaining cum crowning my dick head. I confessed, "I couldn't help it. You are so hot. That ass. Your cock. Your fucking body. I know I told you I was fine earlier, but I needed to make sure you get to the site on time. Shit. As soon as you left the bed with your semen scent still lingering behind, my hand went right for my cock and I couldn't stop myself from jacking off. You left me rock hard, Nykolson. I needed to ejaculate. In your honor." I was sitting up by then.

He met me in the middle with a kiss. His eyes sprung open and his surprised voice said, "You smell and taste like cum, which I like. What else did you do?"

As if he really needed to know, I still told him, "I couldn't resist that stain ejected from your black balls."

He humorously spoke, "So you rolled in it?"

After he started laughing at me, I nodded, my head bobbing hurriedly, the way it would if I was a child in trouble and in agreement with my scolding father. "Well... um... my face did. As well as licked the jiz from my fingers." I couldn't control my grin.

I turned away from Nykolson and glanced at the rooster doodling clock. "Holy shit, you need to get moving and I need to get my ass in the shower." I bounced across the bed on my butt cheeks until I reached the edge.

Nykolson looked down on me and said, "Well then. Go get cleaned up."

I stood and skipped around Nykolson as he spanked my bare ass cheek with an open handed blow. That stung a little bit, but felt arousing coming from him.

By the time I was finished soaping down and rinsing off, Nykolson was fully dressed and ready to go. As he watched me step from the shower, he kindly offered, "Go ahead and pick what you want from the closet. Just be sure to return them tonight."

I liked the way he casually mentioned I was welcome back. Brilliant man.

I walked him to his car that had been stored in the garage the entire time I'd been there. I kissed him through the open window and watched him drive away. That was the first time I'd seen his little Alfa Romeo convertible. It was a cute two seater — racy yellow and he looked like a movie star when he drove away.

"Hot damn, that fine specimen of a man is mine."

Chapter 18

The morning after, I'd walked into the office and found head of security blocking the hallway along with several unfamiliar men wearing blue suits and jackets. A few had gun holsters strapped to their shoulders as well as voice transmission devices attached to their ears with the mics running their jawlines.

"What's going on?"

There was a mass amount of activity from what I was able to see through a wall of officials who appeared to have been blocking drifters trying to get across the border of Mexico. I couldn't tell if they were standing at my office or blocking what was further down the way. From where I had been standing, there were too many of them to figure out what was going on.

I noticed the office rag reporter, Berdella, sitting quietly at her desk. Her face priceless, appearing frightened, unlike the way I'd expected her to have been during a time like that. I would have figured she'd been leaning over the countertop with a pen and pad in her hands documenting everything that was going on for a planned story to sell. I wouldn't have put it passed her to pull off a mousy act that would hide her true intentions. My first thought was she had set what was happening into motion because of what I'd said to her that irritating day I had with her. Did she really have the evidence on me to create such a criminal stir? Couldn't have been. I hadn't done anything that constituted bringing in the cops. However, by the way it looked, I was the one in big trouble, but couldn't believe fraternizing would bring that much drama to the place. *"Should I sneak out the backway or run head on into the oncoming stampede?"*

I felt every wrinkle in my face come to life when it knotted up from the tension building within my center, all stirred up because of a broomstick bound bitch whose lonely vagina had gotten its only thrills from being a trouble maker, and maybe her own finger. If my thoughts were correct, her spasmodic twat had probably gone into overdrive at that very moment. I'd had good mind to swing the edge of my attaché case into Berdella's bird face and knock her flat on her ass for all the anxiety she put me and everybody else through almost every day.

Whatever was going on down the hallway seemed serious, and if it had pertained to me, I hoped Nykolson wouldn't have been dragged into the mess. Keeping my anger toward Berdella in check, I held my arms stiffly at my sides and gripped the handle on my case, forcing all the blood from my fingertips, turning them yellow-white. I couldn't believe that woman had been able to bring the malicious side of me out so easily.

I was actually glad when I saw Ashlund in the distance, whose presence helped curb my urges to bludgeon the bitch's skull with my case. Ashlund seemed to be the single trustworthy person in the office at the moment, which meant I had only one thing to do — trust him. As far as I'd known, he was the only one with actual facts that I'd slept with Nykolson Kannon, and that was because I told him I had. When Ashlund spotted me, he lifted a pointed index finger as if telling me to stay put, and then some weird shifting of his hands that indicated he was coming right over. I nodded back and continued checking out the chaos in front of me, wanting to run away but decided that would have been a bad idea, marking me the guilty target I thought I was.

Talk about an event spoiler.

What I had walked into was just that, putting an instant damper on the great weekend I had with the twins, especially the highlight where I'd fallen into Nykolson, never wanting to leave the warmth of his grasp. I'd been with him for such a short time, but my body and mind already wanted to be with him for the long haul. I felt the strong connection to him in my bones and my heart, and hadn't wanted anything coming between us, not even

my job. If I had to decide between Nykolson and the Probation &
Parole office, I'd have chosen him in a heartbeat. I was resilient
and had smarts, so finding another job wouldn't have been too
much of a challenge. I wouldn't have thought. Shoot, sometimes
I'd even contemplated just being a patron greeter at a large
superstore. That would be fine with me and probably cut out half
of my daily stress.

Standing, somehow feeling helpless in the office at that
moment, seemed as though everything around me was about to
come crashing down, and in my mind, Berdella was the ring
leader who had instrumented all of it.

I stared upward into the lights, perhaps looking for God, or
Jesus Christ, whom I'd talked to when times had gotten rough,
like every day lately. I blinked rapidly as if trying to clear my eyes
of tears or push away the light digging into them. I silently
begged, *"Come on, Lord. Please. Could I have a day or two without
challenges? Everybody else seems to have happy-go-lucky lives. Why
can't I?"*

I wouldn't say my life was worse than everybody else's, but
I constantly felt like I struggled more than the next guy. I was
pretty sure other people had their rough moments—Nykolson
was a clear example of that. He was getting the raw end of the
deal for crap his brother's girlfriend tried to pull.

I'd flashed a malevolent expression over at Berdella, who
had returned the same look at me, yet with a suggestion of worry.
I wasn't sure why that was, but I sensed part of her hadn't been
happy to see me. The other part of that lady had probably been
anticipating the sight of me waltzing into the pit of fire she
ignited, hoping I'd catch fire.

After spotting a blue jacket with bold FBI letters printed on
the back and becoming shocked when I had, I'd pictured myself
being shackled at my wrists and ankles with a set of cuffs. That
sighting of the blue coat was when I acknowledged something
more major was happening and it might not have anything to do
with me putting my dick in Mister Nykolson Kannon during the
time he was under my authority.

Breaking me out of my hex, Ashlund stepped away from the
FBI agent I'd seen him with. When he reached me, I slurred,

"What the fu... huhg?" He hadn't answered, so I rephrased my question. "What the hell is going on, Ashlund? Who's getting busted?"

I hadn't asked a rhetorical question that time, but Ashlund seemed to have thought I had. Instead of telling me what I wanted to hear, he said, "This is some heavy shit going down right here, Michael."

It was irrational for me to have thought the FBI was there because I fooled around with a detainee, but I couldn't get the farfetched idea of that out of my crazy head. I was always dreaming shit up like that, imagining the worst before it even happened and creating stories that hadn't pertained to what I thought it had. If another second had gone by without questioning why they were in the office, I'd have blown to bits right there on the spot. I'd taken a frazzled breath and asked, "This doesn't have anything to do with what we talked about over the weekend, does it?" I'd hoped Ashlund's answer would have been "no", which would have gotten me off the hook regarding my unlikely scenario about being hauled off to do some serious jail time. I wasn't up to getting spit fucked by anybody other than Nykolson. I'd heard that kind of shit goes on in a prison cell and nobody comes to the rescue. I was gay as fuck, however, having a man nicknamed Bubba shoving an unlubricated dick up my ass wasn't my idea of a romance.

I'd kept my next questioning to Ashlund on a more formal basis in the event somebody had been listening. "You have everything in order with Mister Kannon's case, right?" If I hadn't gotten my questions out of the way and answered, the hypertension growing inside me would have taken my head right off and shot it through the ceiling.

Without looking away from the blue coats, Ashlund eased my nerves by answering, "All is taken care of with the Kannon case. This one isn't about you, my friend."

God knew I was thankful to hear what Ashlund had said, and just like that, I felt my blood pressure and heart rate returning back to where they should have been. Lower instead of through the roof.

Turning my way, Ashlund said, "You're not going to

believe this shit. Are you ready for it?" He released a sickened sigh.

If I'd been looking at my reflection in a mirror at that moment he asked if I was ready, I'd have certainly seen my complexion shift to a shade whiter than pale. "Get on with it, Ashlund. For the fifth time, what is the deal?" My voice cracked on a high note, instigating Berdella to swivel in her chair and look at us. Her imaginary pad and pencil followed her turn, appearing as if she was ready to jot down what she was about to hear.

Ashlund shifted, leaning closer to my ear and softly said, "It's the church lady, Sandra Dee."

Chapter 19

"Holy-shit-damn-son-of-a-bitch!" I was not expecting that. At all.

"Sandra Dee, how could you?" I thought I knew her. What I thought I'd read on the inside was so far off from the exterior I had judged. That appears to have proven, the cover is not the book.

Does that mean Berdella is off the hook? Probably not. She still was, and most likely always will be on the top of my shit list.

I'd sent short text messages to Nykolson a few times throughout the day, some lovey-dovey notes, and a few stupid emoji stickers, but hadn't once checked his location, wondering how his sentenced chore had gone. Since I already knew he only had a four hour schedule at the roadside and if he hadn't gone straight home, I or Ashlund would have known about it. I'd also had too many distractions taking up my time to bother him with the bullshit I'd encountered.

I'd been isolated by agents who asked question after question, and my answers were, "No, I didn't know Sandrine Dexter until she started working here. No, I hadn't realized I was one of many on her list of enemies. No, I hadn't known anything about her hacking abilities or that she was connected to some money stealing mob leader overseas. To tell you the truth, I'm stunned by all this about her. I had no idea she was in such a fix."

The questions had gone on for over an hour and my replies

were pretty much the same. "No. No—and No." Regarding the amount of times I said no, the facial expressions of the agent dishing out all the questions displayed signs he was annoyed with me. He must have wondered how I'd worked so closely with a woman and had no knowledge of what she had been up to or had known much about her. My answer to that was, Sandra Dee had never given me any reason to think she was a bad-ass bitch, and from what I'd just witnessed, the lady was a freaking exceptional performer who belonged on stage.

By the time my session with the FBI agents ended, my brain had become mush and at the point of a major meltdown. Even though I wasn't the one on trial, I felt as though I was the sacrificial virgin who was about to be pushed into the fiery volcano. My ass crack was even sweating, and I was pretty sure my wanker had crawled up inside my body, pulling my hairy balls with it. I just wanted out of that place so I could jump in the shower and wash the day away.

It turned out to have been an all-day event with the investigating agents from the bureau, confiscating forms of evidence and putting Sandra Dee's office on lockdown. I couldn't get over what had happened, and was surprised as shit to find it wasn't Berdella being dragged away in wrist cuffs and ankle shackles. Damn, would I have liked to have seen that. Maybe someday. If my intuitions had served me well, she was next.

It was closing in on six in the evening and in all fairness to me, it was time to call it a day and shut down. My eyes were burning and my head was banging. There was only one thing that could sooth my aches and pains, and Nykolson's name was written all over it. I couldn't wait for him to jump on me, wrap his legs around my waist, lock his arms around my neck and take what had been waiting for him all day. I so badly needed him.

Finally, that moment I'd thought about for the past several hours had finally arrived and I lunged for his fantastic body the moment I walked through the door. By Nykolson's welcoming reaction, he seemed as thrilled to see me as I was to see him. His cheerful voice rang, "Wow! I like this kind of homecoming. Glad to see you, too, Mikey."

Even though my parents were the only ones who'd called

me Mikey throughout my life, I liked hearing it from him, too. There was something appealing to me when he said it, and had given me the feeling he was my family, and I was his.

He unlaced his legs from around my hips, and slid them down my thighs until his feet hit the ground. He bent slightly at the knees, leveling enough with my lips to kiss me.

He asked how my day had gone, but before I'd gotten into all the dramatics of what had taken place at my office, I wanted to hear about his morning first, making it seem as though I had asked a question of business. He smiled at me and said, "Why'z you tryna git all up in my bidness? I don't reports to you'z no mo."

"Gah-ha!" I'd always adored his unpredicted hoots of thugliness with good natured humor, and I undoubtedly needed that laugh he'd just gotten out of me. With the little bit of ghetto lingo I picked up from hanging with the Kannon twins, I threw down my attempt at idiom verbiage too, "Jus checkin' tuh make sure you be all right on duh playin' field. If they be messin wid my black man, I be busstin dem up." Yikes. Enough of that. I clearly wasn't able to pull the ghetto slang off like the Kannon brother's. Maybe with a little more practice, I'd have been a force to be reckoned with. Until then, proper English was what I'd stick with. That's when they both laughed—at me trying to be like them.

His day was exactly as I'd imagined it would have been. He told me there was the bus ride to the dump site along the highway, a dayglow vest for safety, over the shoulder garbage holder, and a clawed poker stick for stabbing trash. He even looked a wee bit darker from being under the sun all morning. I'd seen plenty of crime and punishment films on television to know that trash pickup along the highway was a game of stab and grab. Putting it that way, made it seem a bit lighter hearted, not so criminally centered. The one thing that worried me was Nykolson hanging with other offenders who might have been a little bit more dangerous than he was, and who might see him as being so pretty, they'd have at him with their pokers all at the same time. Nykolson was a decent sized guy, built as though he'd been a gym bunny his entire life, so most cases, they'd have been more afraid of him than he would have been of them. He manhandled me a few times already, so I was well aware of what he'd have been capable of, had any of them tried shanking his ass.

Nykolson raised an eyebrow meant for me, and by that, I knew it was his signal to hear about the day I had.

Once I mentioned FBI, he shrieked, "What? Is that a normal day around that place?"

"Not. At. All." I was truthful.

With that answer, Nykolson seemed a little bit shaken, and by automatic actions, he moved closer to me as if his body was there to protect me from whatever danger he had sensed. "Do we need to be concerned about anything?" he asked, including himself in my issue without knowing what it was about.

My thoughts had gotten wrapped around his mention of "we," which made me think he had started considering us companions, by which doing so, he no longer considered himself an individual, but an "us." I was grinning on the inside because I knew couples would do that sort of thing. Everything singular had suddenly become plural at the moment they slept together and discovered they were meant for each other. Putting a dick in another man's ass kind of validated that. Connecting the two as one. Like a bond. And once they ejaculated inside each other, that would really seal the deal.

I reached up and cupped both hands to Nykolson's prickly five o'clock shadowed jaw and assured him there was no need for concern about anything, but the church lady I had thought was an angel needed higher hope, and that she was probably looking at doing some hard time in the slammer for what she'd done.

Without hesitancy, Nykolson hugged me and murmured, "Thank God." I figured he meant that for us, not Sandra Dee. Then he backed away and asked if sharing with him what happened would have been okay.

I looked him in the eyes and detailed, "I don't see why not. It has nothing to do with us, nor had it been mentioned to keep quiet. The media teams blab about these types of events all the time, all using bystanders' hearsay, without having any actual facts from the sources closest to the criminal." I knew whatever I told him, he'd keep between us, with the exception of his brother,

I'm sure. They were too close for secret keeping, and probably were able to read each other's minds anyway, so whatever I told Nykolson, I expected him to mention it to Nathaniel. I knew deep down I could confide in Nykolson with just about anything. That sixth sense was practically felt the first moment I met him.

Before I started speaking, Nykolson cut in, "Oh, hey, by the way. Mister Ashlund seems like he has his shit together. He has me scheduled for a visit with him tomorrow around one in the afternoon. Will you be in the office then?"

That's when I sounded intrusive, "So you think he's better than me?"

Before Nykolson had taken a breath, he immediately blurted out an admission, "Jeez, no. You are the best. At Everything." He'd given me the sidewinder's wink and that half-mouthed grin I liked so much—the one where he meant, grab the tube of lube and get naked. Yeah, that one. All Nykolson had to do was look at me and I popped a stiffy. Yeah, that one—the one on the rise.

But before a good hard banging up his butt had been added to the day's schedule, Nykolson spun on his stocking covered feet and scampered to the liquor cabinet to fix him and me a stiff drink.

Was it that obvious I needed one?

Out of the blue, he said, "Sit tight, sweetheart. I'll whip you up a strong one. Then you can tell me about Sandra Dee."

Wait a second, had he thought I needed a drink or had I spoken my desire out loud? Delirium must have been settling in because I couldn't even remember hearing my own voice ask for a bottle of booze.

"Okay. First things, first." I walked me and my erection over to the cabinet alongside my boyfriend who had already started tipping bottled whisky into an ice filled glass. After handing the throat burning beverage to me, he set out on his next mission at mixing himself a classic gin martini with one of those ghastly green olives resting on the bottom. I loved watching him rattle that shaker over his shoulder, the deep caverns of his triceps and bunched bulges of his biceps held my attention as they flexed. Damn, him. He was even sexy-hot doing that simple task. Was he for real? Was he my boyfriend who I already fucked and would fuck for the rest of my life? I couldn't imagine ever doing it with anybody else anymore. I figured within time I'd have answers about our everlasting relationship.

The minute he filled his glass, he reached down and cupped my ass cheek, giving it a good squeeze at the moment he'd given me a chicken-like peck on the lips. Keeping it short and sweet made me want more. Our glasses chimed when the two rims tapped against the other. He chanted, "To a positive outcome for Sandra Dee."

"Why toast to her? Why not us?" Of course his kind heart would send good wishes to someone who direly needed it, even with full knowledge she was the bad guy.

Right before he'd taken a sip, he said her name again, "Poor, Sandra Dee." Almost singing it that time.

His few hints within minutes sounded like a reminder I was supposed to give up what I knew about the office and the FBI visit that morning. Nykolson seemed to be chomping at the bit to get that out of me. I had already decided to let him have the limited information I knew. If I hadn't fed him the story straightaway, I'd have to deal with his gray-eyed puppy dog stare until I had. That of which, I could not handle. They were too damned hypnotizing and I fell for the look every single bloody time.

"All right, all right. Have a seat," I bellyached good-naturedly as I pulled the chair out from under the patio table. But I changed my seating choice when Nykolson tapped the spot beside him on the settee. "Over here, sweet thang. Sit next to me where it's comfortable."

I hadn't known what I was thinking when I'd chosen the chair at the table instead of beside Nykolson. My brain was fatigued and it was starting to show obvious signs of shutting down.

After I landed in the seat with a huff and put my arm over Nykolson's shoulder to make a comfortable back rest for him against my chest, I'd given up what I knew about the office raid, speeding through it so I wouldn't bore him to tears with the small stuff, yet made sure he was clear as to what had happened with the good stuff.

Nykolson's reaction to most of what I told him was the same

as if we were watching waves smashing against rocky surfs. I kept hearing a lot of whew's, whoa's, holy shit's, and a countless number of gasps. If he had a string of pearls around his thick neck, he would have been clutching those too.

Chapter 20

There was an unnerving perception in the office the morning after the FBI had come in and busted up the place, even smelling like cops, whatever that really smelled like. The place seemed as though all the good air had been sucked out overnight. Even my personal office with the large sunny windows had a dank and dreary quality about it, but I still stepped inside and had taken a seat at my desk. It felt like death all around me. I had good notion to believe everybody was feeling the same way I had, even snarky ol Berdella, who shocked the shit out of me when she'd given up a teensy smile I almost missed seeing when I walked passed her. Knowing the type of person she was, made me think she'd been up to something no good again, or had known another fabricated secret I hadn't been made aware of. Another thought had come to mind—she might have been feeling regret for crap she'd done that aided with getting her friend hauled away in FBI cuffs. Whatever it was with her, I remained cordial and smiled back with an accompanied single roundabout wave of my hand. No words.

As soon as my PC was up and running, I called Ashlund's extension and asked him if we could chat.

I headed down the hall to his office, passing Sandrine Dexter's place on the way. The door to her space had been locked and cross taped with that famous FBI criminal investigation notice pasted at eye level, stating no entry was allowed until further notice. When I saw that blockade, it had physically sunken in that the shit had gotten really real. My body turned cold as if there was a dead body on the other side of that door. I sensed myself shifting my steps to the right, unconsciously taking my footpath further away from her space of work.

Ashlund greeted me at the entryway of his office, and after I walked in, he directed me to sit in one of the chairs as he'd taken a half assed seat on the corner of his desk.

He asked me if I was there to speak about Mister Kannon. Part of it was, but I mostly wanted to bring up the FBI and Sandra Dee. When I mentioned her name, he hadn't seemed too surprised, however, still said, "Oh?" as if he was.

Even though it seemed like I was in his office to talk smack about what had happened, that wasn't the plan at all. I wasn't there to speak ill about Sandra Dee, or spank her for what they found on her PC, what her true plan had been, and the shit she had on me. I simply wanted to get the incident off my chest and rid the fears I had camping out in my head. Since Ashlund hadn't been involved in most of the office crap I had been, he might have a clearer vision on the whole shit storm and speak more logically than the way I'd been thinking.

I felt like a detective with the types of questions I'd asked Ashlund, but in all honesty, I was clueless on the entire Sandra Dee operation while still wondering how she'd gotten to that point and what she would have gained if it had continued. A criminal's mind I didn't have, so the plot she'd planned out was a big blur to me. The main question I asked him was if he'd known of anybody else in the office that might have been guiding or assisting her.

The FBI hadn't released much information regarding Sandra Dee's case and why she'd been taken away. It was private at the time and like most secret operations, was on a need to know basis. Apparently we had no business knowing and we weren't anybody who needed to know, even though we were all in the center of the fire pit trying to save ourselves from getting burned to a crisp.

I figured out most of what she'd done by all the questions the agent had asked. I wasn't certain it was okay for Ashlund to tell me what he'd known, but he had. I guessed it really wouldn't have made a difference. The more we knew together, seemed for the better.

Ashlund made me pinky swear that I'd keep what he was about to tell me to myself. He already knew I was good with secrets, as well as my promises, but as we'd always done with confident information between us, he mentioned he'd feel better about letting me in on what he knew if I locked fingers with him. I'd recognized joining fingers was child-like, but that worked for us, even with something as major as what we were up against. He was one of the closest friends I'd made since coming to San Francisco, and I wouldn't jeopardize breaking that trust over some wretch who'd gotten tangled up in some sort of covert activity. I was quite shocked by how much detailed information he had on her, made me think he was part of it, but I knew he wouldn't sink that low, nor had he seemed like the type of person who'd trade freedom for a prison cell just to get rich quick. I hoped I knew him better than that.

"Jeez. Don't even go there."

Ashlund cleared a lot of things up when he mentioned Sandra Dee's involvement with cracking security codes and getting into the detainee's files. She created false identities with each one of them and organized routing numbers in and out of their personal banking accounts that funneled what little money most of them probably had out of the country. I hadn't known about any of what she'd done until that very moment Ashlund mentioned it. How he knew all that about her, I hadn't dared ask. I had known, however, he was connected to many investigative detectives, reporters and agents, which might have been how he was so up to date on Sandra Dee's situation as quickly as a day after the shit hit the fan. That was my guess so I stuck with it.

Trying to appear more natural than shocked and since I wanted to know as much as possible, I kept Ashlund talking. It wasn't because I was nosey, or planning to verbally spread the information he told me, but instead, I wanted to make sure I wasn't caught up in the mess as much as I thought I might have been.

Ashlund mentioned Sandra was paid large sums of money by an off shore agency as long as she continued feeding them information through the secured servers of the court. The part that had gotten to me the most was how daring she was with processing every transaction right under the roof of the county court house. It had to have been due to the heightened security throughout the building, personnel and networks, which I wondered what kind of criminal would risk doing such business in a place that was so frequented by members associated with the law. That made a lot of sense when I thought about it, and who would have thought to look for such criminal activity in such a secure establishment. With the courthouses network security as it was, there couldn't have been a better place to access and take people's lives away from them. All the information pertaining to each offender was on file — consisting of full names, social security numbers, previous and former addresses, bank information, and even life changing events and history. The court had it all. It was a hacker's jackpot, plinthed on top of golden nuggets. Most of those offenders were sent to do jail time or live a prison term, many never coming out, or by the time they had, their personal funds would have been long gone, making it difficult to trace the money and how it was removed or where it had gone. They were criminals whom nobody probably cared about anyway, and if there were any arguments pertaining to their stolen money, it'd have been a hard sell to convince anyone they were bringing up a believable issue. It would simply boil down to lies and fabricated stories of what might not have been there in the first place.

It amazed me, however, that somebody like Sandra Dee was able to pull something like that off for such a long period of time. She must have been coached, or there was a silent bystander who knew how to keep themselves hidden, let Sandra be the one who left a dirty trail. She'd go in, and they'd be off the hook. Come to find out, she had background training as an Information Technologist, and probably knew how to get at anybody's PC through some sort of back door worm she'd pin to their IP address. People like her were in and out of systems so quickly, it was nearly impossible to trace their trafficking. It shocked me that a skinny church lady like her was a freaking PC bounty hacker. She'd been doing it under everybody's noses for two and a half years. That right there amazed the shit out of me.

What had gotten me riled even more was finding out about

her personal life and how unlikely it was for someone like her to even think about doing what she'd done. The dangled bait must have been very appetizing and had come at the right time when she was at her most vulnerable, snatching it up like a fish takes to a wiggly worm on a hook—hungry for it, but not thinking about the consequences once she'd taken that bite.

From the gossip I'd overheard coming from Berdella, had it been a truth or a lie, to my understanding, Sandra Dee was a frequent church goer. She'd chosen the hymn's they'd sung every week, sang in the church choir along with Berdella, and was instrumental with the yearly Christmas pageant. All that connection to religion, yet she'd chosen to get caught up in a web of dishonesty. The way it seemed, Sandra Dee was a master of disguise and her sweet smile and frequent time spent in church was her cloak for what she really was. The thing I hadn't understood, and neither had Ashlund, was, how the heck had she gotten involved with the creep overseas? Had he had somebody approach her at church, or had she joined the church after she'd gotten involved? I had a good idea that part of the puzzle would become revealed someday soon since every detective, journalist, and news tabloid would be digging into her life to get hold of the ultimate front page headline. The whole thing was big time crime, right on our doorstep. I never would have thought something like that would hit so close to home.

I continued talking with Ashlund behind closed doors, and he nearly spit in my face with laughter when I mentioned Berdella might be next on the FBIs to-do list. I was happy to find what I mentioned had lightened the mood since there was so much heavy shit coming down in his office that morning.

He answered by saying, "That lady might be a stupid gossiping bitch, but I don't think she has the skills to pull something like that off."

I was a bit hesitant with what he said. We thought that same thing about Sandra Dee and look what had come of her. She was all sugar and spice that appeared to be everything but nice. As it turned out, she was an evil genius who might have a few accomplices hidden under her skirt. From what we knew so far, which wasn't much, Sandrine was a full blown criminal. The thing that really sucked, we all unknowingly helped her achieve the goals she had put into motion.

Then my mind rewound and I panicked, practically screaming out, "Holy shit, what about our identities?" — I pointed to my chest — "Us... in this office? Had she gotten hold of any of ours?"

Ashlund answered, "Highly unlikely, but no guarantees. Our information is kept off site with the human resource department, not mixed in with the detainee's that she had access to here. I already checked my accounts. You might want to do the same with yours. She had to have been smarter than that, anyway. I can't see her targeting any of us. It would have been too risky, getting noticed well before this time if she had. She hit the people who hadn't had any access to their bank accounts."

I plucked my phone from my front pocket and immediately went on line to check a few accounts. The first one was my bank, the next, my IRA's. I settled down once I found everything seemed fine. Since I had no messages from my bank regarding suspicious activity, I seemed good there. I decided to also check my frequently used bankcards, making sure there was no strange or high dollar amounts posted against them. Thankfully, they were still active and the balance was what I expected them to have been.

Then I worried about Nykolson's security as well as his personal identity. I knew his documents were made available to her, and I understood that man made a shit load of money as principal editor for that fancy fashion magazine in New York City.

"Do you know how we can check out which files she had stolen and if Nykolson's was one of them?" I asked Ashlund, but he replied by mentioning we couldn't, however, Nykolson could review his personal accounts on his own the same way we had.

Ashlund asked, "Has Nykolson mentioned strange activity with any of his accounts recently? It seems he would have made comments if there were. With any luck, his file was in our possession for too short of a period for her to get her hands on it."

"No, he hadn't mentioned anything, but I'd just met him, so I really don't think he'd discuss financial issues with me." My guess, Nykolson might have said something casually or without noticing he was mumbling about money matters. "He's a smart man, other than getting himself into the silly shit that landed him a parole sentence. I presume he has security checkpoints on all his accounts. I couldn't imagine somebody like him not putting safe measures in place." I was surely planning to ask him that question in a roundabout way as soon as I was able.

Ashland then asked, "Were you aware she had a file on you?"

"I do now. The questions I was asked by the FBI yesterday clued me in on that. I presumed she gathered most of her information from blabber mouth Ms. Berdella Betrayal." I had every right to have been furious, but for reasons of shock helped me keep a level head on my shoulders as well as helped me refrain from flying off the handle the way I normally would have. "I understood she had everything on me and Nykolson, except for photos of the two of us fucking." I saw Ashlund's eyes practically pop out of their sockets after saying what I had, mainly because it wasn't up his alley to be picturing me with my dick poking around Nykolson's back door. I would have laughed at his reaction if the circumstances would have been different, but reality of the situation told me that wasn't the time for jokes and laughter.

I wasn't sure why or what sick plan Sandra Dee had that made her want to document the sex I had with men. I'd found that creepy in a way, as well as disturbing. It seemed she'd been doing it for quite some time while she'd spoken kindly to my face as if I was her friend.

Jeez, what a two faced bitch.

I figured her reasons for that had something to do with being a church-goer, and while there, she'd been convinced I had made a choice in life that was going against the grain of her churches cult-like ways.

"Say what?"

A true Christian would identify the love within a person, wouldn't argue or devalue it, but simply understand through education that true love was the positive way of life. Organized religions seemed to have a mission to make the world believe their creed was the only one, and whoever hadn't sung beneath the same tainted steeple, the church would consider them an outcast, condemning them to hell for not being an unethical follower. My thoughts on that were hogwash. God made every individual exactly the way he wanted them to be and to my understanding he doesn't differentiate a man from a woman, black flesh from white flesh, or even segregate nationalities. Flesh and bone is meaningless—a traveling vessel. What's inside is what matters, and those internal souls are meant to connect and share the love.

Nonetheless, Sandra Dee had shit on me. Since that lady was probably going to spend the rest of her life in a prison cell, I might never find out why she'd done what she had to me. Plus, if my sex life wasn't conclusive to the FBI arrest, it might never become a question in court or ever come up again.

From what I'd gotten out of the FBI questioning, I presumed Sandra Dee was keeping tabs on me as an educational tool, perhaps doing research for a book she was writing or some kind of periodical column she'd planned to submit, but after being interrogated by the FBI agent, I'd understood she had many hate messages and posts on social media condemning and bashing the lesbian and gay community. I found that shocking, but hadn't surprised me, because part of my questioning from the agent was if I knew of, or had any connection with Sandra Dee's lesbian interest, who happened to be a well-known person at the freaking church she was attending.

Was I blown away by who Sandra Dee was eating out? Um… definitely so, and the scandalous kicker brought into the spotlight, which wasn't any of my business, was that I had no idea the preacher's wife was a muffin munching scissor sister who'd been scrumping Sandrine Dexter behind closeted doors.

As soon as I'd come down from my state of shock, without showing the agent I was, I wondered if the pastor knew about his little woman's pussy bumping activities, and had chosen to keep the secret locked away so he appeared holier than thou to his brainwashed congregation. Even if the pastor had that knowledge, he still preached about all 'the gays' were sickened sinners by choice and should be sentenced to a fiery death, however, as he saw it, his religious followers who decided it was okay to hate alongside him were all rising up to heaven as if they were the true angels.

News flash—it doesn't work like that. Heaven is not holding a spot for haters. It's all about love up in there.

After hearing all about the lesbian activity taking place right under the pastors dwellings, it seemed the mass amounts of hating and bashing Sandra Dee had done must have been how she kept her cover on the underground affair with the preacher's wife.

Whoa!

And they call me and Nykolson the devil's children. It wasn't us who deceived people, lied to them, and hid under the holy roof with hopes that there would be exclusions from the several commandments of the ten they all had broken. I wouldn't exactly call me and Nykolson's kettles the black ones.

I was stunned by the amount of garbage they'd found on Sandrine's PC about me, and I'm sure that wasn't all of it. What she had collected over time was outrageous, so my recollected vision of her being hauled away in cuffs surged a dose of satisfaction within me. I was no longer affected by gloom with what had happened to her, but was content. It served her right for bringing hate upon a community she was part of. Whatever administration or religion she belonged to, they were all far more vindictive and malevolent than the people they were pointing fingers at.

Sandra stealing files and hiding the preacher's wife under her panty free skirt had gone beyond corruption of a sinner. The news of that shit and finding out she was the one who turned me and Nykolson into the authorities instead of by whom I suspected, felt like it was all pulled out of my ass with an ungreased fist—a shocking eye opener to say the least.

They had nothing on me because I'd fixed the Nykolson issue before it had a chance to get started, shutting it down straightaway, but it had only added fuel to other shit-bombs she'd been up to. I had always thought I was an excellent judge of character, but after the wool had been pulled over my eyes with Sandra Dee's stunts, I'd need to scrutinize the covers of the books I'd been judging more carefully. That one had come at me like a whirlwind, had never seen it coming. So unbelievable! That

Sandra Dee was one fantastic actress and deserved the Oscar for her two year well-played performance.

Before I left Ashlund's office, I asked him one last thing — to take care of Nykolson during his time under tether while I take care of him at home.

His reply was, "I'll do what's legal."

Chapter 21

To roughly have said I was thrilled another day at the workplace had gone by would have been an underestimation, especially *that* particular Tuesday following the Sandra Dee cuffing incident. Everything about that day was out of sync, and I was having one heck of a time getting my mojo back. I couldn't concentrate to save my ass.

The real thrill had come when I arrived at Nykolson's home, or as he had mentioned recently, "our home," which I was still finding difficult to absorb that term since I was still so new in his life and hadn't had actual confirmation from him that we were boyfriends. To me, it seemed boyfriends should come first, and then the home. The only hazy affirmation of me being his companion was that my dick had been buried inside him a few times already, giving me total confirmation we were technically inching toward being a couple. Once he'd given me permission to shoot a load of cum up his ass without a condom, then that would probably validate me as "the boyfriend"—kind of like putting a permanent mark on my man. Then when he ejaculated inside me, that would definitely make our relationship official next to exchanging vows at the pulpit.

Anyway, when I arrived at *"our home"* I'd done my usual ritual of bulldozing Nykolson with gropes and kisses—one of my favorite moments of the day for sure. Unfortunately for us, Nathaniel was typically standing nearby, begging us to stop even though he was the one who'd egged us on at getting our newly developing relationship off the ground. He had no issues with the two of us giving the other attention, but when we prolonged our periods of going at each other in front of him, it was more than he cared to have been a witness to. I'd told him he was jealous, and his answer was always the same—the fuck you finger or a back and forth pumping fist in front of his crotch that told me to go fuck myself. If he only knew how much I enjoyed watching him do that he'd probably tone that dick jerking gesture down a bit or cease it altogether. When there was anything to do with groping, Nathaniel preferred we carried out our hands on activity more subtly or take it to a more private place where he wouldn't have to see what we were doing. Out of respect for Nathaniel's silent wishing, I pushed Nykolson away.

While I had Nykolson and Nathaniel in the same room, I'd brought up the security concern regarding their funds, asking if they noticed any odd activity and if their accounts had been set up with suspicious checkpoints in place.

Nathaniel made it a point to tell me it was a peculiar question to be asking, whereas Nykolson looked at me in a strange manner, probably thinking the same thing.

Adding humor, Nathaniel asked, "Are you planning on burgling us or what?"

The way Nykolson was looking at me, I immediately assured them both it wasn't me who was trying to get my hands on their piggy banks, but Sandra Dee's team might. I understood Nykolson hadn't filled Nathaniel in on what had happened when he asked, "Who the hell is Sandra Dee?" Then I hacked out a chuckle when he said, "Wasn't she in a musical or something?" That was true, but the Sandra was not the musical Sandra.

I was glad Sandrine had come up in the conversation, which helped avoid having any secrets between any of us or put Nykolson in a position where he was forced to keep anything from his brother. They shared everything and I wasn't interested in being the one person who had anything to do with keeping them from confiding in one another.

I'd gone on telling them what had been found on Sandra's PC, which was the reason she had been targeted by the FBI, and why I asked about the security of their accounts. Nykolson guaranteed, in so many words, that both their accounts were safeguarded, with insurance. His answer settled my mind since I was part of the reason Sandra Dee had access to Nykolson's information.

"Good. Okay. My job is done here. Now you know." I dragged the back of my hand across my forehead as if I was dabbing away nervous sweat beads.

The subject quickly changed as if the idea of me being a burglar hadn't been talked about. Redirecting the conversation, Nykolson asked me what I liked on a pizza pie.

My eyebrows lifted. "Pizza? Who orders pizza on a Tuesday night?"

Nathaniel had given me a flabbergasted look as he balked, "What? What's wrong with you? Who doesn't eat pizza any day of the week?"

He had a point.

Taking over where Nathaniel left off, Nykolson said, "No, no, no, we are making it here. From scratch. Like Italian housemates. Wash your hands and get ready."

I enjoyed pizza. A lot. I'm not against eating pizza midweek, I just couldn't remember if I had ever ordered one on a day other than Friday or Saturday night. It just seemed like a weekend meal to me — with beer. Tuesday pizza was actually the saving grace to a shitty day. It was the perfect distraction from all the crap that had taken place at the office.

While making pizza together, I had my share of tasting Nykolson as I intermittently gobbled the black olives I was supposed to be slicing as part of the topping off his fingertips. I wouldn't have gone after any of them like that, but he was poking around my face with some alien finger shit, those black olives looked like weird finger pads. He thought it was funny and I thought it was too. Nathaniel on the other hand seemed annoyed with our flirty playtime.

We exchanged a kiss just about every three minutes, a grope to the ass every four, and a body against body rubbing here and there as if it had been done by accident. Then had gone through the motions all over again, but juggling the order of all the touchy feely moments neither one of us could seem to have gone without.

All of a sudden a hunk of dough hit the counter top with a sharp smack.

"Holy, what the fuck?" flew out of my mouth because the shocking boom scared the living shit out of me. Nykolson lost his grip on the girthy pepperoni stick he was poking me with and it rolled across the counter top and bounced to the floor as if it had been made of rubber. I cracked up as the tube of meat wobbled under the stool next to me. Yes. It was that funny lying on the floor like a misplaced dildo.

Nathaniel threw flour at the both of us, hitting me in the face and Nykolson in the chest. He laughingly blurted, "Jeez, bro and brozo. Go bang already. Get it over with so you can concentrate on your shit." He stabbed the space in front of him with a pointed finger and ordered us to go, "Hurry up. Get it done with. I'm starving to death."

As much as I'd have liked to have taken Nykolson to the back room, pulled his pants to his ankles and banged his brains out, I instead decided to move away from my hot black boyfriend and take my position to the opposite end of the island to chop the olives I was supposed to have had done already. "I'll stay over here. I promise." My jazz hands snapped in front of me, resting near my ears.

Nykolson stayed where he was and said, "I'll stay right here. Promise." He looked at me with a mischievous grin, then blew me an airborne kiss, which I'd caught in midair with my hand and pressed it to my lips.

I heard Nathaniel grumble, "Ohmigawd. You did not just do that."

Chapter 22

"That was the best pizza I think I'd ever had," I blurted out the moment we stepped through the door of the master bedroom, right before I lunged into Nykolson full force. I actually had planned something romantic with him once we made it through the doorway, but I'd lost my mind and thought less about romance and more about roughly fucking around with Nykolson's naked body.

My cock had been aching the entire time we were tearing into that pizza and downing beer. There was no longer time for flowers and romance, I needed to bed that man, fuck his brains out, and maybe let him stick his fat whopper into me, too. I wanted to give that cock a try, ride it a while. I'd been having those feelings recently about letting Nykolson in. My thought on that was I needed him closer, and there was no better way than for him to sink a part of himself inside me. He was the one, after all.

"You're in a hurry," Nykolson shuffled backward in my grasp.

"Shut up," I snarled, pushing him down on the bed to more easily strip him of the shirt he was wearing. I ran both hands over the hard, muscular planes of his chest, exploring the masculinity of his body, taking in the radiating heat. I gently pinched Nykolson's nipples, followed by a lickety flick of my tongue. He whimpered and pushed his chest to my mouth. His reaction implied he liked what I had done.

195

Nykolson gasped while I slid my tongue across his chest, stopping to nip sharply at his other nub. I figured after that, they needed a good gentle lapping to help ease the sharp pings of inflicted pain. Nykolson's body writhed under the pleasured assault I'd given his chest. I'd even heard a few cries, then an, "Oh gawd that makes me hard. Keep going. Just like that."

I'd gone wild from the effects Nykolson's earthy scent had put me through, and my aroused mind associated it with plunging my beefy erection into him. It was the same pleasing fragrance that dominated my senses the first time I had the man naked and filled with my full length, screwing him until his body sucked the cum right out of me. I would always remember that aroma and hopefully have the pleasure of breathing it in every night and day from that day forward.

Pulling away from Nykolson's nipples, I stripped him of his briefs and pants too, leaving him completely nude and lying defenseless on his back across the mattress. His horse hung dick bending up and over his hip. I licked my lips and said, "Gawd, you're fucking gorgeous."

His legs opened just enough so his nut sack slumped in front of his dark taint and kept his bullet hole hidden from view. I'd have to push those black plumbs aside to get at that sweet spot I badly wanted to penetrate. I extended a hand to his crack, running my full palm up and down the black furry trail that bridged his asshole to his dangling nuts. I liked the way he felt down there—hot and masculine, scruffy with hair. My kind of man.

I toed off my shoes, tugged my own shirt up over my head and dropped my pants. I climbed on top of Nykolson, straddled his hips and settled in, our cocks grinding into one another's, my heavily leaded rifle pressing down on his.

Nykolson reached between us, wrapping his fingers around both erections, slowly stroking from base to flared head, pre-cum already beading from his and my slit.

Looking down, I admired the way Nykolson's muscles shifted as he squirmed under me on the bed, adored the way his forehead crimped with desire, his lips slightly open, moaning and sucking in air. But most of all, at that moment, I loved the feel of my thick cock being stroked by his strong black hands.

I gripped Nykolson's fist, stopping him from jerking my dick. If I hadn't, I'd have shot sperm within seconds. I was that close and that horny. He moved his hands to my chest, massaging the blocky masses. My eyes closed and then slowly opened, the pleasure of Nykolson's touch had sent electric sparks through my entire body, putting me in a spiraling bout of sexual stupor that wasn't going to quit until I'd cum. I leaned in and kissed him, long and slow, just like I'd been dying to do all evening. I parted Nykolson's lips, feeding him my slippery tongue, then sluggishly pulled back, telling him in a soothing voice that might have shocked him, "I want you to fuck me, Nykolson." That was the first time I'd asked anybody to do that to me, and when I brought it up to Nykolson, I really, really meant it. The words had come out of me so naturally, no reason to have given it thought.

The look on his face seemed doubtful, almost reluctant. I'd sensed he might not have been interested, perhaps doubting his ability to be the man on top.

I'd come across men who were strictly bottoms and found it a struggle to perform outside of their comfort zone, coming across as awkward as a fish trying to mount a bird. A lot of men felt more natural on the bottom, and a position switch wasn't of any interest. Maybe Nykolson was one of those men—one hundred percent catcher? Asking him to stick his dick in me might have caused the application of those brakes.

Before I'd made Nykolson feel any more uncomfortable and relieve him from the duty of mounting me, I interposed by telling him, "But you know... my dick might have a problem passing up that role."

As if I'd flipped a switch by what I'd said, there suddenly seemed to have been no question in Nykolson's mind that he wanted to stick his stiff cock into my willing butthole, and with that perception, I felt his dick twitching under me, pressing harder up against mine.

My eager bottom man jabbered as if nervous, "Okay. Yes. I do. How would you like me?"

As I lay on top of Nykolson, I pecked small kisses along his five o-clock shadowed jawline, stopping where ear met skull and whispered, "I want you just the way you are."

When I pulled back, I recognized eagerness in Nykolson as though shockwaves of pure desire had been injected up and down his spine. I reached for the tube of lube and a few condoms left out on the nightstand, and as I stretched, he licked my nipple, sending a jolt of electricity straight to my dick. I stiffened even more than I already had been by what he'd done, having no idea a tit nip could feel so erotic.

His cock was stone hard with a slight up-curved bend, perfectly angled to prod my prostate when fucking me face to face. I knew from experience of giving dick that a punching prostate massage can make a man go ape shit. I'd seen it many times before and really found that out when I jabbed my cockhead into Nykolson's. When the moment had come to put himself inside me, he'd probably get me off without a single stroke of my dick. I was that ready for him to stick it to me.

His cock was steel hard, making me believe he really wanted to fuck me in the ass. He waited patiently as I rolled the oversized magnum down the full length of his thick shaft. He moaned, "Ohmigawd, your hands feel so much better than mine."

That was the first time I'd found an XXL magnum to have been nearly too small for an erection I'd put one on. If his cock had been any bigger, the fucking sleeve would have been way too tight. Incredible. Right then I knew I was up against one heck of a challenge, but I was determined to have all ten inches, and by the way my asshole was going crazy, it wanted to be sucking on his huge dick as much as I wanted it shoved up my asshole.

I looked into his gray eyes with complete desire and said, "Just wait 'til you feel my ass wrapped around that python." I readily grinned as I rolled the brown rubber sleeve over his massive dick, taking my sweet time to build anticipation.

I repositioned myself over Nykolson's hips, at the same time I tucked a lubricated finger into my tender hole, then two, and then three. I lost my breath a few times from the exquisite torture of my own fingers relaxing my bullet hole, gently scissoring them inside myself in preparation at taking something much larger. "O-oh. My. Gawd." I quaked and felt my face changing. My melting expression had to have shown Nykolson how much I was enjoying having my prostate massaged by my own hand, and when I mumbled, "fuck, I want more," must have been a dead giveaway I'd rather have my black man's cock sliding inside me instead. The thought of replacing four fingers with Nykolson's dick had made me grow stiffer and I could hardly keep my mouth shut or my eyelids from fluttering out of sync. Jeez, I wanted his stiff dick reaming my ass. Like... real bad.

"Shit-damn-son-of-a-bitch! I was a bottom, too?" Something about Nykolson made me want to give my ass to him, let him fuck me. Like... really use my hole. My instincts had told me to get on my back, raise my legs and open my hairy hole to him, but I stayed where I was, seated in his lap. I leaned back and lifted higher so he could easily watch me finger-work my hole in front of him. His face was glowing. He seemed eager to make the switch from fingers to dick. I sensed his need and I truly wanted my man's black erection sliding in and out of me.

Where the fuck had that come from? I had suddenly become the eager one. The bottom. A rectal cocksucker.

Nykolson watched as I worked my warm hole with an enthusiastic hand. He lifted my hairy nuts and said, "That's so fucking hot. Open up for me, but not too much, I might like you tight. Plus, I want you to feel my entire dick moving inside you. The tighter the better." How had he known?

His orders had made me even hornier. I could hardly wait to feel him sink into me.

Turning aggressive, I pushed my four fingers into my butthole further, hiding the last row of knuckles inside me. If I had added my thumb, I'd have been fisting my butt. It was hotter than a fire in there, like a stoked up furnace. I rotated my hand as best I could, opening myself, making room for what would come next.

Nykolson's hands reached up and massaged my expanding pecs, my feathery chest hair catching between his black fingers.

"Get ready," I groaned, my dick twitched when my finger pads pressed against my prostate. Pre-cum oozing from my slit. I was ready.

Nykolson started stroking himself, running a slick hand up and down his rubber covered shaft. He blurted out, "Gah Dayum.

Fuck. I feel like I'm gonna explode if I don't get this cock inside you right now."

Then I leaned forward and kissed Nykolson, ravishing his mouth, sucking at his slippery tongue. After stealing his breath away, I growled, "I want that cock so fucking bad." I hadn't known until that moment. Then, I shifted backward, starting out slowly, continuing downward until I felt the course pubic hair scrubbing my nuts. He was in. Completely. It was better than I'd expected. Mind wrangling. Pure pleasure. I was literally trembling from how grand he felt stretching my rectum wide open. I had to gasp for air. The excruciating pleasure was overwhelming. I had no idea he'd feel that good. He was extremely deep. The pressure inside me great beneath my sternum.

I lifted, pulling off him until his fist sized cockhead was all that was inside me. My sphincter gripping his crown. I kissed him. Then like before, I rocked backward, skewering my burning channel with Nykolson's rigid erection, going down hard in a hurry, not inch by inch. I wanted all of it. Digging deep. All at once.

I howled, "Oh my fuck, that's fucking good." My body trembled when my ass cheeks met Nykolson's hips. The trail of fur between my asshole and nuts sounded like crackling fire as I ground against the pelvic hair above Nykolson's cock.

I squeezed my rectum as I lifted and lowered myself again and again, stroking Nykolson's hard-on with my tight slippery chute, making the man beneath me squirm like a virgin teen. I bounced up and down on his curved erection, deliberately rubbing the crown of his dick over my active prostate. I was determined to work a load out of me that would flood his chest and face.

I roared like a beast as I slid on and off his cock, the intense pleasure ruining me, making me quake like I'd been starving for that butt fuck for decades. Damn, he made me want to ejaculate, but I held back, only giving him the pre-cum he worked out of me with the strength of his prodding prick. The string of glistening semen connected my cockhead to his ribs, some pooling in the gutters of his abdomen and chest center. Every time he pushed his cock into me, I leaked a little more. The bulbous head of his dick fucked me so fantastically, pushing the pent up sperm toward its exit. I could feel the electrical charges beginning to ignite.

Nykolson was noticeably gazing up at me, keeping his eyes locked on the muscles across my torso. Pensively observing. I maintained the show, making sure my abdomen flexed and rolled with each stride I'd taken on his stone hard cock. Nykolson moaned as my channel gripped and pulled him in. Sucking for his sperm. He reciprocated the pleasure he must have felt with a growl, "Gah, Dayum. I want you to take my spud."

Wholly satisfied, I rode that dick, squeezing it, sucking it with my ass. I held his cock inside of me, taking his stiff boner as deep as I could make it go, grinding my butt cheeks over his hips on the downslide. My mouth sprung open and I uncontrollably moaned, noises erupting from within me, getting louder with each stride. Riding, I pushed his orgasm to ignition. My own greediness kicked in and I wanted his semen, wished his seed would burst through that rubber jacket and sperm fill my ass channel. I secretly murmured, *"Breed me."*

"Fu-HUck!" Nykolson howled. "We need to stop or I'm going to cum inside you right now." He gripped my hips, restraining my perfect rhythm.

With my pre-cum leaking cock throbbing against Nykolson's black six-pack, I forced myself to hold steady. I was quaking, my legs shaking, finding it difficult to contain the internal orgasm Nykolson had inflicted on me. Every bit of me cried out to continue riding his deeply implanted erection. I had to have it. Wanted it. Needed it. My damn, I wanted his black sperm swimming inside me. I mumbled out loud, "Fuck me, Nykolson. Pummel my hole."

Nykolson pinched his eyes shut while pulling me to him by the nape of my neck. He kissed me and I kissed back. It had begun innocent, but quickly exploded into fevered osculating jaws. I'd begun to lose my shit, nearly crying from being fully impaled. With his slippery tongue in one end and his oily dick in the other, I'd been pushed to orgasmic overkill. I wanted to cum on him as much as I wanted him ejaculating into my manhole.

By itself, I could feel my rear channel sucking on Nykolson's buried erection, impatiently trying to draw semen from his nuts.

My asshole was on fire. I couldn't stop its enthusiasm and I was amazed my rectum was capable of giving such a skillful blowjob. There was an uptick in our lust, quickly changing from smooth and gentle to hard and nasty butt fucking, like bad-ass men would have done during a sweltering moment—coming upon an overpowering need to screw each other's brains out and spit our juicy loads.

Keeping our connection secure at first, I spun around on Nykolson's hard-on, faced his feet and then pulled off his dick with a sputtering pop. Nykolson's thick black dick sprung back and struck his abdomen with a sloppy smack. He gasped with a tone of surprise and muttered, "Wha' the fuck?"

I steadied myself on my hands and knees, aiming my primed sphincter right at him. Looking over my shoulder I found his head lifted off the pillow, catching him peeking at my lubricated knot while tugging on my sagging nuts. My tenderized bullet hole was opening and closing, flexing as if it was missing his dick.

He whispered, "That hole. So fucking sweet." Then I felt him poking what I thought to have been three fingers into me, maybe four. My furnace hot hole had gone to town, sucking aggressively on the digits he'd sunk into me.

I hoarsely ordered, "Oh yeah, use my hole. Pull that hand out and drive that fucking cock into me. Come on. I need your black dick jammed back into my slick chute." Who knew I could have been such a bossy bottom, and the way Nykolson urgently reacted, he fucking loved the way I ordered him around. I dropped to my elbows, my ass lifting, my sphincter opening and closing, begging for his big black dick to return home.

The mattress shifted when Nykolson crawled on his knees behind me and pushed the bulbous head of his cock against my stretched out hole, teasing me with pokes and prods. Then, I felt his head slipping in, and then—

He made me holler, "Fuck an A-oooaaAAH," as he drove his fat black dick inside me all at once, to the brink, as far as he could go. He ground into me, scrubbing my butt cheeks with the course hair at the base of his dick. My back door opened up and pulled him in like a vacuum switched on high, cocksucking his dick, wildly craving the release of his man-spunk. He pushed forward while holding me firmly at my hips with both his hands, reaming me hard and fast. In and out. His thighs crashing into the back of mine. Out low hanging balls slammed together as they swung back and forth under me.

Nykolson suddenly struck my butt cheek with an open hand. I jerked and hollered, "Fuck yeah." The surprise assault had caused me to immediately tense, my channel gripping his cock like a steel vice, instantly becoming tight from the shocking blow.

"Gah, Dayum. Fucking Gah, dayum, your hole got tight," he groaned.

I unclenched and pushed backward into each of his forward thrusts, taking every thick inch of his extended erection. The sensation of being split wide open felt incredible to me. I never imagined I'd have liked it so much.

Nykolson howled, groaned and even grunted, biting his bottom lip as he fucked me. He repeatedly pulled his hips back and pushed forward with hard grinding thrusts.

I'd gone crazy as I accepted all of him. He was a master fucker if he'd known it or not. I could feel it in the way he pummeled my hole.

My entire body shook with unrestrained enthusiasm while Nykolson's cock drilled me, drawing out and jamming back in. We seemed to move in perfect rhythm, rocking, pumping, thumping, pushing and pulling. He was a flawless top, fucking the shit out of me with masterful precision. I was hooked on bottoming for my man and knew I'd want it again, very, very soon.

I felt Nykolson dig deep, extremely deep, hiding his cock to the root. Claiming and owning me. I squeezed my ass around his erection, but that trick hadn't stopped him from pulling out and holding the crown snuggly against my shining star, teasing me with tiny jabs, then asking if I wanted it stuffed inside me again.

He had me shaking by then and I cried out, "Fuck yeah. Don't leave me like this? Shove it in, Nykolson. Fuck me hard. Ruin my hole." I pushed backward when I couldn't stand the emptiness another fucking second, taking every massive inch of Nykolson's stone hard cock, making me stand out as if I'd been a power bottom all along. Putting that thick cock back where it belonged had given me the sensation of feeling totally full. The pressure stimulated my prostate into body burning pleasure. I felt like I was cumming.

"Fucking shit, that ass is nice," Nykolson thundered. I sensed the invasion of his entire dick. He pulled back and rammed it back in, jigging me forward at every thump. Then he picked up the pace, plowing me, in and out like a jackhammer, pummeling me like I'd begged him to do. He rumbled, "Milk my cock with your tight ass. Make me cum in your hole, Mikey."

Mimicking the last time, his dirty talk triggered a part of me that made me turn crazy. I ranted, "Fuck my ass, Nykolson. Stick my virgin butt with your huge black cock. I need to know what it's like having a man ejaculating in my ass." I thrust back and forth over Nykolson's dick, pulling off it and then making it go back in. I realized at that moment I was a total cock slut, and it was his dick that made me feel the way I had. Perhaps the feeling was because of his skillful fucking. He was that good. I'd never wanted it like that before, never imagined I had such drive in me to have a man put his cock into my butthole. It was Nykolson who made everything work just right, turning me into the bottom man I had no idea I was.

Nykolson's face changed quickly—knotting up like he was in pain. He groaned, "Gah dayum. I'm gonna cum, Mikey. But I need to see your face and I want to kiss you when I lose my load."

Even though I was in a great position on all fours, I was more than happy to flip over and see him looking down on me when the time had come for him to ejaculate. I rolled over and passed Nykolson a lopsided grin, gripped each knee and spread my legs. I ordered, "It's all yours, you fabulous black fucker. Dig in and give me your cum." I quickly gripped one butt cheek and pulled, opening up my hairy crack, exposing my slippery fuck hole for Nykolson. I felt a cool breeze grace my button, causing it to flex like smooching lips.

Nykolson moved forward on his knees, grabbed me by the ankles and spread my legs wider. "Damn nice fuck hole from this angle," he commented, breathing heavily as he brushed the hairy trail of my taint with the crown of his rubber covered dick. He then pressed his dick head against my sphincter, appearing eager to get back inside me. I heard him comment, "Fuck, you're one hairy fucker down there."

Breathing hard, I replied, "Can't help that. I'm all man. Your man. Don't you like it?" I pulled one knee to my chest and let Nykolson push my other into my armpit. My ass lifted.

"Gawd no, I fucking love your hole just the way it is. I like to know I'm fucking a man. Hold still a minute. Let me take in what's mine." Nykolson popped the head of his cock inside me, pumping small jabs back and forth at first before plunging all the way in.

I howled when he entered, "Fuck me-eeee-aaAH!" Then I slammed my head backward into the mattress out of sheer enjoyment. My mouth flew open, panting from the thorough pleasure of being plowed by somebody I could love.

Nykolson bulldozed into me, again and again and again, pummeling hard, then backing down slowly, changing the speed and the aggressive power of his artistic thrusts. He wasn't stopping, seemed as though he wanted me to feel every inch of him, to make me his cock lover forever. My eyes must have appeared as if they were about to pop out of their sockets when he plowed into me even harder than before, torturing my prostate as though he was aiming to fulfill my every desire and make me cum indefinitely.

I watched Nykolson's magnificent body shift above me, moving rhythmically like a trained dancer. I couldn't help absorb every bit of him as he bore into my body with magnificent precision. I admired the width of his shoulders, the bulk of his chest, and the crunching knolls of his six-pack as he pushed his hips into me. I let Nykolson use me the way he needed to, and at the same time allowed myself to enjoy being penetrated for the first time in a very long while. He felt so amazing and made every part of my body feel so good. His talented technique helped me understand what I'd been missing all those years.

He'd driven into me with enthusiastic thrusts, pounding roughly, stroking my magic spot over and over again with his perfectly up-curved dick. I moaned and cursed, "Fuck! Fuck, I'm close. Fuck the cum out of me. Keep it going."

Feeling the tidal wave of pleasure coming on fast, my mouth had blown open but hung silently. I could no longer voice how great he felt. I gripped my cock and stroked it. I was about to burst. Then I roared and my body convulsed on cue. Nykolson kept fucking, building momentum as I reached the summit of my own release.

Nykolson bared his teeth, roaring as his face contorted into something savage. Spit flung when he shook his head. Wolf-like, he growled, as if letting me know his pelvis had started buzzing, and by his grizzly actions coming down on me, I knew the electric shock waves were on the verge of shooting up his spine to his brain and back down to his prostate. I'd been there many times myself. I knew what was going on. Then it happened. With violent words, he shrieked, "Gah Dayum! FUCK! I'm cumming up your sweet fucking ass." He collapsed on top of me, ravaging my mouth, kissing me in a beastly manner, sucking and blowing air like an enraged gorilla. He dug into my mouth with his tongue while he blew his entire load of hot semen into the condom up my fiery chute. His pelvis jerked and ground into me. His harsh vocals matched each spurt, "Huh. Huh. Huh. Huh-huh." His body had gone stiff as a board, back arching, his pubic bone pressing tightly into me.

I hadn't wanted to miss my beautiful man loose his shit. I lifted him up and watched him empty his semen into me. His tight body jolted, muscles bunched. His thick dick still inserted deep inside me, spurting. I heard the throaty roars turning raspy as his embedded cock tried splitting me in two.

His actions over top of me had proven erotic. I lost control to hang on. I cried, "I'm gonna cum. Don't pull out." The flood gates had suddenly broken open and my jiz rumbled free, swimming like hungry sharks toward the head of my dick. My pelvis had gone numb, and my pubic hair seemed to have burst into flames. "Fuck! Here it comes," I groaned.

My torso crunched as I jerked forward, letting out a menacing growl. My boiling hot semen shot clear over my shoulders, and pearly ropes lashed my chest and abs, oozing like burning molten down the sides of my ribs. As Nykolson thrust his hips into me, I'd fallen deeper in love. I couldn't get enough of him. He fit me perfectly as he topped me so hard.

Cum had sprayed everywhere, stringing me and the bedding with white juicy pearls.

From our previous engagements, Nykolson found out how much semen I'd produced, but what he'd seen spurting outside of a condom must have blown his mind.

He kissed me, licking my sperm that lashed my mouth and face.

When my gasping finally settled and my heart rate slowed, Nykolson collapsed on top of me and quietly whispered with labored breaths, "That was a first for me in a very long time and one damned awesome fuck I'll never forget."

Eventually our breathing evened out, and I relaxed in Nykolson's arms. "Your first, huh? I never would have thought since you were a fucking maniac. An awesome fucking machine. That was a damn fine fuck I won't ever forget. Now that you had used my butt, dumped a hot load up my hole, I'd say that technically makes me your personal cum dumpster."

Nykolson nibbled my lips. "Damn straight. I mean. Damn gay. Aagh... Never mind. Make that a yes!" His scattered reply made me chuckle, and the sensation of laughter and the final stages of my orgasm made my brain strangely tingle.

Then he added, "You were a brilliant bottom, Mikey. The best I'd ever had. That tight ass wrapped around my dick and your perfectly hairy body beneath me had given me the grit to fuck you like that. I never want to give that up. I need you, Michael. All to myself. Can I keep you?"

Those words were what I wanted to hear and my body's reaction from what he'd said was automatic. I'd instantly gone hard again.

I then nibbled Nykolson's lips and mumbled, "Damn straight. I mean. Damn gay. Aagh... Make that a yes!"

He'd given one last thrust of his hips, sinking all of his lengthy inches into me. I felt his erection glide well beyond my six-pack. My firm body was accepting. I clenched and hollered, "Gah, Dayum, that's good. FUCK! Don't pull out yet."

Chapter 23

My best times had been with Nykolson by far, which was why my evenings with him had always flown by so quickly. It'd always been known that time flew when having a good stretch.

I couldn't believe the night had already gone by. It had turned into the next day before I knew it, and I was back at the office doing the same old day after day crap. The more time I spent away from Nykolson, the more I realized how much I disliked being at work. I used to like my job—maybe because I hadn't anything else to look forward to. But... with Nykolson in the picture, my entire outlook on how I saw things had changed. He was my priority. My job wasn't anymore.

"Jeez, I need coffee."

When I strolled from my office to the kitchen to get a second cup of morning brew, I felt like I was dragging ass. If I had turned to look, I'd have surely seen my own butt cheeks tiresomely lagging on the floor a few feet behind me.

I cringed when I heard, "Mister Mike? Might I have a word with you?"

As expected, I turned around and saw Berdella standing there. I couldn't tell by the tone of her voice if she wanted to have a fist fight or a civilized confrontation. She was the only one who called me Mike, which I hadn't minded. The short name made me feel that much more disconnected to her, almost as though she was addressing somebody else.

We were in the office kitchen at the time, and even though I hadn't felt like getting into it with Berdella again, nor had I wanted to have been anywhere close to her, I still made the effort to turn around and greet her with minimal kindness. I stood rousing my totally black and sugarless coffee with a mini straw. Stirring black coffee was a habit of mine, simply to cool it down before I made that first tongue numbing sip.

Since Berdella was blocking my way out of the kitchen, I leaned back against the countertop, resting my glutes against the ledge next to the sink. I just looked at her and kept my mouth shut. I hadn't had anything but bad words to say, and if I'd said anything, she might have started crying or grasped those invisible pearls strung around her neck like she'd done the last time I'd spoken with her. In my head I thought, *"What the Sam hell do you want now?"*

"May I?" Berdella stepped to my side and reached for her coffee mug that had been drying overnight in the rack beside the sink.

Crossing one foot over the other, I slid my rear end along the edge of the countertop, stopping about two feet from where I had been. As I moved aside, I blew into my mug before taking a cautious sip. *"Oh the goodness!"* Its flavor and hotness helped me feel more relaxed, like I'd just received a warm hug and had been told everything was going to be all right.

I wanted to get the heck out of there, but figured I might as well give the lady a chance to redeem herself, *if* that was what she had planned, and *if* she was even capable of that. I patiently waited, getting annoyed by the second while I'd taken another sip of my superhot coffee.

She started out by saying, "This is not a makeup session, which if it was, I wouldn't expect you to change how you feel about me. There's been a lot of animosity between us, practically from the very first day we met, and I want to put all that behind us. Especially now that we've seen how ugly things can get around here. I'd like to clear the air between me and you and start fresh."

"Fresh start my hairy asshole. No the fuck, way." I'd rather she'd done her thing and left me the fuck alone to do mine. I just stared at Berdella, couldn't bring myself to find truth in anything she said, or anything she had ever said for that matter. The lady

had faked many apologies before, but her screwed up personality never allowed her to follow through on any of her promises for the long haul. She had all the signs of manic depression syndrome — smiling at me one minute, and suddenly growling at me the next. That drove me bat-shit. It was as if she'd forgotten to be friendly or mad at certain times of the day, not limiting them to Mondays, Wednesdays, and Thursdays, or was it Tuesdays and Fridays. Then she'd do it all over again, but switch the days and times. She confused the shit out of me most of the time because I wouldn't know which day I was the bad guy or knew the reason why. There was more to her than my eyes and ears were able to identify. I was sure of it. The twisted bitch had been up to no good, and I wasn't about to become her target as I had been with Sandra Dee. For all I knew, the two of them had consorted together, and Berdella was pissed that she was left standing in the office alone. She had nobody, and if she thought I was going to be her next ear for gossip, she had another thing coming. *"I don't think so!"*

I'd always thought Berdella was a little crazy, evident by her unexpected behavioral shifts. Almost every confrontation I had with her sent my head rambling with, *"What's it going to be today, Berdella? Are you my friend? Are you not my friend? Either you hate me or you don't. Stop leaving me hanging somewhere in the middle, wondering if you're going to like or dislike me today."* She was all over the place with her extreme mood swings, suddenly biting my head off about something silly one minute, and then ten minutes later calling me sweetie as if nothing had ever happened. *Um... What?"* I'd always been playing Russian roulette with Berdella, never knowing when the barrel had that dreadful bullet engaged and aimed at my skull.

The animosity Berdella had mentioned was pretty much all her doing if she realized it or not. I'd decided to give in to that bipolar moment in the kitchen, gone in with a nicer approach, and said, "Okay. Let's clear the air, shall we?" I had come off almost as snarky as she had been to me so many times in the past, and I honestly couldn't have cared less I sounded that way.

I let Berdella talk without interrupting her. She made it clear to me that whatever I heard from Sandrine Dexter hadn't come from her, which I'd known most of that was a lie since there were certain things I had only said to Berdella had mysteriously been mentioned to me by Sandra Dee at a later time. There had never been any truth to what Berdella ever said, which meant it was going to take a lot for me to believe whatever she was planning on feeding me was going to be portrayed as heartfelt and honest. There was an apology attempt out of her that pertained to the time she called me a honkey faggot, which I think meant I was a backwoods cannibalistic gay man. My guess was as good as anybody else's as to what that really meant. On a related note, that title Berdella had given me a few days back was mentioned during my interrogation with the FBI. I'd been told Sandrine had it in a file she kept on me. As far as I knew, Berdella was the only one who'd known about that horrid nickname she'd given me, had probably come up with it at the spur of the moment, and during her stint of anger toward me, had run off and fed the pet name to Sandra Dee.

In the kitchen, Berdella spilled the cream and then dropped the sugar packet when she was adding both to her coffee. That indicated to me she must have been a little bit nervous about what she was going to say next, or for all I knew, she was nervous about something else. I tilted my head to one side, giving her a lifted eyebrowed glare that indicated I wanted her to hurry up and say what she pulled me aside to talk about. By the slow motion mechanics I'd detected coming out of her, I figured she hadn't absorbed the drift of my expression. Then she'd finally spoken about Sandrine. "For the record," —what record?— "I had no part in Sandra Dee not liking you." What a liar. News flash, bitch, "Yeah, ya did."

Looking back on what I'd seen, and some of the garbage the FBI had confirmed to me, I was aware Berdella instigated Sandra Dee's thought process on much of the human race. I hadn't realized Sandra Dee disliked me that much until a of couple days ago when the FBI told me she seemed to have a hate scale for gay men and I was at the top of her list.

Then Berdella told me she had no idea Sandra Dee was hacking into people's lives and trying to take what didn't belong to her, that Sandra was on her own with all of that. I believed her. Sort of. Otherwise I figured Berdella would have been hauled away right along with Sandra Dee, or... I mean, Sandrine Dexter.

Berdella's voice had been shaking a little when she said, "I don't feel good about much of what I talked to her about, but trust me when I tell you, Mike, I didn't say anything to her about you and Nykolson, or discussed your perver..." — she stopped herself — "your chosen way of life." Her face went sour as if she had smelled her own fart.

"*My CHOSEN way of life? Ugh. You make me want to vomit.*" I refused to believe the B.S. that had come out of her shit lined lipsticked mouth, and of course she'd say that since Sandrine was unable to defend herself or call her out on any of the lying. Regardless, Berdella had her reasons for being dishonest all the time, and I couldn't have cared two shits about it anymore. She was only isolating herself from everyone, and all the crap she pulled would come back around soon enough to take her down, and from what I could tell, it seemed to have already started. Part of her probably knew that, which might have been the reason she pulled me aside and started her very own damage control.

When she told me Sandra Dee was who initially said I was a fag, I hadn't believed that either. Berdella had made lude comments to me about my man ass-banging ways well before Miss Dee had started working at the Cumberland Probation & Parole Offices. I found it amusing how she couldn't keep her lies cohesive or the timelines of them in order. The more bullshit she drummed up, the tougher it must have been to keep them all organized.

Berdella asked me if I had planned on saying anything or commenting on the subject, but honestly, what was the point in doing that. She had her mind set, and it would only start a different argument between us, so I left it at that and just said, "No."

Then that familiar look of Berdella's had been released, the one where her eyes had gone dark and her upper lip curled like she smelled her own dirty ass fart again. She was upset that I wasn't agreeing with her or letting her off the hook so easily. Could I have held her accountable for what she'd done to me? Probably not. I had no solid proof, and there was no reason to, but I sure as shit was planning on adding more distance between the two of us, even had she started calling me sweetie again. Jeez, I really hated hearing her call me sweetie. The title wasn't going to fly with me anymore and I'd rather she called me a honkey faggot. At least that was coming from the heart and she meant what she said.

I was no detective, but I'd become convinced Berdella "Deville" had a sinister agenda behind her false compassion. Somebody like her doesn't just change overnight. My thoughts on the reason for her anger with life were, she's a middle aged virgin, or she's pissed at me for being so openly gay and she doesn't have the balls to come out herself, which led me to believe, she might have been after Sandra's twat for quite some time, yet wasn't good enough at being a lesbian to scissor leg the sister the way Sandra wanted. All of the above explained her resentment toward me, "the honkey faggot," and I wouldn't have put it past her to have become a member of the same man hating club Sandrine Dexter had been part of. Shoot, for all I'd known, she might even hold the title as the ring leader who recruited Sandrine.

I thought it was time I'd done some digging.

Chapter 24

Nathaniel and Nykolson were standing on the front porch as though they'd planned on waiting for me once I arrived. I couldn't help but notice how good-looking they were in identical low rise denims and no shirt. A positive appearance that stopped me in my tracks, but prevented my, "Honey, I'm home," entrance I'd been antsy about doing. But damn, damn, damn, it was nice driving up and seeing those two beautiful creatures looking back at me half dressed. The best part of my homecomings—one of them was my boyfriend. How'd that happen? I had no idea. I'm just a simple suit, and he's an A&F model without question, and I guarantee that's not only my opinion.

I stepped up to the twins and jokingly said, "Which one of you is mine?"

I'd gotten the perfect response out of one of them, which included a sweet lip to lip pressure peck, and I hoped it was from the man I'd slept with, even though, I wouldn't have objected had it been from the other brother. They were both as handsome in every way, so whoever laid that kiss on me, it wouldn't have made a bit of difference. When the kisser reached down and cupped my ass with a full strength down the middle of my butt crack squeeze without being shy about applying a three fingered grope to my covered bullet hole, I knew I had my man, and, "Damn, I needed that."—The kiss and the, I want to fuck that asshole again grope.

As we walked inside, I mentioned I was in need of a stiff

drink due to the day I had, but Nathaniel said, "Tonight I thought we'd drink fruit punch instead."

That had better been a name for an adult beverage with a boozy twist, because Kool-Aid is for kids, and I really wanted to get my drink on. "Who the hell at our age drinks fruit punch?"

Nykolson laughed, "Aw, ma-an. We do. We love the stuff."

I hadn't disagreed with that. I remembered enjoying the stuff and having a red mustache all my life as a kid during summertime. But now? How would I explain that one, and who would have taken me seriously when I showed up for work with a thick red caterpillar under my nose? Meh, "All right. I'm in. Bring on the punch."

When Nathaniel actually brought out a glass pitcher filled with red fruit punch he'd prepared that afternoon, the back of my throat cracked right before an out loud laugh had broken loose. "Holy shit, you two were serious about the fruit juice?" I'd gotten an echoing, "Uhm. Like, yeah," out of them both, and then they glanced at each other as if one was standing in front of a mirror and the reflection had done the exact same thing. Jeez, I'll never get over how incredibly identical they were and how that twin shit was really going to fuck with my beautiful mind.

"Let me see that." Luring the pitcher of punch to be passed my way, I rolled my hand inwardly in front of me. "I've got to do this." I drew the iconic smiley face on the outside of the glass decanter. Nykolson was amazed at its likeness and called me quite the artist.

I pulled my phone. "Don't move it. I need to get a photo, document that I'm actually about to drink my childhood summer cool down." After snapping the picture, I stood there at the island and fumbled with my phone, trying to figure out social media on the damned thing, but since I hadn't set up my accounts on my business phone, I was having a heck of a time searching for what I was looking for.

Nykolson noticed my nimble frustration and asked, "You seem like you're searching for a fish in the desert. What are you trying to do?"

His analogy made me laugh and my disjointed answer was, "I should really put Facebook on this fucking thing."

"What? Really? Who doesn't have their social media on

their phone?" Nykolson's surprised expression had indicated he found it abnormal I hadn't linked my accounts to my cell, but I never added them because I preferred keeping my personal life out of the hands of my business life. "It's a company phone, that's why."

"Yeah, but... I can help you add them. Plus you can always purge everything before returning the phone." Nykolson held out his hand, but I refrained from passing him my cell. I just held it, causing him to look at me funny while he questioned, "Are you planning on putting that picture on it?"

Adding the photo I'd just taken might have seemed like the reason for trying to access Facebook without a login, but I let him know I was thinking about doing a quick social media search on, Sandrine Dexter and Berdella "Cruella" Hutcherson, to see if they were linked as friends and belonged to a few of the same groups.

The chuckling tone of his voice had gone higher during his surprised, "What the fuck?" reaction. "Are you serious with that name or are you having me on? That can't be real. Are you Serious?"

I answered, "Dead serious," but immediately told him I added the nickname, Cruella, for obvious reasons.

He quickly remembered who Berdella was from what I'd briefly told him, and she was who he first met when he'd come to the office. As for Sandrine Dexter, Nykolson clearly knew who she was due to recent events, so with that tidbit of knowledge, I figured his WTF outburst was meant for Cruella, only. Nykolson agreed to help me out with doing some digging on those two, and with a sudden movement that surprised me, he'd taken off down the hallway lickety-split after kissing me on the cheek at the uprise. I very much loved when he'd done that. It was charming and helped me feel connected to him while he was away. I'd purposely left his wetness where he'd put it just so I could feel a part of him on me. I believed he felt the same way and had been his reason for always popping me with a cheeky kiss before he split.

He returned carrying his laptop, and I saw his browser home page powering up as he passed by me and Nathaniel standing at the kitchen island. He rolled a hand through empty space as he walked, beckoning for us to follow him over to the sofa.

He put the laptop on the table in front of him where he sat, leaned back and with a pat of his hand on the cushion, had given me the order to have a seat between his legs. No objections from me of course, so I followed his direction and sat where he wanted me to sit. It felt amazing when he leaned forward and pressed his chest against my back, wrapped his arms around me and gently stroked a hand up and down my abdomen before tucking four fingers down the front of my pants.

Trying to ignore the incredible sensation I was feeling from his touch, I chicken pecked the keyboard and searched for Kool-Aid. I'd gotten the love chills when he nibbled my neck and ear, saying with a smirk in his voice, "Are you really looking for a way to turn your fruit punch into an alcoholic beverage? I thought you needed Facebook to search out criminals?" He lifted my shirt a little bit higher and ran his fingers up my abdomen to my chest. I could barely make out what he'd said when he whispered into my ear, but thought it was, "Damn, I love your hairy chest."

Nathaniel, whom which I'd once again forgotten about because Nykolson was giving me so much of his undivided attention, commented, "You guys are confusing the shit out of me with the whole bottom and top thing again. The way you have yourself wrapped around Michael, I'm beginning to think you are banging his ass now?"

I glanced at Nathaniel. "Don't be silly. I'd told you before, there's no way of knowing who's riding the pony simply by looking at them, or by observing their actions. Things aren't always what they seem, Nathaniel. Trust me. For your journal you seem to be writing, this little white guy is pounding your big black brother." There was something arousing about sharing our sexual positions with Nykolson's twin, and I'd gotten a bit of a stiffy after telling him who's doing whom. What I failed to tell him, and he didn't need to know, was that his brother had recently put me on the bottom and fucked me. I couldn't bear to confuse him any more than he already had been on that subject.

As if Nykolson had become disturbed when I'd given up the truth, which his brother had already known, he pulled his hand from my chest and covered my mouth. Within a split moment, I grabbed his hand and put it back where I'd rather it stayed—

caressing my hairy chest he liked so much.

His hot breathy whisper upside my ear mentioning I'd been doing a damn good job at fucking him had sent vibrations through my body that added strength to the erection trying to come to life between my legs. I should have shushed him about how well he thought I fucked him, but I couldn't. I wouldn't. I liked hearing it. Plus, I knew it was the truth.

Settling down from the erotic breathy fire in my ear and the hand petting my chest, I questioned myself, "Whew. Okay now. Where was I?" My train of thought had been blown out the window many moments back for obvious reasons. I had to clear my throat after that one.

When I typed Facebook.com/ into the search field and waited for the browser to open the link I was looking for, the system brought up Nykolson's login credentials, which wasn't surprising since it was his laptop I was using. I leaned back into him, resting my hands on his knees and before I asked if it was okay to clear and continue, he punched the enter key that had taken us to his home page. I couldn't believe I hadn't looked him up yet, but since I had the real thing, it never dawned on me to nose around in his posted business. I commented on his profile photo, "Of course, another effing gorgeous picture. Do you ever have a hideous head shot?" Then I smiled when he said, "It'll be even more gorgeous once I have you in a photo with me."

"Pffft. Okay. Like. Whatever." I sounded like a snob nosed schoolgirl when I said that, and when Nathaniel rolled his eyes, I wanted to take back my silly reaction. But I mainly added that to hide behind my embarrassment for being addressed as anything but average. Sure I'd always thought I was a decent looking guy, but never anything more than that, the way Nykolson continued to assure me. He really thought I was something special to look at, made me feel good about myself in ways nobody had ever done, and I was beginning to like him more and more because of that. Who doesn't like to feel special?

I shifted forward and said, "Let's get this hunt started. See what those bitches have been up to." I rubbed my hands together, giving off a greedy air, typed Berdella's name into the search field, that of which had populated quite a long list. If there was no face to identify her, I'd have to click on every one of them to find the wench.

Cocooning me with his body, Nykolson narrowed the search by retyping her name with the addition of a city and state. I hadn't realized that was possible, but it appeared to have worked.

I scrolled for a couple of pages and found a profile within the city displaying a brief description that seemed to have matched her disturbing personality. The photo used was that of Rosie the Riveter — that Iconic poster was all about woman power, so the profile had to have been her. I clicked it open and found a lot of junky posts. Like a lot of useless junk and stuff. Mostly meme cards stating her opinion on how she thought this and that should be. Of course none of it was her personal thoughts, just a cluster fuck of shared messages from other people's pages. I saw a few things I recognized, like food recipes she'd brought into work and a few printed messages that I had also seen pinned at her desk. Yep, that was her all right. It had to have been. However, since she was supposedly a church lady and a "Christian" woman, I was astonished by some of the things she had posted. That lady subliminally displayed hate for the human race more than the devil would have.

After about fifteen minutes of looking at garbage on Berdella's wall, I needed to move along. "Okay, I've seen enough of this beyotch's crap. Let's see what's going on with Saaandraaa Deeee." I sang her name as I typed Sandrine Dexter, and then S Dexter, and moved on to Sandrine and then just Dexter. It seemed that every one of them were completely nonexistent. Not a single one populated. How was that possible?

The intelligent side of my brain told me the FBI had shut them all down. I figured that to have been the scenario over somebody reporting her for pinning lewd snapshots or vulgar messages. Facebook was most likely ordered to lock those pages up after what had just taken place. I could have probably bet both my peach sized balls on that, and that's saying something solid because I'm in love with my hairy balls. It probably goes without saying, my balls were an additional reason Nykolson had become attracted to me, so losing them would amount to a big downer for the both of us. I could tell he found joy in them as much as I had. I knew that by the way he pushed my hand away so he could hold them during the night while we slept. Might I add that cradling black hand under my nuts was comforting? Not a question.

I was so positive that the FBI closed all the Sandrine Dexter accounts that I hadn't even flinched at taking back the bet I made against my big hairy balls. I was that sure, otherwise there would have been one or two accounts up and running.

That idea had taken me back a few months when my Facebook page was abruptly shut down. There was no reason or notice of any kind, just a populated web message stating it was closed. At the time I figured somebody hadn't cared for one of the shirtless men I posted, or two men kissing, or the hideous one of me on the beach wearing only a pair of board shorts, giving whomever a reason to report me. I had simply snubbed it off as some sort of a glitch, never giving it another thought. After all that's been going on, I'd gone ahead and bet my nine inch boner I was being scoped out by the FBI to find out if Sandra Dee's account was connected to me in some way. Realizing that could have been the case, I panicked over being a suspect in such a major criminal case. Who knew, and it goes to show, nothing is out of the FBIs reach.

It had taken a good week before my profile was reinstated, and again, there was no explanation or notice from Facebook advising what the reason for the shutdown was. I hadn't believed I'd ever come to know why, and honestly at the time it happened, I hadn't cared. I'd never really been a Face-booker, only used it for stupid shit because I found it was just a place for people to brag or be nosey. For that reason, I rarely, if ever put anything personal on my wall, and when I had the time, or if I felt like it, I posted some stupid crap that nobody cared about anyway. That I could tell by the few likes I'd gotten.

Nykolson agreed with me when I mentioned my suspicions regarding Sandrine's Facebook account, so he told me to give Google and twitter a try. I was stunned to find the shutdown carried over to those social accounts as well. Not a single Sandrine Dexter. That seemed impossible. There had to have been at least one in the world, and I was practically living next door to one of them, so I knew the name had to exist somewhere.

Since Facebook was the most popular network of them all, I'd gone back to it and tried to find a group that those two might have belonged to. I searched. No women of power. No man hater clubs. No groups for bitches, or mean girls. I was at a loss. Ready to poop out. How was I supposed to find a group I had no idea existed. Maybe I wasn't educated enough with Facebook to figure that shit out.

Nykolson told me to try the name of Berdella's poster girl with the red bandana and pumped up bicep muscle.

So that I did.

I typed, Rosie The Riveter.

Chapter 25

"Holy shit," flew out of my mouth before I had a chance to stop it. A group popped up and it had to have been what we were looking for. It was an all-women's power group. The description stated it was a place for women only. We three had dicks, big ones, so there was no way we were entering as ourselves. *"How the shit were we going to find somebody who would let us in?"* and fast.

I wasn't favorable with making any dishonest moves. I had a hard time with that, but Nathaniel hadn't seemed to have any issues at all. That was noticeable when he spun the laptop toward himself and said, "People create fake accounts all the time. Let me get into that group. Give me a name."

I jumped in. "Wait!"

Nykolson blurted, "Ah... What?"

"This is so not good. Maybe we can figure things out by reviewing Berdella's page. There should be enough there to see if she had anything to do with putting the screws to me."

Nathaniel said, "Highly unlikely. She doesn't seem like the type of person who would let her churchy friends know she's a sneaky bitch, so my guess would be she's done it all as an alias. Give me a name to create?"

"I don't know about this. I feel like I'm being as dirty as she's been." I was so uneasy about what we were about to do, I'd forgotten why we were prying into her business in the first place.

"Go back to the group." I leaned toward the screen. "I want to see the types of names they have as members. There were a few on the first page, and might be all that exist. If there's any pattern, we can pick one similar that'll make it easier for us to be accepted." The screen flashed when Nathaniel refreshed Rosie The Riveter's introduction page.

I scanned the names on the list, and by the powers of men, there was a Cruella listed as an administrator. I had a laugh about that name, finding it apropos to have been listed as one of the evil queens, giving no thought that it could have actually been Berdella until Nykolson pointed it out. He practically pushed me to the floor when he lurched forward and punched the screen with his finger, hollering, "No fucking way. Berdella Cruella De Ville. Could that be her? I really need to say this. What. The. Fuck?"

As he grabbed me around the waist to keep me from hitting the floor, I huffed, "It can't be this easy, can it?" I privately nicknamed her that, never telling her, yet she might have chosen the alias for herself, thinking it suited her as much as I thought it had. We were about to find out with one simple tap of the mouse pad if that was her.

"What'cha gonna do, boi-ee?" Nathaniel sang. Whoa, he actually had a great voice.

I mentioned there might have been no need to hack into the private group as impostors after all—a relief to me. I hadn't felt good about doing that at all and preferred to keep our slippery back door invasion honest. Somehow, honest and slippery invasion hadn't seemed as though they belonged in the same sentence. Too late and whatever. We were on a mission to put a stop to a hate crime. That's when I moved the pointer and had taken a stab at Cruella's picture posted on the introductory wall. It hyperlinked straight to the profile we were hoping to find.

The profile photo was not of Berdella, which had come as no surprise, but displayed the well-known teeth baring Cruella from the animated Disney version. That was our first clue the profile would display a lot of anger. The banner was a bunch of black spots on a white background, presumed to have been the fur of a Dalmatian dog the bad woman wanted to make a coat out of. Appropriate, yet deceiving as to what we might find while moving through the profile.

There was a top pinned photo of Rosie The Riveter. Not a

surprise with that either since the profile we had been looking at was most likely created as the sole purpose of being part of a secret group, putting on a disguise so others wouldn't know who she really was. I refrained from calling her out on that since we were about to do the same thing. Luckily we'd found another way to get what we needed, and we were still considered decent people.

The more we scrolled through Cruella's profile, the more we'd noticed a ton of similarities to Berdella's account. Mainly, the posted memes on both had matched, and some of the verbiage written had come across as being the same person. We had no proof yet that Cruella was Berdella, but all the signs of the obvious were presented right there in front of us as if put up in Broadway lights. There were so many vicious messages about gay men, and men in general that it baffled the shit out of me.

What the shit had happened to those women? How could they despise men so much?

Then the kicker to the puzzle showed its ugly face and my heart just about stopped beating. That bitch was a fool, made stupid moves and I could easily frame her for the one we ended up finding.

I opened a conversation between Cruella and another person by the name of Miz D, and a single exchanged word was my clue that Berdella was consorting with Sandra Dee. Yep, there it was. "Honkey F*****." Even with the –aggot blocked out, I knew what it said, and that they were talking about me. Some of the messages were clear as day, even without the use of names. Her comment about, *"The honkey f**g**t in the office doing the nasty with a criminal"*, only confirmed she was referring to Nykolson taking my dick up his ass. I hadn't much cared because it was the truth. I liked it up his ass and he certainly liked taking it up his ass, so the statement was fine with me that I was giving it to him up the ass. The only thing I hadn't liked was the H.F. label, but since I'd labeled her a cunt, we were even. I tapped the screen over top of that message and told Nykolson, "This here? Is about me and you."

He asked what made me think that, which I replied, "She called me a honkey faggot in the office, and Sandra Dee had me labeled with it on some list she'd been keeping."

I clicked on the highlighted Miz D, but it hadn't gone any place as if the laptop had frozen solid. I banged my finger against the mouse pad several times as if I was sending signals by Morse code to somebody in the past. I'd become determined to get to that profile if it had taken me all damned day.

Nykolson had soon placed his hand over mine to stop me from my continued efforts that clearly weren't getting me anywhere. With the inability to make the hyperlink open, I was sure it would have gone to Sandrine's alias, and it had been closed out by the FBI due to an I.P. possibly linking to her home PC. I wasn't sure about that, but it was a good guess for an amateur and made a heck of a lot of sense. It was all coming together. I felt we had those wenches cornered.

I'd gone back to reading more of Cruella's page with all the garbage about her opinions on men, how she loathed them, and commented they all deserved to be coats hanging in her closet, very similar to the real Cruella's ideas pertaining to furry little animals, however, her brain had shifted to where mister Hannibal Lector left off. That lady was sick. Really needed help, sick.

Everything posted, I could have placed myself into the comment and it would have appeared she was directly pointing me out. I'd given her kudos for being smart there, as it would have most likely led to finding out whom she really was if a name had been mentioned. I couldn't believe how much Berdella hated me.

I heard Nykolson buzz, his warm breath in my ear again, "Jeez. You weren't kidding about this lady. She is definitely a bad seed." He wrapped his arms around me and kissed my temple. Twice. The second time holding his lips there as if letting me know, He Got Me.

My reply to that was, "I told you. This shit here only demonstrates how much worse she is than I thought. I'm truly stunned she posted all this shit in a public place. What a fool."

"She seems to be the type of person who wants to get her voice heard, but too ashamed to do it out in the open." Nykolson rubbed my shoulders as if he was consoling me. Gawd he always felt good when he put his hands on me. My anger toward Berdella had grown, so the upper arm massage he'd given me helped tremendously.

"A sneaky bitch is what she is. A double sided sword." I clarified my thoughts on her twisted personality, pointing out how she'd befriended a person directly to their face, with an ultimate intention of taking them down behind their back at a moment they weren't looking. I'd sworn to the guys there was something going on with her, I just hadn't been able to put my finger on it.

As I continued scrolling through her wall, fast and slow, trying to bypass all the junk that was simply stupid and downright hateful, I found an older message, clearly in code, that I was sure had been directed at Mizz D. It appeared to have been about somebody who'd caused her heartache, an old pussy bumping flame of hers who seemed not to want her anymore, chose a man over her, and now she wanted help setting the woman straight. No wonder she hated men. One had stolen her pink bumper car.

After all I'd seen on that laptop, I was almost certain Berdella had a little bit to do with Sandra Dee's plan at stealing people's identities. If not directly, she helped feed her what she needed. There was too much evidence—though on the weak side—in her profile that suggested she had carried the flame somewhere along the trek to the games. She might have been blind to the entire scam, which could have been why the FBI hadn't dragged her in that day alongside Sandra. Whatever the case might have been, I knew the lady resented me and Nykolson because we were together. I totally understood that based on the recent discovery where she lost the woman of her dreams to someone with a real dick. A man.

Tired of what we had been doing, I lay back against Nykolson's warm chest and huffed, "Now that I know Berdella had it in for me and the reason why, I've had enough of this detective work, for now. Er, wait. One more thing." I immediately returned to the laptop, searched for my wall under Nykolson's account and clicked send friend request. "Now I'm finished."

Nykolson wrapped his arms around me again, pulling me back against his chest, his kisses pecking at my neck caused me to collapse to my weakest. *"Fuck, I was fucked – again."*

Chapter 26

Once I'd moved the laptop out of the way, Nykolson placed the heels of my stocking feet onto the sofa table in front of us. I had done the same without asking, adjusting myself between his legs with my back to him. It made the whole experience lying in Nykolson's arms that much more enjoyable. I felt him breathing while sensing his heartbeat trying to synchronize with mine. Even though his bodily surface was hard and lumpy, I could have lain there against his chest all night. He was that comforting. His hand moved back under my shirt, dragging a gentle finger up and down the trail at the center of my abdomen and caressing the hair on my chest when he moved it from side to side. His touch—Amazing!

"Kool-Aid, please." I jokingly stretched my arm forward with a snapping finger.

Nathaniel had taken me seriously or had the gentleman gene bred into him. He'd intuitively gotten up from where he'd been sitting and brought mine and Nykolson's punch right to us.

"You guys are pathetic," Nathaniel firmly noted. So much for being gentlemanly.

I related to his comment since my ass had the best spot out of the three of us. Sitting comfortably, I looked up at Nathaniel and mentioned, "All we need now is a good movie and some popcorn. Be a dear and…" I was joking of course, but if he'd taken me seriously with that too, I'd have been okay with that.

Nathaniel had given me a sideways pirate's eye squint.

"Really? You think my black ass is going to make your white butt popcorn now? Isn't it enough I brought you Kool-Aid?" I felt Nykolson quaking under me, my body bouncing as he laughed at his brother's references.

Nykolson begged, "Pleeease. I can't move." Nor had I wanted him to.

"Just stay put. I'll feed you two hobos. But if I catch the two of you mating when I get back, nobody's getting shit from me." He pointed at us, air scribbling his finger from Nykolson to me a few times. "I'm good with what you've got going on here, but I'm certainly not ready to see you two boinking each other yet."

Good-humoredly, I smirked. "Yet, huh? Care to watc..."

By the time Nykolson had his hand over my mouth to stop me from saying anything more, Nathaniel had called me a charming idiot along with giving me the fuck-you finger once again. I knew he hadn't meant any harm when he walked out of the room saying, "The gays. Always gotta be settin' dah trends."

I laughed.

Nykolson pinched my nipple at the same time he licked my ear.

"Gah, Dayum." He might have thought that would have put my mouth to rest, but instead, that nip twist had gone straight to my dick and I'd felt it swelling.

I'd stolen Nykolson's drink from him, set both his and mine on the table, and spun to face him. Our chests pressed against each other's with my lips lightly touching his. I'd spoken quietly into his slightly open mouth, "You make me so hard. All I want to do right now is get those legs of yours over my shoulders so I can power plow that ass." I kissed Nykolson lightly, and had teasingly given him just a little taste of my tongue.

He talked back softly, "You're so fucking hot, Michael Millhouse. Why do you say shit like that at a time I can't give it up? You know damn well I want that fucker bulldozing my ass, but, "you know who" is too close for comfort. You heard the man. No popcorn if he catches you beefing me in the ass on this sofa." Nykolson had given my butt cheek a good harsh squeeze. It stung a bit, but damn I liked it. Rough play must have been my thing.

No doubt I wanted to hide my cock in Nykolson — he seemed ready, too — but I knew it wasn't the place or the time. His debate about getting my dick all up inside him made me laugh. I wasn't really going to do it with his brother watching, "yet," but it was worth getting Nathaniel's reaction on the whole man-on-man action plan when I said it.

I assured Nykolson, "Okay, we'll resort to sweet kisses instead, but once I get you behind those bedroom doors, that sweet ass is mine to do whatever I want with it." I sensed Nykolson's dick repeatedly pulsating against my abdomen as if he was already spurting sperm. He trembled under me and said, "Fuck, Michael. You've got my asshole twitching. I don't know if I can wait for the movie to end."

I joked, "Well you're gonna have to, cuz I want popcorn." I swiftly sucked his nipple and sat beside him. That nip made him whine a whisper, "Damnit, Mikey. You know that makes my dick hard. Shit. I felt that one in my asshole, which now wants that cock of yours more than ever. It might be best if you get off of me."

I was right there with Nykolson at trying to fight a hard-on. I grabbed one of the throw pillows next to me and put it in my lap, planning to keep my lasting erection hidden from Nathaniel when he returned. I was anything but modest around Nykolson, but Nathaniel might not have been too thrilled with what grows between my legs when his brother gets me aroused.

Popcorn let off an aroma that I'd always found comforting. That buttered smell over kernel corn brought back some of the most enjoyable memories I had as a kid. I breathed the warmth in deeply as I listened to the popping sound coming from the kitchen. All of that made my boner deflate, giving me assurance I was able to ditch the pillow.

Nykolson hollered, "Yo, asshole brother of mine. Do you have a movie in mind or are we going to review the channel lineup together?"

"I don't. Go ahead and pick something." Nathaniel was on his way back, carrying two big bowls of popcorn, presumably one for him and the other for Nykolson and me to share.

As I watched Nykolson scroll through the list, I noticed he was becoming agitated with how few movie selections there were out of the nine hundred available networks. He exaggerated, "I don't know why we pay for this shittin' cable service when there's not a thing on any of the billion and one channels we subscribe to. We'd seen everything available about fifty-two times in the past four days. This is crazy shit. I'm canceling it tomorrow. Streaming is the future."

Laughing, Nathaniel mentioned, "You've said that every night since we had the service installed. Go back to channel five hundred and let me see what's in the premium guide."

"I haven't seen all of the latest Tarzan movie yet. What about that one?" I'd spoken up when I saw it flash by, really wanting to see it again—for obvious reasons, and my decision to watch that particular movie wasn't based on the adorable animals running beside Tarzan.

Nathaniel looked at me and smirked. "Of course you do. That guy is stacked solid. Keep going. We can always come back to that if nothing else is on. Let me know if you see any action flicks?"

"Tarzan is full of action. Meaningful action," I said. "I especially like the jungle scene when all the elephants show up." Nykolson smirked at me, glancing from his dick to my eyes. He quietly mouthed, *"of course you do."*

"Of course you'd say that," Nathaniel repeated, still clicking the clicker.

Then I excitedly shouted, "Oh hey... Batman versus Superman. Have either of you seen it?"

That's when they both looked at me, and Nykolson snarled, "We've tried watching it about twelve times, maybe more, but we both continue to doze off about thirty minutes into it. It's a bit dark and pointless. But... Henry Cavill is fucking hot. I'd watch him in an action flick any day of the week."

That remark had gotten me to gruffly look at Nykolson and grumble, "Uh... excuse me?"

Nykolson popped a few kernels into his mouth that almost prevented him from saying, "But you are way hotter, Hun." He rubbed my thigh and squeezed my knee.

Nathaniel chuckled at Nykolson. "Yo-Ass got busted. Can't be speaking out loud like that anymore. Gotsta respect the boyfriend when he's around."

Then I commented, "He saved his ass is what he just did." I weaved my arm under his and patted his thigh. "Keep going, we aren't watching that." I sort of made it clear to Nykolson just then, there'd be no more fantasizing about any white men unless it was about me. Straight up.

It appeared to me there were only two decent movie choices. One we weren't watching because Henry Cavill was in it, and since I resembled the man in many ways, and knowing Nykolson gets turned on by a man with chest hair, my jealous self wasn't going to risk losing him to that beautiful creature in a blue and red spandex suit.

That protective streak brought us back to, "The Legend of Tarzan," which was like soft porn since the lead star was half naked during a good share of the film.

"Tarzan it is," Nathaniel grumbled, followed by a tone that sounded depressing. "I suppose I will have a few minutes with Jane. There is a Jane in this one isn't there?" Hearing Nathaniel mention a female sounded strange to me, only because of the way my mind worked. My attraction was toward other men. With that, I understood how one male found another attractive, but it was strangely odd to me how a man could find sexual fascination in a person with no dick. In my head, I viewed everybody as gay until evident signs showed they were otherwise. Most people I'd figure out immediately, others had taken some time.

I'd become surprised we all made it through the entire film without passing out, or me trying to hump Nykolson, or stick my hand down his pants and stroke that marvelous dick of his. I watched the movie wide awake, not wanting to miss a moment of that ape man running through the jungle and swimming the rivers without a shirt on. If that man's skin tone was that of milk chocolate, I would have totally been hooked. Thank all get out I have my own jungle man who howls as loudly as Tarzan does when being seriously screwed by a hairier being than he himself.

When the movie credits started scrolling from bottom to top, Nathaniel mentioned how much he liked the film — that it wasn't what he'd expected, and it was probably the best version of Tarzan he'd seen. I interrupted, by blurting out, "Holy shit! It's eleven o'clock?"

Nykolson yawned. "Tis... definitely bed time."

ശ ഇ

Nykolson lay back on his side of the bed, appearing exhausted. He rolled his head to look at me where I lay next to him. My eyes already locked on his striking face, his heavy lids dropping as if he was about to crash into a deep, deep, sleep.

Looking into his eyes, I mentioned, "You aren't falling asleep on me, are you?" I fisted my dick, slowly stroking it. I was a horny top and really needed to stick my dick into my man to get my rocks off.

I threw the bedcovers off of Nykolson, revealing every part of his naked body as he laid face up, one arm behind his head, looking sexier than shit to me. I rolled over, landing on top of him, purposely brushing his chest with the hair on mine—arousing him as I knew it would. I'd given him gentle kisses as I sunk between his opening legs, my rock hard dick battling with his, ready to jet-spit my sperm all over him. I knew I'd never get tired of seeing my pearly white semen splashing across his chocolate skin. It was so fucking erotic, and I couldn't wait for the day he let me blow it up his ass without a condom. That right there was total connection with another man and would permanently seal the deal at making him mine.

"That movie was more stimulating than I expected," I confessed. "I'm so fucking hot for you right now that this might not take but a few minutes to ejaculate. I'll probably cum the second the head of my dick starts its journey into you." I dropped the bottle of lube and the magnum to the bed at Nykolson's side and gone back to kissing him. Our mouths tenderly kneaded each other's, transferring sweet and genuine passion. My breathing increased. I wanted to be deep inside Nykolson, moving nice and slow, giving him my love, so passionately, so romantically, making sure he felt me connecting with him, all the way to his beating heart.

As if he'd heard my every thought, he whispered, "I want to feel you, Michael. No separation."

If he was saying what I had just been thinking, I wanted that, too. But was it safe? I rocked against him, sliding my stiff cock alongside his, keeping us both stone hard. I softly asked,

"You sure we'll be okay?" My tone softened even more, "I mean..."

Nykolson placed a thumb to my lips and leisurely nodded. His voice sounded breathy and quiet, "I'm certain, Michael. I've never let another man enter me the way I want you to. How about you? All good?"

There was something about Nykolson I trusted. I completely believed he was being truthful with me, even though I had only known him for a few days. I knew for sure I was harmless, and I needed him to trust me when I told him I was, and not think I was saying that simply because he confessed himself to me, or because I really wanted to empty myself inside him without a rubber sheath that would keep us apart.

I kissed him with tenderness that prefaced my softening voice. "Yes, Nykolson Kannon, I'm certain. You'll be my first encounter with unembellished entry and I'm glad I waited for you. I'll be sure to pull out before I ejaculate."

He chuckled, "Good thinking. I don't want you to get me pregnant."

Smiling, because it was funny, I shut him up with a kiss.

The anticipation of finally penetrating another man completely raw had ruined me. I almost emitted semen by the mere thought of what we were aiming to pull off. I couldn't wait another moment to enter and make love to the man under me, slide my uncovered dick inside him, moving slowly, giving him what he wanted.

I gazed down on Nykolson as I reached for the lubricant and saturated my stone hard dick with both stroking hands—slowly gliding my fists back and forth, shafting myself gracefully to maintain the mood of emotional love.

I laid my body back down on top of Nykolson, placing each one of his legs over my shoulders to lift his rear end where I needed it. I kissed one side of his jaw, then his other, ending with a gentler connection from my lips against his. I reached between us and gripped my dick, hard as stone and slick as an oil stick, located his sweet knot with my slippery crown and pushed into him slowly, so, so, slowly. His flexing ring accepted and wheedled me in. His mouth sprung open with a sharp grunt that turned to a softer moan as I begun to hide my erection. As I slid into him, there had come another strident gasp before his lungs steadily emptied in harmony with my slow gliding cock. A raspy groan seemed to crawl from his throat. "Ye-eaah, Fuh-huck, Mike-eeey. Give it to me nice and slow. Make me feel every solid inch."

Moving slowly at first, then quickly changing my rhythm, jamming my pelvis into him. He hollered, "Fuck!" from the repetitive thumping of my hard hitting hips when I forced my dick deeper.

Flesh against flesh felt incredibly different—total pleasure, romantically raw and sensual.

I'd begun to ease my erection in and out of Nykolson with tenderness, the sensation entirely unbelievable as he gripped me, one so new I couldn't explain. I started losing control, feeling the surge of my orgasm evolving. I knew from the start it wouldn't take but a few minutes to empty my dick and I was so ready to pump my sperm inside Nykolson as long as he'd let me. Every muscle in my body had gone taut and I growled, "O-oh Ga-awd! I knew you'd feel this good."

I violently sucked air from Nykolson's lungs as I kissed him. I groaned again, "Oh my Gawd, I'm close to cumming." I stopped moving for a moment so I could make our new connection last a little bit longer.

Nykolson's eyes had glazed over. He gasped. Then he whispered, "Stay, Michael. Stay inside me when you do."

Those words pushed me to my limit and I collapsed on top of him. My slow sensual strokes ceased and I released a gruff growl. Then that familiar rush hit me and I'd gone light headed, and the searing sensation ripped through my pelvis. My abs instinctively crunched, reacting as it should when naturally breeding was about to take place, forcing my body to curl forward over his, driving my hips into Nykolson so tightly and holding me there. I jerked and hoarsely huffed as the semen within me raced at lightning speed from my strangled soul.

Nykolson's ass stroked all up and down my dick, sucking and pulling like it was trying to yank the sucker off, hungry to feel my load blown up his hole. What his ass had done to my cock had fucked me up. The surge had begun and there was no pulling back.

I pressed my mouth to his. Our kissing furious. I grunted

and groaned from the intensity of my increasing orgasm.

My cock was totally embedded in Nykolson, expanding and contracting as I felt surges of my sperm shooting into the deepest part of him. I growled again, followed by roaring, "Cumming," — I huffed — "inside you." Spurt after spurt after dominant spurt had raced through my cock, determined to breed my Nykolson.

"OhmiGawd," I coughed out. I was heaving, and gasping. Moaning and jerking. It was all so glorious. Growls of pleasure mounted even louder than my tone already had. Gritty roaring expelled as I pumped fertile semen from me to him.

I was no longer in control of my pelvis as it viciously clung to him. I could hardly breathe. My ass cheeks tightened like solid boulders, forcing my dick to drive deeper. My back bowed as I furiously pumped so much sperm into Nykolson that it overflowed from his manhole, leaving his ass cheeks dripping with my ejected juices. I was pumping and shooting and creaming one massive load after another. Every part of my body had turned rock hard, and I clung to him as if we were glued together. I couldn't have pulled back if I tried. The intensity of my orgasm firmly pinned my hips to him, my dimpled ass pushing inward, locking me into a breeding position until I was done. It was a cum dump, and my man was getting every jet.

I'd gone on growling like a savage lion while blowing spurt after gushing spurt inside his slickened chute. "Gah damn. Suck my cock with that ass. Take my spud." I was firmly buried inside him, still, pressed against his butt so tightly I felt as though my nuts were inside him too. My body had taken over, not allowing my connection to break. I rocked into him, yet almost holding still, firmly thumping his ass, steadily pressing against his taint as my prostate squeezed gob after gob into his hot black hole. My mouth remained agape. I gasped and growled like a gorilla until the last wad spit from my cock. "Oh, fuck. Jeez. You feel so fucking good." My entire body trembled with each gush I injected into my man.

Nykolson grumbled he was cumming, too. His body jerked violently under me as his throat let out raspy rumbles from the increasing pleasure I had been putting him through. He was squirming and thrusting upward into me. Crying out at the same time. I felt his trapped dick pulse with each spurt he let go of, discharging his funky wetness between us, soaking both our torsos and chests.

His hands had a tight grip on me, digging into my shoulders, holding me in place. He growled, "Don't... slide out. I want... it all."

There was no chance of pulling out. Everything I felt seemed as it should. His channel clenched me tightly, stroking my deeply penetrated erection, naturally sucking until I had nothing more to give. My kisses soon relaxed, taking us to a gentler place, more caring than shameless. I'd never wanted from anybody what I had done at that moment with Nykolson. He was who I had saved that superior exchange for and I was grateful he let me share the experience with him.

Slowly, we moved together, my dick smoothly gliding in and out of him, partaking in a motion that unified us. My whisper to him was beyond sincere, "I could stay inside you forever, Nykolson. I really could. I'd never in my life felt anything that extraordinary. I have to have you as mine. Forever."

His response was what I wanted to hear. His voice low and earnest, "You just gave me an exquisite part of you that no one else ever had. There's no separating us now, Michael. You're inside me and forever will stay."

I lay on top of Nykolson, kissing him with such desire that I wasn't feeling like a single person anymore. I hadn't realized I could have been so aligned with someone as much as I was with Nykolson. It was as if my body had become part of his and his had become part of mine, sharing an intimate moment that transformed us into a single living being.

Was it possible to have become that coupled with someone in such a few short days? To me it was clearly conceivable, and tells me we were destined to be together.

With the intention of leaving as much of my semen where I'd injected it, I pulled out of Nykolson as slowly as I was able, wanting my sperm to stay, as in keeping my territory marked. I heard him release a depressing sigh as I snaked my dick from his gripping channel. Then he released a disparaging huff the moment the head of my dick popped out.

I smiled down on him. "It's all right. I left plenty of me inside you. Plus, I have lots more where that came from. This fertile cock will be slithering back into that sweet hole again very soon. You and I both know that."

I kissed him softly.

"I'm in love. I'm in love. I'm fucking in love."

Chapter 27

I strolled into the office, passing Berdella, purposely ignoring her phony, "good morning, Mike." I just couldn't reply, or even look at her after what I knew she'd been doing on social media. I heard her mumble, "Whatever."

That empty response from me had done it. She was back to her normal deceitful self, and I was glad about that—I hadn't wanted anything to do with her anyway. Not anymore.

Part of me hadn't cared about her mumbling, nor had I wanted that fresh start she'd mentioned. That was all a bunch of crap, and as I'd found out, that lady was going to town on Facebook behind my back, still.

I'd viewed Berdella differently after what I'd come across on her fake Facebook wall. I was completely disgusted with her after finding all the garbage she'd subliminally posted about me and other people. She was really angry with life, her own mostly, and by the way it appeared, angry at many other people because their lives seemed better than her own. I decided to stay clear of the lady from that point moving forward, since my instincts were telling me the front door was going to be broken down by more FBI agents at any moment, and she was next in line to be hauled away just like Sandrine Dexter had been. I was certain it would only be a matter of time, and for her not to think the same, was crazy. If she had been connected somehow to the recent events, I couldn't for the life of me figure out why she was still hanging around after what the bureau had done to Miz D. I had still been trying to wrap my head around that shit, understanding she was really stupid, or utterly crazy in the head.

I'd met Ashlund in the kitchen, not intentionally, but he'd been there when I arrived to fill my cup with java Joe. I said, "Hey," instead of good morning. His reply was the same as mine. I never really cared for that insensitive style of hello, but that morning was all I felt like saying.

Ashlund stepped to my side, pressed his shoulder against mine, and as if we were in an act of espionage, he whispered, "Meet me in my office as soon as you get settled."

The level of my adrenaline spiked to an immediate high, anxious to hear what on earth he had to tell me that deserved such a sexy whisper? My mind ran porn wild with the scenario of Ashlund asking if Nykolson and I would consider a threesome. That was not going to happen. My dick and body belonged to Nykolson, and Nykolson's belonged only to me. I wasn't sharing him with anyone. I'd shaken the image of us three getting it on from my thoughts and told him, "Lead the way, I'll follow you from here."

"Oh lawd, here we go." I started feeling hot, like my blood pressure had risen and I hadn't even had issues with hypertension. I'm too young for that shit. I had no reason to have felt that way, but since I had one fucked up imagination, my busted thoughts had taken me on a joyride they shouldn't have been on and I was thinking perhaps he decided he wanted to stick his dick into me at the same time Nykolson had.

Ashlund closed the door and squeezed passed me to get to his desk. He wasn't one who normally shut his door, and with that, made me think he was really up to something no good. Was I right? Had I felt an erection against my butt cheek as he rubbed against me to get by? My gay mind had gone porn wild. How stressed out was I? Apparently, very, since my sudden sexual thoughts included the only friend I'd ever had here. I was being ridiculous, but with all the crazy shit that had been happening around the office, a three way rendezvous with a good friend wasn't too farfetched. I really needed to write a book with all my fucked up thoughts. It'd probably make it on the New York Times best seller list.

He started by telling me to pull a chair around the desk and take a seat next to him. If I had spoken at that moment, my voice would have cracked. The singing in my head announced nothing was going to happen, we were in a public place, at work no less, and he was my friend.

Holding my coffee in both hands as if I was cold, I'd taken a noisy sip. I'd done it more as a distraction than anything else, but normally I'd subconsciously done that to cool my sip with an air filled slurp.

"Cool it, Michael." Nobody in the room wants to fuck you.

I set my coffee mug down on the corner of Ashlund's desk where I found an empty spot, gripped hold of the chair and dragged it around to his side of the desk, not too close, but enough so I could see his screen if that was the reason he wanted me to sit down next to him. He grabbed the arm, and pulled it closer.

"Oh Lawd, this is it. Why not just shove me under the desk between your legs, already?"

What the fuck was wrong with me? I hadn't given him any reason to think I'd be interested, so there was no need for me to be creating such a ridiculous story in my noggin. I was sure that maneuver was strictly business—it had to have been. Taking into consideration I had passed Nykolson's file over to him, he probably simply had a few questions he wanted to go over with me. That's all.

I was glad to find out both the ideas whirling in my head were incorrect. It wasn't about him wanting to get closer to me or had anything to do with Nykolson. He wanted to show me a few items he'd found on Berdella and Sandra Dee. Little had Ashlund known, Nykolson and I had already discovered the two ladies were consorting with one another, however, his searches were internal, where ours were through public social media, which were probably fifty percent bullshit and the truth elaborated over the top.

He slipped in, "Can I trust you?"

But before I could answer or hold out my pinky swear finger, he opened up a file on his PC. Within a few clicks, I couldn't believe what I had seen. My jaw dropped. Like hit the damn floor, dropped. It was more incriminating than I had anticipated, and it hadn't stopped with Berdella and Sandrine.

"Holy, sum-bitch! All three of them were in on it?" I was honestly flabbergasted, not expecting any of what I'd seen, and couldn't comprehend those people were stupid enough to be using the office PCs to carrier out their dirty work. It was a total game changer after what I'd witnessed, and at that moment, I hadn't cared to be part of the office anymore. At that very moment, my fucked up fantasy bubble that included Ashlund banging me, burst. Thank the Lord. I was not having that.

Was the entire place corrupt? It certainly appeared as though it had been.

All I wanted to do was get the fuck out of there before I'd gotten roped into the mess those three yay-hoo's had plummeted themselves into. How they thought they'd have gotten away with what they had been doing was outside of my way of thinking.

We were in Ashlund's office behind a closed door, but I still felt the need to whisper, "Should we say something? Alert the FBI? If we don't, they might think we're in on this crap, too. Especially you, now that the information is all over your system."

Ashlund continued staring at his screen. "No need to. I'm sure they already have this stuff and had put the puzzle together, just waiting for the right time to strike and nab the rest of this motley crew. But, the next time they show up, this entire place is coming down. I can pretty much guarantee that."

I finally dared to ask, "How'd you get hold of all this and how the shit did you figure out what they were doing by all the rubbished messages between them? It hardly made any sense until you drew me this picture."

Ashlund admitted he had access to everybody's PC as of yesterday. He himself had at one time been a PC technician and was able to hook into any PC as long as he had access to the main server they were connected to. He wasn't a big time hacker, but able to crack lightweight invasions such as connecting as if transmitting through an approved network.

"Jeez. I didn't know that about you." I looked at Ashlund who was grinning back at me.

Moving on.

"Why did they start with the weakest link, and why had they not taken them all at the same time? If you think about it, the others have time to hit the highroad."

I wasn't expecting an answer from Ashlund, but he said, "I'm no detective, but the FBI has their reasons for how they operate, so I wouldn't put it past them to have what they need already and are waiting for the right moment to strike. My guess is they came in here to stir up the beehive with a single poke of a stick, irritating one insect that would get the rest of them to start buzzing around and lead them to the queen — the one they really want. The way the head master works is they have their worker bees doing all the shit work, buzzing and gathering bits and pieces out in the open, so if anything goes wrong, they're the ones who get killed, and the queen is still hidden somewhere underground, free to move on and start all over again with new bee's."

I never would have been able to figuring out what Ashlund had if I'd come across it myself, but he seemed brilliant at reading between the lines and coming up with conclusive evidence that the three amigos were thieves. "What tipped you off?" I asked.

Ashlund seemed proud of his hacking skills by the way he eagerly answered, "All the messages between them were encrypted in ways only the three of them knew how to decipher, and using their thought process, it wasn't too difficult to figure out what they were doing. Sandrine was the weakest and they knew it. The two leaders seemed to have covered their tracks a bit more than Sandra Dee had. My thoughts on that is, they made Sandrine do the dirty work, making sure all the details moved through her system and not theirs. Now... people, especially the weak ones blab under pressure, so I'm figuring Sandra Dee had caved under the heat lamps and had given out who her sources and teammates are. The FBI will be working quickly now that they have the weakest worker bee. Meaning, I anticipate the FBI will be busting those doors down soon. Be ready. Five, four, three..." He was actually dropping fingers as if he truly knew the clock was counting down at that very moment.

What happened next was the real shocker.

Pulling us away from the PC, we heard shouting. We both stood and I yipped, "What the fuck?"

Ashland then said, "Shit. Soon. Like now. Three, two, one. Move."

Chapter 28

I'd said it again, "What the fuck?"

There was pounding coming from the front entry, as if the doors were coming down by force of a cow herd. I'd have shit my pants if I'd actually heard mooing. Deep voices hollered, "Stand down," and a crash that sounded like plastic shit skidding across the floor and ricocheting off walls.

I'd recognized Berdella's voice crying out as if she was being ass reamed by a prison gang. That would have been disturbing for me to see, yet well-deserved since I already knew that wasn't something she would have enjoyed. Could it have been she was nabbed by the Bureau so soon after Sandrine? Sandra Dee must have broken down under pressure and spilled the beans like Ashlund said she would. I presumed Mizz D ratted her accomplices out with the bright idea there'd have been no way on the green planet she was going down alone.

We hadn't moved very far from Ashlund's office doorway after we heard the ruckus in Berdella's station. There hadn't been much reason too, and hell-to-the-no were we getting hit by flying debris that she or the blue coats were tossing around the freaking room. Staying put was the best idea we had. By the yellow block lettered acronym on the backs of the blue jackets, it was easy to identify the blue coats were FBI. They'd come back to wrangle Berdella to the ground, giving her the full treatment of a true criminal. By the way it appeared with all the scattered shit around the entryway, the bitch must have tried to make a run for the door after her stupid attempt at destroying evidence.

They had her pinned in a position that wouldn't allow her to go anywhere, bent forward with two agents holding her from behind, one gripping her cuffed wrists and the other pushing her face into the counter top. Her beehive hairdo had been quickly turned into a birds nest, and from what I could see, her makeup had been smudged like a frosted cake had been dropped and picked back up. The facial paint was all over the place, and what was most comical, was the streaking line of red lipstick running up her left cheek and over her eye. It looked like Freddy Kruger had gotten to her and that was clear evidence they'd crossed paths in her nightmare.

That moment should have been a highlight of my life when I saw her forced over the counter top and slapped with restraints, deserving of being in that position for all the shit she'd done to people. Any other time, or under nimbler circumstances, I would have laughed, but I was too freaked out by what had been happening to carry through with getting a kick out of seeing her like that. I do have some compassion.

An FBI invasion within our city wasn't normal day to day activity, and witnessing such an act less than twenty feet away was rather startling. For all I knew, bullets would have flown if that wench decided to lose her mind and gone all ape shit on their asses.

Scattered on the floor in a million pieces, I could see Berdella had really tried to destroy evidence stored on her PC by throwing it across the room like she was a bad-ass gorilla whipping a clump of bananas at onlookers behind a glass wall. It surprised me she had done such a thing, and I'd taken that as being one stupid felonious stunt. Had she thought the FBI was actually after that? I could pretty much guarantee they had connected to her computer before storming in the place, and had all the evidence they needed to incriminate her before barging through the door, which would have been why they had come to tag team her ass so soon after hauling Sandrine Dexter off to jail.

There'd been two Bureau raids in less than a week, and it was anybody's guess if there would come a third. My guess would have been, not. A third bust would amount to a lost cause since the perps would have been long gone by then after the follow up raid had gone down.

Berdella seemed to have been second in command with the operation she was involved in, so I couldn't imagine what had been taking place upstairs on the fourth floor with first in command. I imagined the fourth floor judge was most likely being hog tied too, probably more violently than Ms. Berdella Cruella.

As far as I could tell from what Ashlund had shown me, the judge was the ring leader of the entire operation, coaching Sandra Dee on channeling money outside the country to his own and the mobs accounts. The entire situation was startling and I couldn't fathom it was taking place right in front of us, nor could I believe it included somebody we knew. These were incidences only seen on television, not under our own roof, so close to home. How the shit had we not seen any of it all these months, or years. Jeez. When had it all started?

There were about ten men in the front office, maybe more, most of them FBI officials, and a few others I presumed were detectives. I wasn't sure.

While I focused on the Berdella throw down, Ashlund was also tuned in on the action taking place, and the few times he glanced at me, his expression was definitely the same as my *"holy-shit-damn-son-of-a-bitch!"* face.

There had been a lot of robotic voices coming from communication devises, dishing out crackled orders to handle this and that. I couldn't tell what was being said through all the scattered radio noises trying to outperform the other.

Among all the noise, an agent had ordered Ashlund and me to stand back and not touch anything until we were escorted out of the building. We'd been quarantined as if we had an infectious disease, not allowed to go anywhere until strip searched, examined, and approved for release.

Even though I had nothing to do with what had been happening, my nerve endings pricked my flesh as if I was being bitten by a thousand fire ants. For all I knew, I'd been selected as a suspect until proven innocent. I knew very well I wasn't guilty of anything, but that still had my securities slightly shattered. I'd always been fine on my own when facing unusual scenarios, but I recently had become so aligned with Nykolson that I felt the need to have him closer to me. All I wanted at the moment was to call him, to hear the comfort of his voice, be smothered by my boyfriend's support. Being put in such a situation made me realize how much I liked that man and needed him by my side. Like a real couple.

"Oh my gawd. Was I falling in love with Nykolson already?" My entire body was telling me I was. But wasn't it too soon for that? Not if we were truly soul mates, which I was certain we were.

While Ashlund and I wore our invisible restraints, other colleague's in the office had been told the same thing we had, to stay put until proven innocent. Most of them appeared as though they had just witnessed a bloody murder, their mouths wide open and hands clutching their chests. A few were whispering amongst each other. If I hadn't known what I already knew, I suppose my face would have been just as long as theirs. Sweet little Miss Beasley was crying.

I started preparing myself for more questioning, but hoped the FBI had collected all that was needed the last time they were in the office. That had gotten me to think they had more on me than what was on the PC in my office. Because of Berdella and Sandrine's scheme of getting rich quick, the FBI had to have sneakily invaded every part of my life, or at least deeper than they typically would have. It was a no brainer my office PC had been hacked, and I was ninety-nine percent certain my personal computer and cell had been picked at, too. In fact, I probably accepted an agent or two as friends on Facebook and unknowingly helped them investigate everybody at the office. I had nothing to hide, but still worried that one little word or phrase could have been taken out of context and that would have put me in a position of being hog tied right next to the judge and Berdella. I suddenly felt violated, like I'd been standing naked on the golden gate bridge, which had caused me to unconsciously fold my arms across my chest to help make myself feel less exposed.

"Oh gawd." That's when I started to think an error could have been made and I'd have been considered part of the deviants who had started all the shit. I'd have been fingerprinted, tried by jury, found guilty of a crime I hadn't committed, and been sent to prison to become the receiver of a butt fucking rotation machine. There would have been where my sweet tight ass would belong to

Bubba, Jimmy Joe, Harley, Axel and Daddy tattoo, and with my luck, their dicks would have been the size of my entire arm. "Oh, Lawd."

Breaking me out of my loon crazed trance, an agent tapped my arm and corralled me to another part of the office. I was pulled one way, and Ashalund had been tugged another. We weren't the criminals, but it sure seemed that way. Damn that wench.

Then I was alone, feeling even more vulnerable than I had been before. I just wanted the whole thing to have come to an end. My distress was turning into anger, all because of someone else's stupid actions. That turned my thought over to Nykolson and how he'd been tossed into a similar situation because of Dajana and her stupid actions. He hadn't done anything, but because of her, he'd been thrown in the slammer.

The FBI agent—whose belt hooked badge spelled out, Benjamin Bradford Barry—escorted me halfway to freedom where which I figured he'd question me before my big release. His name flowed off the tongue so smoothly, and made me think of a performance actor. It was catchy, very memorable and I liked it. He was handsome, too, so I hoped I wouldn't stutter when giving answers.

As expected, Mister Triple B had asked me the same questions as somebody else had the other day. That right there had proven every investigating agent at the bureau assigned to the case knew everything about me, and the one asking the questions was most likely looking to see if I would change any of my answers, catching me in a lie, or two, or three. I had no reason to fib the first time, nor had reason to bullshit anybody the second time around.

Thankfully, it was a short interrogation, and quickly after, I was led to the far wall at the front entry. I was labeled with a white tag to my lapel, which I figured meant I was free to go. I wasn't too certain about that, though, since nobody mentioned a single thing about it or what the next step would have been. They left us lingering in shades of gray. In my mind, white usually meant the good side, where any other color probably indicated something different, like, *"Bitch, you are going down. Enjoy prison and your new boyfriend."* That's when I pictured Bubba with a greased up arm and Axel coming up behind him with his dick nearly reaching the floor. I was scared all over again. I almost blacked out, but having a white tag, I'd gone with white equaled positive. Even trying to remain optimistic, my nerves had caught fire again and I knew then just how cattle must have felt right before the slaughter. Note to self: Time to become a vegetarian.

I glanced around the lobby in search of Ashlund, but couldn't see him anywhere. I was hoping he had already been sent out the door, and if not, prayed he wasn't cell blocked with chains connecting his ankles to his wrists. That would have sent me packing and on the forward path of trusting no one. I silently begged, "C-mon, c-mon, c-mon. Where the fuck are you?"

My heart settled when I finally spotted Ashlund coming around the corner with that glorious white tag attached to his chest. I wanted to jump up and down like a giddy school girl, let him know I was an angel just like him, but of course, that spastic display of excitement would have been over the top, and most likely produced a pistol pointing contest right at me if I had. Sudden disruption at a time like that was not good, so I kept my thrill of being release along with my closest friend on the down-low.

Ashlund joined me in the same cattle-like line up. A couple people stood between us, however, hadn't stopped either of us from passing an optimistic smile to one another. I winked at him as well because it was in my nature to do so and I wanted him to know I was fine.

Berdella had still been in the office when we were released, which was a total surprise that the FBI hadn't hauled her out of there or moved her to a more secluded location by Paddywagon. But my guess for not doing that was to let her wallow in humiliation for what she'd done. Cops and agents love doing that shit.

She was sitting in her own office chair with her hands cuffed behind her back, her head tipped toward her tightly cinched knees—one of them bleeding, and her feet wedged outward as though they were tied to each leg of the chair. She looked overly pathetic propped in her seat, and I almost felt sorry for her when I saw she was missing a shoe. That particular piece of footwear had been lying on its side at the corner of her desk, looking forgotten.

Everything was so dreamlike, as if we'd been acting out a part in a movie, and Benjamin Bradford Barry had the starring role in that chaotic scene.

The line moved another pace or two, which meant I was getting closer to the door of freedom. I honest to goodness couldn't wait to get out of that place, and once I had, I'd run into my man's arms the way I wanted to the moment those blue coats barged into the Cumberland Probation & Parole Office with their barbaric ramrods in search of a red headed villain.

Chapter 29

Finally, I was standing outside the parole office with Ahslund at my side, but I was feeling a bit shaken. I imagined my anxiety was instigated by the sudden adrenaline rush of what had taken place, followed by coming down from it so suddenly after being set free.

While looking out over the parking lot, I was shocked by all the news vans staged right outside the door behind all the FBI vehicles. How'd they have so quickly gotten wind of what had happened? Those snakes were sneaky.

I fought the reporters who practically gagged me with microphones while trying to get answers to their questions, all of them talking over each other, the voices so jumbled, it sounded like foreign languages to me. It had taken me but a few seconds to curse at all of them because I needed to call Nykolson before he saw all the chaos on the local news stations.

I pushed every mic out of my face with a backhanded swing, and the thump reminded me of Nykolson's dick when it had come straight for me. The length was almost true to size and the spongy head was pretty much spot on. Had they known I would have been able to swallow those things whole, they might have thought twice before shoving such a phallic symbol toward my mouth. And considering the talents of my recent bottoming event, if I'd turned around, the whole damned thing would have disappeared for good.

Before I reached Nykolson's sports car that he'd let me drive that day, I had to cut through ill-mannered reporters who would have taken a seat in the vehicle next to me if I hadn't had all the doors locked and the top in position. The car even wobbled a few times until I honked the horn, which thankfully, frightened most of them off of it. I found their actions very offensive and not in the least bit respectful toward other people's property.

To avoid journalists prying eyes through closed windows at what I was about to type on my phone, I waited until I reached the first stop light to send a text to Nykolson, letting him know I was on my way home.

His reply had come back, *"already? It's only noontime."*
My answer was, *"a full day down. I'll tell U later."*

I kept my messaging short since I knew from previous stops at that particular crossway, the traffic light would have changed from red to green in less than a minute.

I cruised slightly above the speed limit down highway one-O-one, humming the lyrics of a rock-disco-orchestrated song by OMD playing through the audio system. I found it a bit of an upper to know Nykolson enjoyed that group as I had. Shoot, we were going to be good together. I just knew it.

It felt I'd been driving for quite some time even though I knew the route hadn't taken as long as it seemed. According to the dashboard clock, I'd been on the road for less than ten minutes. I started passing orange triangular construction signs every few hundred feet, some alerting a substantial fine if driven over the posted speed limit. Just what I needed. More rocky disruptions that day. The closer I'd gotten to the work zone, I'd eased up on the pedal, bringing the little speedster to a crawl.

Another bridge repair, who would have thought?

Nykolson's Alfa Romeo wasn't engineered for creeping at a turtles pace and it had become agitated on its own, seemed as though it was disobeying the pressure of my lighter foot. The car lurched forward like a grasshopper — the motherfucker seemed to have a mind of its own, and unlike my practical pickup truck, I wasn't used to a car with such peppy power.

Perching myself higher in the seat, I'd sung, "Wait a

freaking minute—hold everything." I lowered my window to get a better view of the well-built hunks busting up the roadway with their heavy-duty tools. Their bodies worked fluently under the baking sun—glistening, nicely tanned, rock solid, and bulging in all the right places with harder than shit muscles. Even though their well fitted jeans were a little soiled, it hadn't made their appearance any less fantastic.

Then I spotted the one man on site handling a jackhammer, the juddering machine strategically positioned between his thighs, his strong stance wide. When our gawping eyes met, I noticed he inflated his chest, forcing his plaid sleeveless shirt to break open at the top. That's when my finely tuned gaydar had gone off, picking up his mating dance that included a willingness to give up that ass during lunch break. With all that on display, my sex-filthy mind had gone to thinking of six different ways I could have helped him use that hammering jack.

The big hammer vibrated audibly against his inner thighs and the thorny tattoo around his right bulging bicep seemed to have been straining to keep the muscle contained. His dark spiky hair snapped like fire flames in the wind and his protected eyes smiled right at me through the rising dust.

"Holy shit! So very nice," I mumbled, keeping my eyes locked on him.

Breaking my goggling concentration, the Alfa's front tire climbed the roadside curb as if looking to find a new way out of there. Flushed with shame as well as guilt, I hid behind my mirrored sun specs and moved on down the street like I should have done in the first place. "Sorry handsome. I got-sta go."

Finally parking the low riding sports car in the drive at Nykolson's home, I grunted like an old man when I was getting out of its ground gliding platform. I crept toward the front entrance like a prowler, dragging my mentally exhausted ass across the pavement as if it had been beaten for being bad. The vision I needed to lift my spirits had been standing bare chested in the doorway, his arms propped in each jam above his head with those damned sexy sweat pants riding low on his hips.

Nykolson watched me slink up the walkway, that ivory grin on his face spanning from ear to ear. "There's my handsome man," he rung.

A huge smile unraveled across my face the closer I'd gotten. "Damn, I missed you." I cradled his jaw in the palm of my hand, kissing him delicately on the lips.

Nykolson's hands had come down from the door frame, landing gently on my shoulders as he kissed me back. He loosened my tie just enough to snap my shirt's top button open with the twist of two fingers while asking, "How was your day, Hunny Bunny?"

I responded with a bit of false energy. "It was eventful. One you're going to enjoy hearing about." My hand skimmed across Nykolson's chest, stopping in the middle to feel his heat and the thump of his heartbeat. I slid it downward, following the deep gutter in the center until I reached his waistband, pulling the elastic open to have a peek. "Oh yeah, I definitely missed you all right." I grinned and snapped his gray sweat pants back into place.

"Let's get you out of these stuffy clothes and into something more comfy." Nykolson had taken my messenger bag from over my shoulder and slung the strap over his, side-stepping me into the house with one finger locked around a belt loop at my hip. He led me to the kitchen and laid the satchel in the middle of the island counter top. "How about another kiss before Nathaniel gets home?"

"Why the shit are you askin'?" I lunged into Nykolson, forcing my tongue toward the back of his throat like there was a diamond in there. He grabbed hold of my jaw to overpower my advances. As he raged on, he walked into me, pushing me into a backward skip. His mouth moved over mine like he was chewing gum, trading spit with his hammering tongue, searching the back of my throat as if trying to get that diamond back.

Losing my balance, I'd fallen backward against the refrigerator door, my arms dangling limply at my sides. I lost my breath. My lust for him had caused a meltdown. I hardened. I trembled. I'd gone weak. My knees had given out and I started to slip into a trance. I surprised myself. I wasn't like that. I was the one who dug in and dominated the situation. But with Nykolson, I felt differently. Defenseless. I wanted him to force himself on me. Take total control. Was I changing for him? Was he the one who

I'd allow to abuse and use me? Bend me over and take what he wanted? I'd begun to think so, and hadn't cared.

Nykolson had taken charge and I liked it. I'd felt it in the grip he had on me. He slipped his hands into mine, palms to palms, our fingers woven between each other's. He rotated my arms out and upward along my sides, pinning them tightly above my head to the refrigerator door. My eyes closed. I inhaled under the pressure of his mouth, taking the warmth of his breath straight into my lungs. He slowly dragged his mouth across my cheek until his lips caressed my ear, nipping my lobe with his tender lips. Hotness flushed over me. I swallowed. I felt my Adams apple bob. I couldn't speak. As if warming a cold windowpane with a breath of heat, he exhaled slowly into my ear and down my neck. I nearly burst into flames. All that steam had penetrated my soul. He teased me. Making me want him more. I was rock hard and probably oozing precum. He pulled back slightly and whispered into my mouth, "How's that for foreplay?"

It had taken me a moment to respond, and when I had, it'd come out as broken words. "Ho. Leee. Shit! That was... the greatest... fucking kiss... I'd ever had." I hesitated then added, "I so needed that today."

"It gets better. Wait 'til later," Nykolson added, running my stubble lined jaw with a single finger.

I blinked until my senses had become clearer. "What had I done to deserve that?"

"Nothing, my love. I had a burst of spontaneous passion and you were in the right place at the right time, there to take what I had to offer. If you liked it, I could do it again. All you have to do is ask."

"You're going to make me ask?"

"Actually, it'll never get to that point, as you'd just discovered. You're way too irresistible. I won't be able to wait for any drawn out invitation." Nykolson stalled for a few moments and then told me, "Don't make me ask either. Violate me at will if you so desire."

He sounded so formal and blunt standing there with his arms extended like wings at his sides, his solid torso rippling, and those low riding sweatpants that had given me a glimpse of black hair sprouting above the waistband. All of him, so damned sexy. I couldn't pull my lustful gape away from him, my attention immediately drawn to the perfect outline of his major sized manhood, the beautiful head predominantly popping out at me along his inner thigh. "Jeez, you shouldn't tease me like that," I groaned.

"Got it. Mouth shut. But... you'll find my ass will always be open," Nykolson let on.

"Oh, gawd. That is it. We've got to stop this before I yank down those pants and bang that black ass right here on the kitchen floor. Scoot. Get outta the way. I need a cooler after that stunt you just pulled." Pushing Nykolson aside, I spun and faced the refrigerator and hunted for something cold to drink. "Aaah. Kool-Aid. Perfect."

Chapter 30

I'd almost forgotten about the shitty day I had after that burst of spontaneous energy Nykolson granted me with against the refrigerator door. The bump to the back of the head hadn't even fazed me. In fact, the dizzying blow might have made for a more euphoric moment of passion.

With both his hands gripping my ass cheeks while standing behind me, Nykolson asked, "Okay, what happened at work today that caused you to leave early? And please tell me you weren't let go because they found out you'd been putting that throbbing cock in my backend."

"How much time do you have?" I was hardly in a position to have been telling a story after what had just taken place. With Nykolson's hands on my ass, my thoughts weren't on anything else but him, like getting his cock all up inside me. Yeah that. I'd been thinking about it more than ever after having him up there once already, wanting to have another go at his sausage sliding in and out of me again, to compare sensations from the last time to make sure I really had liked it.

That thought was silly. I knew I liked it, and liked Nykolson. Liked his dick. A whole lot. I'd do anything for him, even if it meant giving up my top position. I wanted to please that man more than myself, and jolly to shit out loud, all I'd been able to think about was spreading my legs to let him in. What the fuck? The desires of being his bottom sex toy had been getting stronger and I had no clue where the fuck those urges had come from.

Perhaps after the whacked ass day I'd had, feeling frightened and alone, I for once, needed to be taken care of, and by that, I felt a need to have been submissive for a change, let Nykolson run the show, hug and hold me, do whatever *he* pleased with my body. He'd certainly made an impression on me in the kitchen, and with that, he had a good start at bringing me down and getting my legs over his shoulders. My dick had gone completely stiff at the thought of him topping me. He was so fucking fit and confident, I couldn't wait for him to give me that black erection another time.

I'd given my head a wobble, trying to clear the thoughts of being penetrated by Nykolson's cock, but I hadn't been able to shake it. The image was holding strong. I really wanted him to use me. Rough up my ass like I'd done to his. Take care of my hole.

I spun to face him while flipping the refrigerator door closed with a backhanded swing. I stared at him, or more like gawked. His fat free body — so tight and chocked with muscle, tormented me. How'd I get so lucky? I shook my head again, clearing it as best I could, except that time batting my eyes, wondering if I'd be able to make it through a sexual encounter without sticking my dick into that sweet ass of his. I was a natural top, so simply thinking about slipping inside him made rock hard sense.

Nykolson looked at me, his penetrating stare bore deep into my eyes. He backed away and said, "What do you say I grab some glasses and we talk about our day over punch?" My sex crazed reply was, "Yeah... that's... a good plan." Jeez, he messed me up so easily. Nykolson was a magnificent creature with the ability to fuck up my head every time he looked at me, and it hadn't made my matters any better with him standing there without a shirt on. He was fucking handsome as all get out if he knew it or not. He was gentle, kind hearted, pleasingly romantic, and when he looked at me, there was so much conviction in his gaze, I'd sworn he was peering into the other half of his very own soul, that of which was unquestionably living within me. There was no other explanation for how connected we were. Two halves had become whole that first moment we'd met.

I followed Nykolson out to the backyard patio where we sat opposite each other at the dining table. I nearly spit out my punch when he leaned back and clasped his hands behind the nape of his neck, exposing all his sexiness in one smooth move. That chest, those effing abs, and those gah damned pits below those bulging biceps. I'd understood what I'd thought before to have been true, *"Holy fuck, I'm fucked."* Even though I had been fucked.

I was seriously ready for the guy to screw me again, and screw me hard. If he had, and considering the time of day it was at the moment, still blue skies and sunny, I would have referred to that daytime fuck as an afternoon delight.

Nykolson hardly seemed like a snooping person, but the way he stared had me thinking differently. I'd sensed he'd become curious about my day, only because it was unusual for me to have been out of office at noontime and that I had mentioned I'd tell him about it once I arrived at the house.

Keeping it majorly brief, he finally questioned, "So?"

I knew what he was referring to, but before I'd gotten started, I set my glass of Kool-Aid down on the table, feeling the coolness of the red liquid staining my upper lip like it once had when I was a puny little kid. Being silly, I purposely left it there, waiting for Nykolson to make a comment, which he had, along with pointing and chuckling at how cute and childlike it made me look.

I laughed along with Nykolson, telling him the last time I had a red mustache was when I was about ten years old, and I'd missed having one. The taste of red punch brought back all sorts of good memories. Oh how I cherished those handmade tree-branch horses and green wagon wheel days. That little red caterpillar forming above my lip had helped lighten the mood, allowing me to open with a chuckle.

I'd told Nykolson about Ashlund showing me information pertaining to Berdella and then the judge on the fourth floor just minutes before the FBI ramrod-banged the office doors down. Well, not literally, but it sounded more dramatic when I told it that way.

Before I'd gone any further, Nykolson sat taller in his chair and squealed, "What the shit? You were invaded by the FBI again? Holy shit! Why didn't you say something earlier? I thought they already had their perp?"

"I thought so too, but apparently more than just Sandra Dee had been in on it, and hopefully they got 'em all this time around." I flashed back to that morning, explaining the unfortunate event if I had permission to do so or not. Nobody had mentioned anything to me about keeping quiet, otherwise I would have, and besides, I was certain the six o'clock news was going to spill everything they knew about the ordeal anyway, and the story was most likely already on their public social sites.

Moving along, trying not to leave anything out, I mentioned how gratifying it was to see Berdella hog tied and bent over the countertop in a compromising position. Nykolson looked at me weirdly and asked how I could have smiled at a time like that. I clarified quickly by letting him know it wasn't as grand at the time, but after it had ended, I found it easy to laugh at. The bitch deserved it for what she'd done to so many people.

I told him, "You probably would have been laughing too if you'd seen her hair, the smudged make up, and oh gawd, the missing shoe." I started cracking up at the images in my head. I couldn't hold back. At first I felt sorry for her, but after it happened, knowing what she'd been up to and how she had planned to steal more people's money, helped me see the light and that she really deserved what she'd gotten *and* what was coming to her in the near future. For all I knew, she had a few million dollars sitting in an off shore bank account along with Sandra Dee's and the Judge's. "They all deserved to be laughed at, Nykolson. How does the good book tell it? Thou Shalt Not Steal?" For some reason, those churchgoers had chosen to ignore that major commandment.

Nykolson kindly reached for the Kool-Aid pitcher and refilled my glass. I'd taken a good sized gulp, adding a deeper tone to my already reddened lip. "So then what? Did you see them drag her away? Did she lose the other shoe?" I saw him smirk.

"Sorry to say, I missed that part." But I told Nykolson I had the pleasure of seeing her strapped to a chair on wheels, rolled into a corner like a bad girl, and told she was going to be doing some long hard prison time. Thinking back on the event, seeing Berdella on a downward spin was pretty comical, even though it was some serious shit.

Getting back to the office crime scene that mattered and what had gotten me off the hook, was the FBI agent who had questioned me. He'd asked if I had ever helped the three criminals hack accounts? Had I ever socialized with them outside of work? Had I known about any of what was going on around me? My answers were all, no, except for the question about socializing outside of work. That had taken place a couple of times, but only during the holidays and a few happy hour events we'd all gone to. Never had I done a one-on-one with any of them. Even at those events, as a drunken church lady, Berdella hadn't spoken of anything she was up to. She'd have been a fool if she had.

The same as the first time, I'd been isolated by an agent who asked a lot of questions, and my answers were still, "No, I didn't know Berdella Hutcherson until she started working with me. No, I didn't know the judge upstairs. No, I hadn't realized I was one of her main enemies. No, I hadn't known anything about her hacking abilities. No, I hadn't known she'd been stealing money from innocent people. The questions had gone on for about thirty minutes and my replies were all the same. I kept giving the agent a bunch of negatives." Regarding the amount of times I said no, Nykolson's facial expressions indicated signs of being proud of me. He must have wondered how I worked so closely with someone without having any knowledge of what she'd been up to. I'd told Nykolson, none of those three had given me any reason to think they'd been involved in such a grand scheme. I revoked my confession almost as soon as I said it, stating that Berdella was easily identified as a bad-ass bitch, and from what I'd witnessed, the lady, and Sandra Dee were both outstanding stage performers who were masters at keeping their criminal activities hidden. That told me, Berdella's inner office actions were distractions to what she had really been up to.

"Why did that woman have it out for you so badly?" Nykolson asked, licking the red punch from his own upper lip, not forgetting to run a finger over it to make sure he'd gotten it all. I snuck in a smile when he'd done that, secretly wishing he'd left it there to match mine.

"First of all, as we both discovered on her social media pages, she had been bashing and hating homosexuals as a cover for being a lesbian herself. I was her main inner office deterrent. I guess the more she brought up her disgust with my homosexuality, it had taken the telescope off of her wide butt. The thing I had noticed, nobody in the office seemed to have cared I was born the way I was, and they most likely resented her for being such a horrible human for all the hatred she passed on at my expense. Jeez, we should have picked up on that. How could we have been so blind? I wonder if anybody in the office had her figured out but kept it to themselves?"

Nykolson interrupted me, "The way she was, totally makes sense."

"And from the way it sounded during my interrogation, Berdella was planning to create a phony account under your name, with me as the accomplice. That piece of shit was conjuring up a plan to throw us both in a dumpster. But why? I just don't understand people like her."

"That fucking bitch," Nykolson squealed. "How the fuck would she have pulled that off?"

"I'm not sure, but hackers can figure just about anything out if they want the goods they're after bad enough."

"I'm happy to hear they shut that rancid vagina chomper down before she'd gotten that plan underway," Nykolson prompted a laugh out of me by the label he'd given her. It suited her just right and when I pictured it, I scowled, "Jeez, that's gross."

Nykolson laughed at my reaction, which made his face light right up. He reduced his laughter to a chuckle. "Well... It's the truth. If she's going to be that rotten, she might as well be deservingly labeled for what she truly is."

"We should check her Facebook for the fun of it. See if the FBI brought down her pages," I said, prompting Nykolson to stand up so quickly he almost toppled the chair to the ground behind him. He grabbed it, stopping it just in time.

He grunted out loud, "Oooo. Good fun. I'll get the laptop."

I swiped hold of his hand in passing, giving it one of the quickest kisses ever achieved in motion. I barely felt the back of his knuckles touch my lips. "Hurry back," I put a demanding tone to what I'd said.

Nykolson walked backward through the doorway, blowing me kisses I'd much rather have had directly on my mouth.

He was a master at multitasking. I knew because his computer was up and running by the time he'd gotten back, and was already generating his Facebook home page. He set the laptop on the table and told me to take over. He dragged his chair next to mine, bumping the metal arm against the one I was sitting in.

I typed Berdella's name, and was as surprised as if the sun had shined in the night sky, her page had not been purged. I typed to check Cruella. Not deleted either. "Holy hairy manholes, I'm shocked."

Nykolson then said, "Give Rosie The Riveter's group a try?"

I'd taken a stab at that page, and like the others — still live. "I can't believe how quickly they shut Miz D down, but left everything this whore had her hands on up and running."

Nykolson turned the laptop toward himself and closed Facebook out. "Maybe we should quit searching anything more on her and her cronies. The FBI might be keeping tabs on who's attempting to connect with her. They might still be looking for stragglers. This just reached a serious level, and I don't think it's a good idea for either one of us to be linking ourselves to any part of it."

I shockingly answered, "Oh fuck. You're probably right." I told him to put it away. "If we want to know anything, we could simply check out the news feeds. Surely it'll be plastered all over the media by everybody else."

"Really?"

"Yes. Really. Somebody must have blabbed. I mention that because there were a bunch of reporters and news vans parked outside the office when I was set free. I had to run from many of them on the way to your car, which brings up something I need to tell you."

"Oh, gawd. What else?"

"We better go check for dings and dents," I said that as casually as if it was no big deal.

He groaned, "What? Why?" His face turned into a bunch of O's. Every part looked like a circle, and I laughed. Round eyes, round mouth. His ears even appeared to have rounded off.

Was I Kool-Aid drunk?

Not likely. I peered into the center of my glass, checking to see how much I'd ingested, then questioned, "Is there booze in this shit?"

"Not that I'm aware of. Why check my car for dings and dents?"

I set the glass down and thank the lord his face had gone back to normal. Totally gorgeous. No more O's. I answered, "Knowing I'd come from the scene of the crime, those journalists were bouncing off the car to get a story out of me. I had to blow the horn to get them off my ass. Any damages, I'll take care of. I promise. Don't worry about that."

I wouldn't have expected the damage I caused to have been paid any differently, but Nykolson replied, "Don't fret. Fully covered. No deductible."

That was a first. Who purchases car insurance with no deductibles?

"Are you supposed to go back to work soon?" Nykolson asked.

Until we'd gotten reorganized in another part of the courthouse, or wherever, the office would remain closed for several days to continue further investigations, which meant I'd be working from my laptop at home and scheduling visits with my detainee's off site or in a tiny room at the courthouse. In which made me think to tell him, "By the way, Ashlund will be calling you soon to reschedule your appointments."

"That's effing awesome," Nykolson excitedly squealed. "I mean... having you here every day. With me. That's the awesome."

"I'll be on the road quite a bit, but yes, most of the time I'll be here with you." I was honestly thrilled about the new plan and, I supposed we had Berdella to thank for that since she was influential at getting me and Nykolson even closer together. That was one positive thing that had come out of all her deceitful planning. Or... Make that two things—her out of my life on a permanent basis was another.

I'd taken one more drink of the Kool-Aid, holding it longer than normal to really add color to my upper lip. I tried not to laugh at my stupidness, then pulled it away, letting out a refreshing, "Aaaaaaahhh." Then I burped. Jeez.

Nykolson smiled at me and said, "You're doing that on purpose, aren't you?"

With puffed up cheeks and a super tight mouth that might

have resembled a balloon knot, I nodded like a child, and then my famous half grin appeared.

Before the punch above my mouth had a chance to evaporate, Nykolson leaned in and licked the red dew from my upper lip like he was giving me happy-to-see-you puppy dog kisses. "M-mm-mm, you taste sooooo good," he rumbled. "Like sweet redness."

I refused to stop him, letting his tickling tongue lick me clean. With all the punch I'd swallowed, I wondered if my dick would taste like a Popsicle and if the load of cum I'd spurt into Nykolson's mouth would be bursting with a fruity flavor. I decided then, we were definitely going to find out. I'd tell him about that idea later.

I'd mentioned before that I wasn't an alcoholic, but I really needed a stiffy that afternoon. "How about we add a splash of vodka to the pitcher of punch, it might help make all the crap I'd witnessed go away."

Nykolson looked at me from the corner of his eye. "I know an excellent way to get your mind off all that's happened today, and it involves my big black dick finding a place up your ass. What do you say? Give it another go?" Nykolson pulled me from the chair and whirled me around until I'd fallen backward on the settee. He'd come down on top of me quickly after, right between my legs where he wanted to have landed. I huffed when he hit and my feet naturally sprung upward, effortlessly wrapping around his waist. He was positioned so perfectly that if I hadn't been dressed, his cock would have gone right up inside me.

"Damn those pants," Nykolson complained.

I shifted and declared, "Nothing that a swipe of a zipper can't fix."

"You always know what to say in a bind, don't you? I'd noticed that."

"There's a solution for everything," I replied.

Nykolson was propped at an angle above me, arms locked at my sides, looking straight into my eyes, like a panther, pinning its prey. "You going to let me in?"

"Is a frog's ass water tight?" I looked up at him, my hands firmly clamped onto his bunching biceps. Shit, they were solid.

When I asked my rhetorical question about the frog's anus,

Nykolson laughed. "I'll take that as a big yes. However, we're probably gonna need a lot of lube for this one."

"I'm inclined to agree with you on that since I'm determined to take all of you." I moved one hand to the back of Nykolson's head, tugging him downward. "Kiss me, stud."

Nathaniel unexpectedly burst through the door, startling me, and by the way Nykolson jerked, had frightened the shit out of him too. If Nathaniel's voice had boomed any louder, the entire neighborhood would have heard him wailing, "What the man banging shit? Don't tell me you two are connected." He covered his eyes as if he was offended, one finger dropped and an open eye peering at the two of us.

Nykolson turned his head toward Nathaniel, but he stayed on top of me. "Relax your asshole, asshole. We aren't boinking. Yet."

For a minute, I thought Nykolson was addressing me, but then quickly realized it was Nathaniel's asshole he was ordering to loosen up. I had to chuckle at the comment, which helped dissolve my predicament of being watched by his brother.

Nathaniel continued walking toward us and had taken a seat at the table, looking at us as if we were a live action porn show and Nykolson was the butt fucking star. "You guys are confusing the shit out of me. Again." He addressed Nykolson directly, "I thought he was fucking you? What are you doing on top?"

"Why does the positions we hold matter to you so much?" Nykolson started rolling off of me, but stopped. I put a hand over my dick to hide my erection. I don't know why I'd done that, he'd probably seen my boner already, but covering it up was worth a try at concealing the fucker from his wandering eyes.

Nathaniel answered, "It doesn't. I just want to make sure you're working this bonding thing correctly. I like Michael. I think he's good for you and don't want you scaring him away with your freakishly large dick trying to get all up inside his butt."

I grinned and sat quietly while Nathaniel and Nykolson debated which one of us should be sticking a dick into whom.

Nykolson smirked before answering, "So you're the expert on butt fucking?"

"Not exactly an expert, but remember, I did have a ding

dong come at me once, and I knew then I wasn't thrilled about taking it up the ass. A finger, maybe two is all I'm able to take."

So he had been fooling around with assplay. I should have known. That guy had just become cooler. I grinned again.

Nathaniel then blurted out, "From what I understand, two bottoms don't make a right."

"You're thinking two wrongs don't make a right," Nykolson corrected.

"What's the difference?"

Nykolson huffed, "Forget it. Who bangs who here shouldn't matter to anybody but us."

"I was just trying to find a solution to your dilemma," Nathaniel said.

"There is no dilemma, and the solution for all this would have been a locked door."

"Aw, come on. Don't be like that," Nathaniel seemed to be pouting.

"Then relax your asshole and go get a glass so you can join us... for a drink." Nykolson addressed his brother, but stayed on top of me.

That's when I finally chimed in, "You talking to me, Nykolson?"

Nykolson responded, "No silly. I'll be saying that to you later—the part where I ask you to relax your asshole." He chicken pecked my lips with his.

Nathaniel laughed, stood up and headed for the kitchen. "Gah, Dayum. Now I really need some Kool-Aid. With a spike of the good stuff."

I commented to Nykolson, "Holy crap, he sounded just like you."

Chapter 31

Since the FBI seemed to have all they needed, including the three criminals who were stealing money from people they never knew, the blue coats hadn't been back at the office and as a result of that, I'd been left alone.

I couldn't believe a few weeks earlier, everything had suddenly come to a head all at once, turning my smooth sailing life into chaos. Even though it all seemed like I'd been thrown into a pile of shit, I wouldn't have traded it for whatever else I would have faced, since I ended up meeting the man I believed I'd spend the rest of my life with, giving him a part of me, and wow, getting one big thing in return. Life has a funny way of rolling.

It had gotten late, and we'd left Nathaniel alone to himself, ripping up the documents he'd been saving in case the restraining order against Dajana had to be filed. Come to find out, that girl was tossed in jail, pending trial on a boat load of criminal acts she'd committed throughout the years. Every bit of her dirty past had been laid out on the table all at once after the last stunt she pulled on Nathaniel, which was what initiated the investigation for the shit she'd been up to before he'd come into her life. I'm pretty sure the big red flag was due to the sneaky way she tangled with a bag of oranges and a fist bruised twat. That false self-inflicted assault right there had tipped everybody off to dig deeper into the crap she pulled on innocent people.

I'd come across documents stating a few of her past relationships had come forward and exposed her for what she was. They had also been screwed by her. One of the major cases on Dajana was the government subsidized funds she'd been receiving had been annulled until further notice. I was beginning to realize how blessed I was for being gay and it was the men in my life who seemed to have been most stable.

CȜ ȜƆ

I hopped into bed ahead of Nykolson with a gut groaning umph, saw my gorgeous man standing completely nude at his side of the bed, and wondered what he was truly up to.

"What are you doing just standing there?" I asked while slowly stroking my dick with my own hand. I was super hard and horny all over again as I stared at his magnificence, anticipating how good he was going to feel next to me.

As much as I wanted to put my white dick into him and fuck his brains out, I was utterly ready to have him invade every part of my body, including my mouth and especially my ass, with tongue and dick. I continued single handedly gliding up and down my shaft, and with the other, circling my butt ring with a few fingers to get ready for that wide load he'd drive into my back door.

I'd always enjoyed hand fisting my prick, hardly missing a morning or evening when I was alone, and sometimes going at it during the middle of the day. But, I was more interested in having Nykolson lip wrangling or bronco riding my erection instead, sucking the semen right out of me however way he wanted.

Was I surprised to see Nykolson standing there at the edge of the bed watching me stroke my erection? Not by a longshot. I knew he liked how I looked with nothing on and what my hands were able to do to my dick and ass. His grin and rising hard-on made that very clear. His black masculine body was so appetizing, completely nude with his long dick and sagging nuts completely exposed. I tried not to stare, but I couldn't keep my eyes off of him. The overall package was breathtaking, complete with his ballplayers body and his man sized dick that needed both hands to hold it steady. Everything defining him as a grown ass man.

Damn, that chest. Damn those abdominal muscles—all hills and valleys that just wouldn't stop grabbing my attention. I'd been attracted to his type since I was about twelve years old, and with my teenage fantasy standing right in front of me, I couldn't draw my gaze away from his ripped six-pack that deserved the cum gutters title, for sure. I was a horny boy then who turned into a horny man now. Jeez, I wanted to blow my load and flood those dells, splatter his blackness with my whiteness.

As it turned out, by the greedy look in Nykolson's eyes and the way his lashing tongue ran a full circle over his lips, I sensed he wanted to get all up inside me in a bad way. As of which, I'd made it a point to continue the show, stroking my erect dick and fingering my asshole while he watched, keeping it slow for obvious reasons, that of which I'd shoot semen if I'd jerked or fucked myself any faster.

Avidly, Nykolson had taken steps forward until his knees were pressed against the bed mattress, then mentioned a returned favor was in store. I had a good idea what he was thinking, but I still curiously looked at him, raising one brow higher than the other and waited for him to let me in on his plan.

After a slight pause that appeared as though he was going to retract what was on his mind, he mentioned he wanted to ejaculate into my asshole the same way I'd done to his the night before. His voice cracked when he asked and I'd given him my unhesitant response, "Absolutely. You know I'm down with that."

The second I agreed, his dick started getting stiffer. The heavy fucker was trying to lift itself without help. Then when I commented to him I'd been thinking all day long about having his hard-on jammed up my hairy hole, his dick thickened even more and he nearly ejaculated right there in front of me. I could see it coming on. The pre-cum was already glimmering on the tip of his cock head like a sugar glazed cap.

While I watched his heavy dick trying to point straight at me, the head of it like a lightbulb, so big and plump, I thought, *"Yee-haa, I'm about to bottom my man so hard."* I was more eager than I had expected about getting my legs in the air and taking him up the ass again. I could hardly wait to watch how beautifully he'd react once he started cumming inside me. The feeling was overwhelming, one I had never experienced before, like I was finally uniting with a man I wanted to give everything I had to. I felt differently with Nykolson, almost softer, where all I wanted to do was make sure I'd taken care of him before I looked out for myself. That was when I knew I was hooked, or in love.

"Yikes."

The L word had always freaked me out until I'd met Nykolson, but at that very moment, I could tell the word had come easily — because the feeling had come from deep inside me. I was so ready for Nykolson, really needed him to penetrate me, make me his the same way I'd made him mine.

I tried to play it cool by bringing my arms up under my head to lift it from the pillow and holding them there, which might not have been a wise position to put myself in because Nykolson's eyes appeared to have inflated and he started trembling when I'd done it. It must have been the way my biceps bulged when my arms bent, or maybe the way my steely abs stretched and tightened, or could have been the way my hairy chest flexed when I'd taken a breath. I hadn't meant to come off as utterly enticing, it just happened naturally, and the man in front of me clearly had taken notice.

I'd gone fucking nuts when he laid himself out in front of me like that, so by pulling the same action on him, probably amounted to a cruel motion of my doing. A part of me really wanted to turn him on, get him enthusiastic about fucking me. The harder his dick was, the better it would be for both of us. I'd gone on teasing him, bringing one hand down to masturbate while making sure he had a clear shot of my other hand sliding fingers in and out of my softening hole, getting myself excited at the same time. Jeez, my fingers had really worked their magic on my prostate. Holy fucking shit, I could have really gotten off by what I was doing. I never would have expected that. I had to take it down a notch before I shot a wad prematurely and ruined our intended sexcapade.

My open hand gently caressed my chest, moving from one nipple to the other, giving them each a frisky tweak. The exhilarating sensation sent electrifying bolts of pleasure straight to my dick, causing me to stiffen and lose a bit of my breath. Holy shit again, I found I'd gotten turned upside down when I or anybody else flicked and pinched my nubs. I truly believed mine were connected to my prostate. I moved my hand to the middle of my chest, made a sharp turn south and ran the tip of my middle finger up and down the center of my abdomen a few times. I liked the feel of my hairy chest as much as I believed Nykolson liked looking at me touching it.

I let him know I was looking forward to having him shoot me up with his semen, and while I erotically rubbed a hand over my own body, I heard him mumble "Oh... my... gah... dayum. Top or bottom would be fine with me."

Hearing him mutter wasn't the only evidence of how badly he wanted to have sex with me, his plumb sized crown dripping pre-cum had, too. I hadn't completely expressed myself to Nykolson yet, but I wanted to become his cum dumpster in a bad way, swallow his semen or take every shot he had up my willing ass channel. The way his cock dripped and glistened, grabbed my attention, made me want to get to my knees and swab the oozing nectar off him with my tongue, maybe pop the swollen head between my lips and suck it clean. But before I could have at it, he'd already transferred his spice to his own tongue with two fingers. A gah damn turn on was what that was.

His excitement to fuck me appeared to have taken over his mind, evidence displayed by the way he immediately moved toward the nightstand and grabbed the tube of lube. He shook the bottle a couple times before squeezing a shit load of it into his palm. His dick was more impressive than mine when stiff, by which, I knew that meant every oily bit of lubricant he dumped in his hand was going to be needed. He prepped his thick black shaft quickly, coating it well with both hands, making it shine. His half grin and glistening eyes made me believe he was ready to get his cock all up inside my asshole—run my prostate through the wringer—prod the fuck out of it with that large head of his to get me to squirt.

While Nykolson greased his dick from tip to base, I rolled to my side with my ass aimed right at him, lifted my right leg and fingered my hole he'd soon be plunging his dick into. I was so fucking horny, it had taken me less than five seconds to push every one of my slippery fingers inside me, even my thumb, twisting and turning, softening my chute for penetration of a grander scale. His thick as fuck dick. I hadn't had many men put their cock up my ass, yet with Nykolson, I'd become an aggressive daddy's boy—built tough, could take his dick like a champ. No waiting. No drawn out finger fucking to warm me up. I was quickly in ready to go mode and wanted Nykolson to just shove his stiff cock right in and get to the fucking. I was talented like that, wanted to know and feel I was getting fucked by my man's cock.

I heard Nykolson breathing heavily while looking down on me, viewing my asshole so close up for the second time. He growled, "Holy cripe, that asshole is so fucking hairy. It's totally fucking awesome. Gah, dayum, I want in."

I'd gone short of breath when he reached a hand between my legs and dragged his slippery fingertips over my eager anus. His touch felt superb, a different and exhilarating sensation from when I'd done it myself. The mind boggling feeling turned grander when I sensed his thumb poking at my softened star, sinking deeper by the second, searching out that hot spot inside me that would cause me to cum just by simply pushing his thumb pad against it.

I growled on the verge of slurring my words, "Fu-uck that feels great." By the last word I was breathing heat like a dragon. Throat rumbling. I'd gone crazy having another man touching my butthole, and couldn't wait for Nykolson to shove his thick dark meat into me, bring back the memories of what I'd been missing for so long. I was literally shaking at that point, coming apart from his touch.

He rumbled, "Holy, Jeez."

I followed that with a groan while trying to keep it together, "Whaa—?" I trailed off with hoarseness to my tone.

He softly replied, "I can't believe someone as physically strong as you is falling apart at the touch of my hand"—he held his thumb inside me—"it's the most incredible vision I'd ever seen," he admitted as I told him to hurry up and cock plow my ass before all the excitement of him probing me had caused me to blow my spunk prematurely.

Without letting another second pass, Nykolson dropped to the bed at my backside and slipped his lubricated fingers into my asshole. Not one or two, but all four, maybe even his thumb, too. He was fucking me with his hand, twisting and jamming his fingers deep, curling them into my ever blessed prostate.

Ohmigawd, I wanted more. Much more. If he hadn't pulled his hand out of me, I would have cum, but rather his dick had been stuck in me when I let it spurt.

I cried out loud, "Fuck me, Nykolson. I need to feel your black cock reaming me. No more finger probing, pleeAYAAHO! FUCK!" I nearly broke apart when he shoved his thick ten-plus inches right into my puckered channel next to his probing fingers. *Holy fuck me to Jupiter.* My eyes rolled upward as though trying to look at the back side of my skull. Every nerve ending in my body had been set on fire and I felt I just might cum from what he'd done. I was that damned close to ejaculating.

Then, the slippery suction when he yanked his fingers out of me was a fucking turn on, too. The sensation topping erotic. "Jeez. Gah. FUCK!" I howled. I couldn't hold back the outburst.

My sudden flare-ups hadn't interrupted Nykolson's blissful muttering, "So tight. My gawd."

"Fucking cocks, FUCK!" I nearly wrecked my throat when I growled that out. The talent of Nykolson cock jamming me had felt so damned good.

Lying on my side with my back to Nykolson, I gripped the sheet in front of me as if I were trying to tear it to shreds. It wasn't because he busted me going in, but how his sudden invasion felt so fucking awesome. I believed it shocked the shit out of him how easily his cock had sunken into my ass. I noticed that by the way he rattled, "Holy fucking shit, I'm totally in you already."

He pulled half way out and once again speared me fast and recklessly as if he wanted to get inside me before I changed my mind about letting him screw my chute, which wasn't going to happen because, as I had known myself, I was more than eager to have his donkey-sized dick sliding in and out of my cock-sucking channel. If he only knew I had been ready to take him up my ass since the day I met him — to show him I was into bottoming... for him — he might have taken the whole bang daddy's hairy butthole a little slower. There was certainly no reason for him to worry. I had and would continue giving him my ass no matter what. The way I acted with my widespread legs should have been a no brainer how much I wanted it again, and he could have had his way with my hole any way he wanted.

From the corner of my eye, I could see his fuck-face expression. His eyes were slightly open and his mouth was agape, giving up a dream-like appearance. That gorgeous gaze coming over my shoulder from behind certainly indicated he was completely satisfied with being the fucker. Yeah, he was visiting heaven all right.

There wasn't any surprise to me that my asshole sucked his cock right in without flinching or fighting back. It turned out I was an exceptional bottom by the way it was going, and as I accepted Nykolson's dick like a winner, had proven I'd become the perfect mate for him. Once he was balls deep inside me, scrubbing the course black hair above his cock against my firmly toned butt cheeks, I couldn't get over how fucking great he felt sliding in and out of my asshole. I'd discovered then, how much I missed getting fucked in the butt. I couldn't remember anybody else's dick in my ass ever feeling as good as Nykolson's had. Perhaps it was because Nykolson was a mastered bottom and knew all the fancy moves that would get my rocks off, or I liked him so much, my body overpowered my mind and really wanted him.

It astonished me how much I liked the way he forcefully tunneled in, slowly pulled out, and then plunged back in again. Getting drilled by Nykolson's cock from behind was fucking me up like nobody's business and I had to hold my breath a few times to avoid cumming too soon. I even fist gripped my cock like a vice as a secondary precaution. My sperm wasn't going anywhere until I was good and ready. Getting butt fucked was mind blowing and sensual all at the same time. Hotter than hell if that was possible. He had the pummeling rhythm of a revved up jackhammer, yet at intervals, worked himself in and out of my slippery channel with gentler massaging strokes, similar to that of moving a bow across the strings of a cello. He even released the deepest vocal tone a stringed instrument like that would have made.

Fuck an A, he was an awesome fucker. I tried like mad to pay attention so I could do the same to him, but my overblown orgasmic mind was being hammered to bits. Nothing sticking.

When he dropped the tempo of his hips, I knew exactly what he was doing. I'd made that same maneuver on him. My gifted boyfriend had slowed his rhythm, making sure I was feeling every inch of his black erection. I could feel him going after my prostate from the inside, using the head of his cock to repetitively thump against it. I discovered right then how amazing he was at fucking my tight unused asshole, knew he was pushing the limits at giving me ultimate pleasure, and I was fucking glad it was my asshole he was committed to pleasing. With him using his big dick to give me the best prostate massage I'd ever had in my life, I uncontrollably blurted, "Fuck! That's it. Right there. Ram that cock in and out of my ass. Fucking, fuck your daddy's butt. Wreck my hole. Screw it. Give it to me good. Fuck up my butthole. Make me cum." I was completely lost in lust, messed up, sounding bossy and totally out of control.

I lost my mind as he moved rhythmically at my backside while one of his hands smoothly stroked my cock and the other pinched my nipple like a woodshop clamp. As he ground his cock into me, I felt ravenous nibbling at the back of my ear. There was rasp to his voice when he growled, "I'll fucking fuck you good, Mikey. I'll pound you so hard you won't be able to stop cumming. Would you like that? Would you?" He pushed his dick deeper, banging my ass like he was beating a drum he was mad at. He masterfully moved his palm over my chest and back to my nipple, gripping it so tightly, my rock hard cock jumped in his stroking grasp. He roared, "Fuck, your ass is slick. How does my cock feel? You like what my dick is doing to your fuck hole?"

I loved the way he was talking nasty to me and I was thrilled I brought that out of him. At that point, all I could have done was holler like a stuck bitch that needed to keep getting reamed rough and hard, "Fu-u-u-ck. Fuck meee-hee. Ream my fuck hole." I bit down, grinding my teeth together. Spit spewed as I exhaled through them. His awesome fuck job made me screech the words, "fuck me," again, making him aware how badly I wanted to be rammed by his cock for the rest of my life. I was at a loss of control, so worked up, wanting to cum, and almost crying because he felt so good slamming his hard-on in and out of my channel. My ass seemed to have been made for him—like... we were meant for each other. There was no other explanation.

Just when I was at my peak and about to reach down to jack the built up cum from my dick, the unexpected happened. Nykolson abruptly stopped fucking me, pushed his dick deep and held it still. The prickle of his hairy pelvis glued tightly to my ass. He gripped hold of my hips, and said with hot breath against the nape of my neck, "Fuck, Michael. Don't move or I'm gonna shoot my load into your hot as hell ass. Please... Mikey... Don't fucking budge or it's all over." He inhaled, but I hadn't felt him blow it out. He was honestly holding back.

At that moment and remaining steady, I'd done what I was told, because like him, I hadn't wanted what we'd been doing to end either. I could've, without a doubt, let him fuck me all night long and into the next day. I was definitely up for it. I loved his dick inside me that much. I was a top, but he turned me into a bottom the night before and even a bigger one that second time around. It was my turn to hold my breath, working like a mad dog to keep my puckered asshole from auto sucking the fuck out of his cock. Then... I'd heard him whimper at the same moment my hole had lost the lockdown battle and gone into twitch mode, pulling on his dick as my prostate flexed.

After a few moments of stillness, I felt him slowly exhale, and soon, could feel him gradually moving his hips in small circles, grinding, scrubbing the course hair above his embedded cock against my butt cheeks, the prickling sensation of his manhood adding to my pleasure. He was fucking me like the stud I knew he was, working my stretched out hole, bringing me closer to that point of a definite eruption.

I wanted him badly and everything he had to give. It was as though I needed his love, all of his cock, his strong body, and every spurt of his genetic release. I craved his sperm, needed his black cum swimming inside my white ass. When I clenched my sphincter around his hard-on and begged him not to pull out until he flooded my chute with his sauce, his energy level boosted again and I heard him roar, "Holy fucking shit, that ass of yours is so damned hot."

I could actually feel Nykolson's dick expanding and contracting against the depths of my silken channel, hitting the spot that would have made me cum without a single hand stroke to my own shaft. The way his pulsing erection was reacting inside me at that moment felt like he was already pumping spunk into me. I begged, "C'mon. Give me your sperm. I need it. Fill my ass the same way I flooded yours."

At that point, the both of us were overly enthusiastic, our hard pricks raging, so worked up beyond return that it had barely taken another minute of fucking for both of us to blow cum all over the place—or 'I' had anyway—his burning spunk deeply pelted my rectum instead. I felt every jet as if he had shot bullets from a rifle and the entire vital barrel had been crammed up inside me. Every one of his spurts had come so power filled, I'd sworn his semen charged through me and bombarded the back of my throat. By the way he drove his hips against my ass, I knew he wanted every shot of sperm to burrow deep and stay where he'd sent it. Our bass vocal rumbles, grunts and groans blended while we ejaculated together, sounding identical.

We finally settled down and lay connected for a while, I for one refusing to let him go and he seemed to have wanted to stay inside me, too.

Nykolson eventually pulled out, and the way his dick snaked so gradually from my cum soaked hole, it seemed he was trying to keep as much of his sperm in my ass as he could. When the large head of his cock finally popped free, my overfilled ass spit his semen back at him, burrowing into the hair above his dick. The slopping sound of suction I heard when he withdrew was erotic as fuck. I then felt his fingers circling my stretched out hole before using them to push the seeping semen back in. He punched several fingers in and out of me a few times before hooking all four inside my opening as if trying to hang on to a bowling ball.

"Hot Damn! Your asshole feels nice and soft. I didn't ruin you did I?"

"Fuck no," I hurried my answer. "Everything you did felt incredible." I hooked my arm around my knee and pulled my leg against my chest to give him better access, prompting him to go on probing my relaxed sex hole with every finger, feeling the slickness his semen left behind as his fingers continued pushing the spunk back inside me.

"Awesome hole." My fuck-proud Nykolson gently stroked the wet hair surrounding my pucker while alternately plunging his fingers in and out of my used asshole he thought he'd ruined. The sensation was gently pleasing even after I had his wide dick rooting around inside me moments earlier.

After a short time had passed and before the semen around my sphincter had a chance to vaporize, he repositioned himself on top of me and entered my body again. Gentler that time. Face to face, making love to me. Moving ever so slowly. He was such a master fucker, one as gifted when slow screwing me as when he was rage reaming me. He was a stud. Or, my stud, and certainly knew how to work that dick of his inside a man's cum needy asshole. Or, my cum needy asshole. If I hadn't known better, he'd fucked a lot of guys before me. He was that good at it. I hadn't asked or wondered any further, because at that moment, I wanted him to be mine, no one else's.

He tenderly kissed me at the same time he gently slid his dick in and out of my cum filled rectum. His body immediately had gone taut, he moaned, and when he released a ravenous growl and his hips pressed against me with extreme pressure, I knew exactly what was happening. My asshole must have felt that good to him all over again.

As soon as he ejaculated that second time, so quickly after entry, he lay convulsing on top of me, looked into my eyes and mentioned he wanted me to do to him what he'd just done to me.

There was no need to ask twice. I quickly answered "of course" as we flip flopped positions by log rolling across the bed.

Chapter 32

I'd gotten to my knees in a hurry before my man had changed his mind. Not gonna happen by what I'd seen laid out in front of me. If I had been honestly thinking, I missed doing the banging. That was my comfort zone, and I was damned good at it.

I looked down on Nykolson who had laid himself back with his knees pulled to his chest, giving me full access to that gorgeous black hole of his. *"Wow "*, had I certainly liked all that had been put on display. By the way everything looked down there, he was positively a full grown man. I'd noticed that the first time I'd seen him completely nude, and my memory had been jogged the moment I laid gaze on that stunning package again. The same as before, seeing his big black dick, sagging black nut sac and puckered black asshole flexing as if trying to suck my dick before I'd even gotten near it, had turned me so rock hard I couldn't contain my excitement to have at it. All I wanted was to blow his mind with the best butt fuck ever.

Appearing impatient, Nykolson blurted out how much he wanted me to hurry up and jam my dick into him, start fucking before the sight of me towering over him alone had made him lose his rocks another time that night. His excitement was clear by the way his throbbing cock kept lifting and falling against his flat stomach, perfectly cradled by his abdominal gutter that would soon become a river of cum.

I knew exactly how he was feeling at that moment. I'd been in that exact position a few minutes earlier, overcome by the overpowering desire of having the shit pounded out of me by a stiff dick.

It had become his turn to take my cock. I couldn't let him wait a moment longer.

I'd gotten to what mattered—prepped my dick and his asshole with a ton of oil.

While chattering for me to start fucking, he pulled his knees tighter against his chest, opening himself up even more than he already was. *"My Gawd."* He looked so incredible lying back like that, waiting for me to slide my dick inside him, I'd nearly forgotten I was supposed to fuck him in the butt.

Snapping out of my daze, I added more lubricant to my hardened rod while positioning myself closer to his ass. I generously pressed the bulbous head of my dick against his starry pucker, lightly punching my target by rocking back and forth, softening him for the grand invasion, each time giving him a little more of my enlarged head. His oily hole was unbelievably soft, felt like silk, and when I glanced down, his sphincter was opening and closing, sucking on the tip of my dick as if trying to pull it in. His body was reacting as though his hole was begging to be invaded, and if I hadn't jammed my dick in soon, the fucker was going to open up like an alien and pull my entire body right in. I couldn't hold back speaking my thoughts, so I said, "You like that dick, don't you?"

"Ye-hes," he muttered. "I wanted it the whole time I was fucking you." Nykolson nodded, leaving his mouth open where I could almost see steam of desire coming out of it.

With each jab, I sunk a little deeper until the entire head of my cock was swallowed up by his butthole knot. The ringed fucker instantly snapped round the rim of my cockhead. The grip tighter than shit and I could feel his asshole wasn't letting go until he'd been fertilized with my semen. I growled a phrase he'd recently repeated a few times while screwing me, "Gah Dayum, your fuck-hole is awesome."

I was still several inches away from being completely inside him, yet watching my thick shaft disappearing into his asshole just about made me cream his chute right then. I was so fucking ready, all I wanted was to plow right in, give him the big white shaft with one rapid plunge, to let him know what it felt like to have nine inches of thick meat stuffed inside him all at once, but, I'd taken it easy on him. If I shoved every inch of me in too quickly, it might blow the deal I was invested in and possibly ruin any chance I had of using his chute to get my rocks off. That shocking blow would have required some healing time.

I pressed my hands to the back of his thighs, pushing his knees against the mattress at the sides of his ribcage, his kneecaps tucked into his armpits where I needed them. The adjustment shifted his butt cheeks higher, causing most of my dick to snake out. His asshole maintained partial hold on my shaft. His pucker blossomed pink and quickly turned black when it snapped shut. Repeating, I could feel his butthole milking my dick, sucking as though eating my cock.

When Nykolson open handedly slapped my hips and pulled me into his ass, I knew then he wanted my full erection burrowing back in, ramming his channel the same way he had done to mine only minutes earlier. Then he'd given me the confirmation I was waiting to hear when he said, "Shove it in, Mikey. I've had you before. I can take that fucker whole. Don't make me wait."

Even though he seemed ready to have gotten plowed hard and recklessly, I was still apprehensive about giving into his slapdash desire. I rooted gently instead of driving my full blown cock in with one unforgiving plunge. The thickness of my shaft was more concerning than the length. A jam-packed intrusion would have been a shock to anybody's system, not easy to take a wide cock like mine in one fell swoop. Understood that I'd fucked him before, and he'd taken me like a champ, however, a cock like mine would take more than a few times to get used to, every primary insertion would feel like a fresh experience. With that fact, I'd sunk into him slowly, giving him time to get used to my bulk. Plus, gradual penetration would allow him to feel every inch of me gliding in.

While I pushed inward and onward, I treasured how warm and tight his hole felt around my erection, and worried if I increased my rhythm more than I already had, I'd cum at that very moment.

Yes, he felt that incredible wrapped around my cock. AGAIN. I wanted to cum, real bad.

As I gradually slipped into him, the expression across his face was complete satisfaction. He looked amazingly angelic lying under me with his eyelids dropped at half slits and his soft lips slightly opened. His wet tongue had come out of his mouth and swiped his upper lip. When he threw his head back into the pillow and let out a begging whimper, I knew then I had him where I wanted him. I used the head of my dick to thump his prostate, keeping the pace of my nudges gentle, taking care of him the way I had done before, and making certain he wouldn't regret that I had been inside him once I'd finished.

Each time I pushed passed his prostate, he trembled with a breathless moan that sounded like he was on the verge of crying. That had been my indication not to stop the internal massage. I could feel the way his hole flexed that he'd given in to my oversized cock, taking every inch like a professional, not once fighting my invasion. He gripped my ass cheeks with both hands, cried for me to go at it with forceful pounding, pleading me not to stop until I filled his ass with cum. That's what he wanted all along.

His squirming body and those needy words had done a number on me I wasn't ready for, and before I knew it, I'd felt my crotch catch fire. The concentrated sensation sent numbing sparks to my brain and back down my spine, igniting my own prostate into an intensified discharge. I growled, "Fuck... I'm cumming." The sound of my voice was insanely vicious, and at that point there was no way I'd have been able to stop myself from ejaculating.

Every muscle in my body had gone rigid. I was fixed with convulsions while shooting my thick load into my boyfriend's vice-tight channel, hitting him up with my usual ten to thirteen jet powered spurts. I was so wound and horny, it might have been more than thirteen.

My dick filled man hollered between pleasured moans that had gotten louder and louder. "Pound my hole. Don't stop dicking me-eee," he begged. There were groans and whimpers combined together. "Harder... Pound me harder. Fu-huck... I'm there... shit... here it comes. Keep going. Keep going."

His crying outbursts changed to gritty growling as ribbons of semen shot from his hard-on, wet pearly gobs splattering his dark chest and abdomen, adding slickened artistry to the black beauty under me. The rising scent of his pungent semen kept me rock hard, intensifying my ongoing orgasm. Every shot I let go appeared to have traveled straight through him and out his dick. We'd become that closely unified. Spurt for spurt.

I collapsed on top of him, his cum soaked torso sticking us together. I kissed him while we trembled — panting as though the air around us had gotten thinner.

As the orgasm washed through him, his airy vocals sounded strained when he said, "That was fu-hucking excellent, Michael."

When I regrettably shifted to vacate his body, he hollered, "Wait. No. Don't pull out."

Staying was definitely a good plan and one I'd continue to practice. I'd given him a slight forward hip nudge, cock prodding the pleasure emporium inside him. His reaction was another, "Gah, that's excellent. I need a lot more of this."

I was thrilled to have heard he wanted it again and again, and again. I dived for his mouth with a tongue filled kiss, in a way that seemed I couldn't get enough of him. I had him skewered. Tongue and dick. He masterfully reciprocated, sucking my tongue with greedy desire. I countered by giving him more of my dick and holding it there. As I lay on top of Nykolson, I whispered, "Are you going to be okay once I pull out?"

Nykolson released a weakened whimper that seemed to have meant he'd survive once I had. I rolled off to his side expecting to snake from his rectum, but as if we were tied together, he rolled right along with me, propping one leg over my hip and one hand resting on my chest. I felt comforted when he'd done that and knew the soothing feeling would probably continue for the rest of our lives.

I turned my head and kissed the top of his head, letting go of a long drawn out breath, finally feeling content for the first time in days. It wasn't because I just had great sex with a beautiful man, but it was because I knew everything was going to be okay, inside and outside our home. All we'd recently gone through over the past few weeks had felt as though it was finally behind us. It was a good feeling, and I hoped like heck I was right about that.

The FBI had their perps, and I had my man, who someday I knew was going to be my husband.

Hot damn, white dress wear and fuchsia flowers would look excellent against his beautiful chocolate skin.

Epilogue

Meeting Nykolson the way I had was never how I'd expected, yet on that very day, I had a good feeling the two of us would become a true romance love affair. What seemed to have started out as a great depression—my biggest complaint was the day being Monday, and Nykolson's was being under house detention—had put me and him on a path of discovering what true love really was. Strong as shit, true love.

Our happily ever after started on the day he stepped into my office, and I was determined to hand that man the best days of his life. Fate has an interesting way of working out—it sneaks up when least expected, when looking for it wasn't even a thought.

I knew the very second I looked into Nykolson's eyes, I'd been hooked. They pulled me right in and captivated me, never letting up.

"Who would have thunk a crappy Monday morning would have turned out so fantastically?"

As for my archenemy, Berdella and her motley crew of identity thieves, it was understood they are all sitting in the slammer, doing prison time for the rest of their shitty days. Quite well deserved as far as I was concerned. But, the way the system worked, that miserable trio most undoubtedly would get early parole in less than five, and with my bloody luck, I'd be the one assigned to keep tabs on their psychotic asses.

"Hell-to-the-no!" I'd fight that one tooth and nail.

Of course that wouldn't have been permissible, but shit, the scenario had come to mind, elevating unwanted heart palpitations behind my own ribcage at the same time constricting my windpipe so I couldn't breathe normally. If by chance they had been released sooner than later, I certainly wouldn't have wanted to run into any of them in this lifetime. In my opinion, bad times and badder people needed to be put away for good.

Pertaining to the subject of Dajana Washington, she'd been sent to small time jail for several piles of shit she had put her grubby hands into, all of her crap unraveled after a file had been opened up on her. The domestic violence cases she falsely accused men of inflicting on her wasn't what tipped the iceberg, but cheating the State into allotting her with subsidized funds, had been what did her in. That girl was total bad news and I couldn't for the life of me figure out what her worn out pussy had that those men found appealing. It was as though that twat had put a spell on them and their dysfunctional peckers had fallen trap by it.

In regards to Nathaniel, who was finally free of that tramp, Dajana, he still clung to me and Nykolson like gum on a poor man's shoe. I never minded, though. I liked that thug-wannabe goof-ball and enjoyed having him around. I'd already gotten used to the idea that he'd become part of the deal, would always remain connected to Nykolson and me, clear into infinity.

After a while, Nykolson and I stopped talking about those displeasing times that followed the day we'd met. Sure, we had reminisced about how the two of us and his twin brother Nathaniel had gotten started, the good stuff, but had chosen to leave all that other crap in the past. In a crazy way, we'd reached a point where that part of our lives seemed like a dream. Even that bloody tether around his ankle was out of our lives, but, before it had been ditched, undeniably, that strappy foot handle had come in handy at times during our sex games.

I was all in when it had come to playing good-guy, bad-guy with my man in bed, however, handcuffs and ankle shackles brought back memories Nykolson and I preferred to have forgotten. Instead, when he felt like being naughty and the time had called for it, we pulled out the silk ties to strap his wrists and ankles to the bedposts. Those kinky times had been when I found out how much Nykolson liked being spanked during penetration in the backdoor.

Even before Nykolson's parole had completed its course and that attractive anklet had been removed, he'd become a permanent fixture in my life. That was a no brainer and known from the very day we'd taken that car ride to Starbuck's, and I believed, the two of us meeting the way we had, happened like that for a reason. There's no fighting fate or the collision of two destined souls. Ours were introduced when his twin brother had a messed up desire to have at some bad ass pussy.

To celebrate months of companionship between Nykolson and me, and so I'd have been able to tell him apart from his brother at a glance, I surprised him with a silver chain he could wear around his neck. It was a bit thug-chunky, but I picked it because he and his brother had always thought of themselves as hooligans, and what better way to hold claim to him as my badass ruffian than with a thick silver chain dangling around his neck. When I put it on Nykolson and the silver gleamed against his brown bare chest, I admitted then, the brilliance had attracted me to him on a different level. I couldn't deny how I felt about that. He was so fucking sexy with it on and a little part of me was enticed by his secret thugness.

Jeez, he could wear anything and make it look like a million bucks. So unfair.

Nykolson had worn the chain respectfully, telling everybody who'd asked about it that his handsome boyfriend had given it to him on our midyear anniversary. He was so proud of that chain and what it symbolized. That's when I knew the man had fallen in love with me as I had with him. He'd never taken it off. Come to think of it, I couldn't come up with a time I'd ever seen him without it since the day I'd placed it around his neck. He told me he liked having it on, that it reminded him of me every time it swiped against his chest. He said if he removed it, he'd surely have separation anxiety from the man he'd fallen in love with. I blushed when he said those words, and in a roundabout way, I said I loved him back. Logic won the battle of the chain, so other than wearing it out of love for me, I'd come to believe he actually liked the thick gangster chain because it made him feel like that macho thug he always wanted to be.

As for a home we could call our own? Nykolson and I had been slowly clearing a place on a lake just south of San Francisco. A low populated area outside the city, however, only about an hour's drive from door to downtown. The preparation of the land had been taking some time, but slowly and surely we'd come up with that finished product. The dream house Nykolson and I decided on was a cozy craftsman, not too large, but spacious enough to include a corner for Nathaniel whenever he'd come to visit, which would amount to quite often considering the two are practically fastened at the hip. That's a twin thing that'll never get broken. I accepted that a while back and am okay with sharing the minds of twins.

Our idea of a cozy home included a stacked stone fireplace that would bring down the chill during those cold winter evenings, and would serve as a romantic perk for cuddling with the man I love. I'd also have a great spot in front of a crackling fire on Christmas Eve where I could make holiday love to my husband like I'd always imagined doing since I was a teen.

Clearly, I mentioned husband. I plan on wedding that man, permanently making him mine and tagging him off limits if any hounds in the village thought about sniffing around. The engagement ring I'd put on his left hand would also ward off most of those scoundrels. Nathaniel had given his blessing without argument, probably long before I had the nerve to ask Nykolson to be my husband.

Complementing the glimmer of that ring—I would have been extra thrilled to bring him those bracelets in the Cartier window as well, however, my stumpy pocket book wasn't that damned deep. I couldn't afford those gems even if I'd won the lottery, but, I had picked up two equally snazzy trinkets that resembled the two we'd seen, and wholeheartedly, had come with every bit of the same meaningful significance.

My big strong black Nykolson teared up when he opened the package, telling me he'd have been thrilled if I'd so much as given him a string of yarn to tie around his wrist, that the meaning behind the idea would have been more important than the Cartier branded silver & gold. Then *my* eyes misted over.

Yeah, that's right, I also sniveled like a love sick teenager.

Gah, Dayum. I love him.

Even his twin brother, Nathaniel, had gone a bit weepy that day, proving to me, he wasn't as tough and boi-ghetto as he thought he was. That guy *just* might have been one of the coolest people I'd ever met, and I'm pleased as all get out Nathaniel will be a permanent part of my family someday. I enjoy his company and indeed love that man. Not like love-love, but more like Luv Ya, love. Brotherly love. Carry the trash to the corner together, brotherly love.

Anyway.

Even though Nykolson and I shared everything, his identical twin brother wasn't part of any sexual arrangement. That man was off limits. I was only allowed manly bear hugs and a smack to the butt like the athletes do. That I could live with as long as he smacked me back.

I couldn't imagine getting it on with Nykolson's brother anyway, even with his appearance so identical to my boyfriend and it would have felt I was doing him. Nathaniel had already come clean in so many words he'd never give man sex a try. It wasn't his idea of a good time. That experience where a dildo had been aimed at his asshole told the story loud and clear, and from that, I was pretty sure he'd stick to the lady bits instead of taking on man meat and a set of pear shaped nuts — unless they were his own as he'd told us many times before how much he liked his own balls. I'd caught him holding them a few times while we were watching movies together — the real reason I decided he'd always lap his own bowl of popcorn on movie nights.

I'd be the first to admit, Nathaniel is definitely a hot piece of ass, as in a real boner builder, and thankfully I have his identical brother to keep my appetite contained, whom of which, I'd rather get with any day of the week, give his black ass the big white erection, shoot him up with so much semen it would gush out around my stiff dick like the grand falls of Niagara.

I'll never get tired of seeing that spurting fountain of joy surging from my man's cum dumped hole. The contrast of my bubbling spice against his dark skin continually appeals to me in a major way. I'd challenged him a few times at holding onto all that

I'd emptied in him, and many of those times he hadn't been able to succeed that contest. I laughed every time Nykolson clenched his butt cheeks together, trying like mad to hold it all in. He'd done what he could to lock that baby up tight, yet, my boys found their way out of that cozy home inside him. He'd even gone as far as clamping a hand across his crack, but that five digit blockade hadn't corralled any of my wild running seedlings. There had always been too much to hold onto. It was all downhill once he stood to have a go at walking. It was funny to witness, and had gotten a laugh out of me seeing him skivvy away with dimpled butt cheeks and both hands holding his crack shut.

Yeah, he was cute doing that too.

God bless him.

When filled by him, I'd tried pulling off that same butt clinching maneuver, but failed worse than he had. I wasn't in control of my asshole the way Nykolson had been. He was the bottom master, I wasn't.

At any rate, the times Nykolson climbed aboard and fucked the crap out of me the way I found pleasurable, we still established he was the favored bottom between the two of us. Even though it visually appeared otherwise, we worked perfectly in that order — the smaller white guy boning the larger black dude.

How fucking hot is that?

Observations of many all-male relationships had been assumed the larger of the two should be dominating the small fry. But in a few cases and as with ours, the big guy favored laying back to receive the plunging dick, and I certainly enjoyed the position I held on top of my big black muscular macho man. Things aren't always as they seem.

To spice things up from our regular routine, we made it a point to trade places on occasion, and the swap had taught me a lot about how to give good dick to Nykolson. I learned from him. An experienced bottom can certainly teach a top a thing or two.

As much as I enjoyed bottoming for Nykolson, I was always ready to take my place back on top where I was able to carry out my best work. The proof I'd done well was the way Nykolson reacted. Screaming and begging. It was breathtakingly erotic to watch him go through each stage of an orgasm while my dick was burrowing nine inches deep. I loved hearing his profound growl at that peaked moment his prostate squeezed his caged semen free. I liked the way his face scrunched when he started cumming, thoroughly enjoyed seeing the muscles in his chest swell with each breath he'd taken. What had gotten me the most was the way his abdomen flexed with each spurt of cum that rushed from his body and pooled in the deep gorges of every ripple. It was almost as though his body knew what was about to come and shaped the deep abdominal gutters to catch it all. His body was amazing the way it reacted to the way our bodies joined.

Other than my desire to bottom for him from time to time, Nykolson had told me he enjoyed being on top, mentioning how much he liked his cock stuffed in my cum hungry rectum, said I was hotter than fucking shit when I reached my orgasm while being penetrated by him—that the sight of me trembling, jerking, splattering semen over my abs, chest, face, and shooting it everywhere else had made him want to continue fucking me into eternity.

Witnessing another man's cum shooting everywhere? A gay man's dream come true.

Without a doubt, I'm definitely one of those gay as fuck men who can't seem to get enough of another man's cum—blasted in my face, down my throat, soaking my body, and as recently discovered, blown up my ass. I seemed certain by Nykolson's aggressive riding skills he'd taken on my stone hard dick, he was just as eager at being a cum slut as I'd come to be.

Proving I was correct, it was midafternoon on Saturday when Nykolson had come at me with an extreme urge to be that cum slut. He grabbed my wrist, twirled me like a dancer and pushed me backward onto the sofa in the living room. As soon as I landed flat on my back, he pulled my pants to my ankles, ripped off all his own clothes and straddled my velvet hips—his hands pressed to my bare chest, holding his position for that desperate ride.

Anticipation building, I grinned at the way he was handling me, rough and recklessly—the way I liked it. I could tell the upcoming fuck I was about to encounter was going to be a wild and crazy quickie. Like a wham-bam-thank you-man kind of bang, full of hard driving cock.

I was so ready for that and if there had been anything I really wanted at that moment, it was embedding my hard-on inside Nykolson's rear end, spurting semen.

I gripped his hips firmly, pressing my thumb pads into that glorious deep pelvic V at his waistline. I lifted my butt off the sofa, driving my cock toward his inviting back door I couldn't see but knew was there. I just needed him to back up a few inches and let my erection slide inside.

When he resisted, confusion swathed every part of my face.

Malevolent behavior had come over Nykolson, his ominous grin had told me that much.

What was my boyfriend up to? Whatever it was, I was certain I was in for a treat.

He reached behind his back, shifting my hard-on between his butt cheeks, propping my tall erection passed his tailbone and up the center of his lower spine. He stroked it a few times before letting go. His touch arousing. I almost burst.

He slid further forward, his ten inch prick slithering along the center of my abs to my chest, burrowing through hair as if it were a grassy valley, his sagging nuts dragging behind. I wanted him to keep coming, eager for his swollen black cock head to be forced between my lips.

I opened my mouth with an extended tongue, but he stopped.

Dammit! I was so ready to suck and swallow.

At that point, I was overheating with butt fucking desire. I looked up at him and asked, "Why'd you stop?"

He smiled at me like an evil genius, combing his fingers through my silken chest hair. "I like teasing you. Builds sexual tension so I get the biggest load out of you."

He slid backward down my abs, bowing his back as he leaned in to kiss me. The heat of his breath transferred to my mouth. I inhaled as if it was my only way to breathe air.

Every hair on my body stood on end when he licked my lips. My entire body buzzed when he skimmed his tongue over my jaw and flicked the wet tip along the network of my ear. His warm breath had come next, turning me inside out when he told me he wanted to dick fuck my chest, soak my hairy pectorals with his steaming sperm—pump a few shots down my throat as well.

I felt the pressure of Nykolson's dick trapped by his two thumbs at my sternums center. His hips gyrated back and forth, gliding his cock over my chest hair. Every thrust inched his erection closer to my throat, pre-cum crowning his swollen knob and clinging to me.

His body vibrated.

His breathing tripped.

His eyelids fluttered, too.

He moaned and then mumbled, "Gawd, I love your hairy chest. It's so fucking sexy and feels amazing stimulating the base of my dick."

My breath caught as I watched the head of his erection sliding between my muscled mounds, coming inches from bumping my scruffy chin.

His body quacked as if on the verge of cumming.

I wanted his sperm, eager to feel it flowing across my chest, burrow into the hair until it warmed my flesh.

Nykolson's thighs thickened, the top muscles bulged. He grittily groaned, "Gaaah, Damn. I'm almost there."

"That's my man. Let me have it." I bowed my back, my abs crunched and my chest lifted, putting more pressure against the base of his cock. I reached up and pinched his nipples. Tweaking hard. His reaction untainted.

His chest pushed forward into my hands, voice trembling, "Ye-eah. Ju-husst like that. Pinch them hard. HardER. HARDER! MAKE ME CUM," he ended up yelling.

I wanted his semen so bad. Needed it. "C'mon. Soak my chest." I clamped his tits with my fingers and thumbs, pinching more aggressively. My teeth bit down, elevating my desire to get him off.

He spit in his hand, transferring the wetness to my pre-cummed dick. His ass followed, backing into my stiff cock and popping my hard knob just beyond the ring of his flexing channel. He shouted, "Gah, dayum. Fuck."

With sudden force, he jerked forward and back again, sucking in my cock. His dick slid back and forth over the gutter of my abdomen, moving faster and faster, my dick head popping in and out of his slippery rectum as he glided.

I pinched his tits even harder. He whimpered between grinding teeth. Spit bubbling over his bottom lip as if my cum was already filling him.

His voice turned raspy, "Gah. I'm cumming." Right then, the head of his cock inflated and dug into my sternum. His lungs filled with air, projecting his brown chest forward. His six pack crunched tightly and a ribbon of cum powerfully assaulted my chest, diving in and out of hair before back spraying off my chin and splattering Nykolson's torso. The thick white pearls dripped into the black curls above his thick shaft. It was stunning.

My head lifted just in time to get a second shot that found my open mouth, striking the back of my throat. I swallowed. The third and fourth squirted my left and right pectorals, one at a snap second after the other. The sensation of his sperm gracing my nipple made me lose my breath. I buckled forward, my abs bunched, forcing my cockhead deeper into Nykolson's slickened rectum.

Nykolson yelped, "Gah dayum." His body lifted with me.

Another spurt from his dick sped across the left side of my chest, skimming my sensitive nipple and soaring over my shoulder where it slammed into a pillow above my head. The thud was that of a bullet hitting airy feathers.

I opened my mouth again, waiting for another glorious jet of my boyfriend's sperm. Without delay, I'd gotten my wish. It had come at me hot and musky. The way I liked it. Two more quick spurts laced my tongue and the eighth jet splashed my tonsils. A ninth immediately followed, hitting me above the eye.

Fuck, my man was loaded. I kept after his prostate. I wanted more.

As soon as I swallowed, the tenth powerful charge hit the roof of my mouth. I gulped that one down before the next shot had a chance to reach me. I was hungry, wanted as much as I could eat. Spurt eleven and twelve had come at me like a bullet from a semi-automatic — pop, pop — splattering my left and right cheek within seconds of each other. Stray globules sputtered to my temple, dripping downward into my ear. His thirteenth spurt lazily burrowed into my chest hair at my center, the fourteenth had too. I was in spunk heaven, but was greedy for more.

He huffed the entire time he ejaculated all over me, his hard abs flexing until the end, concaving deeply as if aiding each discharge that had made a wet mess of my upper body, face and much of the sofa around me.

He was growling, and huffing — body jerking.

The pungent scent and taste of Nykolson pushed me over the edge and I could no longer hold my own cum. I'd lost my mind and my shit, couldn't take what was happening another second. I needed to ejaculate, dump my load inside Nykolson's butt.

I lifted my hips and sunk deeper into him. That single intrusive thrust was all it had taken. No more friction required. I started ejaculating, my discharge powerfully filling him like the gushing effects of a broken dam. My cock was blowing up inside Nykolson, flooding him with so much cum it flowed from his hole and soaked the seat so bad my butt cheeks were swimming in my own semen. My body lurched up and down in harmony with every explosive surge. Fourteen if I had been able to count. Just like my boyfriend. The last jet almost as robust as the first.

I threw my head back and growled while I finished filling my man's sexhole. He had me so wound up, I turned beastly on his ass. I hollered, "Fucking suck the seed from my dick. Take it all if you can. Use that cock sucker of an asshole on my dick."

He slobbered as if he was overflowing with the semen I'd blasted up his ass.

Deeply kissing him, I sounded angry while moaning my pleasures into his mouth. My body was still jerking, hips thumping upward, pumping the last few shots of cum into him. My nostrils flared to get air.

I dropped back. Heaving. I was saturated. Soaked in body fluids. His and mine. The scent of cum was everywhere. I'd become consumed by the intense orgasm my boyfriend's cock sucking ass had made happen.

Nykolson pressed his chest against mine, licking cum from

my mouth, tasting his own semen while murmuring, "That was excellent."

As I snaked my dick from his butthole, I heard slippery sounds of suction, and when the head reached his gripping ring, there was a sputter, a spittle, and a sloppy sploosh. When I pulled and popped the plug, his asshole squirted as if a garden hose had sprung a leak.

Nykolson rambled with laughter, "Jeez. My asshole just ejaculated the sperm you dumped in there."

His back arched, and I heard another sputtering squirt. I gripped my dick and pushed it back into Nykolson's chute, putting a stop to the spurting sperm. I felt the flooding over my knuckles as more of my semen squeezed free.

Before I had a chance to add my comment, I was suddenly startled, and sure Nykolson had been too, by the way his brother burst into the living room and hollered, "Holy crime scene batman, someone's been shot in the butt."

True.

I groaned, "Oh, Gawd," and tried to hide the cum on my chest and face before Nathaniel had come around to see the magnificent mess his brother made of me.

Nykolson glanced over his shoulder and shouted, "Just look away, my brother. Nothing to see here. Just look away." He hadn't even tried to get off me, just pushed backward with my dick driving further upward into his ass. Hiding my erection, I supposed.

I reached for a pillow and tried concealing what we'd just done, hoping Nathaniel hadn't gotten a birds eye view of how connected we were.

Too late.

Nathaniel blurted out, "Shit, white boy, yo dick iz thick. And check out those Gah, Dayum, droopy nuts. You sure you'z white? How deep inside my brothuh does that muthuh fucker go? You be elephant trunk impressive, bruh."

"He's very deep," Nykolson quickly confirmed.

Jeez. Nathaniel was so descriptive. Had he gotten down on his knees and shoved his face between my legs or what? All I knew, the time was not good to be carrying on a conversation or answering questions about my cock size with Nathaniel, so I only groaned, "Oh, Lawd."

By the sound of Nathaniel's reaction, he wasn't opposed with finding my dick embedded in his brother's rear end. In fact, I believed he was thrilled with the idea when I heard him make another comment about what he'd been trying to prove all along. "Now that position makes sense to me. Jolly good show, boys. Jolly good show."

Was he really clapping?

Nathaniel turned and walked away. Laughing. "Finally, the proof I needed. Mystery solved."

Nykolson had also laughed as I groaned out loud, "Ohmigawd. I'd never been caught with my dick in a man's ass before." I wasn't sure if I was humiliated or turned on by being seen. My true thoughts—I was immensely turned on since my cock was still hard and comfortably tucked up inside my boyfriend's butt hole.

"Don't worry about him, Michael. He's a grown man and already knows I like it when you put the meat in me."

"Yeah, but..." I covered my eyes with my hand while Nykolson returned to licking cum from my face, acting as if sharing with his brother what we had just done was no big deal.

All the jokes I'd made about Nathaniel watching me fuck his brother had come true, and that isolated incident had not been limited to the only time he caught me with my dick in his brother. Since we all lived under the same roof, being seen was bound to happen sooner or later. One memorable penetrating occurrence was when he walked into the living room at the exact moment I started cumming inside his brother's asshole. I'd reached that point of no return, unable to stop ejaculating to benefit his virgin eyes. Pulling out was not a possibility. I was too far invested and could only go on fertilizing the man. One supposed good thing had come of it though, he found how insanely crazy I look and sound when ejaculating up his brother's butt, so there's no need to hide that act from him anymore. If he wanted to keep watching, I'd let him.

From that day on, I figured it best to carry out our intimate moments behind locked doors. But, I couldn't promise anything — Nykolson was too irresistible and I wouldn't put it past myself to attack and screw the man's ass on the fly.

We fucked constantly, like fresh-weds or wild rabbits. A day hardly passed where I hadn't propped Nykolson's feet over my shoulders to pound the living shit out of his cum hungry hole with my nine-incher. I turned him into my personal cum dumpster, and I couldn't seem to get enough of giving him every burning load I had. He was an addiction I couldn't quit, and he couldn't seem to get enough of me either. Many nights he'd come to bed completely ass lubed and ready to go to town on my dick. Those were some special times.

My priority in life would always be to please Nykolson any way I could, be it covering him with romantic kisses, holding him against my chest, or sitting next to him on our brand new porch overlooking a babbling brook. I loved him so much. He had that incredible effect on me.

Nykolson and I still act as though we'd just met, interrupting each other's sleeps during the night just to make love, or simply touch so we know the other was still there. I don't foresee our frequent mating rituals coming to an end any time soon. The love we have for the other refuses to weaken.

It's difficult to explain how much we care for each other, but I can say and probably speak for Nykolson, too — when we're apart, there's an ache so bad I feel as though I had my wings clipped and I can no longer fly.

THANK YOU

Thank you for reading SHAKEDOWN. If you enjoyed Nykolson and Michael's story, please consider leaving a review. They help immensely at getting the story out to more people.

Be the first to know about upcoming releases and special events when you subscribe to my webpage at:
gregoryjonathanscott.com

Also, be sure to connect with me on Instagram, Twitter, and Facebook.

Gregory Jonathan Scott

ABOUT THE AUTHOR

Gregory Jonathan Scott was raised in the small town of Belmont, Michigan, survived the city of Grand Rapids, before relocating to South Florida with his longtime companion, Scott.

Growing up with a creative imagination and the artistic ability to sculpt and color another world was what prompted his goals to be a writer, which ignited the desire to captivate readers with short columns in magazines pertaining to art and leisure. From there, it continued. Finding the joy of writing, along with an artistic hand, had given Gregory Jonathan Scott the inspiration to design and write M/M romance & erotic Novels.

Gregory Jonathan Scott is currently enjoying air conditioned living with Scott and their pets in a scorching village off the coast of South Florida.

Gregory Jonathan Scott

OTHER WORK BY

Gregory Jonathan Scott

TAKE TO THE SKY TRILOGY
INTO THE HEADWINDS – 2ND BOOK
TAKE TO THE SKY – 1ST BOOK

STAND ALONES
SHAKEDOWN
INTENSE ATTRACTION
ENCOURAGED BY SPARKS
CRASHING INTO LOVE
THE PRINCE OF ALMOND MANOR
(PREVIOUS VERSION; THE PLANTATION AFFAIR)
HEARTBREAK BEAT

www.ingramcontent.com/pod-product-compliance
Lightning Source LLC
Chambersburg PA
CBHW031251170626
46807CB00001B/83